# THE F

Sam Bourne i

Freedland, an award-winning journalist and broadcaster. He has written a weekly column for the *Guardian* since 1997, having previously served as the paper's Washington correspondent.

In the annual What the Papers Say Awards of 2002 Jonathan Freedland was named Columnist of the Year. His first novel, *The Righteous Men*, was chosen as a Richard and Judy Summer Read in 2006 and hit Number One on the *Sunday Times* bestseller list. His second novel, *The Last Testament*, was a top ten bestseller and has sold over 250,000 copies in the UK alone. He lives in London with his wife and their two children.

By Sam Bourne

*The Righteous Men*
*The Last Testament*
*The Final Reckoning*

SAM BOURNE

# *The Final Reckoning*

HARPER

This novel is entirely a work of fiction.
The names, characters and incidents portrayed in it are the work of the author's imagination. Any resemblance to actual persons, living or dead, events or localities is entirely coincidental.

*Harper*
An imprint of HarperCollins*Publishers*
77–85 Fulham Palace Road,
Hammersmith, London W6 8JB

www.harpercollins.co.uk

A Paperback Original 2008
2 4 6 8 10 9 7 5 3 1



A catalogue record for this book is available from the British Library

ISBN: 978 0 00 7302062

Typeset in Meridien by Palimpsest Book Production Limited, Grangemouth, Stirlingshire

Printed and bound in India by
Thomson Press (India) Ltd.

For Sarah: *Ani l'dodi, v'dodi li.*

# PROLOGUE

*My pen has hovered over these pages many times. I have wanted so badly to set down my story here – but I have hesitated. Each time I begin a sentence only to pull back. Even now the pen is heavy in my hand.*

*But there is not much time, I see that now. I understand that if I were to leave these pages blank, all that I have witnessed would be forgotten. Our story would be lost forever.*

*So forgive me if what you read here is harsh, if it haunts you the way it haunts me. But there will be no exaggeration, no lies. I may not tell everything, but what I will tell will be the truth. This is what happened. Some of it you know already. Some of it you don't. It is my story now, but soon it will be yours.*

# CHAPTER ONE

The day that changes a life, or ends a life, rarely comes with a warning. There are no signs in the sky, no dark ravens on a post, no soundtrack in a minor key. To Felipe Tavares, security officer at the United Nations building in New York, September 23 had started as a regular Monday.

He had come in on the Long Island Expressway on the 6.15 train, picked up a cappuccino and a muffin – a skinny blueberry one, in a concession to his wife – waved his permit at the guys on the door and headed to the basement of the United Nations building, headquarters of the institution he had served for the previous three years. There he opened up his locker, pulled out the blue uniform of an officer of the UN Security Force, complete with the Sam Browne belt and the brass badge that still triggered a charge of pride, and dressed for his shift.

Next, he went to the armoury to pick up his weapon. He handed over his smartcard photo

ID, taking in return a 9mm Glock, standard issue for most serving members of this miniature police force, charged with protecting the international territory that was the UN compound and everything within it. Felipe took the ammunition from the pouch on his belt and loaded up, carefully pointing the weapon into the loading barrel to guard against any misfires. Once his gun was holstered on his belt, alongside his truncheon, a P38 baton with handle, pepper spray and cuffs, he headed for the basement's 'ready room'. There he would stand in his place for the line-up, where he and his fellow guards would be reviewed by an officer, checking to make sure his men and women were tidy, sober and fit for duty.

That done, he headed back to the main entrance on First Avenue between 45th and 46th Streets to begin what he assumed would be another long day checking permits and answering tourists' questions. It was warm enough, but rain was in the air; he put on his orange-and-black waterproof cape. The work would be boring, but he did not care. Felipe Tavares had yearned to escape from the drudgery of small-town Portugal where he had been born and grown up, and where, if he had not moved fast, he would have died – and he had made it. He was in New York City and that alone was excitement enough.

* * *

At that same moment, across town in a Tribeca side street that was no more than an alley, Marcus Mack conducted his own morning routine. African-American and in his late twenties, wearing loose, frayed jeans, with a full head of dreadlocks and with a grungy Crumpler computer bag slung across his shoulder, he checked on his parked car. Anyone watching would have assumed he was merely proud of his souped-up, if aged, Pontiac and that when he knelt down by the driver's side rear wheel he was checking the tyre pressure. They probably wouldn't have seen him feeling in the well above the wheel and finding, stuck there with duct tape, a cellphone. He took it and walked on.

Perhaps a minute later the phone rang, as Marcus knew it would. The voice that spoke was familiar but Marcus knew better than to say hello. It said four words – *'Athens coffee shop, seven-thirty'* – then hung up. At the corner of the street, and without ceremony, Mack dropped the telephone into a garbage can.

The café was full, the way his handler liked it. Marcus spotted him instantly, on a stool in the window, just another grey-suit reading his newspaper. Marcus took the seat next to him and pulled out his laptop. They made no eye contact.

The handler's phone rang and he pretended to answer it. In fact, he was speaking to Marcus, whose eyes remained fixed on the computer screen in front of him.

'We've picked up activity in Brighton Beach. The Russian.'

He did not have to say any more. Marcus knew about the Russian, as did the other member of his unit in the NYPD Intelligence Division. The Russian was an arms supplier who had been spotted a year ago. The Division had enough to shut him down immediately but the order had come from on high: 'Keep him in play.' It was a familiar tactic. Leave a bad guy in business, watch who comes and goes and hope he leads you to some worse guys. Throw back the minnow, catch the shark.

'Surveillance camera caught a man in black entering the Russian's place last night, leaving an hour later. Traced him to the Tudor Hotel, 42nd and Second.'

Marcus did not react, just kept tapping away at his keyboard, for all the world an urban guy reshuffling his iTunes collection. But he knew what the location meant. The Tudor was perhaps the nearest hotel to the United Nations building. And this was the UN's big week. Heads of government from all over the world had piled into New York to address the General Assembly. US Secret Service were crawling all over the place in preparation for the President's visit later in the week, but there were more than a hundred other prize targets already here, all jammed within a few Manhattan blocks for seventy-two fraught hours.

In a week like this, anything was possible. A Kurd bent on assassinating the head of the Turkish government, a Basque separatist determined to blast the Spanish prime minister, ideally on live television: you name it.

'Placed a tap on the Tudor Hotel switchboard last night. Recorded a guest calling down to reception this morning, asking about visiting times to the UN. "Is it true tourists can go right into the Security Council chamber itself?"'

'Accent?' It was the first word Marcus had spoken.

'Part British, part "foreign".'

'OK'

'You need to get down there. Watch and follow.'

'Description?'

'White male. Five-eight. Heavy black coat, black woollen hat.'

'Weight?'

'Hard to tell. Coat's bulky.'

'Back-up?'

'There's a team.'

Felipe Tavares was now outdoors. Behind him was the temporary white marquee that served as the UN visitors' lobby – still up after five years. Not much tourist traffic yet, too early. So far it was just regular UN staff, permits dangling like necklaces. Not much for him to do. He looked up at the sky, now darkening. Rain was coming.

* * *

Marcus stationed himself on the corner of 42nd and Second Avenue – still called Nelson and Winnie Mandela Corner – tucked into the doorway of McFadden's Bar. Diagonally opposite was the Tudor Hotel. The first drops of rain were a help; the shelter gave him an excuse to be standing there, doing nothing. And it meant the Tudor's doorman, in cape and peaked cap, was too busy fussing with umbrellas and cab doors to notice a shifty guy in dreads across the street.

That was how Marcus liked it; to be unnoticed. It had become a speciality of his back when he was doing undercover work in the NYPD's narcotics squad. Since he had moved over to the Intel Division a year ago it had become a necessity. The thousand men and women of what amounted to New York's very own spy agency, a legacy of 9/11, kept themselves secret from everyone: the public, the bad guys, even their fellow cops.

He had been waiting twenty-five minutes when he saw it. A blur of black emerging through the hotel's revolving door. Just as it turned towards him, the doorman stepped forward with his umbrella, blocking Marcus's view of the man's face. By the time the umbrella was out of the way, the blur of black had turned right. In the direction of the UN.

Marcus spoke into what those around him would have believed was a Bluetooth headset for a cellphone. 'Subject on the move.'

Without waiting for a response he started walking, keeping a few paces behind the man on the other side of the six, traffic-filled lanes of 42nd Street. A voice crackled into his ear, sounding distant. 'Do we have a positive ID?'

Marcus shot another look. The man was swaddled in the thick, dark coat the handler had mentioned; his head was covered in a black woollen hat pulled low, and he was no more than five feet and eight inches tall. The subject matched perfectly the description of the man seen at the Russian's last night. He pressed the button clipped to his sleeve: 'Affirmative. We have a positive ID.'

Suddenly the man in black began to turn, as if checking for a tail. Of course he would: trained terrorists didn't just let themselves get followed. Marcus swivelled quickly, switching his gaze to the steps that led up to a small city playground. In his peripheral vision he could tell the subject was no longer looking at him, but was marching onwards.

Something about the man's gait struck Marcus as odd. Was he limping slightly? There was a restriction to his movements, something slowing him down. He walked like a man carrying a heavy weight.

Suddenly the East River came into view. They had reached the corner of First Avenue: UN Plaza was visible. The rain was getting heavier now, making it harder to see.

The man in black had reached the crossroads, the traffic heavy. Marcus hung back on his side of the street, all the while keeping his eye fixed on the subject, who had now stopped by the first entrance to the United Nations, reading the sign: 'Staff, Delegates and Residents. Correspondents Only.' Now the subject moved on, separated by the black iron railings from a procession of flag-poles, each one empty. Further back loomed the trademark curve of glass and steel that was the UN headquarters.

Marcus cursed his short leather jacket, feeble against this downpour. He pulled his collar up to stop the rain running down his neck. The man in black seemed untroubled by the weather. He moved past another UN gate, this one for cars, and another green-tinted sentry box.

Marcus stopped for a moment in the doorway of the Chase Bank. The second he did so an over-sized tourist bus – doubtless full of oversized tourists – pulled up into the slip road that fronted the UN between 45th and 46th.

'Lost visual, lost visual!' Marcus urged into his mouthpiece.

'I got it,' said another voice over the air, instant and calm. 'Subject has halted outside main gate.'

Marcus walked on, trying to get ahead of the tourist bus without revealing himself. His headset crackled again.

'Subject back on the move.'

OK, thought Marcus with relief. A false alarm.

The man in black was not trying to enter the UN building after all.

At last the bus pulled out, giving Marcus a clear view of the subject, now walking further down First Avenue. His pace was quickening slightly, thanks to the steep downward slope. But this was no relaxed stroll. Marcus could see him studying the garden on the other side of the railings intently. He had drawn level with a large, heroic sculpture – the slaying of a dragon, the beast apparently fashioned out of an old artillery cannon – and stopped as if looking for something.

Marcus squinted. Was he searching for another, unguarded, way into the UN compound? If he was, he clearly had not found it. Now, with renewed purpose, the man turned around, heading back towards the main entrance.

Felipe Tavares' radio was bulky, low-tech and in this rain barely audible. It was hard to separate the static crackle from the rest of the noise. But the word 'Alert' came through clear enough, especially when repeated twice.

'Watch Commander to main entry points, this is the Watch Commander to main entry points.' Felipe recognized the accent: the guy from the Ivory Coast who'd started three months ago. 'We have information on a possible threat to the building. Suspect is male, five foot eight, wearing a heavy black coat and dark woollen hat. No more details at present, but stay vigilant. Please stop and apprehend anyone fitting that description.'

Felipe had barely digested the message when he saw a blur of black striding, head down, towards the gate he was guarding.

Marcus was now halfway across First Avenue, struggling to hear the voice in his ear above the traffic.

'. . . enter the UN compound. Repeat, agents are *not* to enter the UN compound.'

He stopped as he reached the kerb of the slip road, now just yards away from the man he had followed for more than ten minutes, and watched him walk briskly through the gate and up the few steps to the small piazza in front of the white marquee. He had crossed into UN territory: he was now officially beyond reach. All Marcus could see was the man's back. He felt his heart fill with dread.

From this angle, at the side of the piazza, Felipe could only see a little of the man's face in profile, the hat and the collar of his coat obscuring even that. But he fitted the Watch Commander's description perfectly.

Felipe watched him stop, as if contemplating what stood before him. Then he took three more paces forwards, then stopped again. What was he doing?

The security man could feel his palms growing

moist. He was suddenly aware of how many people were around, dozens of them crossing between him and this black-coated figure. So many people. He wondered if he should say something into his radio, but all he could do was stare, frozen, his gaze fixed on the coat. It was raining, but it was certainly not cold. Why was the coat so thick, so heavy? Answering his own question spread a wave of nausea through him, starting in his stomach and rising into his throat.

Felipe looked around, desperate to see half a dozen of his fellow officers descending on this scene, men who by their very presence would take the decision for him. He wanted to use his radio – 'Believe suspect could be armed with a bomb. *Repeat, believe suspect could be armed with a bomb!'* – but what if that only provoked him to act? Felipe Tavares was paralysed.

The man was on the move again, now just yards away from the marquee. Felipe thought that perhaps he should wait, let him go through the doors and be stopped by Security. He wouldn't stand a chance: he'd never get past the detectors or a frisk. *But he wouldn't care.* That, Felipe realized as the blood drained from his head, was the absolute horror of it. Nothing could scare this man.

Now the subject changed course again, still showing his back to Felipe, but turning to face the street. Felipe wanted to cry out, demand that the man freeze and put his hands in the air. But that, he understood, could be no less fatal. Once the man knew he'd been discovered, he would push the button immediately, right here. And there were just so many people around . . .

Felipe did not *decide* to do it. That much he would remember later: there was never a decision. He simply reached for his gun. And at that moment he saw ahead of him, through the black iron railings, two men, one of them young, black and dreadlocked, both raising their hands, showing their palms, as if in surrender. The sheer alarm on their faces, the mortal panic etched on them, settled it for him. In a single motion, he pulled out his weapon and aimed it squarely at the man in black.

The next moment was one Felipe Tavares would replay over and over until his last breath, usually in slow-motion. For the rest of his life, it would be the last image he would see at night and the first when he woke up each morning. It would sear itself behind his eyelids. At the centre of it were the faces of those two men. They were aghast, not just frightened but shocked by what they had seen. One of them shouted the single word: *No!*

Felipe was certain what had happened. The man in black had obviously undone his coat, revealing the explosive vest underneath. The two men, on the other side of the railings, had seen that he was about to blow himself up. The sound of that cry, the look of horror on the dreadlocked man's face, coursed through Felipe, sending a charge of electricity down his right arm and into his finger. He squeezed the trigger once, twice, and watched the man collapse at the knees, falling slowly, even gracefully, like a chimney stack detonated from below.

Felipe couldn't move. He was fixed to the spot, his arms locked into position, still aiming at the man now lying in a heap no more than five yards before him.

He heard nothing for a while. Not the echo of the gunshots. Not the cries, as the crowd scattered like pigeons. Not the alarm that had been set off inside the UN building.

The first voice he heard was that of a fellow officer, who had dashed out of the marquee at the sound of gunfire. She now stood over the corpse, repeating the same word over and over, 'No. No. No.'

Unsteadily, dumbly, Felipe walked over to the pile of black clothes now ringed by a spreading puddle of blood. And, in an instant, he understood. There, at his feet, was not the body of a suicide bomber. There was no explosive vest filling that jacket. All it had contained was the flesh and bone of a man, now broken and unmoving. Felipe could even see why he had been wearing a heavy coat in September. He understood it all and the horror of it made his knees buckle.

Felipe Tavares, and the growing crowd of security officers now circling him, were all looking at the same thing.

The corpse of a white-haired and very old man.

# CHAPTER TWO

There was a moment, lasting perhaps two beats, of silence and then the noise erupted. There were screams or course – a man first, yelping in a language few around him understood – and then the cries of three women who had been posing for a photograph by the Pop Art sculpture of a gun, its barrel twisted into a knot. They had fallen to the ground, their larynxes temporarily stopped in fright, but now their fear pealed as loud as church bells. Soon there was crying, shouting and the sound, just audible, of a man contemplating the shard of human bone that had landed at his feet, murmuring in his own tongue, 'Good God'.

Some in the marquee began to panic; one sounded the fire alarm. The rest remembered the drill they had practised. They abandoned their posts at the scanning machines, rushing to stand like sentries at the doors of each entrance, their pistols brandished. The United Nations headquarters was going into lockdown.

Felipe Tavares was now flanked by two colleagues, guiding him away from the corpse which lay, still uncovered and untouched, on the ground. Tavares was talking feverishly, babbling about the men he had seen at the gate, describing the horror on their faces – but when his fellow officers looked, they could see no one.

The noise soon got much louder. Less than ninety seconds after the shooting, the first of forty NYPD squad cars converged on UN Plaza, their lights flashing, their sirens wailing: this was the 'surge' they had practised nearly a dozen times since 9/11, the full might of the New York Police Department rapidly converging on a single spot. Several cars disgorged SWAT teams, the men, their flesh buttressed in Kevlar, armed with assault rifles, charging forward like GIs storming a Normandy beach. Soon they ringed the entire UN perimeter, their guns trained on the terrified men and women within.

First Avenue was free of traffic now, thanks to the NYPD officers armed with 50mm machine guns who had sealed the road from both north and south, 30th Street all the way to 59th. The UN headquarters now sat in the centre of a 'sterile zone' thirty blocks long. Since First Avenue was a main artery for the eastern half of Manhattan, New York City was about to seize up.

In the air, four NYPD Agusta A119 helicopters equipped with high-resolution, thermal-imaging 'super-spy' cameras now hovered, together policing an impromptu no-fly zone over the entire area. At the same time, on the East River, police launches took off from their bases in Throgs Neck, Brooklyn and along the Queens shoreline. No one would be able to enter or escape the United Nations compound by air or by water.

Not much later, the NYPD's Chief of Detectives arrived with his own lights and sirens. To his pleasure, he had got there ahead of Charles 'Chuck' Riley, the Police Commissioner, whose motorcade and motorcycle outriders pulled up a few moments later. Both nodded with satisfaction as they observed a lockdown utterly complete. As their aides would brief reporters for the rest of the day, there had been a suspected terror attack on one of the city's 'high value targets' and New York had responded 'with swift and deadly force'.

But as they stepped out of their cars and shook hands with each other, the two men instantly saw the nature of their problem. They could approach the now-locked steel gate of the UN but go no further. They had reached the limit of the NYPD's authority, the very boundary of United States sovereignty. They were able to look into the eyes of the two men on the door, one a policeman from Montenegro, the other from Belgium. The Commissioner was sure he could see their hands trembling.

Inside, on the thirty-fourth floor, the United Nations Under-Secretary-General for Legal Affairs heard the fire alarm before he heard anything else. Henning Munchau leapt to his feet. He checked his outer office: nobody there, too early. He called down to front desk security but the phone just rang and rang. He checked his window, wondering for a moment if he was about to see a 747 steaming through the air, larger and lower than it should be, about to pierce the glass skin of the UN headquarters, killing the eight thousand people who worked within as well as a good number of the world's heads of government.

It was only then that his deputy, a Brazilian, rushed in, the blood absent from his face. He struggled to speak, and not just because he was out of breath. 'Henning, I think you need to come right away.'

Eighteen minutes after Felipe Tavares had fired his fatal shot, Henning Munchau was standing close to the lifeless body that had still not been touched, save for the waterproof cape placed over it. The rain was still coming down.

At his side stood the Under-Secretary-General for Safety and Security, stunned into silence. Both had just received an instant briefing, giving them the roughest outline of what had happened. Munchau saw the discotheque of lights that now ringed the UN compound and the small army of NYPD men that surrounded it and felt like the inhabitant of a medieval castle on the first day of a siege.

And now he could see, standing on the other side of the railings, a face he recognized, one rarely off the front page of the city papers, the man they called 'The Commish'. This was one legal conference that would have to take place outside, on foot and in the rain.

'Commissioner, I am Henning Munchau, chief lawyer of the United Nations.'

'Good to meet ya, Henning,' the Commissioner said, his face and tone conveying nothing of the sort. 'We appear to have a situation.'

'We do.'

'We cannot enter these premises and respond to this incident unless you formally request that we do so.' The language was officialese, the accent down-home Southern.

'Looks like you've already responded in quite a big way, Commissioner.' Though German, Munchau spoke his eerily fluent English with a hint of Australian, both accent and idiom, the legacy, so UN legend had it, of his service in the UN mission in East Timor.

Riley shrugged. 'We cannot enter the compound without your consent. And I'm assuming you don't have the resources to handle a terrorist incident.'

Henning tried to hide his relief. It meant the NYPD had not yet heard about the dead man. That would give him time.

'You're quite right,' Munchau said, struck by the strangeness of speaking through metal railings in the rain, like an outdoor prison visit. He envied the Commissioner his umbrella. 'But I think we need to agree some terms.'

The policeman smiled wanly. 'Go ahead.'

'The NYPD come in but only at the request and at the discretion of the United Nations.'

'No discretion. Once you let us in, it's our investigation. All or nothing.'

'Fine, but none of this.' He gestured towards the SWAT teams, their guns cocked. 'This is not the UN way. This is not Kabul.' Munchau saw Riley bristle, so he went further. 'This is not Baghdad.'

'OK, minimal show of force.'

'I'm talking one or two armed men only, to accompany your detectives.'

'Done.'

'And your investigation to be shadowed at all times by a representative of the UN.'

'A representative?'

'A lawyer. From my team.'

'A lawyer? For Christ's—'

'Those are the conditions.'

Munchau saw the Commissioner weigh it up, knowing he could hardly refuse. A suspected terror attack in New York, the NYPD had to be involved. 'The Commish' couldn't go on television saying that the department was sitting this one out, whatever the explanation. Munchau knew that: Riley would want to be on the air within the hour, reassuring New Yorkers that he had it all under control.

Now a black limo pulled up, with a whole new battalion of lights and sirens. Behind it were two satellite TV trucks, clearly given special permission to come through. The Mayor had arrived.

'OK,' the Commissioner said, glancing over his shoulder. 'I accept.'

Munchau offered his hand through the railings and the policeman took it hurriedly. Munchau nodded to the UN guard on the gate, who fumbled with the lock until it opened.

Watching the TV reporter heading his way, Munchau made a point of raising his voice to declare, 'Mr Commissioner, welcome to the United Nations.'

# CHAPTER THREE

It took time for the Chef de Cabinet of the Secretary-General of the United Nations to convene this meeting. Besides Munchau and his counterpart in Security, the UN's most senior officials, the rest of the elite quintet of USGs – Under-Secretaries-General – had been on their way to the building when the shooting happened. (The UN tended to work late, but did not start especially early.) Thanks to the shutdown of First Avenue, none reached UN Plaza much before ten a.m.

Now, at last, they were gathered in the Situation Center. The more cynical folk in the building always cracked a smile at that name. Built in the aftermath of 9/11, this heavily armoured, lavishly equipped and top secret meeting place was clearly modelled on the legendary Situation Room of the White House. But of course the UN could not be seen to be aping the Americans: the United States' many enemies in the UN would not tolerate that. Nor could the Americans be allowed to believe that the UN Secretary-General was getting ideas above his station, imagining himself a match for the President of the United States. So the UN would have no Sit Room, but a Sit Center, which made all the difference.

At its heart was a solid, polished table, each place around it equipped discreetly with the sockets and switches that made all forms of communication, including simultaneous translation, possible. Facing the table was a wall fitted with state-of-the-art video conferencing facilities: half a dozen wide plasma screens that could be hooked up rapidly by satellite, across secure links, to UN missions around the globe. The Secretary-General was never on the road for less than a third of the year, but the existence of the Sit Center meant that he did not always have to leave New York if he wanted face-to-face talks with his own people. Above all, it was there for when disaster struck.

There had been no need for video links this time: the danger was right here in New York. The Chef de Cabinet, Finnish like his boss, began by explaining that the building remained in partial lockdown, with authorized access and egress only. No one would be let in or out without the express permission of the Legal Counsel. That had been agreed with the New York Police Department who wished to interview every witness, even if that meant interviewing the entire UN workforce.

The Chef de Cabinet went on to confirm that

the Secretary-General himself had not been inside UN Plaza at the time. He had been at a breakfast at the Four Seasons held in his honour and was now heading over through horrendous traffic. He had told his audience that he had made a deliberate decision to continue with his planned engagement, that to do otherwise would be 'to hand a victory to those who seek to disrupt our way of life'. Apparently that had elicited an ovation, but it made Henning Munchau wince. Not only because it felt like a crude pander to New Yorkers, echoing their own post-9/11 rhetoric of defiance, and not only because he reckoned it would have been smarter politics for the new Secretary-General to have stood with his own people as they appeared to come under attack, but largely because the SG had now opened up a gap between public perception of the morning's incident – a terrorist outrage, bravely thwarted – and what Henning knew to be the reality.

The Chef de Cabinet explained that technicians were trying to connect the SG via speakerphone.

'In the meantime, I suggest we establish what we know and work out some options that we can present to the Secretary-General. Can I start with you, Henri?'

The Under-Secretary responsible for the security of UN personnel across the globe glanced down at the note he had hastily written when being briefed by the Watch Commander, translating from his own handwritten French.

'We understand that a man was shot at 8.51 a.m. today by a member of the UN's Security and Safety Force in front of the main visitors' entrance between 45th and 46th Streets. He had been monitored by a team from the NYPD Intelligence Division who had been in liaison with ourselves and they had cause to believe he posed an imminent danger to the United Nations. That information was passed to the Watch Commander and he passed it onto the guards on duty, including the officer who fired his weapon, believing the man to be a suicide bomber.'

'And the man is dead?'

'Yes.'

'And what else do we know? Is the building in any danger?'

'The lockdown procedure was followed perfectly. The building is now secure. We have no reason to believe this was the start of a series of attacks.'

'And why is that?'

Henri Barr hesitated. He looked over at Henning, who gave a small nod. 'Because we strongly suspect that the man killed does not match the profile put together by the NYPD.'

'What the hell does that mean?' It was the USG for humanitarian affairs, a white South African ex-communist who had made his name in the anti-apartheid movement. His bullshit detector was famously robust.

'It means that the man who was shot was old.'

'Old?'

'Yes, he was a very old man.' Barr lost oxygen at the end of the sentence and gulped. 'But his clothes fitted the description and they seemed to be the clothes of a suicide bomber.'

'Oh come on. He was *dressed* like a suicide bomber and that's why we killed him?'

The Chef de Cabinet stepped in. This was no time for grandstanding or arguments, though he could feel the adrenalin rising in the room. 'When you say "old", Henri, what do you mean?'

'We estimate maybe seventy, perhaps more.'

'Did he even look Muslim?' It was the question that several of them had wanted to ask but had not dared. But Anjhut Banerjee, the Indian Under-Secretary for Peacekeeping, had none of their inhibitions.

'No,' said Barr, looking down at his notes. 'It seems not.'

'Good God,' Banerjee said, falling back into her chair. 'You do know what this mcans, don't you?' she said, looking directly at the Chef de Cabinet. 'I was in London when the police shot some Brazilian electrician on a train because they thought he looked like a suicide bomber. Completely innocent man.' She exhaled sharply, shorthand for 'You have no idea the shit that is coming our way'.

'What is our vulnerability, Henning?' The Chef de Cabinet looking towards the lawyer.

'You mean our liability?'

'Yes.'

'We can look into that, but I don't think we should get too hung up on compensation claims and the like. That's not the nature of the problem.' He paused, forcing the man at the head of the table to press him.

'What is the nature of the problem, then?'

'Same as with most legal problems in this place. It's not legal. It's political.'

'So what do you suggest we do about it?'

'I think I know exactly what needs to be done. And, better still, I know just the man to do it.'

# CHAPTER FOUR

Tom Byrne was jolted awake by a sound both unfamiliar and unpleasant. These days if he ever set the alarm, he used the iPod docked in his Bose bedside player, waking up to the soothing welcome of a song from his own collection. Yesterday it had been Frank Sinatra, serenading the morning with *I've Got You Under My Skin*. What an improvement on how he used to begin his day, with the dreary drone of the BBC bloody World Service.

But this noise was worse than the radio. It was a repeating chime, with a long, echoing sustain, the sound lingering in the air. Tom could feel his heart thumping in his chest. And then he saw the culprit: his new BlackBerry, fresh out of the box just yesterday. He hadn't got around to setting it to silent.

He squinted at his watch. Half past ten in the morning. That was OK: he hadn't got to bed till five, having worked through the night on the Dubai contract. Then he remembered: he hadn't spent *all* night working.

'Hey, Miranda. Wakey wakey.'

There was a groan from the pile of brunette hair resting on the pillow next to him, followed by a lift of the head and a grunt. 'It's Marina.'

'Sorry.' Tom swung his legs out of the bed and headed over for the blinds, which he louvred open, flooding the room with light. 'OK, Marina, I mean it. Rise and shine.'

The woman in the bed sat up, shielding her eyes from the glare of the sun. She didn't bother to cover herself, affording Tom a daytime view of the generous breasts he had been enjoying just a few hours earlier. Maybe young Upper West Side brunettes had their drawbacks, but right now he wasn't seeing any. Perhaps he could hop back into bed for another half hour . . .

The BlackBerry sounded again, a single high-volume chime to herald the arrival of a message. Bound to be his clients: he had sent them the first draft of the paperwork in the middle of the night, and here they were, already demanding revisions. You could say what you liked about organized crime, but you had to hand it to them: they worked long hours.

His new clients were what you'd call 'a family of Italian-American descent with long and historic roots in the New York construction industry' – that is if you were their lawyer. They were now seeking to expand into property in the Persian Gulf, all legal and legit, but there was a pile of international papers that had to be filed first. A friend of a friend had recommended him and the family were happy to have him – they liked being represented by a big-shot international lawyer, British-born and with several years at the United Nations on his resumé – and he was happy to have them, earning more in a week than he had earned in a year working for the blue-helmets of UN Plaza.

He watched as Marina slunk out of bed, nodding her in the direction of the shower, then looked back down at the BlackBerry. *1 Missed Call.* He pressed it to see a single name displayed: *Henning.*

Now there was a surprise. Henning Munchau, Legal Counsel for the United Nations, hadn't called Tom from his personal cellphone all that often even when Tom worked for him. But that had been more than a year ago.

Tom would listen to the message first, before calling back – a habit picked up at the UN, an institution whose organizing principle could be boiled down to three little words: *wait and see.* His younger self had always been in such a hurry, but Tom had learned from the best that it paid to take your time, give yourself a moment to think, let the other guy show his hand first, even – especially – when the other guy was your boss. Or former boss. A few seconds' thinking time might make all the difference. Christ, the rule even applied to face-to-face conversations in that place. It was as if Harold Pinter had written the dialogue, the way UN officials would pause to read each other's expressions and divine their motivations.

'Hi Tom, it's Henning. We need to talk. I know what you said about . . . Meet me at that coffee shop as fast as you can. Tom, I . . . don't call me back.'

Not even a 'long time no speak', the prick.

So the UN's most senior lawyer needed to discuss a topic so sensitive he didn't dare do it on the telephone or in his own building. That was hardly news: everyone knew there was not a word spoken in UN Plaza that was not monitored, by the Yanks at NSA, by the Brits at GCHQ and by God knows who else. But 'meet me at the coffee shop' was especially interesting. That meant Henning didn't even want to give away a specific location. And why on earth, given everything that had happened, had he called Tom? If it had been anyone else from the UN, Tom would have hit delete and not given it another thought. But this was Henning.

He walked into the closet, reviewing the line of suits arranged like conscripts on parade. Big meeting like this would normally call for the Prada or Paul Smith. But Tom didn't want to rub Henning's public sector salary in his face; he'd go for something plainer. Pink shirt and cufflinks? No, the plain blue would do. He caught a glimpse of himself in the mirror: wrong side of forty, but he could still scrub up all right. No time for a shower today though. He shot two bursts of Hugo Boss aftershave onto his neck and mussed up his close-cropped, dirty blond hair.

The BlackBerry was now winking with the arrival of an email. Subject: Dubai. Sure enough, the Fantonis had been reading the small print. They'd noticed the legal obligation to pay compensation to the fishermen whose villages they were about to destroy to make way for a luxury high-rise development. 'Can't we make this clause go away?'

Tom got ready to draft a reply that would explain the moral obligation on all developers to ensure that anybody rendered homeless would be adequately . . .

*Fuck it.* Using his thumbs, he typed: 'Leave it to me: it's gone.'

He gathered up his things, admiring again the vast, open space of this loft apartment. He wondered about firing up the plasma TV, to check on the news but decided against it: Henning was waiting. Instead he poked his head around the bathroom door and called into the cloud of steam: 'See yourself out, Miranda.'

# CHAPTER FIVE

The cab driver shook his turbaned head, muttering that he would get as far as he could, but the road had been blocked for the last hour. 'On the radio, they say something about terror attack. You here on 9/11?'

Tom handed him a ten dollar bill and got out at 39th Street, walking as far as he could. He could see the clutch of police cars, their red lights winking, and behind them the glare of TV bulbs already illuminating a jam of trucks bearing satellite dishes. In itself that was no surprise during General Assembly week. He assumed the Russian tsar was in town – no point calling him anything else – or any one of the usual procession of African, Central Asian and Middle Eastern despots in New York for the glory of a stroll up to the podium of the General Assembly when they were lucky not to be in the dock at the Hague.

But now he could see a city cop, a woman, turning people back from the first entry gate to

UN Plaza. Along the railings, stretching for several blocks, apparently encircling the entire compound like a ribbon on a Christmas gift, was a continuous thread of yellow-and-black plastic tape: POLICE LINE DO NOT CROSS.

He walked on, noticing how each successive entrance was blocked off. The gate used by the public was thronged by a pack of reporters, photographers and cameramen. Tom was tall enough to peer over their heads, to see, in the middle of the paved area in front of the security marquee, a small tent constructed from green tarpaulin. Around it fussed police officers, a single photographer and a forensic team in overalls, masks and white latex gloves.

He crossed the road, threading his way through the cars. Facing him was the concrete phallic symbol that was the Trump World Tower and a skyscraper decorated with a damp and limp German flag: Deutschland's mission to the UN. The Nations' Café was just next door.

He saw Henning Munchau immediately, earnestly studying the map-of-the-world pattern that decorated the vinyl table top. Funny how easily men of power could be diminished. Inside the UN, Munchau was a player who could stride through corridors, winning deferential nods of the head from everyone he passed. But take him out of the building and he was just another New York suit with a briefcase and thinning hair.

To Tom's surprise, Henning rose the moment

they had made eye contact, leaving his coffee untouched. His eyes indicated the door: *follow me*. What the hell was going on?

Once outside, Henning raised his eyebrows, a gesture Tom took a second or two to understand. 'Of course,' he said finally. Munchau was one of those smokers who never carried his own cigarettes: he believed that if you didn't buy them, you didn't really smoke them. Tom reached into his jacket pocket, pulled out a pouch of Drum rolling tobacco – one of the few constants in his life these last few years – inside which was a small blue envelope of cigarette papers, and in a few dexterous moves conjured a neat, thin stick which he passed to Henning. He did the same for himself, then lit them both with a single match.

'Fuck, that's better,' said Henning, his cheeks still sucked in, refusing to exhale the first drag. He looked hard at Tom, as if seeing him for the first time. 'It's been a long time. You doing OK?'

'Never better.'

'That's good.' Henning took another long drag. 'Because you look like shit.'

Tom let out a laugh, which triggered a broad Henning grin, the smile that had made Tom instantly like the man when they first met all those years ago. That and the Munchau patois, flawless English with an Australian lilt and the earthy vocabulary to match. Tom had seen it take shape: they had served on the Australian-led East Timor mission together. Their friendship had been one legacy of that experience. That the Legal Counsel had become that rarest of creatures – a Hessen-born doctor of jurisprudence with a mouth like a Bondi surfer – was another.

'So you don't miss the old place? Working for the family of nations and all that?'

'No, I don't miss it. So, Henning, we're both busy guys. What is it you need?'

'It's about this—' he trailed off. 'About what happened here this morning.'

'Yeah, what is all this? I saw the police line and—'

'You don't know? Christ, Tom, all those fat corporate fees and you can't afford a radio? A man was shot here about two hours ago, a suspected terrorist.'

'OK.'

'Not OK,' said Henning. He exhaled a plume, then checked left and right. In a whisper, his eyes intent, he said, 'Turns out we got the wrong guy.'

'He wasn't a terrorist?'

'Apparently we killed some pensioner in a woolly coat.'

'What do you mean, "we"?'

'Don't go blabbing a word about this, Tom. I'm serious, mate. Not a fucking word. Media don't know yet.'

'Of course.'

'The shooter was from our own bloody security force.'

'Jesus.'

'Jesus is right.' Henning took a long, final drag, sucking the life out of the tiny, hand-rolled cigarette, then threw it to the ground. 'Just unbelievable bad luck. NYPD Intelligence tipped us off about a suspect who'd been visiting an arms dealer. Dressed in thick black coat, black hat. Which just so happens to be what the old boy was wearing when he went out for his morning stroll.'

'Bad luck all round then.'

Henning gave Tom a glare. 'This, Tom, will be the biggest nightmare to hit this place since oil-for-fucking-food. Can you imagine what the Americans will do with this? Can you imagine tomorrow's *New York Post*? "Now the UN kills geriatrics on the streets of New York".'

'Picked the right week to do it.'

'Oh yeah, when we've only got every world leader from the King of Prussia downwards here. Not exactly the start Viren wanted, is it? Imagine, the new Secretary-General spending his first General Assembly on his knees apologizing.'

'He knows?'

'That's where I called you from. For the last hour, we've been in the Situation Center with his Chef de Cabinet, all the USGs. Secretary-General wasn't there: he was getting his dick sucked at some society breakfast. The building's in complete lockdown. USGs are the only ones allowed out.'

'What are you going to do?'

'Well, that's what I wanted to talk to you about.'

'Oh no.'

'Hear me out, Tom. I know you said you'd never work for us again. I understand that.'

'Good. So you'll understand me when I say, "Nice to see you, Henning but I've got to go".'

'But this is not working for the UN.'

'Who it for, then?'

'It's for me. Consider it a personal favour. I think I have the right to ask for that.'

Tom examined Henning's face. It was the one argument to which he had no response, the same unarguable fact which had made him desert the pleasures of Miranda/Marina and come straight here. It was true: Tom owed him everything. 'What do you need?'

'Turns out the one good thing about this situation is that the dead guy was British.'

'Why's that good?'

'Because the Brits are the only ones who won't go ape about the Yanks murdering one of your citizens. Inside America, it'll be the pinko faggot UN who fucked up. Everywhere else, it'll be America who gets the blame. Trigger-happy cowboys, all that. Not the British government, though. Your boys will bend over and bite it.'

Tom would have liked to argue, but he couldn't. He remembered the campaign to get British citizens released from Guantánamo. The British government had barely raised a peep in protest, lest it offend the Americans.

'So? Was it an American who pulled the trigger?'

'No. Portuguese. Name of Tavares.'

Tom digested this. 'So what do you need me to do?' He envisaged the complex documentation that would have to be filed on the occasion of a homicide on the international territory of the UN. He could see the jurisdictional issues looming. Who would do the investigation? The NYPD or the UN Security Force itself? Who would be in charge? Henning's answer surprised him.

'First, I need you to shadow the NYPD guys on the case. They'll have seen the body by now: they'll know we screwed up. I need you over their shoulder. Just for this first day: I stuck my balls out, made a big deal of it, so I can't send out some novice to do it. It would make us look like pricks. Get a sense of what they're doing, then hand it over.'

'And then?'

'Then I need you to close this thing down, Tom. Make it go away. This is just too much of an embarrassment. We can't have the grieving family on television holding up pictures of Grandpa, wanting to send the bloody Secretary-General or fuck knows who else to jail. You need to go to England, find the family and do whatever it takes to make it go away. Put on the English accent, do the whole thing.'

'I don't need to put on an English accent.'

'Even better. Play the charming Brit and offer a gushing apology, massive compensation package, whatever they want. But no grandstanding, OK?

No photo-ops with the Secretary-General or any of that bullshit. He's new. We can't have him associated with this.'

Tom took a drag of his own cigarette. He could see the politics clearly enough: his departure had left no Brits in the Office of the Legal Counsel. Plus it probably helped to have an outside lawyer do this: arms' length, so that the UN itself would be less tainted by whatever shabbiness Tom would have to resort to in order to get a result.

But it was hardly a top-flight legal assignment. He would not have to liaise with Foreign Office lawyers or diplomatic officials. He would probably have to deal with some London ambulance-chaser desperate to get his hands on a pot of UN cash. Bit of a waste of his CV: eleven years as an international lawyer with the UN and before that a legal resumé that included spells doing litigation in a City firm and three years as an academic at University College, London.

'There are plenty of Brits around who could do this, Henning. Maybe not at the most senior level, but just below. Perfectly capable lawyers. Why me, Henning?'

'Because you're a safe pair of hands.'

Tom raised an eyebrow: a lawyer who'd left the UN the way he had was not what you'd call a safe pair of hands. *Come on,* the eyebrow said, *tell the truth.*

'OK, you're not a conventional safe pair of hands. But you're someone I can rely on.'

Tom made a face that said flattery wasn't going to work.

Henning sighed in resignation. 'You know what they're like, the young lawyers here, Tom. Christ, we were both like that not so long ago. Full of idealistic bullshit about the UN as "the ultimate guarantor of human rights" and all that crap.'

'So?'

'So we don't need any of that now. We need someone who will do what needs to be done.'

'You need a cynic.'

'I need a *realist*. Besides, you're not afraid to put the rulebook to one side every now and then. This might be one of those times.'

Tom said nothing.

'Above all, I know that you'll regard the interests of the United Nations as paramount.' The hint of a smile playing around the corner of Henning's mouth gave that one away. He couldn't risk some British lawyer who might – how would one put it? – lose sight of his professional allegiances. Always a risk a Brit might give a call to his old pals at the Foreign and Commonwealth Office, just to keep them in the loop. Lunch in Whitehall, a bit of chit-chat, no harm done. But there was no risk of that with Tom Byrne, graduate of Sheffield Grammar and the University of Manchester. He could be relied on not to betray the UN to his old boy network for one very simple reason: he didn't have an old boy network.

'You know me: I'm a citizen of the world.'

'I knew I could rely on you, Tom.'

'You did a lot for me, Henning. I haven't forgotten.'

'After this, we're even. Really. Which is not to say you won't be properly rewarded.'

'Not the usual crappy UN rates?'

'Separate budget for this, Tom. Emergency fund.'

'So I'm to give the family whatever they want.'

'Yep. Your job is to make sure that, after today, none of us ever hears another word about the dead old guy. When he gets buried, I want this whole thing buried with him.'

# CHAPTER SIX

Henning led them through the press gauntlet, the pair of them using their shoulders to carve a passage. Reporters threw questions at Henning even though they clearly had no idea who he was but he said nothing until they had reached the entrance of the makeshift tent that contained the dead man's body.

'Tom, this is Jay Sherrill. The Commissioner tells me he is one of his elite, first grade detectives.'

'First grade? That sounds junior.' He couldn't help it: the guy looked about nineteen. Maybe early thirties, tops. Neatly pressed shirt; studious absence of a tie; sleek, hairless, handsome face. Tom could have drawn up a profile of Jay Sherrill then and there: one of the fast-track Ivy Leaguers favoured by all urban police forces these days. They were the young guns who spoke and dressed more like management consultants than cops. Had probably done a fortnight on the street and was thereafter catapulted to the first rank of the force. Tom had read an article about men like this in the *New York Times* magazine, how they never wore uniform – they were 'out of the bag' in NYPD jargon – and how they did their own hours. They were the new officer class.

'Young, sure. But with a ninety-six per cent conviction rate.' The accent was posh Boston; he sounded like a Kennedy.

'Ninety-six per cent, eh? Which one got away?'

'The one with the best lawyer.'

Henning stepped in. 'All right. As you know, Commissioner Riley and I have agreed that the UN and NYPD are going to work closely on this one. And that means you two fellows. Are we clear?'

'We're clear,' said Sherrill, making a pitch for the high ground of maturity. 'Mr Byrne, I'm on my way to meet the head of security for this building. You're welcome to come with me.'

Tom dutifully followed, noting Henning's schoolmasterly gaze. He would behave himself. 'Let's hope you're the first person he's spoken to,' he offered, in a tone he hoped suggested a truce.

'You worried he might have talked to the press?'

'No, I'm worried he might have talked to someone in this building. It leaks.' Tom was thinking of his own mission to London, what he would say to the family. He didn't need a whole lot of rumours reaching them before he did.

As they walked through the visitors' marquee,

now closed to the public, and into the eerily quiet foyer of the main building, Tom raised a palm in farewell to Henning, off to a meeting of the top brass. He realized what a pushover he had been. The Tom Byrne of more than a decade ago would have been appalled. But that Tom Byrne was long gone.

They rode in an empty elevator to the first floor. For Tom, being back in this building was at once instantly familiar and yet, after more than a year's absence, oddly nostalgic too – like coming back to your own city after a long trip abroad.

Harold Allen was waiting for them. Tom had never spoken to him before, but he recognized him. He'd once been the most senior African-American officer in the NYPD before he had famously sued his own force for racial discrimination. Once tipped as a future commissioner, he was now in charge of a mere corner of the city he might have led – and, thought Tom, even in this small patch he had managed to run headlong into a weapons-grade scandal. The anxiety was carved into his face. He showed his guests to a round table in the middle of the room, a few paces ahead of his own desk. Tom noticed the multiple framed NYPD citations for bravery on the wall.

Sherrill wasted no time on pleasantries. 'As you can imagine, I've got a few questions for you, Mr Allen.'

'Yeah, you and this whole goddamn building.'

Tom listened and took notes as Allen talked

through the sequence of events: the initial tip-off from the NYPD about the Russian; the recorded phone call from the hotel room to reception; his own instruction to his watch commanders to be on the lookout for a man fitting the description the police had provided; how that message had been passed onto the guards at the gate, including one Felipe Tavares; the confusion and finally the shooting. A tragic case of mistaken identity.

'Where is Officer Tavares now?'

'He's with one of the NYPD support officers.'

Tom's forehead crinkled into a question mark.

'Getting counselling.'

'Counselling? I see.' That would look great in the *Daily News*. 'Minutes after they'd murdered a pensioner, the authorities sprang into action – pouring out tea and sympathy for the killer.'

'Yes, Mr Byrne, counselling. I guess you've never been on the front line in law enforcement. Tavares is in a state of grave shock. He's a good man. Just came from him now.'

'How's he bearing up?' It was Sherrill, his voice softened.

'Keeps moaning and repeating, "That could have been my father. That could have been my father". He's in a bad way.'

'Do we know how old the dead man was?'

Allen got up and walked back to his desk. He was heavy, wide; probably had been fit enough as a young man, thought Tom, eyeing the commendations on the wall. But somehow he had let it go. He returned with a single sheet of paper. 'Seems like he was seventy-seven years old. Name of Gerald Merton. Place of birth, Kaunas, Lithuania.'

'Lithuania? Not many Gerald Mertons there,' said Sherrill, with a smile that conveyed he was pleased with himself. 'Does it say when he went to England?'

'Nope. Just the date and place of birth.'

'What is that you're looking at, Mr Allen?'

'This is a photocopy of his passport.'

'His what?' No softness now.

'His passport. One of my men removed it from the pocket of the deceased, seconds after he was killed. Wanted to check his ID.'

'I strongly hope you're joking.'

'I'm afraid not, Mr Sherrill. We put it back, though.'

'Have your men never heard about preserving a crime scene, about contamination of evidence? My God!'

'Handling a homicide is not what we do here, Mr Sherrill. It's never happened before.'

Tom saw an opening. 'Can I see that?'

Allen handed over the piece of paper, but with visible reluctance. That was par for the course at the UN; people were always clinging onto information, the only real currency in the building.

Tom stared at the copy of the photograph. It was grainy, but distinct enough to make out. The man was clearly old, but his face was not heavily lined, nor thin and sagging. Tom thought of his own father in his final months, how the flesh had wasted away. This man's head was still firm and round, a hard, meaty ball with a close crop of white hair on each side. None on top. The eyes were unsmiling; tough. Tom's eye moved back to the place of birth: *Kaunas, Lithuania*. Under nationality, it stated boldly: British Citizen.

He passed it to Sherrill who scanned it for a few seconds and then said, 'We'll need to have copies of all the paper you've got in this case.'

'You got it.'

'And I think we need to speak with Officer Tavares.'

'That may be difficult. He's not in a state right now—'

'Mr Allen, this is not a request.'

Allen's temples were twitching. 'I'll see what I can do.'

# CHAPTER SEVEN

Tom understood that the NYPD had made a priority of this case: the deployment of *summa cum laude* Sherrill proved that. He understood why they had done it, too: the politics of New York City meant that even a terror-attack-that-wasn't, since it involved an iconic target, had to get the full-dress treatment. Still, it was hard not to be impressed by seeing it in action.

By the time Sherrill had returned to the makeshift tent the corpse had already been zipped up in a body-bag and despatched to the Office of the Chief Medical Examiner. The post-mortem would begin immediately: preliminary results would be in within a few hours. Sherrill gestured to one of the multiple police cars still idling outside UN Plaza, its driver clearly a personal chauffeur, urging Tom to get in and join him on the back seat. This, Tom guessed, was not how the NYPD investigated the average crackhead slaying in Brownsville. The journey was short, a quick zip south along First Avenue, which had once been Tom's daily route home. The traffic was circulating again; people were out shopping. For them, the death at the UN had been a morning inconvenience that had now passed. Just past the Bellevue Hospital, Sherrill tapped on his driver's shoulder and leapt out when the car halted. 'Ordinarily no one's allowed to witness an autopsy,' he explained to Tom. 'But I find a sheet of results doesn't give the full picture. And they don't say no to first-grade detectives.'

They waited only a few minutes at reception before a middle-aged woman in surgeon's scrubs appeared. When Sherrill introduced Tom she gave him an expression he translated as, 'OK, Mr UN Lawyer. Prepare yourself for an eyeful . . .'

She opened a pair of double doors by punching a code into a keypad and led them down one corridor, then another. There was no smell of rotting flesh. Instead he saw fleetingly, through one half-opened door, the familiar paraphernalia of an office: zany decorations, including a stray thread of ribbon leading up to a sagging helium balloon; he heard a radio tuned to some Lite FM station. At last she walked them into what seemed to be a hospital ward. The odour of disinfectant was high.

'All righty, let's put these on.' She handed them both green surgical gowns and hats, pulled back a green curtain and there it was. A slab on a gurney, under a rough sheet.

She moved a pair of spectacles from her head and settled them on her nose. 'Here's where I got to before I was so rudely interrupted,' she said, pulling back the sheet.

The body was on its side, a vast hulk of pale white flesh like the underside of a fish, though now tinged with green. Was that the light reflecting off the curtains? Tom couldn't tell. Strangely, his eye found the unbroken flesh first. The wound, the torn opening in the back, ringed by frayed threads of red, he only saw later, and when he saw it he could not look away. It was the depth of it that appalled him, the deep, red depth of it.

'. . . consistent with severe trauma to the trunk, shattered shoulder blade, ruptured lung and exploded right ventricle . . .'

Tom was not listening. His eye was still gazing into the crimson gash, now congealed. It had the broken, rough edges of a hole in a plaster wall, as if a fist had punched right through it.

'Let me turn him over for you.'

The two men had been standing opposite the pathologist, with the body between them and her. Now, they moved around so that they were alongside her. There was no smell yet, but the sight was powerful enough. Tom felt a hint of nausea.

'You can see the exit hole here. Which means you'll have to be looking for a bullet.'

Tom focused on the dead man's face. The passport photograph must have been recent; the same full, roundness of head was still visible, hard as a billiard ball. He moved his hand forward, contemplating a touch.

'Don't!'

He looked up at the pathologist, who was holding two latexed hands up in the air. 'You don't have gloves.'

Tom gestured his retreat and took the opportunity to ask a question. 'Can I see his eyes?'

She stepped closer and, with no hesitation, pulled back one eyelid, then another, as roughly as if she were checking on a roasting chicken.

For that brief second, the inert lump of dead flesh, a butcher's product, was transformed back into a man. The eyes seemed to look directly at Tom's own. If they were saying something, Tom had missed it. The moment was too short.

'I'm sorry, can I see his eyes again?'

'Pretty striking, huh?'

Tom hadn't noticed it the first time but now, as she pulled back both lids, pinning them with her latex thumbs and holding the position, he saw immediately what she meant. They were a bright, piercing blue.

'He was strong, wasn't he?' Tom pointed at the thickness of the dead man's upper arms. When his father had hit his seventies his arms had thinned, the skin eventually flapping loosely. But this corpse still had biceps.

'You bet. Look at this.' She pulled back the rest of the sheet revealing a flaccid penis, its foreskin drooping limply, before prodding the man's thick thighs: the butcher's shop again. 'That's some serious muscle.'

'And that's unusual for a man this age?'

'Highly. Must have been some kind of fitness freak.'

'What about that?' It was Sherrill, anxious not to be forgotten – and to remind Tom who was in charge here. He was gesturing at a patch of metal bandaged to the dead man's left leg like a footballer's shin pad.

'That appears to be some kind of support. It's unusual. When plates are used in reconstructive surgery, they're inserted under the skin. This is obviously temporary. Maybe it was used as a splint after a muscle strain. Odd to use metal though. It will probably become clearer once we see the deceased's medical records.'

'What about that?' Sherrill asked pointing at the lifeless left foot. There was a big toe, another one next to it and then a space where the other three should have been.

'I hadn't got to that yet,' the doctor said, with a welcome implication that he was ahead of her – and Sherrill. She moved to the end of the gurney, so that she could examine the foot from above. 'These are old wounds,' she said. 'Maybe an industrial accident as a much younger man.'

'Can you tell how old they are?'

'Put it this way, I don't imagine this playing much of a role in your investigation. I would estimate these wounds are no less than sixty years old.'

## CHAPTER EIGHT

Sherrill resumed with a battery of technical questions, most of which seemed to centre on ballistics. He and the pathologist were now trading in a technical dialect Tom didn't speak, all calibres and contusions, and that was when he noticed, lying casually on the top of a small cabinet of drawers, several clear, ziplocked plastic bags, the kind airport security hand out for valuables. One of these contained a plain white plastic card that looked like a hotel room key, another a clunky, outdated mobile phone. These had to be the possessions of the deceased, removed from his pockets prior to the post-mortem and carefully bagged up. Tom remembered Sherrill's scolding of the security chief over the passport.

As casually as he could, Tom picked up the first plastic bag. Sure enough, the card inside bore the imprint of the Tudor Hotel, suggesting once again that this poor old buffer was no suicide bomber: he probably planned to go back to his room after his ‘mission’ to UN Plaza, no doubt to have a nice cup of tea and a lie-down. There was Merton’s passport, a few dollar bills, a crumpled tourist information leaflet, probably taken from the hotel lobby: *Getting to Know . . . UN Plaza.*

Sherrill’s stream of technicalia was still flowing when a head popped round the door, summoning the pathologist outside. Tom seized the moment to beckon the detective over and show him the bag containing the phone. Through the plastic he reached for the power button, then brought up the last set of numbers dialled, recognizing the familiar 011-44 of a British number and then, below that, a New York cellphone, beginning 1-917. Instantly Sherrill pulled out a notebook and scribbled down both numbers. Tom did the same. He was about to bring up the Received Calls list, and then take a look at the messages, when a ‘Battery Empty’ sign flashed up and the screen went blank.

Sherrill waited for the pathologist to return, peppered her with a few more questions before making arrangements for a full set of results to be couriered over to him later that afternoon. Then he and Tom went back to the UN, to the security department on the first floor where, on a couch and armed with a cup of sweet tea, sat a pale and trembling Felipe Tavares.

Despite himself, Tom had to admit, Sherrill was a class act. He spoke to the Portuguese officer quietly and patiently, asking him to run through the events of that morning, nodding throughout, punctuating the conversation with 'of course' and 'naturally', as if they were simply chatting, cop to cop. Unsaid, but hinted at, was the assumption that if Sherrill had his way no police officer was going to be in trouble simply for doing his job. All Felipe – can I call you Felipe? – had to do was tell Jay everything that happened.

The part of the narrative that interested Sherrill most seemed to be the moment Tavares had received the alert from the Watch Commander supplying the description of the potential terror suspect: black coat, woollen hat and the rest. Sherrill pressed the officer for an exact time; Tavares protested that he had not checked his watch. What about the precise wording? Felipe said it was difficult to remember; the rain had been coming down so hard he had struggled to hear properly. Other officers must have heard it too: it was a 'broadcast' message to all those on duty. 'That's right,' said Sherrill. 'I'll be checking with them, too.'

The detective did his best to sound casual asking what was clearly, at least to Tom's legal ears, the key question. It came once Felipe described the moment he pulled the trigger.

'At that instant, did you reasonably believe your life was in danger?'

'Yes. I thought he was suicide bomber. Not just my life in danger. Everyone's life.'

'And you thought that because you saw some kind of bomb?'

'No! I told you already. I thought it because of the message we had, the warning about a man who look like this. And because of the faces of those men I saw. The way they looked so shocked, and the black man screaming "No!" like he was desperate.'

'And you now think they were screaming because they could see the man was, in fact, very old. Not a terrorist at all. They were shouting "No!" not to him, but to you, urging you not to shoot.'

Felipe Tavares' head sank onto his chest. Quietly he replied, 'Yes.'

'Yet that black man, and the man with him, when you looked later, you say there was no sign of them?'

'No sign.'

'Isn't that a little strange? Two men watching what happens close enough to see the old man's face, involved enough to urge you not to shoot, just vanishing into thin air?'

'It is strange, sir. But that what happen.'

Tom watched carefully. He noticed that Sherrill was writing nothing down. The detective continued.

'And, just to conclude, Felipe, you have no idea why the Watch Commander gave his warning then? At that particular time?'

'No. I just heard the message and then I saw the man they describe.' Tavares looked down at his feet again. 'Well, I thought I saw the man.'

Tom could see the cogs in Sherrill's mind

turning, as if he was getting what he needed. Quite what that was, Tom had not yet worked out.

By now he had done what Henning had requested: he had overseen day one of the investigation. It was time to say his goodbyes if he was to make the overnight flight to London. Tom briefed the lawyer Munchau had chosen to take his place at Sherrill's side – a Greek woman specializing in human rights – and then introduced her to Sherrill. To Tom's surprise, the detective did not shake him off, but promised to keep him up to date, to let him know whatever the forensics guys and the medical examiner turned up. He took Tom's cellphone number then insisted Tom take his – at which point the nature of Sherrill's collegiate generosity made itself apparent. With no men of his own in London, he wanted Tom to pass on whatever he discovered about the victim.

In a cab on the way back to his apartment – it would take just a couple of minutes to pack a bag before dashing off for the airport – Tom made the last call he needed, as arranged, to get briefed by Harold Allen on the details he would need in London.

'How are things, Harold?'

'Not great, Tom, I'll be straight with you.' He sounded rough, like a man whose career is flashing before his eyes.

'Have the family now been notified?'

'USG made the call nearly an hour ago.'

'Widow?'

'No widow. Just one daughter apparently. I'll email the co-ordinates.'

'Press?'

'They haven't got the name yet. Just confirmation of a Caucasian male.'

'Has his age been announced?'

Allen sighed. 'Not yet.'

Tom felt sorry for the guy. Depending on how nuclear the media went on this, Allen was shaping up to be the obvious fall-guy. Just senior enough to be culpable, but not so senior his sacrifice would actually cost the high command. Tom knew the battle cry always raised when trouble hit the UN: 'Deputy heads must roll!'

He offered some bland words of reassurance and hung up. As he looked out of the window at the late-afternoon mothers pushing buggies, picking up their kids from day-care, he wondered who he should phone. No need to speak to the Fantonis: BlackBerry and cellphone contact would be fine for them, no matter where he was. He thought of the guys from his five-a-side team, all Brits, most of them former City boys trousering a squillion a week on Wall Street. He should tell them he'd be missing the Wednesday game. Otherwise, he had no one else to call.

The afternoon traffic on the Van Wyck Expressway was heavy. Tom pushed back into the worn, fake-leather seat of the cab and closed his eyes. He reached into his pocket to check his passport when he felt the hard cover of his notebook. He probably ought to call Sherrill, tell him that the family had just been informed, which meant the press would soon get the dead man's name.

He flicked through the pages looking for the detective's number but instead came across the scribbled note he had made at the medical examiner's office.

Now, in his other hand, he fired up his BlackBerry. A message from Allen's office, as promised. A name, a London address and two phone numbers, the second clearly recognizable as a mobile. Rebecca Merton, it said. Tom glanced at the long UK number he had seen on the phone in the Ziploc bag. Sure enough, they matched. Gerald Merton's last telephone call had been to his daughter.

Without thinking, Tom tapped out the digits of the second number he had found on the dead man's cellphone, beginning 1-917. The number sat there, lighting up the display for several seconds. He knew that he ought to leave this to Sherrill; that the NYPD would, as a matter of routine, check out the numbers on the victim's phone. There was no reason for Tom to do it himself. Tom looked out of the window, weighed it up – and then pushed the little green button to activate the call.

It would probably just be the number for a taxi service the old guy had used to collect him from the airport. Or perhaps some relative he had been planning to visit.

Tom put the phone to his ear, hearing it connect and then the long tone of a first ring. A silence and then one more ring. And then a male voice.

At first Tom assumed it was a wrong number. Either the old man had dialled it incorrectly or Tom had scrawled the digits down too fast, both eminently possible. He was about to apologize for his mistake when instinct silenced him. He heard the voice again, first speaking to someone else, as if winding up another conversation, then calling out *hello, hello* – and a shudder passed through him, making even his scalp turn cold.

It wasn't the accent, though that was what had first alerted him, nor even that tell-tale half sentence Tom had heard, spoken in a language Tom had studied back in his university days. No, it was the tone, the brusque hardness. Tom disconnected before saying a word and held the phone tight in his hand. With relief, he remembered that these new BlackBerries came with an automatic block on Caller ID. That man would not be calling back.

A quick call to Allen – and from him to a friend in the NYPD Intelligence Division who took pity on a former comrade clearly in the wringer – confirmed Tom's hunch. He had Allen read out the number his NYPD source had passed on twice over. When Allen asked why Tom needed it, he deployed an old party trick, speaking a few apparently broken words, and then hung up. It would sound to Allen as if Tom had disappeared into a tunnel and lost signal.

The choked roads gave Tom Byrne some time as the car crawled the final few miles to John F Kennedy Airport. He knew he should relay his discovery to Jay Sherrill immediately, but he hesitated. He wanted to think this through. Besides, Sherrill would get there soon enough; just a matter of dialling the number they had both written down.

If he did that he would hear what Tom had heard. He would be able to confirm that the man whose number had been in the late Gerald Merton's telephone was the arms supplier the New York Police Department had branded long ago as 'the Russian'.

# CHAPTER NINE

They never did say welcome home. Tom always imagined they did, or that at least one day they would, but they never did. The immigration officer on the dawn shift at Heathrow had simply glanced down at the passport picture, glanced back up, and then nodded him through.

You couldn't blame him. For all he knew, Tom might have been back after a two-day trip. No big deal. He wasn't to know that this was always an unsettling moment for an Englishman who had made his home in New York since his late twenties. Whenever he came back Tom felt the same curious mix: the familiarity of a native and the bemusement of a stranger.

The country had changed so much. When he had left London the city had been in the doldrums of a recession, the place still creaking from a post-war period it had never really left behind. But now London seemed to crackle with energy. Every time he came back, Tom noticed the skyline was filled with new buildings or cranes putting up new buildings. You only had to look at the shop-fronts, the hoardings, the street cafés to smell the money. The contrast with New York used to be sharp: in Manhattan the skyscrapers were taller, the restaurants better, the shops open for longer. Now the two places looked more alike than ever.

But the biggest change was the people. There were Russian billionaires in Park Lane, Latvian cleaners in Islington and Poles everywhere. He had seen a black British comedian on cable TV lament that these days if you saw a white person in London, you could no longer assume they spoke English.

He took the Heathrow Express into town with one thought still preoccupying him: why was the Russian's number on Gerald Merton's mobile phone?

First, Tom had wondered if the old man had been the victim of a very skilful and cunning case of identity theft. Perhaps terrorists had spotted him, then deliberately dressed like him in order to confuse their pursuers. Maybe, at some point, they had even used – and then returned to him – his mobile phone, knowing that anyone listening in, or tailing them, would be led to the dead end of an aged British tourist.

But it all seemed a stretch. The simplest explanation was that Gerald Merton had indeed phoned the Russian arms dealer himself and gone to see him on Monday, just as the Feds said he had. There were not two men in black, just one.

The very thought made Tom smile. It meant that his old friend Henning Munchau might not be in such deep trouble after all. If Tom could prove that the UN had not shot an entirely innocent man they could put aside the sackcloth and ashes. Henning would be off the hook; Tom would have done all that had been asked of him and more. His debt to Henning would be discharged and there might even be a cash bonus in it for him.

Sure, it was unusual: a suspected terrorist aged seventy-seven. But, hey, these guys were crazy. Children had been used as suicide bombers, women, too, even pregnant ones. Why couldn't Gerald Merton have been the first pensioner accelerating his entry to paradise? He might not have been wearing an explosive belt when he was shot, but Tom could argue that Merton's stroll to the UN had been a reconnaissance mission, timing the walk from the Tudor Hotel to UN Plaza to see what obstacles he encountered, work out how far he could get before he was stopped. He was probably planning to return the very next day, strapped into a bomb supplied by the Russian.

Motive would be the big problem. Most likely Merton had been promised a cash payment for the family he would leave behind. After all, what cause could this old man have believed in so passionately that he was ready to wreak havoc in the headquarters of the United Nations?

Tom reached for his notebook, looking again at

the bare details he had gleaned from Allen. A date of birth as far into the past as Tom's dead father's. Place of birth: Kaunas, Lithuania.

Maybe that was the key fact. He'd read magazine stories about the rise and rise of the Eastern European mafia for years now. This 'Gerald Merton' could have been one of them, recently arrived in the UK and either an elderly godfather himself or, more likely, a jobbing assassin paid to whack somebody at the UN.

Still, the UN would need more evidence than a single number on a mobile phone to justify the gunning down of an elderly man. And the place to get it was London.

The TV screen on the train announced that Paddington was approaching. He remembered from his last visit the giant screens at railway stations, usually carrying a twenty-four-hour news channel. There were screens on the sides of buses now, even at bus stops. Cameras on every corner too, many more in London than you'd ever get away with in New York. George Orwell got more right than he realized.

At Paddington he took a cab. There was no time to check in to the hotel or catch some sleep, however tempting. He needed to see Merton's daughter as soon as possible, before the entire membership of the Amalgamated Union of Lefty Lawyers and America Bashers had descended on her doorstep, offering to put her father's face onto posters in every student bedroom in the land. He could imagine their excitement at the prospect. The protests against the Met's shooting of Jean Charles de Menezes had been lively enough, but in that case the target had only been the humble Metropolitan Police. So long as they could make New York, and therefore America, the bad guy, the death of Gerald Merton offered much richer pickings. Tom knew these people, he knew how their minds worked. He knew only too well.

He was just a short distance away now from Merton's daughter's address, watching as people closed their front doors and headed for work. Most of the buildings were old Georgian houses divided into flats. He had imagined her living in a tidy suburban semi, with a husband and at least a couple of kids. But this was not that kind of neighbourhood. He was in Clerkenwell, the residential pocket just west of the sleaze and grime of King's Cross.

As the cab turned into her street he saw immediately which house was hers. People were emerging from a front door with baleful expressions: making an early morning condolence call. He paid the driver, jumped out and headed in their direction. As he came closer, they looked up at him with the nodding half-smile of acknowledgement that strangers reserve for each other on these occasions. He didn't need to press the buzzer: the door was open.

He hadn't quite planned for the presence of

other people. From the hallway he could hear voices on the stairs, saying goodbye. He headed up.

For a second, he was confused. In front of him were two women in an embrace, one of them sobbing loudly, the other, taller woman, offering comfort. Yet he felt certain that this calm, tearless woman was the daughter of Gerald Merton. It was her eyes that confirmed it. They were as striking as the ones that had stared back at him on the mortuary slab in New York less than twenty-four hours earlier.

'Hello,' he said, extending a hand. 'I'm so sorry to come unannounced like this. My name is Tom Byrne and I'm from the United Nations.'

She fixed the extraordinary eyes upon him, then said in a clear and penetrating voice. 'I think you'd better leave.'

# CHAPTER TEN

Taken aback, it took Tom several seconds to realize that she was not speaking to him, but to her departing guests.

'You call us if you need anything, Rebecca,' said the husband, who Tom guessed was roughly her age, in his early thirties. The wife tried to say something too, but the eyes welled again and she shook her head in defeat.

Throughout Tom kept his gaze on Rebecca, who was standing tall and straight-backed in this wobbling, sobbing huddle. Everything about her was striking, nothing was moderate. Her hair was a deep, dark black; her nose was not short or button-neat, like the *Vogue* and *Elle* girls he dated in New York. Instead it was strong and, somehow, proud. Most arresting were those eyes of clearest green: not the same colour as her father's, but with the same shining brilliance. They seemed to burn not with the grief he had been expecting but with something altogether more controlled. He found that he could not look away from her.

'You can come in here,' she said.

He followed her into a room whose clutter he rapidly tried to interpret. The polished wood floors, the battered, and tiny, TV in the corner were predictable enough: urban bohemian. The books surprised him. Not the first couple of shelves of fiction, contemporary novels alongside Flaubert, Eliot and Hardy, but the rest: they seemed to be journals of some kind. He took a glance at the rest of the flat. No sign yet of another person. No sign of a man.

She sat down in a plain wooden chair, gesturing for him to take the more comfortable couch opposite.

He was about to speak when a phone rang: hers, a mobile. She looked at the display and answered it without hesitation.

'Not at all: I said you could call. What's happening?' She began nodding as she received what appeared to be a staccato burst of information. 'She's hypotensive now, you say? Despite good gram-negative coverage? Poor girl, this is the last thing she needs. Remember, she's been treated for AML. I'd make sure she's on Vancomycin and call intensive care to let them know she may need pressors. And, Dr Haining? Keep me posted.'

Tom looked back at the shelves, packed with what he could now see was an apparently full set of the *Journal of Paediatric Oncology*. He waited for her to close the clamshell phone and began, his opening line now duly revised. 'Dr Merton. You know why I'm here. I've flown into New York this morning because of a grave mistake.'

'London. You're in London.' She showed him a brief glimpse of a smile. It was crooked, the teeth sharp between full lips. He worried that he was staring. He could feel his pulse quicken.

'Sorry. London. Yes.' He tried to collect himself, to handle this like any other meeting. *Remember your objectives: placate this woman without anything resembling an admission of liability*. 'The Secretary-General of the United Nations asked me to come here as soon as this tragedy occurred to convey his personal sorrow and regret at what happened to your father. He speaks for the entire—'

'You can save the speech.' She was staring right at him, her eyes dry. 'I don't need a speech.'

He had planned on her breaking down, needing comfort and solace. Or else hurling abuse at him in a righteous fury. This was not in the plan. 'There's no speech.' Tom lifted his hands away from his briefcase.

'Good, because I don't want a string of platitudes. I want answers.'

'OK'

'Let's start with this. How on earth could any police force in the world not recognize a seventy-seven year old man when it saw one?'

'Well, identification is one of the key issues that—'

'And what the hell happened to shooting in the legs? Even I know that when police want to immobilize a suspect they shoot in the legs.'

'Standard procedure in the case of a suspected suicide bomber is to shoot at the head—'

'Suicide bomber? Fuck you!'

He paused, shocked by the obscenity, the silence filling the air. 'Listen–'

'Fuck you.' Quieter this time.

'I understand that you—'

'Have you ever come across a seventy-seven year old suicide bomber, Mr Byrne?'

'Look. Perhaps it would help if I walked you through the events of Monday morning, as best we know them.' He didn't even sound like himself, resorting to the plodding legalspeak he hated. He was finding it hard to concentrate; every time he so much as looked at this woman, he felt he was being shoved off his stride.

'OK. So my Dad's on a little retirement vacation and decides to be a tourist and visit the UN. Then what happened?'

Tom reached into his bag for the sheaf of papers he had brought, the timelines and FBI reports he and Sherrill had got from Allen so that he would be able to maintain at least the pretence of full disclosure. He had seen enough of these cases over the years to know that it was that above all – the lack of openness, the sense that the authorities were concealing the truth – that always enraged the grieving families. He had planned to give

Rebecca Merton every detail, show her the precise sequence of events, each split-second decision, until she would, despite her loss, have to concede that it was a tragic but innocent mistake and that the UN security team had been in an impossible position: how could they risk a suicide bomber killing tens, scores of innocents? They had taken one life in the sincere belief that they were saving many more. That was what he needed her to accept.

'Don't start giving me some presentation, Mr Byrne. I don't want you trying to bury me in papers, blinding me with science. I'm a doctor, I know that trick.'

'All right.' Tom put the papers back and leant forward in his chair. 'Tell me how we can help.'

'I want an apology.'

'Of course the United Nations feel the deepest—'

'Not from you. From the boss. I want a face-to-face meeting with the Secretary-General. I want him to look me in the eye and admit what the United Nations has done. This was not some minor slip-up; this was killing my father. For no reason. And that means a full apology, in person, from the man at the top.'

Tom remembered Henning's sole condition: no grandstanding, no photo-ops. 'Look, a tragedy happened yesterday. We know that. And the United Nations wants to show that it recognizes the scale of that tragedy. We'd like to make a gesture, to establish a fund available to you for whatever purpose seems appropriate. It could be a memorial—'

'Sorry, I think I misheard you. What did you say?' There was a second flash of that crooked smile.

'I said that the UN is willing to acknowledge the life of Gerald Merton with a one-off payment.' He immediately regretted *one-off*.

'Christ.' She shook her head, the full lips slowly colouring a deep red, as if her rage was filling them with blood. 'Maybe the headbangers are right after all. So the UN's not just anti-Israel, it's anti-Semitic as well.'

Tom frowned. 'I'm sorry?'

'You'd better be more than sorry, Mr Byrne. Is this really what you think of us? That you can buy us off with blood money?'

'I don't underst—'

'You think this is what Jews are like? That we'd let you kill our parents so long as the price is right?'

'I had no idea—'

'That's right. You have no idea at all.'

Her mobile rang again. He was trying to digest what she had just said, but as she stood up, all he could focus on was her shape. She was slim, but not skinny. He could see that even in thrown-on jeans and a loose black top, she had the figure not of the anorexic dolls you saw in Manhattan but of a real woman.

'Hi Nick. How's she doing? How's her chest X-ray look? That's not good.' She began nodding, murmuring her assent to the voice on the phone. 'Sounds like she's developing ARDS. That's what I'd worry about with strep, *viridans sepsis*. All right, tell the parents I'll call them soon. They've been through the wringer: they need to hear a familiar voice. Thanks, Nick.'

He was trying not to stare, but it was an unequal struggle. The intensity of this woman seemed to be burning up all the oxygen in the room. There was a strange butterfly sensation in his chest, as if his heart was trembling. He told himself it was coffee or lack of sleep or jet lag. But still he couldn't look away.

So Gerald Merton was Jewish. Tom had never even considered it. Everything had thrown him off course, the name, the passport – *Place of birth: Kaunas, Lithuania* – and especially the corpse. Tom Byrne knew what a circumcised penis looked like and Merton's was not it.

She finished the call and turned to him. 'I have to go: there's an emergency at the hospital.'

'I'm sorry to hear that.'

'Yeah, sure you are. Anyway, I don't think we have anything more to talk about, do you?' She turned around and disappeared into the kitchen, where he could hear the jangle of car keys being scooped up.

He turned to the pile of unused documents next to him on the couch and began pushing them back into his case when he saw it: a small, black notebook on a side table. For a moment he thought it must be his own Moleskine. But as he looked closer he could see it was thicker. It was hers. On impulse, he shoved it into his bag. He would say he'd taken it by mistake: that way he'd have an excuse to come back.

He stood up and followed Rebecca Merton down the stairs and out of her front door.

'Here's my card,' he said, successfully repressing his surprise that she took it. 'If you think of anything more you'd like to discuss, call me.'

She studied it for a moment, then looked back up, those emerald-clear eyes boring into him. 'So you're not even a UN lawyer. You're the hired help. The guy they brought in to do their dirty work. Goodbye, Mr Byrne. I don't think we'll be seeing each other again.'

## CHAPTER ELEVEN

Tom watched her stalk across the road, get into her old-model Saab and drive off, then stood as if paralysed for a minute or more, trying to work out the effect she had had on him. It wasn't the usual feeling, the sensation he would often get at a Manhattan party or during drinks at the Royalton: spotting some young beauty and lazily deciding he wanted her, the way you might pick a delicacy off a menu. That was how he had kept his bed filled in New York, but this was different.

He felt as if he had just run ten kilometres around Central Park. There was a flush in his cheeks; his pulse was elevated. He remembered, abruptly, how he had felt at the age of sixteen when he had first met Kate, four years his senior, a student at the university and the convenor of the Sheffield youth branch of the Campaign for Nuclear Disarmament. Even saying the name – Kate – brought back the glow. She had inducted him into the ways of the world and although he had been with many women since he had never felt that same, palpitating excitement again. But he had to admit to himself, with a tinge of shame, that he was feeling something like it now. *For God's sake,* he told himself firmly, *grow up.*

A sudden deep need for coffee prompted him to walk to the top of the street where there was a small parade of shops. Mercifully one was a café. He went in, sat down at the smallest table so that no one would join him and ordered an espresso.

When it arrived he downed it in two gulps, then sat back, closed his eyes and breathed deep. Only then did he remember the book in his bag. Could it be Rebecca Merton's diary? He knew he shouldn't open it, but he couldn't help himself.

The notebook was filled, page after page, with tiny, neat blue handwriting. Instantly he knew these were not the writings of a thirty-something woman. It had been a mistake to pocket it. But he only had to read the first few sentences to realize that he – and not only he – had made a much, much graver mistake.

## CHAPTER TWELVE

*My name is Gershon Matzkin and I was born in Kruk, Lithuania. My British passport says I was born in Kaunas because Kruk is such a small town and no one has heard of it. And also because the name of that place should be cursed a thousand times and it is better that it is never written down.*

*I was the second of four children of Meir and Rebecca Matzkin. I was different from the others. My sisters had dark hair, their features proud, while I was blond and had blue eyes and a small nose. I did not look like a Jew at all.*

*My father would joke that maybe my mother had been too friendly with the goatherd in the village. He could joke about such things because he knew they were impossible. These days, they would say that my genes were different, mutant. But then, who knew of such things?*

*I was born too early. My body was tiny; they said my life was hanging by a thread. When I was eight days old the rabbi said I was too weak to have my* brit milah, *too weak to be circumcised. Afterwards, because of everything that happened to our family, it was delayed. Maybe my mother did not want to think about it. And after that it was too late.*

*The little village whose name I do not want to mention did not have many Jews, maybe a few dozen families. We kept ourselves quiet, trying to get by. But every now and then there was trouble . . .*

I was frightened even before it started. At that age – I was perhaps seven years old – the sound of the rain on the windows was enough to scare me. I liked snow, which we had plenty of, but the rattle of raindrops against the glass frightened me: it sounded like fingers, tapping, demanding to be let in. There was no rain that night but it was very dark and that scared me too.

But this night I was not the only one afraid. My sisters too were awake and crying. Local Lithuanians were running through the streets where the few Jews lived, banging on doors, shouting: *You killed Christ! Come out, you Christ-killers!*

This happened every now and then, especially at Easter. Even then, when I was just a child, I could recognize the slur in their voices. They were drunk, on vodka, no doubt, but also on hatred – the hatred of the Jew fermented by their faith and distilled for nearly two thousand years. I know this now: then I was just scared.

There were more voices than usual. We waited for them to fade as they went past, but they did not. They remained loud and near. My mother sat on the bed with us – all four of us children shared a single bed back then – telling us to hush. She was holding the youngest of my sisters, little Rivvy, cradled in her arms and was singing an old Yiddish melody:

*Dos tzigele is geforen handlen*
*Dos vet zein dein beruf*
*Rozinkes mit mandlen*
*Shlof-zhe, Yidele, shlof.*

It means:

*The little goat went out looking*
*Just as you'll do some day*
*Bringing raisins and almonds*
*Sleep sweet baby sleep.*

The men outside were still bellowing, *Zhid! Zhid!* Jew! Jew! But she carried on singing that song. *Shlof-zhe, Yidele, shlof.* Sometimes, even now, when I remember everything that happened afterwards, I hear that song again.

At that moment none of us knew what was going on outside. My mother thought my father was downstairs, peering through a gap in the curtains, watching for the moment when the thugs grew bored and moved on. She was partly right: that was why he had gone downstairs, so that he could look and tell us when the coast was clear.

But then something had caught his eye. He had seen smoke coming from the barn.

We were not farmers, but like most people in our village we kept a few animals, some chickens and a cow. And now, late at night, my father could see smoke. Surely the men from the village had thrown a torch into the barn. He thought only that he had to rescue the animals. So he ran into the barn.

I don't know when my mother first realized what had happened but she suddenly called out. 'Meir?' Then she saw the first orange flames. 'Meir!' When there was no reply she threw Rivvy aside as if she were a rag doll and ran down the stairs. We watched from the window as she fled out of the house towards the barn. I was so frightened that I stopped crying.

We saw her tugging at something, bent double, as if she were dragging a sack of seed from the barn. In the dark it was almost impossible to see that she was, in fact, pulling at the ankles of a man. Hannah made out the shape first. 'It's Daddy,' she said.

We never knew for certain what had happened. Perhaps the smoke was too much. Perhaps he had hit his head on a wooden beam. Maybe one of the thugs conducting the pogrom had followed him into the barn and beaten him. Whatever had happened, our mother had been too late.

She was never the same person after that. Her hair went grey and she let it fall loose; her clothes were sometimes dirty. She would wear the same skirt and blouse for days on end. She no longer laughed and if she smiled it was a strange, misshapen smile, crooked with regret and sadness. And she never again sang the lullaby.

She decided we could no longer live in that place, whose name she would never say out loud. She had a cousin who had once lived in Kovno and so we moved there. She felt we needed to be in a big city, a place where we would not stand out. A place where there were not just a few Jews, but thousands of us. I suppose she thought there would be safety in numbers. So we headed to Kovno. If you look on a map now you will see no such place. Today they call it by its Lithuanian name: Kaunas.

We arrived when I was eight years old and I have happy memories of our first two years there. My sisters and I went to school and I discovered that I was good at learning languages. The teacher said I had an ear for it. Russian and, especially, German. I found it easy. I only had to hear a word once to remember it. Of course 'bread' was *Brot*. What else would it be? The pieces clicked together like a jigsaw puzzle. I learned and learned.

In Kruk, we had followed only the essentials of Jewish tradition and – as my own penis testified – not even all of those. We lit candles on Friday evening to mark the start of the Sabbath, but we did not do much more. In Kovno it was different. Nearly a quarter of the people of this city were Jews and in the area where we lived, everyone. There were synagogues on every street, Yiddish schools, Hebrew schools, a famous religious academy, the yeshiva at Viriampole, even a Jewish hospital. There were people to teach me how to say Kaddish for my father. We did not feel like outsiders here, even if I now looked like one.

I wish I could say my mother was happy, but she was not. We lived in a couple of rented rooms on Jurbarko Street. I do not know how she paid for them. The rooms were dark, even when the sun was shining outside. During this time, I remember my mother's eyes were always empty.

And then, one day in 1940, a different flag was flying.

It was hot that day, the sun so warm it felt as if it would dry out the damp of what had been a long winter. We were playing in the street, as usual, me trailing behind Hannah while my sisters played a game of hopscotch. I was the first to notice it. I pointed upward at the deep red flag, billowing in the breeze. I couldn't quite work out the gold shapes in the top corner; I wondered if it was a letter in some foreign alphabet. Later I learned that these were the tools of the industrial worker and the farmer, the hammer and sickle.

The Russians had arrived to make Lithuania part of the Soviet Union.

At school, the teachers seemed nervous. My Russian teacher vanished. Hannah explained to me that the Russians were arresting people. They were shutting down some of the Jewish buildings because they were against 'the revolution', whatever that was. Hannah heard that some of the men were taken away to Siberia. She said it was the coldest place on earth. I imagined the men standing on a huge sheet of white ice, shivering like penguins.

We were frightened of the Russians but it was not they who frightened us most. Because we soon heard that there was a resistance to the Communists, local Lithuanians who were determined to kick the Soviets out of their country. It was these people who scared us. We remembered from Kruk how these men could behave once they were angry and stirred up.

One day I saw the girls whispering. At first they would not let me see what they were all looking at. 'No, he'll tell Mama,' Rivvy said.

'Tell Mama what?'

'Nothing.'

'What have you got there?'

Eventually, they gave in. Hannah made me swear to secrecy and then she showed me. It was a leaflet she had found on the street. It said the Jews were to blame for the Communists occupying Lithuania. *Without the Jews, we would be a free people!*

In whispers, Hannah issued our orders. 'We must not let Mama see this.' I was not yet eleven years old and I knew nothing of Communism or occupation but I understood that my mother was frail, like a cup that had broken once before and must not be dropped. We succeeded too. She never did see that leaflet.

A year later I thought our troubles were over. At school, the headmaster announced that the Russians had gone. They had simply run away. Good, I thought: now the Lithuanians won't be angry with us, the Jews, for bringing the Soviets into their country. But the headmaster seemed more worried than ever.

This was June 1941. It was only after the headmaster stopped speaking, when I heard the boys in my class talking, that I understood that the Russians had not just left because they wanted to leave us in peace. They had vanished because they were frightened: the Germans had begun an invasion of the Soviet Union.

The next day I was in the street, playing catch with two other boys from school. Suddenly there was a noise, distant at first: the sound of faraway whistles and faint drums. We thought that people were celebrating, a marching band parading through the streets because the Russians had gone. But then there were new sounds: women screaming and children crying. My friend took his ball and ran. I stood there on my own for four or five seconds before a man grabbed my wrist and told me to get out of the street. 'Go home,' he said. *'Go home now!'* I must have looked dumb and uncomprehending because he stared at me hard. 'Pogrom,' he said. *'Pogrom.'*

I ran as fast as I could back to Jurbarko Street.

The screams were getting louder: the Lithuanians were marking the great occasion of the Russian withdrawal the best way they knew how, by attacking any Jew they could find. On Kriščiukaičio Street, I saw a man pulled out of a shop by his ears; three men began to beat him, hitting him on the head over and over. I saw other Jews dragged off. I don't know where these Jews were taken or what happened to them afterwards. But I can guess.

The Lithuanians were wearing strange uniforms, ones I had never seen before. They were black, with the flag of Lithuania on their sleeves, like an armband. These jackets were not all identical, like the uniform of real soldiers. And the men did not march in columns, but rampaged through the streets, shouting slogans: 'The Jews and Communists have brought shame to Lithuania!' They called themselves the Lithuanian Activist Front.

Later we found out that they took dozens of Jews to the Lietūkis garage, in the centre of Kovno. They killed hundreds of men there. Afterwards, in a book, I learned that on that night of June 23 1941 and on the three nights that followed, they killed more than three thousand eight hundred Jews. They used axes and knives, as well as bullets; they burned people out of their houses and out of any hiding place. They drowned others in the Neris river. They torched synagogues. At the time we knew no numbers. We knew only what we could see.

I was running as fast as I could, darting in and out of entrances and into alleyways, to avoid the men in black. I thought that if they found me they might beat me up too. After all, I was eleven years old now and I was tall: they might have thought of me as more of a man than a child. And I assumed they would know that I was a Jew.

Just outside the tenement where we lived, I ran into my sisters. Hannah was so relieved to see me that she clutched me in a tight, long hug. She bundled us into the building and up the stairs so that we could warn our mother what was going on. We wanted to tell her what we had just witnessed, the terrible things that were happening. But she already knew.

I understood what had happened when I heard Hannah's cry. So small, as if she was just a little girl, which of course, now that I am a grown man, I know that she was. She tried to stop us, my other sisters and me, from seeing it, but it was too late. I saw it and I can never forget what I saw.

My mother's feet were in the air, her body dangling from a beam in the ceiling. She was hanging there, swinging like the pendulum in a clock – a clock that said we had reached the end of time.

# CHAPTER THIRTEEN

Tom closed the notebook and looked up. This was a nightmare. Truly, a waking nightmare.

He checked his watch. Too early to call Henning. He imagined what he would tell him. 'I've got good news and bad news. The good news is that the dead guy may not be so innocent after all. The bad news is, you killed a Holocaust survivor.'

PR calamities didn't get much worse than this. Rebecca Merton would simply have to pop this notebook into an envelope and send it to any newspaper in London and the United Nations name would be caked in mud. He could see the headline, across a two-page spread: '"My father's wartime hell", by daughter of UN shooting victim', complete with full colour photo of 'raven-haired Rebecca Merton, 31'.

Tom rolled a cigarette, before seeing the wagging finger of the waitress. Of course, London now had the same bloody puritan rules as New York. He kept it unlit and ordered another espresso. He went back to the notebook and girded himself for the next revelation.

*I remember very little about those next few days. We moved around as if in some kind of trance. My sister Hannah the least. She did not allow herself to be stunned for very long. She had to be our mother now . . .*

My job was to be the provider of food. I was a child, but I looked older and my looks held another advantage. I could pass for one of the local Lithuanian lads, not marked as a Jew. I would scavenge wherever I could, turning up at a baker's shop just before closing time, my hand out for any scraps. If there was a woman there I would try to catch her eye: women were more likely to take pity on me. 'Such a sweet face,' they would say, handing me a loaf-end of bread or a hardened rock of old cake.

'Where are your parents?'

'I'm an orphan.'

'Hear that, Irena? He's an orphan. What happened to your mum and dad, little one?'

'The Russians.'

'Oh, those evil animals. And here I am giving you a hunk of stale bread. Irena, fetch that meat we have in the back. Come on, quick now. Here you are, young man. Now you be on your way.'

None of us told the truth. If anyone ever came near Hannah, she would lie outright. 'My father will be back soon,' she would say. 'My mother has just popped out.' At the time I thought she was simply ashamed to admit we were orphans. Now I understand better. She did not want people to know that in our two rooms, there were only children. She must have worried that someone would send us away or steal what we had. Or worse.

This time, between the Russians and what followed, did not last long. The books say there was, in fact, no time at all, that an advance group of Germans was already there, from the very beginning, even organizing the pogroms the night my mother ended her life. But when the Germans arrived in force, we knew it.

In fact, we heard them before we saw them. I was in the apartment, watching Hannah carve up the crust of bread I had brought into four pieces. As the boy, the man of the house, mine was always the largest. Rivvy and Leah had equal chunks – and the smallest Hannah gave to herself. The girls had learned patience and would eat their food slowly, making even a bite of bread last as if it were a meal. But, at that time, I could not control my hunger. I gobbled up whatever I was given as soon as it was in front of me.

At first, I thought it was a storm. But the sky outside was bright and clear. Yet there it was again, the deep rumble of distant explosions. 'Shhh,' Hannah said and we all held still. Hannah closed her eyes so she could concentrate. 'Aeroplanes,' she said eventually.

Soon there was a different noise. It was the thunder of an army marching into a city. And then there were sounds that were not nearly so far away. Hard, mechanical sounds of motorcycles and infantry and mammoth field guns on wheels and finally tanks, all rolling into Kovno.

Hannah edged towards the window, not daring to press her face too close. I barged ahead and took a good look. What I saw confused me. The windows of the building opposite to ours, and the one next to it, were opening. Out of them were unrolling large, billowing pieces of cloth: flags. Girls were leaning out, smiling and waving, throwing flowers at the men below.

'Is everything going to be OK now, Hannah?' I asked.

'Maybe, Gershon. Maybe.' But she looked unsure.

We went to school the next day and I knew immediately that even if our Lithuanian neighbours were glad to see the Nazis, we Jews were not. Everyone was tense. The headmaster spoke to the whole school and his face was carved with anxiety. 'We are a people who have been tested many times,' he said. 'Children, you all know the story of Pharaoh. And of Haman. Men who came to destroy the Jews. And what happened each time?' No one wanted to answer; this didn't seem like a normal lesson. 'Each time they failed, because God protected us. We survived. Children, this may be such a test now.'

I'm not sure if it was that day or the next but

it happened very soon. Notices went up in German. I stood on tiptoe, my neck craned, to read the one posted on a lamppost near the school, translating it first to the boys in my class and then to a small group that gathered around. The sign said that from now on all Jews would have to wear a yellow star on their outer clothing, to be visible at all times. And there would be a curfew: not for everyone in Kovno, but for the Jews. After dark, every Jew was to be indoors; there were to be no Jews on the streets. And we were not allowed to walk on the pavements. Those were reserved for Aryans only. We would have to walk in the gutter.

Even then, I don't know whether I was scared. These were new rules that we would have to live by, but it seemed better than the Lithuanians and their pogroms. If this was all they planned to do to us – make us wear a yellow star and stay home after dark – then it was better than being beaten on the streets.

But I could not comfort myself like that for very long. A few mornings later, we were woken by a loud banging on the door. I sat bolt upright. My chest was banging. For the first, confused seconds I wondered if it was my mother at the door: I imagined her, smiling, her hair combed and neat, come to take us away from here. I must have been about to say something because Hannah, who was also now sitting up, placed her finger over her lips and fixed me in a glare that told me to keep very still.

The banging on the door started up again, louder and more insistent. We could hear the same noise repeated up and down the corridor and outside on the street too: Nazis pounding on the doors of the Jews.

Hannah got up, grabbed something to cover her nightclothes and opened the door.

He was tall, his back straight. I couldn't stop staring at his boots. They shined like glass and when they moved, the leather creaked.

'You have ten minutes to gather everything,' he barked in German. 'You are moving!' And with that he turned and headed for the next door. There were more men repeating the same instructions up and down the staircase, above and below us. Now we heard those same words coming from the street below, amplified by a megaphone.

When Hannah turned around her face was serious. 'Get dressed. Rivvy and Leah, don't just wear one skirt. Wear two or three. As many as you can, one over the other. Do the same with sweaters and shorts. You too, Gershon. As many clothes as you can.'

Then she scurried around the two rooms, shoving whatever she thought essential into suitcases. She moved fast, but she was not panicked. And because she wasn't, we weren't.

After a few minutes she added, 'You can take one thing each that you really, really want. Just one. Everything else stays behind.'

I reached for a book of adventure stories. Leah

grabbed her favourite doll, Rivvy took a hairbrush. And Hannah calmly removed a picture of my parents from its frame and placed it in her pocket. Then she ushered us to the door and closed it, for the last time. We waddled down the stairs: I was wearing four or five shirts and two coats, as well as carrying our largest suitcase. By the time we reached the street, I thought I might boil with heat.

We saw many Jews like us, trying to carry as much as they could. Many were carrying bags of food, tins or sacks of flour. Some had piled up makeshift wagons or trolleys. Hannah scolded herself. She had not thought of that.

Within a few minutes, we were ordered to walk. We would be crossing Kaunas, they said, to our new homes. We were surrounded by men with guns and, more frightening to me, dogs. We did as we were told.

Some people lasted just a few steps. They couldn't carry what they had taken and they began to drop plates and cups, which broke noisily on the ground. 'Quiet, Jew!' one of the Nazis shouted. Some of the older people collapsed.

All the time, the Lithuanians stood and watched, as if this were a street carnival. Sometimes they shouted and taunted us. If they saw something they liked they rushed forward and grabbed it. They knew the Germans would not stop them from stealing. I kept on staring at this crowd. And then suddenly there was a familiar face.

'Antanas!' I called out. 'It's me, Gershon!' It was the boy I used to play ball with; we had had a game a week earlier. But he just stared back at me, holding tight the hand of his father.

A lady began to walk beside us. She said to Hannah, 'I hear they're taking us across the river, to Viriampole. We're all going to have to live there.'

'All of us? But Viriampole is tiny.'

Hannah thought the Viriampole district would be too small for all the Jews of Kovno, who numbered in the tens of thousands, and she was right. What she did not know then, none of us did, was that there were more who would be crammed into those few small streets of Viriampole. The Germans had sent army patrols into the countryside searching for any Jews there, looking in every last village, little places like the one whose name my mother would never mention. If they found one Jew here or three Jews there, they too had to move into Viriampole. If a Jew refused to move, he would find his house set on fire. So he moved.

Years later, people always asked us, 'Why did you obey? Why did you not rise up and resist?' But we did not know then what we know now. We did not know that we were being marched into a ghetto. I remember thinking maybe things will be better for us if we are all together in one place. At least we will be far away from those Lithuanian murderers.

The walk was long and hard. I kept shifting the suitcase I was carrying from one hand to another, tilting like a reed that was about to break. But I did not stop. I was the man of the family now and I knew that Rivvy and Leah needed me to keep going.

Finally we came to the narrow concrete bridge which marked our crossing into Viriampole.

'Quickly, quickly,' Hannah said, shooing us over. I think she was hoping we would not notice the barbed wire and the watchtowers. Or perhaps she was hoping I would have no time to read and translate the German signs that marked the entrance. 'Plague! Entry forbidden!' said one and directly underneath there was another: 'Jews are forbidden from bringing in food and heating supplies – violators will be shot!'

Once we were inside, the soldiers were no longer walking beside us. Now that they had herded us into the ghetto, their job was done. We waited for a few minutes, not just us but everyone. We were waiting to be given some kind of instruction or at least a plan. But slowly the penny dropped. One man broke away from the crowd and dashed into the first entrance he saw. He then appeared from a first floor window and beckoned the rest of his family to join him. Immediately another family followed and then another and then another. It took a second or two for Hannah to understand: this was to be a free-for-all, you lived in whatever corner you could find.

We went to Linkuvos Street with the lady Hannah had been talking to. Later I wondered if Hannah had given her something, perhaps some jewellery of my mother's, because I know Hannah wanted us to be with a family. She understood even then that there would be times when she would need someone else to keep an eye on us. And so we crammed thirteen people into two rooms, the other family and us.

It seems idiotic now, but I remember thinking that, yet again, this would be the end of our troubles. Yes, it was a ghetto. But we were all together and there was work for those who were fit – and work meant food. I lied about my age and got a permit to work. I was twelve now but tall enough to pass for sixteen. And so each morning I would cross the narrow bridge out of the ghetto in a detail of thirty men, all of them older than me. We were given special yellow armbands to wear on our right sleeves, then loaded onto trucks and driven a short distance to Aleksotas, where our job was to build the Germans a military airbase. We had to do the work of machines: lifting rocks and breaking stones. We worked from dawn till dusk, twelve hours or more, until every sinew, every tendon was screaming for rest. We stopped only for a few minutes, to drink thin soup and eat a crust of bread.

But at least it was food. Hannah, though, was struggling to find enough for the others to eat. And the girls were getting sick. Everyone was. The ghetto was so full, maybe thirty thousand people stuffed into an area fit for one thousand. People were sleeping on the streets, even in the cold. The synagogues became dormitories. One morning, I stepped over a man who I thought was sleeping. But he was not asleep. He had died and no one had buried him.

It was around this time that Hannah decided she too would have to get a work permit. If she had one of those precious yellow pieces of paper, then she would earn food for herself but, more importantly, she would have a chance to get out of the ghetto, somehow buy food and smuggle it back in: that way she could feed Leah and Rivvy something more than the starvation rations provided by the Nazis. It was the only way.

I don't know what she did to get that permit. I like to think she met up with the resistance, who were forging papers all the time. But sometimes I think something else. Because Hannah was a pretty girl and when you are hungry and your family is hungry you will do desperate things.

And so Hannah began to leave the ghetto each morning, along with me and the rest of the workers. There were checks at the gate, but the guards were not German. They were Lithuanian police. Perhaps this fact has been forgotten, but the Nazis did not do all this alone. There were very few Germans in places like Kovno. They relied on the local people to help them.

Then came that cruel day, the one that changed everything. Hannah never told me about it in so many words, but I have pieced together what happened and have made myself set down those events here. So that the memory of it will not die.

Hannah got through the check without any problems. She worked in the normal way. But at some point she must have broken away from the rest of the work detail, because when she came back that evening she had some bread. Not a whole loaf, but a chunk of bread that she was saving for our two sisters who had no permits and no food. She hid it under her coat. I think of her now, a little girl standing there with her heart thumping.

Perhaps in the queue at the gate she looked nervous. Something gave her away. Not to the rest of the policemen on duty: they were too drunk to notice anything. But to the son of one of the Lithuanian guards, a boy not much older than me, perhaps thirteen or fourteen at most, who often used to hang around at the gate with his father and his pals. The older men would laugh and joke with him, as if he were a team mascot. He even had his own uniform. But we called him the Wolf, because even though he was so young, he was as cruel as a beast. His face seemed to shine with evil. The smile was wide, baring teeth that seemed ready to drip with blood. Once you saw that face, you could never forget it. The Wolf would plead with his father to let him search the Jews and the men would laugh at his eagerness. That night he asked to search Hannah.

I can imagine how she trembled as he pushed

and prodded at her clothes, feeling at her bony frame. He was about to let her go when he gave one last poke, under her armpits. And it was there he found the lump of bread.

The Wolf turned around to the cheering guards like a novice fisherman who has just reeled in a prize trout. Nodding, he soaked up their applause.

'So what will be your reward, son?' his father beamed, his truncheon dangling at his side. 'Name it.'

The Wolf paused while Hannah stood there shivering. The rest of the ghetto inmates stared down at the ground, wanting this moment to be over.

'Let me punish her myself.'

There was a loud, lecherous roar from the guards. Several placed their left hand on their right arm and pumped their biceps. They began a chant, a Lithuanian song about a boy becoming a man. The Wolf led Hannah to the ghetto cells, where the jailer recognized him. With pride the Wolf explained what had happened; the jailer stepped aside – and away.

'Take off your clothes,' the Wolf told Hannah.

Hannah stood still, unable to move.

'I said, take off your clothes.'

Hannah was cold, her fingers like stiff shards of ice. She did not move fast enough. He punched her in the face. 'Listen, Jew! I won't tell you again. Take off your clothes!'

Hannah did as she was told and stood there naked

with her head down. She would not have seen the Wolf reach for his truncheon and hold it high before bringing it down onto her arms, her back and thighs. Her cries of pain must have sounded as if they were coming from a creature other than a human being. When she fell to her knees, the Wolf kicked her in the face, in the ribs, in the kidneys, in the place she always cherished as the womb of her future children. Soon she lay prone on the floor, waiting for unconsciousness, or death.

Then it stopped. The Wolf seemed to have grown tired, or bored, and he stepped back. Hannah let out a brief sigh; her ordeal seemed to be nearing its end.

There was a clink of metal, the sound, Hannah realized, of a belt being unbuckled. Was he about to flog her?

But now she felt two cold hands on her hips, hauling her up from the floor like a joint of meat. He was not trying to make her stand up, but rather forcing her into a kneeling position, so that she was on all fours.

She could barely feel her legs, let alone move them. She collapsed back onto the floor several times, but each time he pushed her back up. She was confused. Why did he need her to kneel like this?

Suddenly she sensed him near her, too near, his body arched over hers. She heard the unfastening of a zip.

The sudden realization made her scream in

protest, but he brought his hand down over her mouth, clamping her jaw tight so that she could not bite, and thrust himself inside her.

How long it lasted she did not know. Her mind left her, it fled to the same place it had gone when she had seen her mother's corpse hanging from the ceiling. She vanished from herself. But then as his assault endured she saw something on the ground, just a few inches away. The mere sight of it brought the decision instantaneously, as if the object itself had determined how it should be used. She would merely follow the impulse that seemed to emanate from this small, random thing: a bent and rusty nail that lay loose on the floor.

She reached for it and curled it invisibly into her right hand, a new resolve powering through her. He was too focused on his pleasure to notice her movement: she could hear him panting and moaning as he struggled to grip her hips and keep her still. She did not hesitate. In a single movement, she pushed back, pulling his arm away from her face with one hand and wielding the nail, held between her fingers like a blade, with the other.

She found his left arm, the one that had been gagging her, its underside exposed. The nail tore through the cotton of his shirt and scored down the flesh. She had never known such strength inside her. It made her roar, louder even than the scream he let out as he felt his arm ripped open.

She shook him away. Instinct made her flee

from there as fast as she could, first in a crawl, then in a crouch, grabbing her clothes from the floor. She ran and ran, only noticing once she was three streets away that no one was chasing her. She later told me what she guessed, that the Wolf was too ashamed to admit that he had allowed a naked girl – a snivelling Jewess – to get the better of him. He would claim the deep gash in his arm, which took many weeks to heal, was the result of an accident.

But it was Hannah who was wounded. Not just her face, which was no longer hers. But her soul. She could not be our mother any more. She would stay all day and all night in our small room. I had to keep on working, even though I was now very thin and forever hungry. I would bring back what food I could, deciding at the gate whether I could risk bringing it in. If the guards were drunk, I would try it. If the Wolf was anywhere near, I would pass what I had hidden to someone braver, or more foolish, than me.

Then, in late October 1941, a decree was plastered on every wall and lamppost, announcing that all inhabitants of the ghetto were to gather at six o'clock the next morning at Demokratu Square. No one knew what was coming. All through the night you could hear different sounds coming from the street: religious men praying, women wailing, others feasting and getting drunk, as if to enjoy what they feared would be their last night of life.

I looked to Hannah for advice on what we

should do. But she was not the same Hannah. Her eyes were empty, just as our mother's had been. I was the one who took charge, collecting up a few scraps of food, ensuring the girls wrapped up warm. We left our doors unlocked. Those were the orders: so that no one would try to hide.

There was a light dusting of snow on the ground that morning, sleet really, the gloom broken only by the odd candle or lantern. Everyone was holding on to papers, either a work permit or an educational certificate, anything which might prove they had some worth, that they could be of use to the Germans.

We waited in the damp cold for more than three hours until finally SS Master Sergeant Helmut Rauca stood on top of a mound, where he could survey the tens of thousands of people huddled there, and nodded for the first column of people to be brought before him. I noticed there were machine-gun nests all around the square; further away, on the hill-sides, stood local Lithuanians, anxious to exploit the good view they had of proceedings.

Rauca was the man to watch. With the tiniest movement of his hand, he would send some people to the left, some to the right. My sisters and I were lucky: where we had been waiting turned out to be the front of the queue. But it meant I had no time to work out the pattern: was it good to be sent to the left or better to be directed right? I couldn't tell.

My sisters and I picked up Hannah and stepped

forward. Rauca made a parting gesture: he wanted the girls to go to the right and me to the left. I protested that we had to stay together. 'As you wish – to the right!' he barked, with what I thought was a smile.

And then I felt a hand grip my shoulder.

'Not you,' a man's voice said.

I turned around to see a policeman. Not a German or a Lithuanian, but one of the Jewish policemen that worked in the ghetto.

I tried to wriggle away from him and join my sisters, who were now being shoved ahead. Rivvy was reaching out for me, but I couldn't grab her hand. Leah began to cry. It was no use though. The policeman was holding me back. 'Not you,' he said again.

I began to cry out, pushing and punching at him. How dare this traitor separate me from my sisters? I tried to pull his hand off me, but he held me tighter. Now Rivvy and Leah were screaming – they could see what was happening – but he would not let me go, no matter how much I struggled. My sisters were disappearing deeper into the thick scrum of people sent right by a flick of Rauca's finger. Rivvy and Leah had vanished. The last thing I saw were Hannah's eyes, vacant and staring.

The policeman finally pulled me off and frog-marched me away, down a side alley, until we were gone from the square altogether. I had no idea who this man was or why he had done what he had just done.

# CHAPTER FOURTEEN

Tom rubbed his eyes; the overnight flight was catching up with him. It had been a long time since he had read an individual story like this: case histories, they used to call them. When he had first started at the UN he would pore over such documents, absorbing each detail. After a few years, he would skim read them, seeking only the pertinent legal details. One person's horror story was pretty much the same as anyone else's. But he was reading this one attentively: must be out of practice.

*The Jewish policeman – and you must remember we despised these traitors as much as we hated the Germans and the Lithuanians – left me there, where we stood. Once he was gone, I realized the street was completely silent. It was a terrible silence. It was quiet because all the people had gone.*

I walked back to our little stretch of Linkuvos Street, past buildings that were now empty and still. I felt as if I was the last child on earth. Four thousand people had gone that day. Everyone else was either outside the ghetto, doing forced labour, or they were hiding. No one was on the streets.

I was twelve years old and I was all alone. I felt jealous of my sisters, imagining them living somewhere new.

I carried on working, still pretending I was sixteen. I did not dare tell even the other workers the truth about my age. Some were nice to me, as if they knew I was just a child. But some were so desperate they were no longer the people they had been. They were so hungry, they had become like animals. Such people would have betrayed me in an instant if they believed it would have made my ration theirs.

I lived in the same room we had shared, though now with a different family. The other lady and her children had been on the convoy to the Ninth Fort with my sisters. Now, the rooms were not so cramped. In fact, there was more space throughout the ghetto, because so many thousands had left. We did not know where they had gone or why we had not heard from them.

Nobody I knew was around. The children I had once gone to school with were all gone. The only familiar face belonged to that policeman who had stopped me getting on the convoy, that pig of a traitor. I only had to look at him to feel revulsion. And yet he seemed to be around often. I would return exhausted after twelve hours working on the building site, my legs and back aching, and there he would be, at the entrance to the ghetto. Or he would be patrolling outside the building where I slept. Sometimes he scared me, the rest of the time he just disgusted me.

Then one night there was a knock on the door. An urgent knock, three times, four times. At first, the woman in the apartment looked terrified. She believed it was the Gestapo. She glared at me in terror. What misfortune had I brought down on them? Had I been seen smuggling?

Then we heard the voice on the other side of the door. 'Polizei, open up!'

It was the Jewish police of the ghetto. Everyone knew they could be as vicious as any Lithuanian collaborator. I looked over to the window, wondering if I should jump down onto the street and make a run for it. We were two floors up: could I drop down on the ground without breaking any bones? I saw that my hands were trembling.

Before I had even had a moment to make a plan, the woman had made her decision. She opened the door and there he was, the policeman who had pulled me off the convoy some three weeks before. Here, at my door, in the middle of the night.

'You, boy, come now.'

I was frozen with fear. I did not move.

'NOW!'

I was still wearing all the clothes I had. You did not dare take them off at night because they might be stolen. I let the policeman lead me away.

He marched me down the stairs and into the street, loudly promising to take me to the authorities for what I had done. I did not understand what I had done.

Eventually, he turned left and right, then into an alley and down an outdoor stairwell to the entrance of a cellar. This, I knew, was not the police headquarters. By now he had stopped shouting about how I was going to be punished. I felt the fear tighten in my stomach.

Then the policeman knocked on the door. Not a normal knock, but in a strange rhythm. Three quick blows, then two slow ones. A voice spoke on the other side of the tiny basement door.

*'Ver is dort?'* Who goes there?

*'Einer fun di Macabi.'* A son of the Maccabees.

The door creaked open and the policeman darted in, grabbing me with him. Inside were three other men, their faces lit by a single candle at the centre of a small, rotting table. To me they looked old, their eyes dark and sunken, their faces gaunt. But now I know they were young, one of them barely twenty.

They stared at me until one, who seemed to be the leader, said finally, 'It's a miracle.'

Then another nodded and said, 'He's perfect. Our secret weapon.'

The leader then spoke again, his face harsh. 'Take off your trousers.'

I hesitated and he repeated it until I realized I had no choice. I lowered my trousers slowly.

'All the way down! So we can see.'

And once they had seen, the three men all gave

a small smile. One even managed a brief laugh. None spoke to me. 'Well done, Shimon,' they said and the policeman nodded, like a child praised by his teacher. 'You have truly brought us a Jewish miracle.'

I had heard about the Jewish underground, but I had not believed it. The kids spoke about a resistance that was coming, how some Jews were trying to get guns to fight the Nazis, even to break out of the ghetto. But we had seen no sign of it. I believed it was a fairy tale, the kind of story boys tell each other.

Now though, I understood where I had been taken. The policeman had called himself a 'son of the Maccabees': that had been the password. I knew that the Maccabees had been the great Jewish fighters, the Hebrew resisters who had battled to save Jerusalem.

I was a blond-haired, blue-eyed boy with an uncircumcised penis. I could pass for an Aryan. Perhaps they would use me to smuggle food into the ghetto. I was excited; I knew I could do it. After all, had not Hannah sent me out as a little Lithuanian orphan boy, to beg from our gentile neighbours who might take pity on a gentile child?

But then the leader of the men sent Shimon away and began whispering in Yiddish with the others, oblivious to the fact that I was still there, standing right in front of them. One said they could not afford to wait: 'The boy has seen our faces.' Another nodded. 'He knows about this place. We can't afford to risk it.' I did not know what they were going to do to me.

Finally, the leader raised his hand, as if the discussion was over. He had reached a decision. Only then did he turn and look straight at me. He told me his name was Aron. 'Are you brave?' he asked.

'Yes,' I said.

'Are you brave enough to perform a task that carries with it a grave risk – most likely a *mortal* risk?'

'Yes,' I said, though of course I had no idea of such things. I was saying what I thought would save me.

'I am going to give you a task on behalf of your people. You are to travel to Warsaw, to an address I will give you. You will give them this message. Are you ready?'

I nodded, though I was not ready.

'You will go there and you will say these words. Do not change them, not even one word. This is the message: "Aunt Esther has returned and is at Megilla Street 7, apartment 4".'

'But I don't understand—'

'It's better you don't understand. Better for you.' He meant that if I were tortured I would have nothing to reveal. 'Now repeat it back to me.'

'Aunt Esther has returned and is at Megilla Street 7, apartment 4.'

'Again.'

'Aunt Esther has returned and is at Megilla Street 7, apartment 4.'

'OK.'

The policeman came back into the room and led me away. Standing in the alley outside he told me the plan. He repeated every detail, so that I would not forget.

And so it happened that the next morning I left the ghetto with my work company as always. Except this time that same Jewish policeman was on duty at the gate, to ensure there was no trouble as I peeled away from the others.

A few seconds after I had crossed the bridge over the river, I did as I had been told. I removed the yellow star from my coat and immediately stepped onto the pavement. I was no longer a Jew from the ghetto but an Aryan in the city of Kaunas. I held my head high, just as I had been told.

I walked until I reached the railway station. It was early, there was still a mist in the air. Even so, there was a group of three or four guards standing outside, with one man in an SS uniform supervising them. I spoke in Lithuanian. 'My name is Vitatis Olekas,' I said, 'and I am an orphan.' I asked for permission to travel to Poland where I had family who might look after me.

As I dreaded, and exactly as Shimon, the Jewish policeman, had predicted, it was the SS officer who took charge. He circled me, assessing me, as if I were a specimen that had been placed before him. One of the Lithuanians asked where in Poland I was headed, but the SS man said nothing. He just kept walking around me, his shoes clicking.

Finally, from behind, I felt a tug on the waist band of my trousers.

'*Runter!*' he said. *Down.*

I looked over my shoulder and saw that he was gesturing at my trousers. 'He wants to see you,' said another one of the Lithuanian men, a smirk on his face.

I looked puzzled, as Shimon had said I should, and then the officer barked, 'Come on, come on.' Hesitantly, I lowered my trousers and my underpants. The SS officer looked at my penis, eyed its foreskin, then waved me away.

So began my journey, armed with the right Aryan identity papers and a travel document for Warsaw. I can't remember if I pretended to be fifteen or older or younger, but the truth is that I was just a twelve-year-old boy travelling alone through Europe in wartime, showing that precious *Kennkarte* to Nazi border guards in Marijampolé and Suwalki and Bialystok, over and over again. The *Kennkarte* made everything possible. It was not a forgery, but the real thing. With that paper in my hand, I was an Aryan. No document was more precious.

And finally I pulled into Warsaw. It was midday and the place was bustling, but no one was going where I was going. My destination was the Warsaw ghetto. Most people then were desperate to break out of the ghetto: I was the only one who wanted to get in.

I dug into the hole I had made in the lining of

my coat, the place where I had hidden my yellow star, and pinned it back on. I waited for a group of workers to return and I tagged along. Shimon had promised it would be like Kovno: workers only had to show papers when they went out, not when they came back in.

And so now I was inside streets as crammed and infested with disease as the ones I had left behind. There were corpses in the gutter here, too. But I found the house I was looking for and told them who I had a message for.

'Tell us and we'll tell him,' they said.

'I can't do that,' I said. 'I have to give the message to him and to him alone.' And so I waited.

It was only after the war that I discovered what had prompted my mission, why those three men in the candle-lit cellar sent me away that night. My mission was a response to something that had happened three days earlier.

Some Jews working outside the ghetto had seen a young girl, barely clothed, her eyes wild and staring. She was covered in dirt and smeared with blood; she could say nothing and her face twitched and shook like a mad woman's. They brought her back to the ghetto and once she had been dressed, and had managed to eat and drink a little, she eventually began to speak, though the words came slowly.

She had been one of those pushed to the right at Demokratu Square, along with my sisters. The selection had gone on all day, past nightfall, Rauca on the mound, smoking his cigarette or eating his sandwiches, all the while judging the column of people that shuffled before him, ignoring their cries and blocking out their pleas. Eventually there were ten thousand of them, pushed through a hole in the fence into an area known as the 'small ghetto'. Some had felt relieved, concluding that this had been nothing more than an elaborate exercise in rehousing. Apparently, people began to argue over who would get which apartment; committees talked through the night, planning for their new lives.

But at dawn the next morning, they realized their mistake. Lithuanian militiamen burst in and began beating and pushing the Jews out of their new homes, herding them into a column and ordering them to march. They were to make the four-kilometre trek to the Ninth Fort, the old encampment built in Tsarist times and designed to keep the Germans out.

It was an uphill walk and it took hours; the aged and the sick falling by the wayside, sometimes helped to their deaths by the rifle-butt of one of the militiamen. The route was lined, from beginning to end, with local Lithuanians, curious to see these strange creatures emerging from the ghetto – just as they had been curious to see us all led inside.

The Nazis had a name for this route. They called it: *Der Weg zur Himmelfahrt.* The Way to the Heavenly Journey.

They did not arrive till noon and once they had there was no respite. The Lithuanian thugs were quick to grab any jewellery, pulling off earrings and bracelets, and then ordering the Jews to strip naked. Only then did they lead them to the pits.

These were vast craters dug into the earth. Some said they were one hundred metres long, three metres wide and perhaps two metres deep. Others said they were not as long, but twice as deep. Each one was surrounded on three sides by small mountains of earth, freshly dug. On the fourth side, there was a raised wooden platform. And it was here that the SS men stood with their guns.

Those who had survived the march now began to scream; they understood where this heavenly journey had led them. Some tried to escape but they were shot instantly. And so the killing began.

First the Nazis tossed the children into the pit; then the machine gunners, in position for precisely this purpose, opened fire. The women were lined up at the edge of the crater and shot there, in the back, so that they would fall in on top of the children. The men were last.

They killed them in batches of three hundred, with no guarantee that one batch was finished when work began on the next. They had to work fast. Besides, ammunition was rationed so that the Nazis could not afford more than one bullet to the back per victim. And most of the gunmen were drunk.

The result was that many Jews were not dead when they fell; they were buried alive. This was the fate, especially, of the children. But not only them. Those who saw it told of how the pit moved for three days, how it breathed.

This is the event they call the 'great action' of October 28 1941, when ten thousand Jews were driven out of the Kovno ghetto and put to death.

And this is how my sisters were killed.

The girl who had found her way back, shivering and starving, to the ghetto, was one of those who had been buried but not shot. She had passed out as she fell, but some time later she had awoken to the realization that there were corpses all around her, above and below her. She was wedged in by dead flesh, pressing on her so hard it made her choke.

Most of those buried alive were too weak to climb out of the pits, to use the limbs of the dead as rungs on a ladder. They gave up and suffocated under the bodies. Those who did manage to haul themselves out were usually spotted and shot, and this time with no mistakes made. But this girl, she was nervous and cautious. So she waited till the middle of the night, when the drunken chanting and singing of the Nazi gunmen and their Lithuanian comrades had faded into sleep. And so she had escaped, out of the Fort and back to the ghetto.

This was the story she told once she was clothed and fed and could speak. And this was the story which had reached the leaders of the Jewish underground in Kovno, those men in the cellar. Perhaps for the first time they understood what kind of threat they faced. And so they had decided they must spread the word to those who were also trying to fight back. Which was why they sent me to Warsaw.

And so, many years later, I came to understand the meaning of the message I had carried. I also understood why the men in the cellar did not explain it to me. It was not just because I might be tortured. It was also because they did not dare tell me what had happened to my sisters. Perhaps they thought I would have been so blinded by anger, so broken, that I would not have been able to carry out my mission.

But I did carry it out and I met the man I was meant to meet in Warsaw. I waited for him for three hours, but I met him. He was the leader of the underground in the Warsaw ghetto; he too was a young man who looked old.

When I said the words, 'Aunt Esther has turned up again and is at Megilla Street 7, apartment 4' he looked bemused. But then he asked for someone to bring him a book, a holy book rescued from the ruins of a synagogue in the ghetto. It was the Book of Esther, which Jews call the Megilla of Esther. It is the book we read for the festival of Purim, which commemorates a plot many hundreds of years ago to destroy the Jews.

This leader of the underground turned to chapter seven, verse four and then he understood everything. He read it out loud, as if it would help him think. '"For I and my people are sold to be exterminated, slain and lost; but if we were only being sold as slaves and maidservants, I would have stayed silent".'

# CHAPTER FIFTEEN

The more Tom read of Gerald Merton's life story, the more he found himself thinking about Rebecca. How ironic that a woman who seemed to bubble and throb with life, as if she were keeping the lid on an almost volcanic vitality, should have emerged from a world choking with death. She was even named for a grandmother who had hanged herself.

He tried to focus on his task, the job of work Henning Munchau had asked him to do. There was no denying it: the bind from which he was meant to extricate the UN was only getting tighter. They had not only killed a survivor of the Holocaust but apparently one of its heroes: the young boy who, in disguise, had travelled across occupied Europe carrying word of the Nazi plan to exterminate the Jews.

And Tom had accused him of being a suicide bomber. Thank God he had kept to himself his earlier intuition: that old man Merton, birthplace

Kaunas, was some kind of Baltic war criminal who had sought post-war asylum in the UK. He had been as stupid as the German and Lithuanian guards young Matzkin had dodged again and again: he had seen the blue eyes and the uncircumcised penis of that corpse on the pathologist's slab and he had never once considered that he might have been looking at a Jew.

His phone rang; a New York number. If it were Henning, he would explain the depth of the trouble they were in and suggest he needed more time. This was going to require diplomatic footwork of great dexterity if it were not to turn into a grave blow to the reputation of the United Nations.

'Tom? It's Jay Sherrill. I have some news.'

'OK.'

'That New York number we saw on the cellphone? Belongs to the Russian, to the arms dealer.'

'Really? Wow.'

'I know. Incredible, isn't it? That's not all. Overnight I had a team do a deep search of Merton's hotel room, unscrewing floorboards, the works. They found something hidden in a wall cavity in the bathroom, just by the extractor fan. Very professionally concealed.'

'What is it?'

'A state-of-the-art, compact, plastic-build revolver. Russian. ·357 Magnum calibre. A gun specially designed and marketed to escape detection by security scanners. All you have to conceal are the steel inserts and the bullets; the gun-frame itself gets through unnoticed. Ballistics have examined it. Get this: apparently it's the weapon of choice in the assassin community.' Tom could hear Sherrill's amusement at his own joke.

'Hold on, Detective.' There was the beep of a call waiting. Tom looked at the display: a London number he didn't recognize.

'Tom Byrne? It's Rebecca Merton. You need to come here right now. Do you hear me? RIGHT NOW!'

# CHAPTER SIXTEEN

'I want to go to the funeral.'

'I can see the case for that, Secretary-General.'

'So you think it's a good idea? I'm glad, Munchau. My political staff say it would be unwise.'

'Why do they say that, sir?'

'Gowers here says it could be seen as an admission of liability. I said that was a legal point, not a political one. Which is why I was so keen to see you. If you see no legal problem, then we can go ahead. You're the boss.'

At that, the Secretary-General dipped his head in a small, courtly nod as if to say, 'over to you'. The *Time* magazine profile had been right: 'the world's top diplomat has world-class charm'. He embodied everything people liked about the Nordics: wholly professional, yet without Teutonic efficiency; informal, without American over-familiarity; progressive, without Latin fervour. The magazine had said that, just as some argued the

Olympics should always be in Athens, so the world would be a better place if the top post at the UN was permanently in Nordic hands. The rotation system wouldn't allow such a thing, of course, but once Asia and Africa had had their turn, and a European seemed possible, then the long-standing foreign minister of Finland rapidly became the obvious choice. The Russians had been expected to object but, to everyone's surprise, they didn't and so Paavo Viren had glided into the post unopposed.

'Why are you so keen to go, sir?'

'I think it's the right thing to do. This man was killed on our soil, in our care. I think we have to take responsibility for that and make amends for it. Don't you?'

'I can see that.'

'You keep *seeing* things but not telling me what you think. Please Dr Munchau, give me your opinion.'

Before he had a chance, the Secretary-General's Chef de Cabinet leaned forward to speak. The three of them, plus a note-taker, were in the SG's private office, arranged on the two couches which he had installed within days of his arrival: the essential tools of diplomacy, he had called them.

'While you think on that, Dr Munchau,' the Chef de Cabinet began, 'let me just game out some of the scenarios here. Best case is the SG flies to London, has a handshake and photo-op with Merton's daughter, and that draws a line under the whole episode. Worst case: he turns up for the funeral, gets spurned, maybe even faces protests and barracking and then we've magnified a problem into a larger crisis.'

'All right, that's enough, Marti. We need to hear what the Legal Counsel thinks.'

'Well, sir. Strictly speaking, there is no legally meaningful admission implied by your visiting the family. As you say, you are paying condolences simply because this terrible accident happened on our soil.'

'Good.'

'But.'

'Ah, a but. In this building, there is always a but, no?'

'Such a move will inevitably be seen as an act of contrition. Secretaries General ordinarily attend only the funerals of heads of government or heads of state. For you to go to London would be such an extraordinary gesture, it would imply we had something to apologize for.'

'Well, we do.'

The Chef de Cabinet looked aghast; Henning Munchau smiled tolerantly. 'That's not something we would want to say publicly, sir. Certainly not at this stage.'

'Oh, for heaven's sake.'

'I'm quite serious, sir. We cannot possibly make any kind of apology or statement of regret until we have all the facts. Which we don't yet have.'

'We killed an innocent man!'

'But, sir, the crucial point is that the UN guard did not know that at the time. The officer on duty seems to have believed the man in question posed an immediate threat to the life of our personnel. Which would make this a killing in self-defence.'

'OK, so we apologize for that then. It was a genuine mistake, but we apologize for it. What's wrong with that?'

Henning shot a quick glance at the chef de cabinet, a look that said: 'Christ, have we been saddled with a boy scout as Secretary-General?'

Detecting the dissent, the boss sat back. 'Look, I'm not naïve. I see the risks. But you're not thinking politically. If I'm photographed with the widow, or daughter or whoever it is, showing humility, that makes me look good. Transparent, honest, human. A new approach from the new man at the UN. This could be wonderful PR.'

Over my dead body, thought Henning. 'Sir, let me speak with my man in London. If he's managed to square the family, then your idea could be a very good one. I'll get in touch with him right away. I don't think he'll let us down.'

# CHAPTER SEVENTEEN

The front door was open, just as it had been earlier, but this time there were no other voices. He reached the landing where he had first met Rebecca Merton three hours earlier. Now all he could see was her back, as she surveyed the wreckage of her apartment.

The floor was covered with books, every shelf methodically emptied. Their pages had been flung open, their bindings ripped. On the wall hung frames denuded of pictures; posters and canvasses lay torn among broken glass.

The sofa had been slashed, its stuffing bursting out like unkempt hair. The TV had been upended; even the plants had been shaken from their pots. Tom had never seen a place so comprehensively trashed. This was no ordinary robbery.

Suddenly she wheeled around, her eyes ablaze. 'Well, this bloody confirms it. Did you watch them do it then? Did you stand and watch?'

'What the hell are you talking about?'

'I'm talking about the fact that my home just happens to have been smashed up straight after you came here. And look, five minutes after I call you, you're back. Were you on the corner the whole time, making sure they did a good job?'

'Are you mad? This had nothing to do with me.'

'It's a bit of a coincidence, isn't it? First the UN kill my father and the next day my flat – which has never once been burgled by the way – is suddenly wrecked.'

'You think the *UN* did this?'

'What were you looking for? Dirt?' There was a hint of the crooked smile. 'Is that why you sent the boys in, Tom Byrne? To see what discrediting filth you could dig up on the dead man's daughter? So if I dared to demand justice from the organization that killed my father, you'll start telling the *News of the World* who I fucked at medical school? Jesus, and this is the holier-than-thou United Nations.'

'Look, you're getting hysterical.' He regretted the word instantly. Call a woman any name you like, but never, ever say she's hysterical. 'You think the UN goes around smashing up people's houses? You don't think that, at this particular moment, we're in quite enough trouble with the Merton family without adding this to the pile?' He gestured towards the debris of her apartment. 'The UN doesn't have the people to do *anything*, let alone household burglaries in WC1.'

She looked at him hard, as if scrutinizing his face for signs of truthfulness. He found the gaze unnerving, because all he wanted to do was look back. Then she turned around as if remembering something and sprinted upstairs.

Tom saw his chance. He swiftly reached into his briefcase, pulled out Gershon Matzkin's notebook and was about to throw it onto the pile in the centre of the room when something stopped him: he wanted to be straight with her. He put the book back inside his bag, waiting for the right moment.

A few seconds later, she was back, brushing past him into the kitchen. She only touched him for a second but it was enough: he almost rocked back on his heels from the charge of it. The arousal was instant. Was he the kind of man to get turned on by the sight of a woman in distress? He didn't think so. Or was it just the combined effects of fatigue and adrenalin? He had no guide; he hadn't felt this way since adolescence.

She came back past him, and he caught the musky smell of her. The urge to grab hold of her wrist and pull her close nearly overwhelmed him. He felt as if his powers of reason were shrinking, the space filled up by a growing, expanding desire.

He followed her on her tour of devastation: what on earth had happened here? It would have been extremely rapid; she and he had barely been gone an hour. And expert, too: the perpetrators must have seen both of them leave. The superficial items of value – TV set, stereo – were still in place. This wasn't the work of crackheads out to make fifty quid. They had been desperate to find something specific.

And now Rebecca was searching, clearly panicked that some precious object had been stolen. She went back up the short flight of stairs, past a bedroom, to a study. Here she gasped, as she saw box files in heaps on the floor, their contents scattered like feathers from a pillow.

She stood still for a while and then turned to Tom. 'If you're behind this in any way—'

'For God's sake—'

'I will get in my car, drive to the nearest newspaper office and give them the story that will ruin the reputation of the UN – and you. Do you understand me? All I have to do is tell them the truth of what happened here – and what kind of man the UN killed yesterday. After that, I'll make sure you're prosecuted for murder and robbery.' She shook her head in disbelief. 'No wonder you wanted to cut a deal.'

'Now, why don't you just calm down? If anyone should be trying to cut a deal here, it's you.'

'What the hell is that supposed to mean?'

'It means that there's a few things for you to explain too.'

'Like what?'

'Like the fact that the number of a known arms dealer was on your father's cellphone. Like the fact that a gun favoured by assassins and hitmen was hidden in his hotel room.'

Something passed across Rebecca Merton's face, but it was so brief, so fleeting, Tom couldn't catch it. Was it doubt or shock or panic? It was gone too quickly for him to tell.

The pair of them stood there for a full three or four seconds, facing each other and saying nothing, like medieval knights ready to joust, until finally she stepped backwards and sat on what had once been her couch. She remained very still, as if thinking through a decision. Finally, she sighed heavily and then spoke in a voice that was new and quiet. 'Listen. I think you need to know the truth about my father.'

At last, thought Tom.

'There's something you need to read, but I can't—'

'Is this what you're looking for?' Tom produced Gershon Matzkin's journal from his case.

'Oh, thank God.' She grabbed the book and held it to her chest, her eyes closed, like a mother clutching a child lost in the park. Then her eyes opened into a wide stare. 'Where did you get this?'

'It was a mistake. I thought it was mine.' He took out his own, near-identical notebook and held it up. 'I was going to come right back here and give it to you.'

She held the book tight again, her face a picture of relief. He half wondered if she was going to thank him for inadvertently ensuring this heirloom had been kept safe from the break-in. But then she looked at him hard, her gaze powerful enough to make his muscles weaken. 'I don't know whether I can believe a word you say.'

There was silence before she spoke again. 'Did you read it?'

He hesitated. 'Bits.'

'Well, now I'd like you to read it properly.' And she placed the book in his hands.

She went back upstairs where he soon heard the scraping and banging of furniture being moved and objects being returned to their rightful places.

He wondered if her plan had been to keep this book, this story, a secret. She hadn't mentioned her father's past when he had made his first visit here, even though it would have silenced him if she had: a suicide bomber, indeed. Would she have spoken about it eventually? Or did it take his mentioning of the concealed weapon, the assassin's gun, to make her feel the need to exonerate her dead father?

He flicked through the pages, finding the place he had reached when Sherrill phoned. He let his eye skim across the pages.

*I carried the same message to ghetto after ghetto: 'Auntie Esther has returned.' Everyone understood what it meant, that we Jews did not face mere slavery or a random death here and there, but a plan of complete extermination. My job was to tell the Jews of Europe that the Nazis wanted there to be no more Jews in Europe . . .*

Tom turned the page.

*You never knew who was going to help. Sometimes a peasant woman would find me in a barn and give me a hunk of bread. But once, in Krakow, it was a doctor, a pillar of the community, who tipped off the authorities when he saw a young boy – me – slip into the ghetto at night.*

*. . . We thought once we had escaped the ghettoes and had made it to the forests our troubles would be over. But no. We learned that even if we all hated the Nazis, the Polish or Lithuanian resistance could still find time to hate the Jews . . .*

Tom flicked through the next few pages, scanning for anything which might shed light on the circumstances of Merton's death more than sixty years later.

*. . . I had somehow found my way back to Kaunas, or at least the forests outside. I met up with the handful of resistance fighters who had survived. Their uniform was no uniform: perhaps a coat stolen from a Russian, boots taken off a Lithuanian, a gun bought from some Polish black marketeer. I joined them and we did what we could, blowing up a bridge here, derailing a train there. We killed the enemy in ones and twos. On a very good day, tens.*

Tom skipped to the next page.

*. . . It was in the forest that I met my Rosa. She was older than me, but I was an old man no matter my age. To be a Jew in Europe in those years was to be old in the world . . .*

*. . . Rosa had met someone who survived the Ninth*

*Fort. They said that the Nazis had not even needed to press-gang the local Lithuanian boys to take part in the mass killings: they had volunteered eagerly, including, of course, the Wolf. They all wanted to take a turn, firing bullets into the backs of naked Jews. Rosa told me the ghetto was finally cleared on July 8 1944. The last Jews to survive were sent off to Dachau. 'There is no point going back to Kaunas,' she told me. 'There is nobody there. They are all dead.'*

There was a space on the page, as if to denote the passage of time. Good, thought Tom: after the war.

*Those of us who had survived were the only ones who understood each other. We could look into each other's eyes and see the same darkness. We wandered across Europe, looking for each other. Those of us who could not forget what we had seen. Those of us who were determined to—*

The facing page was blank. Tom turned it, only for it to come loose in his hand. He looked up, hoping Rebecca had not seen him damage the book she had hugged like a baby. He wedged it back in, but as he did, he noticed the next page and the one after that also came loose. He held up the book, to examine the binding.

He could see what had happened. He remembered the same problem with his childhood exercise books: tear out one page from the front and a corresponding page from the back would come loose. It always happened where a book was bound down the middle. To be sure, he followed the page he was reading, to see if its other half was intact. It wasn't. Indeed, each of the last five or six sheets was ragged along its edge. Several pages of this notebook were missing, ripped out.

He read again the last line of Gerald Merton's testimony. There was nothing that came after it, just a sentence as elusive as the man himself.

*Somehow we found each other . . . those of us who were determined to—*

# CHAPTER EIGHTEEN

The adviser asked for a private room. This was not their office and they had to tread carefully. Inside UN Plaza even still or sparkling was a political choice. They could pull rank, of course, demand whatever they wanted. But in a delicate matter like this, it was not a good idea. It would only draw attention.

There were only two of them in there now, the adviser made sure of that. Still, he wished his boss had listened to him and waited till they got back to the hotel to have this conversation. It was far too risky. Perhaps the bugs of foreign intelligence agencies posed no great danger, but they were at least vulnerable to the eavesdropping ears of their own side.

There were telephones here, used for conference calls no doubt. How could the adviser be certain they were not set on speakerphone, either by accident or design? Perhaps there was some kind of intercom system. Or maybe the head of mission here had established a taping system, so that his own meetings could be recorded. Plenty of ambassadors to the United Nations and elsewhere had done that. Hell, even his own boss, back when he was foreign minister, used to do that.

'Has it happened?' his boss asked, in that trademark baritone.

'Yes. They sent people in a couple of hours ago. It's done.'

'Did they find anything?'

'So far, nothing.'

'Nothing? Come on.'

'They took some papers, a couple of documents, a computer with a few files which they're examining. But, so far, none of it seems to relate to the, er—' His throat was dry. He was struggling to find the words. He wished his boss had kept him out of this operation. If they were back home, he knew he would have done. He'd have relied on his chief of staff, the man who had been with him since the beginning. But here in New York the boss's team had been pared down. The only one he trusted to get this done was him. The adviser tried to finish his sentence. 'They have no bearing on this issue.'

'Damn,' the boss said quietly, his eyes faraway. 'I thought this had gone away decades ago. I mean it, decades ago. I'm old now, but still it comes back. Even in death, he's come back to haunt me. He did it once before and he's doing it again. Gershon Matzkin, the man who comes back from the dead.'

# CHAPTER NINETEEN

Tom's next move was one he had learned from his mother. He went into the kitchen, sidestepping the pile of cutlery and shattered crockery on the floor, and put the kettle on. Eleven years in the States had not muted his appreciation of the value of a cup of tea in moments of crisis.

He was looking for an unbroken mug when his cellphone rang. Henning. Tom glanced upward at the ceiling: too near, Rebecca would hear everything. He headed downstairs, rolling a cigarette – an excuse to stand on the pavement outside – and answered. 'Hi Henning.'

'Too early to ask what you got?'

'I've got good news and bad news.'

'Bad news first, please: I like to have something to look forward to.'

'Bad news is, Gerald Merton was not just your average old man. He was a Holocaust survivor.'

'Good God.'

'A hero in fact. As a boy he went from ghetto

to ghetto, under cover, warning the Jews what was about to happen.'

'Jesus.'

'I know. Not good.'

'Especially for me.'

Tom had thought of that: the horror of a German legal counsel defending the UN for killing a Jewish victim of the Nazis.

'Don't tell anyone else, OK? Not yet.'

'Sure.'

'I think I need to hear the good news.'

Tom was watching a man across the street, also talking into his phone. Was there something odd about the way he was pacing?

'Merton may not have been just an elderly tourist. He had a gun concealed in his hotel room. A polymer-framed revolver, apparently designed to escape detection. Seems he got it from a Russian arms dealer in New York, regular supplier to Terror Incorporated.'

'So you want me to claim we didn't make a mistake at all? That we got the right guy?'

'I think it could fly,' said Tom.

'No way. Not with his history. Court of public opinion, mate. That's where we'd lose this case before we'd said a bloody word. No one's going to believe some geriatric posed a threat to anyone, no matter what you found in the hotel room.'

'It was an assassin's gun, Henning.'

'I don't care: circumstantial. What's the link with the arms dealer?'

'His number was on Merton's phone.'

'Also circumstantial. Back to Plan A, Tom: pay the daughter whatever she wants and come back home.'

'She's rejected that out of hand. Says it's blood money. She wants an apology from the SG, in person. Which I've obviously declined.'

Henning let out a sigh. 'Can't you turn on the legendary Byrne charm? I've never known a woman refuse you anything.'

'Somehow I don't think that's going to work.' Tom heard the slight wobble in his own voice. 'She's not like that. She's a very, I don't know, unusual—'

'Don't tell me you've gone and fallen for the grieving daughter.'

'Henning—'

'You have! You're becoming one of those death row lawyers who end up knobbing the widow! Tom, just wrap this up and come back.'

'Seriously, Henning. I need to work out why Merton was in New York. If he was up to no good, we can see off any legal claim against us. The UN would be completely in the clear.'

'Look, Tom. You'll still get your fee, if that's what's worrying you.'

'No, I'm just trying to do what's best for the UN.'

'Long time since you've talked like that, Tom. Do you really think she'd sue?'

Tom remembered Rebecca's tirade of a few

minutes earlier. *After that, I'll make sure you're prosecuted for murder and robbery.* She hadn't meant it; it had been an outburst. But it would do. 'She's been making threats, yes.'

'All right, then. Do what you have to do. But I stress: my overwhelming preference is that you close this thing down. It's the bloody GA this week, remember. I don't have time for another headache.'

Tom went back inside, concluding, not for the first time, that Henning Munchau was the most perceptive man he knew.

He returned to making tea, carefully carrying the two warm mugs upstairs. In the doorway he watched Rebecca replacing chipped and broken picture frames onto the shelf, a cellphone cradled to her ear. She was speaking softly.

'I know, it's just terrible to see your little girl like this. But please, try to believe me when I tell you that this is only an infection and we can beat it. And once we have, she'll be well enough for the transplant operation.' Her gaze flicked over Tom. She took the mug he offered and carried on speaking. 'That's right. We've had the typing back from Anna's brother and he's a ten-antigen HLA match. Sorry, Mrs Reid, that means your son's the perfect donor. We just need to get Anna through this infection and . . . that's OK. You call whenever you need. Goodbye, Mrs Reid.'

After she had disconnected, he gestured towards

the photographs. 'You should leave that alone,' he said as gently as he could. 'For the police.'

'I'm not going to call the police.'

He tried to hide his relief: the last thing he needed was for this burglary to become public knowledge. If Rebecca Merton had assumed the UN was behind this break-in, there'd be a thousand online conspiracy nutcases ready to jump to the same conclusion. 'Why not?'

She looked right at him, the green clarity of her irises so bright it was hard not to look away. He had a sudden flashback to the Marvel comics of his youth – an addiction which lasted a good two years – and to Cyclops of the X-Men, the mutant superhero who could fire devastating 'optic blasts' from his eyes. Did Rebecca Merton have some similarly mystical power, a gaze that could instantly paralyse any man caught in its path?

'In the last twenty-four hours,' she said quietly. 'I've discovered that my father has died a violent death, shot down in cold blood. My home has been burgled and I've surrendered my father's life story – which I've spent my life guarding with great privacy – because it was clearly the only way to persuade you that my father was not some kind of terrorist.' The volume was louder now, the face redder. 'Do you think I can cope with a whole lot more people traipsing all over my home, asking me more questions and more questions and MORE FUCKING QUESTIONS!'

At that, she hurled her mug, still full of tea,

across the room so that it hit the wall. There was silence, the two of them watching the hot liquid streak down.

'Listen, Rebecca—'

'No, you listen to me.'

Something in her voice made him freeze.

'You said you wanted to cut a deal, so let's cut a deal.'

'About the financial contribution, I understand—'

'I don't want your money, I want your help. It was you – the people you work for – that started all this and now you're going to damn well help get me through it.'

'I'm listening.'

'I want to find out the truth of what happened to my father in New York and what it has to do with all this.' She gestured at the detritus of the room. 'I can't do that alone. But you're a lawyer, you've got the UN behind you. You know how these things work. I want you to help me.'

'Deal,' he said. 'But no police means we'll have to do this ourselves. We have to start at the beginning. Can you see anything missing?'

They looked around, surveying afresh a room in which every last item had been either displaced or smashed. She caught his eye, both of them thinking the same thing, when the hint of that wonky smile appeared around her lips. He noticed it and smiled back. The absurdity of his question now hung in the air – asking a passenger on the Titanic if he noticed anything out of place – and at last she released a laugh, a laugh powered not by humour or joy but their opposites, by tension and grief coiled up for too long.

The sound coming from her changed. She tried to cover her face, but he could see a tear falling down her cheek. He stepped forward, hesitated a moment, then put his hand on her arm and drew her towards him. She let her head rest for a moment on his chest and in that instant every one of his nerve endings felt as if it were on fire.

But then, just as suddenly, she sprang back, dabbed her eyes and signalled that the moment had vanished. 'Let's get on with it.'

She started methodically, in the far left corner of the room, picking up books not to replace them but to divine a pattern. She would try to work out which areas had interested the thieves; only then could she begin to deduce why. Tom watched her, noting the concentration engraved on her face. He imagined her as a child, sharp and studious, running to bring home happy news of A grades to a father whose own childhood had been consumed by darkness and evil. She hadn't said so explicitly, but Tom was sure Rebecca Merton had been an only child, the bond with her father almost supernaturally intense.

After a few minutes, she moved back to the desk, working now with greater intensity. Tom watched her head to a specific drawer. As she bent over, he was engulfed by a new surge of desire, like a wave breaking over his head.

She tugged at the drawer and it moved easily. She looked up, as if a hunch had been confirmed. 'The lock's been broken,' she said.

'What was in there?'

'My father's papers.'

'What kind of papers?'

'Legal documents, bank details, things he wanted me to look after. In case . . .'

Tom stepped closer, examining the desk: a mug of pens, a photograph of Rebecca and another woman sitting on a rock on some sun-drenched beach taken, Tom guessed, about ten years earlier. A rectangle on the wooden desk, marked out by dust, was darker than the rest: from the dimensions, Tom could see what it meant. The monitor, unplugged and useless was still there, but the computer had been taken.

He turned to tell Rebecca, now trying to reassemble the contents of a filing cabinet, when he saw something straight ahead of him, pinned to the corkboard above the desk, that made him start. Two words, filling a single sheet of A4. There was no mistaking it: though clearly scribbled in haste, they were written in the same hand as the notebook he had read that afternoon. The message read simply 'Remember Kadish'.

'What's this?'

Rebecca glanced up and for a moment looked utterly startled.

Tom shuddered. 'Was this not here before? Has this been pinned up just now?'

'Oh no, it was here before,' Rebecca replied softly. 'It's something my father wrote a while ago. He's reminding me to say the memorial prayer for my mother.'

'For your mother?'

'Yes. She died six years ago. My father was always very insistent that we do the prayers on the anniversary of her death. That's the name of the Jewish prayer for a dead loved one.'

No wonder she had looked so shaken: that simple piece of paper must have looked like a message from the grave, Gerald Merton pleading to be remembered.

In the silence, pregnant with poignancy, she didn't hear the dull vibration of Tom's BlackBerry, tucked inside his jacket pocket. He waited till she had turned back to the bookshelves to pull the device out and watch the screen light up. It was a message from Jay Sherrill and it consisted of only a single line:

*Prints on gun match Merton's.*

## CHAPTER TWENTY

'Thanks for seeing me, Commissioner.'

'No need to thank me. Me who asked you to report direct to this office.'

'Yes, sir.'

'So what you got, Sherrill?'

'Progress, sir. And in an unexpected direction.'

'Usually say "shoot". Not quite right in this context, I grant you. Why don't you go ahead?'

'The starting assumption yesterday morning was that Gerald Merton was an innocent old man, a tragic case of mistaken identity.'

'That's right.'

'Well, some of our early findings shed doubt on that basic assumption.'

'Do they indeed?'

'Yes, sir they do. The first alert Intel Division had was a meet-up at the premises of an arms dealer—'

'The Russian.'

'Yes. His phone number appears on the

cellphone of Gerald Merton. Second, an overnight search of the deceased's hotel room has produced a weapon, a polymer-framed revolver, with steel inserts, Russian made.'

'Hitman's friend.'

'Precisely, sir. Serious calibre. It was secreted in the room at the Tudor Hotel where Mr Merton was registered. And third, the gun has Merton's fingerprints on it, sir. All over it.'

Riley sat back in his chair, testing its recline mechanism to the full. He did not break eye contact with the detective. He was assessing him, like a head teacher weighing up a bright pupil. 'That's all fascinatin', Sherrill. Really is. Anyone else in NYPD know about this?'

'No, sir. You asked that I report only to you.'

'Good work, Sherrill. Let's keep it that way.' He let his seat spring forward, then he leaned forward some more. 'How'd your interview with the Watch Commander go?'

Sherrill went back to his notes, flicking through to the right page. He hadn't expected this. The Watch Commander's testimony had been wholly predictable, nothing compared to what Sherrill had found on Merton. Why had the Commissioner not reacted to what was clearly the biggest news here?

'Watch Commander Touré reported that a phone call had come to him from his liaison at the NYPD, suggesting a heightened state of vigilance in respect of a man wearing dark black coat, woollen hat and—'

'And when'd this come through?'

'At approximately 8.49am, sir.'

'And when was the shooting?'

'8.51am, sir.'

'Now, what do you notice about those two times, Detective?'

'They are two minutes apart, sir.'

'My, that Harvard education is worth every cent! Exactly, Mr Sherrill. Exactly! Which tells us what?'

'Well, it could be a coincid—'

'No coincidences in police work, Mr Sherrill. It tells us there was *live* intelligence, that's what it tells us.'

'You mean that someone had seen the suspect approaching the United Nations building?'

'That's exactly what I mean. Now, what was the precise wording of the message received by the Watch Commander at the UN?'

Jay Sherrill turned one more page of his notebook. He looked back up at the Commissioner. 'It was an urgent warning, sir. Urging UN to be on the lookout for a possible terror suspect.'

'Urgent, you say. Almost as if they knew he was on his way.'

'But that makes no sense, sir.'

'And why's that, Mr Sherrill? Why does it make no sense?' Riley was leaning back again. He was enjoying himself.

'Because anybody who actually *saw* Gerald Merton would have seen that he was, in fact, a very old man. The very opposite of a terror suspect.'

'You'd think so, wouldn't you, Mr Sherrill? You and I would certainly have done that, wouldn't we?'

Now it was the detective's turn to study the face of his boss. Slowly, out of the darkness a picture was emerging, a glimpse of what might be in the Commissioner's head. He didn't yet fully comprehend what his boss was after, but now at last, he had an inkling of it. Whatever else, it was not a simple resolution of the killing of Gerald Merton.

'What do you want me to do, Commissioner?'

'An excellent question, Detective. I want you to find out who exactly fed that urgent advisory to Watch Command at the UN and on what basis they gave it. Because a crucial mistake was made in this case, the mistake that led that unlucky Belgian policeman—'

'Portuguese.'

'Whatever. It led an unlucky, terrified cop to make a fatal error. We need to find the precise source of that original error. I want to know which part of the law enforcement apparatus of this city—'

'But it may not have been a mistake, sir. The gun, the fingerprints—'

Riley held up his right palm, in a gesture of hush. 'All in good time, Mr Sherrill. All in good time.'

## CHAPTER TWENTY-ONE

Luckily Tom had set the BlackBerry to silent; Rebecca hadn't heard Sherrill's text message arrive and now was not the time to tell her what it had said. Besides, it was only confirmation of what Tom had already told her he suspected: that her father had been in New York with a hitman's weapon.

Above all, he didn't want to break the mood that had entered the room, established first by that fleeting embrace and, now, by his sighting of the message on the noticeboard, the plea for the remembrance of a dead mother. There was a hush in the room, a quiet that somehow seemed to connect them. Occasionally Rebecca would meet his gaze, say nothing, then return to prodding the now-limp sandwiches her friends had brought over that morning.

'Your mother, was that the girl I read about in your father's book?' It was the first chance he'd had to speak about what he'd read.

'Excuse me?'

'Rosa. Was that your mother?'

'Oh no. That's a long story.'

'I've got time.'

She smiled, the warmth of it moving across the table and spreading through him. 'I never met Rosa. She and my father did stay together after the war. And she came here, to England.'

'But?'

'But I'm not sure they loved each other in a normal way. They clung to each other. They needed each other.'

For an instant an image floated before Tom's eyes, two teenage children who had witnessed the gravest horror. He pictured young bodies and old faces.

'They had no children. My guess is that she was infertile. Sustained malnutrition and emotional trauma in the early years of puberty prevented regular ovulation.'

'Is that your medical opinion?'

There was a glimpse of the crooked smile and it was gone.

'My father always said the light had gone out. That she had no light left inside her.'

'Maybe you were both right.'

She turned to look at him, the X-Men power-beam now at half-strength. 'She died in 1966. My father was still young, relatively speaking. He grieved but he was not a man who could be alone, and a few years later he met a woman here, in London. They married and a few years after that they had me. He was forty-five.'

'Did that make a difference, having a dad who was a bit older?'

'Not as much as having a dad who survived the Holocaust.'

Tom nodded, accepting the scolding. He was aware that he had avoided so much as uttering that word.

'Besides,' she went on, 'he was always really fit. Took great care of himself.'

I saw that for myself, Tom thought, the memory of her father's autopsy coming back to him.

'Did the experience of the war— did the experience of the Holocaust leave a physical mark on him of any kind?'

'Well, he never had a number on his arm, if that's what you're asking. Sometimes I wish he had.'

'What do you mean?'

'Well, that's what people expect, don't they? Holocaust survivor, tattoo on the arm. But they only did that in Auschwitz. Did you know that? That was the only place where they branded the Jews with a number.' She was speaking faster now, her voice different. It seemed to jangle somehow, like broken glass. 'But my father was never in Auschwitz or in any death camp. So people couldn't *see* it. They couldn't tell, just by looking, what he'd been through. And he couldn't say it in one word either. Couldn't just say, I was in Treblinka. Or Sobibor. Or Belzec. Or Majdanek. Mind you, not many could say they were from there because hardly anyone ever came out. Hardly anyone survived those places. So my father either had to tell people the whole story – of the village and the burning barn and the pogroms in Kovno and his mother hanging there from the ceiling and the ghetto and the pits – or he had to say nothing. So most of the time, he chose nothing. He kept quiet. He made no speeches. He went on none of the remembrance tours. He never went back.'

She paused, thinking.

'I didn't answer your question.' The tone was the same one he had heard on the phone, Dr Rebecca Merton. 'You asked about physical signs. There was one.'

'What was that?'

'His left foot. He was missing three toes. He lost them to frostbite in the forests, I think. When he was fighting with the partisans. It's in the notebook: how they had to wear felt shoes in the bitter cold. They didn't have any boots. You had to wait for someone to die and take theirs.'

'And did that affect him? Missing those toes?'

'Not really. He walked with a slight limp. As if he was carrying a heavy bag on one side. But it didn't stop him keeping in very good shape. He swam, he ran, he used to lift weights.'

There was no point hinting at it. He would have to ask directly. 'I'm told that your father was found with some kind of metal plate on his leg, taped to his shin. Why might that be?'

She looked at Tom again, her gaze lingering, examining him. 'I saw my father regularly, including before he made this trip and, I can tell you, he had absolutely nothing wrong with his leg. You must be mistaken.'

Tom wouldn't push it. He would just file the metal shin pad that he had seen with his own eyes among the ever-lengthening list of mysteries attached to this case.

'And what about you?' she said, taking the plates to the sink. 'Do you have family here?'

'I have a mother in Sheffield. My father's dead.'

'Will you go and see her, while you're here?'

'I don't think so. I used to do the dutiful son thing. Now I save the nostalgia for Christmas.'

The phone rang, the landline this time; another condolence call. Rebecca took the cordless phone and headed out into the hall.

While she was gone, Tom surveyed the damaged kitchen. Whoever had come here really had spared no mercy. They had turned the place over with brutal efficiency. Between saying goodbye to Rebecca on the doorstep and her phone call ordering him to rush back, no more than an hour had passed. They had managed to trash this place in less than sixty minutes. What had they been looking for? Was this break-in connected to the killing at UN Plaza or could it have been a coincidence? Either way, some unseen and brutal enemy now clearly had Rebecca Merton in its sights. The thought of it made him bristle.

He looked up to see her, breathless, in the kitchen doorway.

'I just saw this downstairs, on the doormat.' She was holding up a large white envelope. 'Hand-delivered.'

'What is it?'

She handed it over, sitting herself on the bench next to him, so close their thighs touched. She leaned across as he examined the blank envelope. He could smell her, the scent flooding him with lust. He tried to focus. Inside the envelope were two sheets of paper, soft to the touch, almost furry with age, held together by a single staple. On each of them was the distinct print of a manual typewriter; it was hard to tell, but it could have been a copy, the kind made by an old-fashioned stencil machine. Tom had been taught at Manchester by a professor who had clearly been setting the same reading lists since the 1950s: back in his seminars was the last time Tom had handled a document like this one.

There was no title or explanatory heading. Instead the first page featured only a list of names, apparently arranged alphabetically:

Wilhelm Albert
Wilhelm Altenloch
Hans Bothmann
Hans Geschke
Paul Giesler
Odilo Globocnik
Richard Glücks
Albert Hohlfelder
Friedrich Wilhelm Krüger

Kurt Mussfeld
Adalbert Neubauer
Karl Puetz
Christian Wirth

In each case the names had been neatly crossed out by two inked lines forming an X, the way a prisoner strikes out days on a calendar. Tom turned to the next page. The font was slightly different this time and the names were no longer sorted alphabetically:

Hans Groetner
Hans Stuckart
Joschka Dorfman
Otto Abetz
Theo Dannecker
Karl-Friedrich Simon
Fritz Kramer
Jacob Sprenger
Georg Puetz
Herbert Cukors
Alexander Laak

These names too had all been crossed out, though this time less neatly and in strokes that were not uniform, not even in the same colour ink. It seemed as if the first list had been marked in one sitting, the second at different points over time.

Other than that, the document in his hand gave no clues. Yet the more Tom looked at it, the more convinced he became that this list would explain at last the mystery of Gershon Matzkin.

# CHAPTER TWENTY-TWO

'This is all that came, nothing else?'

'That's it.'

'No note?'

'Nothing.'

'Did they buzz on the door when they delivered it? Do you know when it arrived?'

'It was on the mat when I went down just now.'

'OK.' Tom went straight to the window, looking for the man he had seen before: no sign. He began to pace, working out his line of questioning, when he caught Rebecca looking at him, her eye sweeping up and down his body. Aware that she'd been noticed, she looked away.

'First off, do any of those names look familiar to you?'

She looked unsure. 'No.'

'Could you have met any of them? Might they be friends of your father's, business associates?'

'My father owned a dry cleaning shop on Stoke Newington Church Street.'

'Right. So not much in the way of business associates then.' He attempted a smile. 'Could any of them be relatives, distant family members?'

'I'm telling you, I don't recognize any of them.'

Tom looked back at the list. A hunch was beginning to form.

Her computer was gone – proof, along with the upended bookshelves and filing cabinet, that it was information, not saleable goods, that the intruders had been after – but the cables and modem were all still in place. He took out and connected his own laptop and, once the Google page was displayed, Tom entered the first of the names. An entry on Wilhelm Albert, fifth Duke of Urach, born in 1957, appeared: not what he was expecting. He tried the second name. Wilhelm Altenloch was a major in the Nazi SS in Bialystock. He looked up at Rebecca, standing over his shoulder.

Hans Bothmann was identified as the Kommandant of the Chelmno death camp, where he had directed mass killing operations from spring 1942 to March 1943. Google drew a blank on Hans Geschke but Paul Giesler had a Wikipedia entry all his own. He was an early recruit to National Socialism, signing up to Hitler's fledgling movement in 1924, rising to be Gauleiter of Westphalia South and, by 1942, Munich and Upper Bavaria. His claim to fame was the supervision of the Dachau concentration camp; apparently, when the liberators were approaching, he drew up a last-minute plan to ensure they arrived too late – by exterminating all the camp's Jews.

Rebecca leaned forward to get a closer look at the screen, one loose curl of her hair brushing Tom's face.

Odilo Globocnik had an entry too, one befitting a senior SS apparatchik and former police leader in Lublin, credited with overseeing the Einsatzgruppen, the mobile killing units who massacred Jews throughout Poland from 1942 to 1943.

The pattern grew clearer with each entry. SS Colonel Albert Hohlfelder, decorated for his work sterilizing Jews and other slaves through mass exposure to X-rays. SS Lieutenant General Dr Friedrich Wilhelm Krüger, member of the planning staff responsible for the comprehensive liquidation of the Jewish ghettoes of Poland. SS Lieutenant Kurt Mussfeld, supervisor of Auschwitz crematorium number two in 1944. Christian Wirth, assistant to Globocnik, and responsible for implementing the principles of the T-4 euthanasia project, in which the disabled were gassed or killed by lethal injection, on a dramatically larger scale by developing extermination camps which served as state-of-the-art, industrialized factories of death.

'So we have a list of big-time Nazis,' Tom said finally, pushing the chair back from the desk.

'I don't understand.'

'Can you think of any reason why anyone would want to hand-deliver this to you? Anonymously?'

Her eyes were aflame with something Tom could not quite interpret. Was it grief, burning anew? Was it anger, at such manipulation? Was it fear at being menaced by violent intruders and anonymous callers? Tom could have looked and looked into those eyes, without ever being certain.

'I have no idea what any of this means, Tom,' she said, shaking her head. 'But I know someone who might.'

# CHAPTER TWENTY-THREE

Rebecca drove them through a north-east London landscape that would have been utterly alien to the Tom Byrne who grew up in Sheffield more than three decades earlier. A single, endless street seemed to pass not through neighbourhoods so much as entire continents. Turkish newsagents and kebab sellers gave way to clusters of Vietnamese restaurants, which in turn were replaced by Polish delicatessens, then storefronts promising internet access and cheap calls to Nigeria and Sierra Leone.

Out on the pavements were women whose heads were covered by hijabs, and others concealed behind the full-face niqab, a tiny letterbox slit for their eyes. Brushing past them were ultra-orthodox Jewish men whose costume was familiar to Tom from New York: dressed head to toe in black, their heads covered either in homburgs or, occasionally, striking fur numbers from a mysterious, long-vanished age. Also hurrying to prayer, though in a different direction, were Muslim men, some in the knee-length kurta, with a kufi, a netted white skullcap, on their heads. Tom eyed up a crowd at a bus stop: a student in the shirt of the Brazilian national football team, two black men, a turbaned Sikh and three white women with prams that looked sufficiently rugged to negotiate serious off-road terrain. His expression must have been obvious because Rebecca, from the driving seat of her ancient Saab, said, 'I see this is your first visit to the Kingsland High Street.'

They parked up and walked past a Kurdish greengrocer and a newsagent promising Muslim-friendly, porn-free shelves, until they arrived at a shabby shop front that announced itself as the Kingsland Law Centre.

Rebecca pushed the door open in a manner that suggested to Tom she had been here before. Inside, a bicycle was propped up in the entrance corridor which led to a staircase and, Tom guessed, some above-the-shop flats. There was a second door on their left which they went through.

The front half of the office was laid out like the waiting area of a down-at-heel doctors' surgery: three chairs arranged around a forlorn, fake wood table. On it were copies of *Hackney Today*, dated from three months earlier. The chairs were taken by men who Tom, expert in these matters after eleven years at the UN, would have guessed were Somali. One was holding a leaflet entitled *Your asylum rights in the UK*.

Behind a flimsy partition, a conversation that was clearly meant to be private was audible.

'Sorry, Lionel, I need to ask you again. Have you stopped taking your medication? Do I need to call someone for you?'

Even without trying, Tom could see over the screen. Towards the back, seated in front of a desk like a customer visiting a bank manager, was an unshaven man in a baseball cap, surrounded by half a dozen plastic bags. He was muttering, not pausing to interrupt his own monologue even when spoken to directly.

Behind the desk was a man no more than thirty years old with looks that were also familiar to Tom now, though they would have been downright exotic in the Sheffield of his youth. He was handsome with a head of dark curly hair and tortoiseshell glasses. In New York, Tom would have bet with confidence that this was a Jewish lawyer and he guessed the same now.

Rebecca smiled in the man's direction with a look that suggested the indulgence of an older sister; he held up a hand in silent greeting, without interrupting his discussion with Lionel.

The unanswered phones, the threadbare carpet, the chaos: it all combined to trigger a wave of memory. Tom had briefly worked in a legal aid practice like this one when he had returned to Sheffield soon after graduating. His father's emphysema had finally caught up with him and his mother had asked Tom to return, to 'give your old man a decent send-off'. The clientele was not quite as diverse as this lot, Tom acknowledged, but the atmosphere was the same: a tiny, no-budget practice permanently on the brink of drowning in an ocean filled with sharks.

'Rebecca, I'm so sorry.' The lawyer had come over now, leaving Lionel to gather up his bags. His voice conveyed condolences for her father in a tone that suggested he knew them both. 'I've been trying to call, left a couple of messages. I guess you've been swamped. We're all so shocked.'

Rebecca waved the apology away, then swivelled to make introductions. 'Julian, this is Tom Byrne from the United Nations. Tom, this is Julian Goldman, legal linchpin of the Hackney community – and the grandson of one of my father's oldest friends.'

Julian's smile at that, his bathing in Rebecca's recognition, told Tom all he needed to know: that this was a bright young man who had been in love with Rebecca for years, probably since childhood.

'Lequasia, can you get us some coffee?' he called out to a secretary Tom hadn't noticed.

Seated at a desk next to Julian's, Lequasia was surely no more than eighteen, with extravagantly straightened hair and a current commitment to admiring a set of improbably lengthy nails rather than answering the phones. She looked up now with an expression that combined indolence and derision in equal measure.

'Come, sit over here.' Julian grabbed a couple

of stiff-backed, plastic chairs and arranged them in front of his desk.

Tom noticed that he had placed Rebecca's chair close to his own.

'What about funeral arrangements? Is there anything I can do?'

'When they rang to tell me what had happened, they said there'd be a delay. For an autopsy.' She was speaking softly, Tom noticed. He wondered how much she would tell him; they had not discussed it on the way here. In New York, Tom Byrne would never have gone into a meeting to discuss the monthly stationery order without some kind of game plan. Yet here they were, winging it, with no strategy whatsoever. It was another reminder that he was losing control of this case – if he had ever had it.

'Are you thinking of taking action against the—' Julian shot a glance at Tom, '— at the people responsible for this?'

Here comes the ambulance-chaser, thought Tom.

'I'm not thinking about that right now,' Rebecca said, as if Gerald Merton's status as an innocent victim was beyond doubt. 'But there are some things I need to find out. About my father.'

'Well, you know everything, Rebecca. You were everything to him, anyone could see that.' He turned to Tom. 'You have never seen a father and daughter who were closer. Even when it was just the two of them, they were a family. A two-person family.'

'What about the will?'

For the first time, Julian turned upon Rebecca an expression that was not undiluted adoration. He seemed shocked, the little boy who's just seen Snow White having a fag. 'You can't be thinking of that now, surely.'

'I want to know if there's anything he left for me.'

'Oh, Rebecca.'

'I don't mean money, Julian,' she said with an impatience that pleased Tom. 'I mean anything else he might have left here for safekeeping. To be given to me in the event of his death.'

Julian recovered himself. 'You know he arranged his affairs when my father was still his lawyer, before Dad retired. I didn't actually do any of that with him myself.'

'Can you check?'

Julian looked over at Lequasia, was about to ask her, shook his head and got up. 'I won't be a minute.'

Tom looked over at Rebecca and raised his eyebrows, a gesture which in UN Plaza would have said everything but which here, he appreciated, needed explaining. 'What's the story?'

'My father was sentimental. He and Julian's grandfather came to this country together. I think he was also a partisan, though much older. When his son became a lawyer, my father became his first client. Out of loyalty. Then when the son retired, Dad moved onto the grandson.'

'Did your father need a lawyer for any reason?'

The steel returned to Rebecca's eyes. 'Not once.'

Tom got up, stretching his legs. The three Somali men were still waiting, their faces blank with weariness and disappointment. Quite a contrast, Tom thought, with the corporate suits and Mafia property developers who formed his own client base these days.

Julian emerged at last from a back store-room carrying a container structured like a shoe-box, though double the width, made of strong cardboard with metal reinforcements on the corners. The colour, once red, had faded to a pale pink; it was veneered in dust.

'This is it, I'm afraid. Not exactly a house in Barbados, I know.' He laid it on the desk.

'How long has this been here?' she asked, not touching it.

'We had it transferred over here about two years ago, when my father retired. He started his law practice in 1967. So he could have got it from your father any time between those dates. It looks pretty old, doesn't it?'

Slowly, Rebecca removed the lid. Julian removed himself to the reception area, where he could be heard enunciating an apology to the three Somali men.

The moment the lid was off, Tom felt a surge of disappointment. He did not know what he had been expecting, but it was not this. The box seemed no different from the kind you might find in the homes of most pensioners: a collection of once-important documents, expired passports and the like. What had he hoped to find in there, a gun?

Carefully, Rebecca took each item out, as if handling precious stones. The old passports were bundled together with a rubber band. Next to them she placed a document which elicited a wistful smile. It was titled Certificate of Naturalization, the sheet of paper issued by the Home Office in 1947 which accepted Gershon Matzkin as a loyal subject of King George VI and magicked him into a new creature: Gerald Merton.

There were more certificates, including the incorporation of his dry cleaning business in Stoke Newington and one for the purchase of premium bonds. The long-gone world of post-war Britain seemed to rise from this box like a cloud of dust.

'Tom, look at this.'

Crumpled at the bottom was a thin pile of newspaper cuttings. Rebecca lifted them out especially gently, to prevent them disintegrating in her hands. Some were yellow, others an anaemic shade of beige. Only a couple were in English. Several were in Spanish, two in Portuguese and half a dozen in German. Handwritten at the top of each was a simple date. They seemed to be collected in chronological order, the first few, almost all in German, clustered in the same period, the second half of 1945, the rest spread through the 1950s and 1960s.

'Do you speak German?' Tom asked.

Rebecca shook her head: 'That was one language I never wanted to learn.'

She turned the first fragile clippings over, until she came across one from *The Times*. It was hard to tell which of the four or five news items on the page they were meant to look at, until Rebecca noticed a fine, faded pencil line boxing a story just a paragraph long.

> *Odilo Globocnik, former SS leader, was found dead yesterday in an alpine hut, high in the mountains near Weissensee. Occupying authority sources said Globocnik, notorious for overseeing the liquidation of the Warsaw ghetto, had most likely taken his own life . . .*

There were two more in German, one from *Die Welt*, originally published by the British occupying forces after the German surrender. It too was a single-paragraph item, in the news-in-brief column, marked out in a square of black ink. Tom's schoolboy skills were just about adequate to translate.

> *The military spokesman yesterday announced that another high ranking official of the Third Reich had been found dead. SS Lieutenant Kurt Mussfeld had been a senior officer at both the Auschwitz and Majdanek death camps . . .*

Tom now reached over Rebecca for the envelope that had come through her letter box an hour earlier, his hand briefly brushing against hers and an electric charge coursing through him.

Forcing himself to concentrate, he laid out the hand-delivered list of names, then looked through the cuttings at the top of the pile, the 1945 ones, pulling out of the German news accounts the names of the men reported dead. He saw a Wilhelm Albert and a Karl Puetz. He glanced back at the list: there they both were, a cross by each of their names. He went deeper into the pile, finding names from the 1950s. They were on the list too, also crossed out.

An image of Gershon Matzkin floated into his head: prematurely old, hunched over his ledger, recording the deaths of ageing Nazis the world over. He imagined him scouring the newspapers, visiting the local library, crossing them off his list one by one, each death a balm to the terrible sorrow that must have devoured him. The deep tragedy of it – a man consumed by such grief and hatred, living only to hear of the faraway deaths of others – struck Tom. How powerless Gershon Matzkin must have felt, a boy whose family had been destroyed by these men, now grown up and watching from his dry cleaning shop, waiting for the day when a road accident here or a faulty electrical cable there might leave one less Nazi in the world. Is that why he had stayed fit, so that he might outlive them all, so that he might see the day when there were none of them left?

Or was that not how it was at all?

'Rebecca, pass me the passports.'

Tom peeled off the rubber band – and he saw it straightaway. There were three old black, hard-cover British passports, each in the name of Gerald Merton. But there was also a large, stiff, navy blue passport of the French Republic, issued in the name of Jean-Luc Renard – with a photo that was unmistakably the young Gerald. There was a travel document for Hans Borchardt, loyal citizen of the Federal Republic of Germany. It too came attached to a photograph of Gerald Merton. Tom looked at the dates inside: most were issued in 1952, though there were also passports for Paraguay and Argentina valid for a full decade later. Tom stared at one passport in particular. Issued in 1952, it identified one Fernando Matutes as a Spanish citizen – even though the picture inside showed the same, unsmiling face of Gerald Merton.

Quickly now, sure that he was right, Tom flicked through the pages of the Spanish passport and saw that the first and last time it had been used was in August 1952. Quickly, he pored over the pile of newspaper cuttings until he found one in Spanish. And there it was. Faded and yellowing but nevertheless clear: *El Correo*, the newspaper of the Basque country, from the second week of August, 1952.

# CHAPTER TWENTY-FOUR

**El Correo August 12 1952**

***Tourist found dead in San Sebastián hotel; wife discovers body***

*Police in San Sebastián have launched an inquiry into the mysterious death of a holidaymaker, whose body was discovered by his wife in their room in the Hotel Londres. Mrs Schroeder said she and her German-born husband had been enjoying a week's vacation and that he had shown no signs of distress or depression. 'I had only been out shopping for an hour or so, and when I came back he was, he was—' a grief-stricken Mrs Schroeder told a reporter, before breaking down in tears.*

I found the abundance of food the biggest shock. I had never seen such plenty, treats spilling out of every opening. Fresh fish laid on a bed of ice, their heads still intact; the counter brimming over with delights, from rolled peppers to the congealed potato omelette which somehow, even cold, managed to be delicious; the slices of salami and cheese, all ready to be munched down with a wipe of a paper napkin promptly dropped to the floor – and, of course, the rows of cured hams above the bar.

I confess, I had to stop myself staring at those suspended hams. I had never seen anything like it. Not in the ghetto of course, where there had been no meat, let alone a pig. And not in London where I had made my home, where food was still a precious rationed commodity. If this was what it was like to lose the war, why had we all fought so hard to win?

I sat on my own. I was used to that by now. I was barely twenty-two years old, but I had travelled all around Europe – France, West Germany, Austria – and beyond, to South America and Canada, always on my own. I had learned how to sit in a restaurant and read without drawing attention to myself. The trick was not to hide. No trilby hats or newspapers in front of the face, like in the movies. Show yourself, act confident, act like a local or else, unembarrassed, like a tourist. That way no one would notice you.

A shelf suspended above the bar was packed with every conceivable variety of liquor: five different types of whisky, more vodkas than I could count and a line of brandies. Had it been like this here during the war? Had the wine flowed and the tables groaned while Rosa and I had lived like wild animals, scratching for our very lives? An image of my sisters floated into my mind. That happened a lot when I was on a mission.

I needed to stay clear-headed, to keep my focus on the task in hand. I had been given that advice by one of the leaders, before he himself was killed on duty. 'Don't hate them,' he had said. 'Hate them before and hate them afterwards. But don't hate them when you do a job. If you do, you will fail – and they will win.'

Usually, I managed to follow that advice. When I had crept into the hospital in Bochum in the far west of Germany, dressed in a doctor's white coat, and told my 'patient', a former Gestapo commander, now tucked up in bed with a thermometer under his tongue, that everything was on track for the minor operation in the morning, but that first he would need to do a brief test – one which entailed injecting kerosene into his bloodstream, as it happened – I had felt only a cool sense of purpose.

When I stamped on the accelerator in Paris, having pursued SS Captain Fritz Kramer down a side street, I did not feel hot anger course through my veins. Not even as I watched the mass murderer run for his life. No, I was calm as I caught up with the former officer of the Birkenau camp, the front of my car ramming him at speed, sending him flying fifteen feet until he landed spread-eagled, like a scarecrow, on the station railings.

I kept a memento of each operation, a report from the local newspaper recording the 'death in mysterious circumstances' or the 'tragic accident' which had deprived the community of one more Nazi war criminal posing as an upright citizen. It gives me no pleasure to record the fact that I had become one of the group's most accomplished executioners, able to slip in and out of most countries without impediment. Of course it helped, as it always had, that my hair was blond and my eyes blue. Occasionally my prey would look at me with warmth, imagining they were about to have a reunion with a young comrade. Sure, they couldn't quite place the face, but I looked the right sort. Where did we know each other from? Was it Sachsenhausen, or perhaps the Ukraine? Did we serve together, Mein Herr? Not quite, no.

So I was not usually fazed by my work. But this job was different. My target now was Joschka Dorfman, who had served the Reich with distinction as one of the senior men at the death camp of Treblinka, about a hundred kilometres north-east of Warsaw. For my comrades, that was the chief item on the indictment: some 840,000 people, almost all Jews, had perished at Treblinka, 'processed' through its gas chambers at a rate of ten thousand per day, an efficiency that was the envy of the other death camps. From the entire time in which Treblinka was in operation little more than a hundred people survived.

But that was not the cause of the small bubbling of sweat I could feel on my back, threatening to stain my shirt. The source of that could be found in another line on Joschka Dorfman's curriculum vitae. Because the lieutenant had won his promotion not in Poland but in next door Lithuania, in the city of Kaunas to be precise. At the Ninth Fort, where he had been one of those charged with filling the pits with the corpses of fifty thousand people, most of them Jews. I knew that, among those Dorfman would have seen shot in the back – if, that is, he had not fired the bullets himself – would have been my Hannah, my Rivvy and my Leah.

He would be here soon, I didn't doubt it. So far all the information we had received from our man in Spain had proved entirely reliable. Dorfman and his wife were indeed in town on vacation, as promised. Their home was in Alicante, in the Spanish south-east. Hundreds of them had gone there: it had become a haven for former servants of the Führer. Dorfman's movements were known; it would have been perfectly possible to hunt him down there. Possible, but risky. An operation in the heart of a retirement village of ex-Nazis would alert the others; they might flee or, worse, attempt to come after us. Better to take care of it here, at the opposite end of the country, where word would not spread.

Our source had discovered that the Dorfmans, husband and wife, liked to vacation here in the Basque country. They had developed a particular fondness for San Sebastián and I could see why. The whole town curved around the bay; its beaches were wide and fine. I had seen the couple swim in the morning, letting their skin dry in the sun. Then they would come here for a late lunch; she would drink wine, he preferred beer. Sated, he would return to the Hotel Londres for a siesta while she went strolling through the cobbled streets, idly window shopping. It looked like a pleasant routine and they had followed it on each one of the three days since they had got here.

I checked my watch the instant they arrived: ten to two. They looked tanned and handsome, the glow of a good holiday. She was smiling as she came in, removing a large, floppy sunhat and shaking the last grains of sand from her hair. He was wearing sunglasses, which gave me a surge of anxiety. What if he did not take them off? It would be impossible to make a one hundred per cent positive identification without seeing his eyes. But then they reached the counter and, keen to peruse the *pintxos* on offer, he removed his glasses and I was certain.

I ordered some mint tea and remained immersed in my newspaper: a man idling away the afternoon. When the Dorfmans eventually paid their bill and left, I quietly placed a wad of notes on the table, enough to cover my meal with plenty over, grabbed my bag and made my own exit.

I kept a fair distance behind them, much further than those who have never done such work would imagine. I let them disappear out of sight, turning left or right, knowing that I would catch up with them again. I had the great advantage of knowing where Dorfman, at least, was heading.

I watched the couple part, she giving him a light peck on his cheek, her right heel kicking up coquettishly, and I wondered what words she had used, whether she had said goodbye to her husband or merely *au revoir*. My heart was beginning to pound in a way I did not like.

I let her meander down one of the narrow, sloping passageways before picking up the pace. Dorfman was walking briskly now, the seafront to his right, the water a sparkling blue. Had the sun carried on shining in places like this when my sisters and I lived in the ghetto? I had always assumed that the skies had darkened across the whole world.

Dorfman crossed the promenade, waiting for a group of teenage boys to cycle past, before entering the hotel through one of the sliding doors facing the sea. I decided not to follow him but to go around to the street entrance.

With a purposeful walk I had perfected back on that train trip from Kovno to Warsaw, I strode past the reception desk, ignored the lift and climbed the stairs. Our informant had even supplied the room number. Before I touched the handrail, I pulled on a pair of tight leather gloves.

I paused halfway between the second and third floors. Looking upwards, I could see Dorfman emerge from the lift and watch his feet pad down the carpeted corridor. I held my breath, waiting for the sound of his key in the lock.

Outside Room 212, I did not give myself a moment to hesitate. I knocked twice and called out, in Spanish, *'Servicio de habitaciones!'* Room Service!

I reached for the holster under my left shoulder and withdrew my Beretta 1951, so that its barrel became visible just as the door opened. It would be the first thing Dorfman would see.

I gave him no time to react. I used my left hand to shove him back into the room, just in case he had any ideas about trying to slam the door on me. With the gun held steady in my right hand, I closed the door with my foot.

*'Guten Tag,* Herr Dorfman,' I began, swiftly moving to the telephone at the side of the bed, yanking its cord out of the wall with a single tug. 'Don't scream or I will kill you instantly.' I was relieved my voice gave nothing away, no treacherous wobble. 'You are SS Lieutenant Joshcka Dorfman of the Treblinka death camp and previously of the Ninth Fort at Kovno where you were personally responsible for the deaths of hundreds of thousands of Jews. I act in the name of the Jews and I have come to administer justice.'

There had been much discussion in the group about this stage in the process. Some believed it entailed an unnecessary risk, that any delay was foolish. I did not argue with that: in some cases, it was indeed impossible. I had had no chance, for example, to address Fritz Kramer when I smashed him off the road, nor to speak to the others who had wound up in road-side ditches or in flaming cars on the autobahn. But where it was possible, as it was now, then it was worthwhile. The leader of our group – Aron, the same grave, intense man who had sent me on my first mission as a messenger, from that candlelit cellar in Kovno – had argued it with great passion. 'Those who are guilty of the greatest crime in human history should know, even as they draw their last breath, that their victims did not let this crime go unavenged. That Jews cannot be murdered with impunity. That the Jews will fight back.'

Dorfman's tan vanished, the sight of the gun draining the blood from his face. There was also, I noticed, a glint of confusion in his eye, a perplexed expression which I had seen more than once. *Why are you, a young, strong Aryan man, saying these things?*

'No. You have made a mistake, I am—'

'I am a Jew and I am here to avenge my people.'

'But I have done nothing wrong. You have the wrong—'

'Don't worry. I'm not going to shoot you.'

At that, Dorfman slumped in relief. He tottered backwards and sank onto the edge of the bed. 'Thank God,' he said. 'Thank God.'

I kept the gun trained on him and said nothing.

'You want money, yes? That's what it is. Of

course. You want money. How much money do you want, to keep this information, er, confidential? Name your price. There are plenty of people who could arrange a wire transfer, you need only—'

'I am not going to shoot you because that would be too quick. I have in my bag two syringes and a small tank of gasoline. I am going to inject the gasoline into your heart. Death takes at least – but you know how long it takes. From the experiments of Aribert Heim at Mauthausen. He ran this particular experiment many times. Surely he shared the results with you?'

'Please, don't do this to me. Please. Whatever you want, you can have it. Names. I can give you names.'

This, too, was part of our procedure. The plea for mercy, in return for information on other war criminals in hiding – their whereabouts, their new identities – we always listened to that patiently.

I opened my bag and pulled out a notebook and pen. I wrote down what Dorfman told me. Occasionally I told him to slow down. The stream of words, powered by his fear, was flowing too fast for me to keep up, a pen in my right hand, the revolver in my left.

But I was also aware of the time. I knew that Frau Dorfman would soon tire of her shopping. I closed my notebook and returned it to the bag. The Nazi exhaled deeply, believing his ordeal was coming to an end.

'Now, where were we?' I said. 'Oh yes. I was explaining how I am going to kill you.'

'You dirty Jew! We made a bargain!'

'You'd better call your lawyer.'

At that, Dorfman lunged for the gun. But he miscalculated. I was still holding the weapon in my left hand, freeing my right hand to deliver a swift, but meaty right hook to his jaw.

For a moment, I was worried that I had knocked him out. That would be no good. Dorfman was flat out on the bed, his hands clasped to his face – but he was conscious.

'As I was saying, the gasoline will go straight to your heart. Fortunately, I have two syringes. One for each of you.'

There was a stirring from the bed and a low grunt.

'Sorry, I can't hear you.'

His voice slurred, the blood bubbling in his mouth, Dorfman tried again. 'What do you mean, each of you?'

'For you and your wife, of course. We will wait for her to come back and you can die together. Though, as you know thanks to Dr Heim, it may take some time.'

With mammoth effort, Dorfman pulled himself upright. His eyes were fierce with fear. I noticed a patch of damp spreading across the Nazi's trousers; he had soiled himself.

He began to beg. At first he pleaded for both their lives, his wife's and his, repeating his offer of money until he could see it was futile. He promised he could give more names, if only he had more time. Eventually, I heard what I was waiting to hear. 'Take me, but not her. And allow me to die like a man.'

He wanted the revolver, but I refused: too noisy. Instead, I opened my bag and pulled out a long rope. Our source had told me there were ceiling beams in this hotel and that the height was good enough.

I, a Jew, handed him, a Nazi, the rope. I positioned a chair. I watched as Dorfman made the noose around his neck then tied it, and I kept watching as he tightened it. My gaze did not waver when he kicked away the chair: I watched his weight fall. I showed no expression as SS Lieutenant Joschka Dorfman of the Ninth Fort gasped, his body convulsing in the last spasms of life, until his legs were swinging, as dumb and fleshy as the hams on Puerto Street.

Quietly, I holstered my gun, gathered up my things, including a bag which now contained a range of unused weapons, including a spare revolver – but certainly no syringes or petrol – and closed the door of room 212 softly behind me.

# CHAPTER TWENTY-FIVE

'Rebecca, I'm afraid there's no other way to understand it. Don't you see the pattern?'

They were standing next to each other, their arms just touching, poring over the papers spread out on the table.

'For every date stamp on a passport, there's a cutting. Look.'

Methodically, Tom set out the pile of newspaper clippings alongside the passports. There was one from Liberation in late 1952. He translated, falteringly, out loud: 'Detectives in Les Halles are seeking witnesses who may be able to help them with information about the death on Tuesday evening of a man apparently hit by a speeding car and flung onto the railings of a Metro station. Police said the man's injuries suggested he had been hit at top speed . . .' In neat handwriting, a hand Tom recognized, a short sentence had been pencilled in the margin: *SS Captain Fritz Kramer, Birkenau.*

And there it was: a stamp in Gerald Merton's

British passport establishing that he had flown into Orly airport two days earlier and left the day after the reported accident.

Next, a news report of a corpse found hanging in a Rio suburb later that same year. Tom checked the date and, sure enough, 'Fernando Matutes' had arrived in Brazil four days before the hanging and had left the same day. The passport showed he had travelled direct from Brazil to Argentina, just in time, it seemed, for the mysterious road traffic accident which would strike two days later – the newspaper account of which had been carefully preserved in this same box.

An explosion in an apartment building in Lille, a botched operation in a Munich hospital: each time, Tom could find a passport stamp that coincided. There were reports of men killed in car accidents, some of them only months apart. One was found dead in a gutter. The pencilled note identified him as *Hans Stuckart, Ministry of Interior*. An account from 1953 reported police bafflement after a driver was burned alive, his car having suffered a rare steering failure which sent it spinning across the highway. The handwritten note added that the deceased was *Otto Betz, deported Jews of France*.

Now Rebecca was working through the cuttings herself, rapidly turning them over, one after another, in date order. After the first set from 1945 and 1946, they jumped to 1952, then paused again before the final item, which dated from the early 1960s in the *Winnipeg Free Press*. It reported the death of an Estonian immigrant, found hanged in his home. The police were looking for no one else. In pencil, the suicide was identified as *Alexander Laak, commandant of the Jägala concentration camp in Estonia*.

Silently, Tom tucked each news story into a passport, inserting it alongside the page where there was a matching stamp. By the end he had done that for nearly three quarters of the news reports; all that was left was the small pile of German items from 1945.

'Rebecca, what languages did your father speak?'

'Lots,' she said quietly, staring down at the table. 'German, Russian. French, I think. Maybe Spanish.'

A sentence from the notebook surfaced. *My sisters and I went to the school and I discovered that I was good at learning languages. The teacher said I had an ear for it.*

Tom didn't know what to say. First the shooting in New York and now this: the father Rebecca thought she knew had been killed twice over.

She fell into a chair, biting her lip so hard he thought it might bleed.

He dragged his gaze away. 'Look, Rebecca, this is—'

'Don't say anything.'

'I don't know what else we—'

'I need time to think.'

Tom retreated, clearing up the items from the table and putting them back.

At last, Rebecca stood, picked up her father's box and strode over to Julian. Tom watched her hand it back to him, and then ask for what appeared to be a favour. Julian scribbled down a number, kissed her on the cheek and said goodbye. Tom ran after her as she went out the door and onto the street, feeling like a dog on a lead.

'Where are we going now?'

'To see the one man who might know the truth about my father.'

# CHAPTER TWENTY-SIX

The convenience stores and fast food restaurants rapidly gave way to the sparkle of steel and glass. As they passed by the Gherkin, another London landmark that had sprouted in Tom's absence, Hackney receded and the glistening towers of Canary Wharf became visible.

'You drive,' Rebecca had said as they walked away from the Kingsland Law Centre. 'I want to think.' And she had sat there in the passenger seat, her face grim with determination.

In a court of law, Tom could have just about constructed an argument that all the evidence they had uncovered was circumstantial, that there was no ironclad proof connecting Gershon Matzkin to any one of the killings, let alone all of them. Most had been recorded as suicides or road traffic accidents; there was nothing that could establish beyond doubt that foul play had occurred. And even if it had, young Gershon might have served as only a minor accomplice, perhaps a lookout. There was no proof that he was a killer.

And yet, neither he nor Rebecca doubted that Gershon Matzkin had been an assassin. Who else would keep a score-sheet, a roll call of war criminals, their names crossed out on the occasion of their deaths, but the man responsible? This, surely, was the record of his labours, maintained with pride. (It was something Tom's friends in the criminal lawyer fraternity had told him often undid felons: sheer professional pride, the desire to be credited for one's work. One way or another, consciously or otherwise, they had wanted their endeavours to be recognized. It was a basic human impulse.)

As they drove on, Tom began to see everything slip into place. Of course Gershon had always eschewed publicity, refusing to address seminars or be interviewed for oral history archives: he could not dare risk his story slipping into public view. No wonder those last few pages of the notebook had been torn out. Carried away by the equally human desire to shape the narrative of one's own life, he must have begun to set down his story in full – only to realize that what he had written amounted to a confession of serial murder. Tom could picture him realizing his error, frantically tearing out the incriminating sheets of paper, shredding or burning them, until their remarkable reminiscences were once more consigned to oblivion.

He thought back to the corpse he had seen little more than twenty-four hours ago in the Office of the Chief Medical Examiner, how he had been struck by the toned muscle, the body of a strong man who had fought to keep his shape. Now that strength made sense. He had been a human weapon, deployed to hit back at those who had nearly wiped out his entire people. He had chosen to do what the Jews had barely been able to do when it counted: to fight back. Of course he had to be strong. He needed to be a Samson, with enough muscle in his arms to smite every last one of the Jews' murderous enemies. This man had been their avenging angel.

Tom's phone rang. 'It's in my pocket,' he said, his eyes on the road. 'Take it out, but don't answer it. Just tell me who it is.'

Rebecca reached across, trying to find the opening in his jacket, her fingers brushing against him. There were layers of clothes between them, but still the sensation sent a charge through him. He gripped the steering wheel tight.

'Unknown caller,' she said.

He took the phone from her and pressed the green button. 'Tom Byrne.'

'Tom, how you doin'?'

'Who is this?'

'A very satisfied customer, that's who.'

'Oh, Mr Fantoni. Nice of you to call.' He could hear himself enunciating more clearly, ramping up his Englishness. It was a cheap tactic, but the high-paying clients seemed to like it. 'As it happens, I'm in London just now. I wonder if—'

'Look, this won't take a minute. We were real happy with the job you did for us: the sale's gone through. My father's very pleased.'

'I'm glad.'

'So pleased, he wants you to work on another big job we have here. Similar time scale.'

'Well, we could meet next week and—'

'Too late. We need this done right away. I'll book you a first class ticket on the next flight out of there.'

'Unfortunately—'

'We'll pay triple rates, Mr Byrne. What can I tell you, my father likes what you do.'

*Triple.* That would be a quarter of a million dollars for no more than a fortnight's work. He shot a glance at Rebecca, her face in profile as she gazed out of the window. Just that brief sight of her was enough to send a surge into his chest.

'You know what, Mr Fantoni. I'd love to, I really would. But I'm on a case here in London I cannot abandon. I hope—'

The voice on the phone adopted a stage Italian accent. 'I make-a an offer you can't-a refuse!' The accent disappeared; the tone became chilly. 'You're making a mistake, Mr Byrne.'

In the silence, Tom felt his throat dry. 'I'm sorry. It's just bad timing.'

'I hope you don't regret it.'

'I hope not, too.'

Tom passed the phone back to Rebecca, hoping she had not heard Fantoni's booming, mugging voice. She gave no hint that she had. He would try to put Fantoni out of his mind for the time being, call when he got back to New York, hope he could smooth things over. For now, he had to focus on this case. Should the contents of Merton's secret box affect his advice to Henning? Could the UN argue that the man they had killed was himself a proven killer? Hardly. Those deaths had taken place five decades ago; the trail of evidence would be frozen, let alone cold. If the UN tried to mitigate its error, its crime, in killing an unarmed seventy-seven-year-old by claiming he had, back in the 1950s and 1960s, been some kind of hitman, it would probably backfire. The organization would sound unhinged. The press corps would demand hard evidence, beyond a ropey shoebox containing a few crumbling press clippings. They probably wouldn't even get to that stage. They would ask the question that had been throbbing in Tom's mind ever since they had opened that dusty container: What does any of this have to do with the United Nations?

The instant he had decoded the fading evidence of that box, he had tried to come up with an answer. Is that what had taken Gerald Merton to the UN, one last assignment, one last Nazi to kill? Decades back, the Secretary-General from Austria, Kurt Waldheim, had been exposed as having lied about his military service in the Wehrmacht, glossing over his knowledge of Nazi war crimes – an affair which older hands in the UN bureaucracy still recalled with a shudder. But that was in the 1980s. There was no one who could possibly fit that bill now, no one old enough for a start. He thought about Paavo Viren, the new Secretary-General. Now in his late sixties, he would have been a toddler during wartime. Besides, he was Finnish; the country had stayed out of the Nazis' clutches. Tom vaguely remembered reading a profile of the SG after his appointment, noting his cleric father's long-time record, out in the Finnish sticks somewhere, as a preacher of tolerance and peace. He cast his mind over the rest of the UN staff, but couldn't think of anyone who came into the right age range.

On the other hand, it was General Assembly week: the place was teeming with representatives of every country, each bringing large delegations in tow . . .

They found a parking space and while Rebecca fumbled for change for the meter, Tom stepped a few paces away and dialled Henning's number. They were in Canary Wharf now, an area that Tom had never visited. Back when he lived in London, Docklands had still been largely desolate and empty, a wasteland dotted with the odd over-priced apartment and served by a Toytown light railway. People spoke of it as a kind of Siberia, a place remote from the hubbub of 'real' London. Now, it seemed, all that had changed. The tower blocks that had once lain empty were brimming with offices, with new, taller buildings arising like spirits from the swamp. The area had built-up a serious high-rise skyline, something London had always lacked. And it oozed money.

'Munchau.'

'Hi Henning, it's Tom.'

'You've either fucked her or she's just filed suit. Which is it?'

'Neither.'

'OK, I give up.'

'Henning, I won't bore you with all the details, but there's some information I could use.'

'Bore me.'

Tom looked over at Rebecca, now placing the pay and display ticket in the front windscreen. 'It's just a hunch at the moment, nothing more.'

'Don't really have time for hunches, mate. At the risk of repeating myself, General Assembly, General Assembly, General Assembly.'

'That's what I'm thinking about too. Could you get someone in the OLC to compile a list of every official either in New York for the GA already or due to arrive this week who's aged seventy or above?'

'Are we still on the hitman theory?'

Tom paused. 'It's a bit difficult to explain right now.'

'Oh, she's with you! Why didn't you say? Is she really, unbelievably gorgeous?'

'Thanks, Henning. I appreciate it.'

'All right, I'll see what we can get. Seventy? That's the cut-off?'

Tom did his sums once again: even seventy was pretty young, anyone below that age would have been a baby. Still, best to err on the side of caution. 'Yes. Seventy. Heads of government, foreign ministers, ambassadors, obviously. But anyone else: aides, translators, anyone coming in for the week.'

'What about the entire UN staff, while we're at it?'

'Actually, that's not a bad idea. Start with—'

'Tom, I was joking.'

He hung up and hurried to catch up with Rebecca, already walking towards the offices of Roderick Jones & Partners, one of the grander City law firms that had moved into Canary Wharf in the late 1990s. The recently retired senior partner was Julian Goldman's father, Henry. But, Julian had told them with a roll of his eyes, Goldman *père* couldn't quite make the break, so spent at least two days a week in the office, nominally as a 'consultant' to his erstwhile colleagues but, Julian had implied, more accurately because he didn't have anything else to do.

The moment they walked into the lobby, Tom smiled to himself: just seeing it instantly gave him the measure of the young man they had left behind in Hackney. A steel-and-glass affair, it had a vast atrium, tall enough to house an impressive, if vaguely absurd, indoor tree. The marble floor stretched for acres before reaching a white desk as wide as a Politburo platform, with not one, but three different receptionists, each equipped with a telephone headset. It was a textbook example of the paradox of corporate relations: the easiest way to impress clients was to show them just how profligate you were with their money.

What options had that left poor Julian Goldman? Born on the top of the mountain, where else could he go but down? He had clearly turned his back on Daddy's riches and gone the ethical route, opening his battered legal aid practice in deepest Hackney on a street which probably lay in the direct shadow of his father's corporate palace. Julian's career would be a rebuke to Henry Goldman; he would be a lawyer driven not by money but by conscience. Tom smiled to himself at the predictability of it all. While men from Tom's background were striving with each sinew to climb up the prestige ladder, the likes of Julian Goldman were in a hurry to slide down.

When they stepped out of the lift, Henry Goldman was waiting for them. He stretched his arms open to embrace Rebecca, but clumsily, as if handling a new-fangled device he had not yet mastered. He shook Tom's hand, then ushered them both into a conference room more plushly furnished than even the grandest meeting place in the United Nations.

'Rebecca, I was so sorry to hear of your news. We all were.'

Rebecca nodded. 'My father always said your father was his best friend.'

'That's true. I think my father regarded Gerald as a kind of younger brother.' A wounded expression briefly flitted across his face. 'Maybe even another son.'

'I presume he told you things. As his lawyer.'

At that, Goldman stretched out his legs and smoothed a hand over his tie. Tom recognized the colours of the Garrick Club.

'You've come here from Julian's office, you say? You know the key,' Goldman paused, *'materials* are kept there now.'

'I know,' said Rebecca. 'I've just seen them.'

'I see.'

The lawyer got to his feet and began to pace away from the table, towards the window. The light was fading; Canary Wharf was beginning to glitter in the twilight. 'I cannot claim to be wholly surprised by this turn of events. No matter what we tell our clients, it's a simple truth that nothing can stay secret forever. Isn't that right, Mr Byrne?'

Tom was barely paying attention. He had not got past the clipped English accent, straight out of a Kenneth More movie. *This* was the son of a Holocaust survivor, underground fighter and forest partisan; this stuffed-shirt in a Garrick Club tie? He should have been used to it by now, having spent the last decade in the ultimate city of immigrants, but this seemed such an extreme case.

Perhaps this is what people meant when they talked of becoming 'more English than the English'.

Rebecca didn't give Tom time to answer. 'Can you tell us what you know?'

Tom fought the urge to inhale sharply. What an elementary blunder: there would be no mistaking Rebecca Merton for a lawyer. *Let the guy warm up.*

'I did know that one day this would come out. But, for some reason, I always suspected it would be Julian who would discover it and confront me over it.'

'Can you tell me—'

Tom gritted his teeth, worried that she would scare Goldman off. But he needn't have worried: Henry Goldman simply talked over Rebecca.

'Of course my father knew it all and he brought me into his confidence on some of the key aspects. I will not deny that it became a source of great tension between us, especially when I was a younger man first reading jurisprudence at Cambridge and, later, as an articled clerk and so on. I imagined Julian and I would re-run some of those arguments, with my son in the role of my father.'

Tom asked his first question. 'And has Julian ever confronted you about this?'

'No. It makes me wonder if perhaps he has not worked it out. But it's hardly Fermat's Last Theorem is it, Mr Byrne? Once that box is opened, it is a matter of adding two and two to reach a round and clear four.'

'Perhaps Julian never opened the box.' Tom didn't like taking over like this. But the Garrick tie had convinced him: a man like Henry Goldman would speak to a fellow white, male lawyer more openly than with a non-male, non-lawyer. For men of Goldman's ilk, that would be like communicating with another species. The fact that Rebecca was Jewish, while he, Tom, was not, did not seem to make any difference. The tie suggested Goldman was not that kind of Jew.

Goldman sat down at the table and gave them both a straight look in the eye. 'It's difficult for me to talk about this without letting my own views show, and I am sure what you are both in need of is an uncoloured account. For which reason, perhaps it is best if I pass on – without too much commentary on my part – the arguments advanced by my father.'

'Actually, a few facts at this stage would be an enormous help,' Tom said, adopting the excessive politeness he affected whenever speaking with the English establishment.

'Very well.' Goldman leaned forward. 'As you now know, Rebecca's father was involved in the—' he searched for the right word, '—*removal* of certain men associated with the events of the Second World War.'

Tom could see Rebecca's leg oscillating up and down in a constant vibration.

'Well, I have to tell you. He did not do this work alone. He was part of an organization. We would call them Holocaust survivors now, though no one used that word at the time. They were men, and a few women, who had seen unspeakable horrors. Unspeakable.' Goldman gave a little shake of his head. 'At the start, in the final weeks of the war and immediately afterwards, there were no more than fifty of them, with maybe two hundred more offering help on the outside. Almost all had been involved in the resistance in some way.'

An image floated into Tom's head of the young Gershon Matzkin, posing as Vitatis Olekas, hopping on and off trains as he criss-crossed occupied Europe, cheating death and desperately trying to warn others so that they might live. *Aunt Esther has returned and is at Megilla Street 7, apartment 4.*

'They were ghetto fighters, my father included. And I suppose this effort evolved quite naturally out of that. They had been trying to kill Nazis before and they were killing Nazis now. Churchill and Roosevelt had declared the war over , but "it wasn't their war to finish". That's what my father used to say. Hitler had declared war on the Jews long before he declared war on Britain or America or Russia. The Jews had their own score to settle.

'But there was more to it than that. More to what we—' he meant Tom and him, fellow lawyers, '—would speak of as *motive*. To understand that, you have to start from first principles.'

Tom didn't even have to look over at Rebecca to know she was squirming in her seat. He felt it too. Goldman had no appreciation of the urgency of their situation. They hadn't told him about last night's break-in for fear it would make him clam up. He hadn't become the emeritus senior partner of Roderick Jones, with a corner office view of Docklands, by wading balls deep into trouble. They would have to be patient.

'You have to remember that Jewish resistance to the Nazis was impossible.' Goldman raised his palm in protest, anticipating an objection. 'I know, I know. There *was* resistance. My father and your father, Rebecca, were part of it. Nevertheless, the logical starting point is that Jewish resistance was impossible. You have to understand that to understand anything.

'As you know, Nazi control was absolute. Even the slightest act of defiance would be punished by swift and lethal retaliation. Dare to raise a hand to a Nazi and they would kill you, your family and your whole community, without compunction. For one of them, they would kill a thousand of you. But that's not the main thing.'

Rebecca was now drumming her fingers on the arm of her chair.

'The Jews lacked the essential requirements of any plausible resistance. They had no arms, no tradition of fighting. They had no army, no barracks, no arsenals. The Poles and the French had been sovereign nations, with their own armies;

there were resources – arms dumps and so forth, even in the middle of the countryside – they could call on when under occupation. The Jews had none of that.

'Above all, they had no friends. No one would help them at all. I'm sure you know the stories, the lengths the Jews had to go to, the bribes they had to pay, to get the Poles or Lithuanians or Ukrainians to sell them so much as a single pistol. And if they ever got out, ever escaped the Nazis, woe betide them if they ran into the rest of the resistance. The Poles or Lithuanians or anyone else for that matter hated the Jews so much, they were only too glad to finish off anybody the Nazis had been foolish enough to let slip away. As my late father, who loved English idiom, used to say, "We went from the fire into the frying pan".'

Tom could feel Rebecca shuffling, desperate for Goldman to get to the point. 'Could I—'

The raised palm again. 'You'll soon see where this is leading.' He cleared his throat. 'Add to this the fact that the Nazis did not exactly advertise their plans. They hid behind euphemisms: "resettlement in the east", and so on. And of course the Jews swallowed it up. "Never underestimate a man's inability to imagine his own destruction." Those were the words of a member of this group. A rabbi, as it happens. Oh yes, there was a rabbi. A poet too. A couple of journalists. Farmers, merchants, doctors. They were a very mixed bunch. Anyway, this rabbi used to speak of Hitler's bus.'

He leaned forward, his eyes bright. 'You know about Hitler's bus, yes? That he was planning to exterminate every single Jew, except twelve? These twelve would be saved, as specimens. Human exhibits. They were to travel the world in a specially equipped bus, a mobile display of "the extinct Jewish people". That was Hitler's plan. And you know what this rabbi would say? "Every Jew in Europe believed he would be one of the twelve who would make it onto that bus".

'This is the context in which your father, Rebecca, and mine acted. They believed that the Jews, for all the reasons I have mentioned, had accepted their fate too passively. A few individuals had fought back, but the damage they had inflicted amounted to mere pinpricks. They were just children, the leaders of the resistance. Even the most senior commanders were in their very early twenties. There was so little they could do. You know the phrase, "Like sheep to the slaughter"? That was coined by the poet of the group. He said the Jews had walked into the gas chambers like sheep to the slaughter.

'It was this that those three hundred men could not stand, that Jewish life had been extinguished so cheaply, without punishment. They wanted to teach the world a different lesson: that to kill a Jew came at a price. That such a crime would be avenged. And so they looked back into history and found an ancient vow: *Dam Israel Nokeam.* "The blood of Israel will take vengeance". They took the first letter of each Hebrew word of that slogan to form another word, DIN. A word in itself, it means "judgement" and that became the name of this group. Your father and my father, they were both in it. And I believe, Rebecca, that your father was its very last member.'

Tom was thinking hard about everything he had seen: the passports, the press clippings, the evidence in New York. Had there been any pointer to this word, DIN; some clue he had missed?

'In the beginning, it was quite straightforward. By the middle of 1945, the Allies ruled Berlin and DIN could operate relatively freely. They cultivated informants in the British and American bureaucracies, especially in the prosecutors' offices, finding men who for their own reasons were only too happy to leak information on Nazis who had melted back into civilian life. One way or another, DIN acquired a target list. Then they used all the old techniques of the ghetto resistance to acquire the uniforms and IDs they needed. My father was good at this work: he would follow a military policeman and knock him out cold, taking great care to steal everything he had: wristwatch, wallet, belt. The soldier would come to a few hours later, stark naked, unaware that the only things his attacker had really wanted were his uniform and military ID. But I believe the female members of DIN were especially adept in this task – though they didn't use force to part the MPs from their uniforms.'

Goldman allowed himself a smile at this, but it passed quickly. The earlier ebullience and pomposity had gone now; his face appeared to be in shadow, a shade entirely of its own making. The more of the story he told, the greater the weight it seemed to press on him.

'Posing as military police made the job easy; they could walk right up to a target and "arrest" him, just like that, bold as brass. Or they could do a "snatch", an abduction. They could do all this because DIN were wearing the uniforms of the Allied authorities – and the Allies were the masters now.

'Then they would act like a court, reading out the charge sheet, listing the prisoner's crimes. Only then would they announce themselves: *"We act in the name of the Jews and we have come to administer justice."*

'Afterwards, they would go to some lengths to hide the body. That way the investigation into the victim's disappearance took longer, giving DIN time either to get away or to strike again. Ideally, the death, once discovered, was recorded as a suicide.'

Tom thought back to the sheaf of cuttings he had seen in the cardboard box that afternoon: most of the deaths reported there were either car accidents or suicides.

Goldman continued. 'This approach had the obvious advantage of ensuring that no other ex-Nazis would know there was a group actively pursuing them; they would not raise their guard. But, you have to realize, the way DIN saw things, that was also a *disadvantage*. They *wanted* the Nazis to know the Jews were out for revenge. They wanted the Nazis to fear the Jews.

'I must stress that they went only after those who had a hand in the Final Solution. SS men who had staffed the extermination camps, those who had served in the mobile killing units, the Einsatzgruppen. You know about those, Mr Byrne?'

Tom nodded, remembering the story in the notebook, the same story recounted in countless history books: the pits, the shooting, the pile of bodies, still writhing even in death.

'I see that I have avoided speaking of the actual *executions* themselves, as my father would have called them. I should correct that.' Goldman sighed. 'My father hinted at all kinds of exotic methods. A punishment fit for the crime was one approach: a Nazi who had been involved with the gas chambers might be locked in his garage, properly sealed, with his car engine left running. Carbon monoxide was a poor substitute for Zyklon B, but at least the point was made. I heard about another method, also involving the garage. The target would be forced to stand on the roof of his car, while a noose, suspended from the ceiling, would be placed around his neck. Then a DIN member would drive the car away, leaving the target swinging.

'Still, I'm not sure I believe these accounts. My best guess is that DIN preferred to kill with their bare hands – strangulation – or maybe a knife.'

'Mr Goldman,' Rebecca cut in. 'What we saw today was nothing to do with this wartime period. The actions my father took were much later, in the fifties and sixties.'

Henry Goldman fell back in his chair, the air escaping from him like a punctured tyre. 'I'm sorry. I've talked too long.'

'No, not at all, I only—'

'You see, I knew, of course, that this day would come, that one day I'd have to tell this story. But that does not prepare one for it.' He gave a forced smile, an expression not of pleasure but of containment, of holding back a great floodtide of emotion. 'I have not shared it with my wife or my sons. I have carried it, as it were, for many, many years. I don't know how else to tell it, except as I heard it.'

Tom decided to act as diplomat. 'There's no problem with the way you're telling it, Mr Goldman. You take your time.'

Goldman nodded his silent thanks, cleared his throat and went on. 'The killings I have described were known as "the first hunting season". They arose out of the strong belief that there would be no other kind of justice. The Allies had promised it of course, fine speeches about bringing every last Nazi killer to book. But even before the war was over, those promises were fading. Soon there was the suggestion that only those in charge of the Third Reich would face prosecution. Which is how we came to have the great show at

Nuremberg, in which a grand total of twenty-four men were brought to account. Twenty-four!'

There was something strange about Goldman's narrative, and suddenly Tom realized that he was witnessing an act of ventriloquism. He was channelling the arguments, even the voice, of his long-dead father. He told the story the way it had been told to him. It had been preserved, as if on a reel of quarter-inch magnetic tape, inside his head for nearly fifty years.

'DIN were repelled by the spectacle of the Nuremberg trial, the pretence that only two dozen men were responsible for this massive, international crime. They had seen with their own eyes the men who had whipped Jews to death for sport, who had herded them onto trains and shot them into pits, the men who had shoved them into gas chambers and then shovelled their bodies into crematoria – they had seen all this, and they knew it was not the work of *twenty-four* men. It was the work of tens of thousands, hundreds of thousands, maybe even millions!'

There was no interrupting Goldman now, the words poured out of him in a hot torrent.

'As the crimes began to be revealed, as people saw the newsreel footage of those mountains of naked bodies, people in the West demanded better. The Russians were executing Nazis by the thousands; people here and in America expected something similar. The Allies felt they had to do something. By the end of 1946, they had jailed nearly half a million Germans, holding them before trial on charges of direct participation in mass murder. There were another three and a half million listed for "significant criminal complicity". Think of that number: *three and a half million.* But the United Nations War Crimes Commission drew up another list, made up of all those liable for automatic arrest as former members of the Nazi Party: in the American occupation zone alone the total was more than thirteen million people.'

'They'd have ended up jailing the entire male population,' said Tom quietly, a memory of his own now surfacing. But Goldman was listening to only one voice: the one in his head, belonging to his father.

'At last it seemed as if they were going to get justice after all. And not simply by grabbing it for themselves. They had a hard debate but concluded that, if justice was truly on its way, they had no business carrying on as judge, jury and executioner. They decided to lay down their weapons, to disband and go their separate ways, start their own lives. My father and yours came here to London. Some went to America, many to Israel. They believed it was all over. But it was not to be.

He paused, as if remembering himself. 'Are you fond of statistics, Mr Byrne?' He did not wait for an answer. 'I am. I like nothing more than a neat table of numbers. My father was the same way. "One number can tell you more than a thousand words." That's what he would say. There's a table in a book by Raul Hilberg, one of the great historians of the Holocaust. A very revealing table. My father would look at it often. You just put your finger on the column of numbers, move it downward and there you are: it tells you all you need to know.

'It starts off with the *Fragebogen*, the "registrants", those thirteen million or more who were part of the Nazi apparatus. Then you move your finger down a line, to the total number of men charged. And this figure, you notice, is much smaller: just three million four hundred and forty-five thousand one hundred, if I recall. The figure on the next line relates to those who, having been charged, were released without so much as a trial. A blanket amnesty, if you like. It's large, this number: two million four hundred and eighty thousand seven hundred. They just walk away. If you have a head for mental arithmetic, as I do, you can work out that the gap between those last two numbers is just shy of a million. That is the number of Nazis still in the prosecutors' sights.

'How are they punished? Just look at the table. Precisely five hundred and sixty-nine thousand six hundred of them are fined. The slate is wiped clean with a cash payment. Go down to the next line and you see that a further one hundred and twenty-four thousand four hundred men had to suffer the indignity of employment restrictions. Unfortunately, for certain jobs, being a Nazi mass murderer was an immediate disqualification. The same was true of eligibility for public office.

Twenty-three thousand one hundred Nazis were told their political careers were on hold.

'If memory serves, another twenty-five thousand nine hundred had their property confiscated. I say "their" but this was property acquired through a rather unorthodox route. Those deemed guilty had seen their neighbours in Hamburg or Frankfurt dragged off to the camps, shed a tear – and then ransacked their homes once they were gone.'

Goldman's eyes were bright. 'The table then speaks of "special labour without imprisonment": I suppose we would call that community service now. Thirty thousand five hundred get that. And nine thousand six hundred are sent to labour camps.

'If you tot it all up, it leaves about ninety thousand convicted Nazi war criminals who were meant to go to jail for various sentences of up to ten years. But then we look at the very last figure in the table, the most important number of all: "Assignees still serving sentence". And that figure is,' he paused, as if expecting a drum roll, 'three hundred.

'Now remember these statistics were compiled in 1949. What this little table is telling us, is that within just a few years of the war fewer than three hundred of those Nazis were still behind bars. Do you see where this is going, Mr Byrne? Out of more than thirteen million men once deemed complicit in the horrors of the Third Reich, we have eleven death sentences at Nuremberg and three hundred men in jail. That's all.

'And when the West Germans took over responsibility for war crimes prosecutions, they were no better. They convicted, to take just one example, Wilhelm Greiffenberger for involvement in *eight thousand one hundred* murders – and sentenced him to three years' imprisonment and three years' "loss of honour" even though the court found he had a role in the deaths of *eight thousand one hundred* people. I could name cases like that for a week and still not run out. Almost every man convicted melted back into German society. They walked free from those prisons, as if they were guilty of nothing more serious than a parking fine. They were so arrogant, so certain there would be no consequences, they didn't even hide what they had done. They were in the phone book.

'And this, you see, is the dirty little secret of the Second World War. We're told, over and over again, that the attempted extermination of the Jews was the greatest crime in human history – and yet hardly anybody was punished for it. The guilty men got away with it. It was a crime that was unavenged, a genocide for which there was no reckoning.'

At last, Goldman slumped back in his chair; he seemed exhausted, emptied out, like a medium once the spirit has departed.

Rebecca and Tom sat in silence. It was Rebecca who spoke first.

'And that's why DIN reformed.'

'Yes,' he said softly. 'In 1952.'

'And the killing started then. Except now it was

all over the world. Wherever the Nazis were hiding. Your dad and my dad.'

Goldman nodded. 'I found one of their lists. I was looking for something else, and I came across a file for his poker club. That was the cover they used: five Jewish men who met on Thursday nights to play poker. My father always said it was a secret society because if their wives knew how much they gambled there'd be hell to pay. So we could never know who was in it. Not even my mother was allowed to know.

'When I saw the file I had to look. I wanted to know about this secret gambling world of my dad's, a man who did nothing more interesting than sell ladies' outerwear to department stores. Little did I know.' He gave a rueful smile. 'Inside the file was a wad of foreign currency, several passports and a list of German names, crossed out one by one. I understood immediately. I was twenty years old, I think.

'We had a fierce argument. We never stopped having it, from then until his dying day. I said I would alert the authorities. I was a newly qualified lawyer, an officer of the court. It was my duty.' Tears began to appear in his right eye. 'But I never did. I should have told the police what I knew, that my father was involved in a criminal gang.'

'But they were hardly murderers,' Tom said quietly. 'They were ensuring that a grave crime did not go unpunished.'

Goldman looked at him anew. 'I confess I am

amazed to hear a man like yourself speak in such a manner, Mr Byrne.'

Tom could feel the veins on his neck begin to throb. His anger was rising: he would have to repress it. 'I'm sorry. But I'm just thinking of what you said a moment ago. That the men behind this monumental crime got off scot-free.'

'Mr Byrne, as you should well know, I was merely doing the job of an advocate, putting the case for DIN as best I could, so that you might understand it.' The steel shutters were down again now, the moment of communion with the spirit of his dead father vanished. 'The right course of action was the law. That was the course these men should have pursued.'

'Except the law often leads nowhere. We both know that, if we're honest, don't we, Mr Goldman?' Tom could hear a tremor in his own voice. 'And isn't that because, when all's said and done, there's no such thing as "the law"? We like to imagine some wonderfully impartial, blind goddess of justice – but that's no more real than fairies at the bottom of the garden, is it?'

'Tom—'

'No, Rebecca, I know about this at first hand.' His temperature was rising, unwelcome memories surfacing. 'We think there's law. But the truth is, there's only politics. And politics never finds it convenient to pursue the guilty.'

'Tom, really—'

'I'm sorry, but it's true. The bigger the crime,

the less convenient it is. When there's a clash of "reconciliation" and justice – and there's always a clash – reconciliation wins out every time. I've seen it again and again.' There was that crack in his voice again, he could hear it. 'So, inappropriate though it might be for a lawyer to say this, I have some sympathy for what this group, what DIN, were feeling. They had seen their whole families wiped out. Of course they wanted to hunt down those responsible. The law had let them walk free. I do wonder if, on this point, Mr Goldman, your father got it right and you got it wrong.'

Goldman was about to respond, when Rebecca stood up. Glaring at Tom she cried, 'That's enough.' Her eyes were burning. The unspoken reminder that she had just lost her father shamed them both into silence.

In the calm, she turned to Goldman and asked in a manner that conveyed both patience now exhausted and the desire for a brief, straight answer to a straight question, 'Is there anything else at all, any other element in the DIN story, that you haven't told us? Some secret perhaps which someone, somewhere, might not want to come out?'

Tom, his pulse still throbbing, could see that Goldman was weighing his answer. As he leaned forward, about to speak, the air was filled with the brain-splitting sound of an alarm: not some distant siren, but one coming from inside the building.

## CHAPTER TWENTY-SEVEN

Jay Sherrill would have admitted it to no one, not even his mother – her least of all – but today he was feeling his inexperience. Ever since his meeting with the Commissioner he had had the novel sensation of a conundrum that might exceed even his expensively educated powers of understanding. If it were simply a matter of logic, he was confident that no problem could defeat him. But this required something more than deductive reasoning, more than what Chuck Riley would doubtless call, adopting his best Boss Hogg accent, 'book-learnin'.'

At least Sherrill had reached the stage of knowing what he did not know. And this knowledge, he concluded, was not taught at Harvard or anywhere else. It was acquired over years, accreted like the lichen on an ancient stone. It was what the older men in the New York Police Department, those he could regard with condescension in every other context, already had and what he, unavoidably, lacked. It was the advantage of dumb chronology, years on the clock. He would have it eventually but right now he was defeated by it.

He had followed the Commissioner's cue and made contact with the NYPD Intelligence Division. He had asked to see those involved in the surveillance operation of Gerald Merton. He had heard nothing back. He called again, adding this time that his need was urgent since it related to an ongoing criminal investigation designated as the highest possible priority by the Commissioner himself. No one returned his call.

He had weighed his options, including alerting Riley to this foot-dragging by a section of his own force, but ruled that out: what could look worse than a Harvard boy running to Daddy because the tough kids wouldn't play with him? It would get around, confirming every prejudice he already knew existed against him.

And then, this morning at 8.30am, the call had come. The head of the Intelligence Division, Stephen Lake, would see him at 10am. It made no sense. Sherrill had made a request at the operational level; he wanted to see an officer – or did Intel Division call them agents? – from the field, at most a unit commander, but someone involved in the hands-on work of monitoring the Russian and subsequently tailing Merton. That request had apparently been refused. Instead he was due to see the man at the very top.

This too he would not have admitted to anyone, but he was nervous. Lake had been top brass at the Central Intelligence Agency, a wholly political appointment made by the city after 9/11, when New York decided it could no longer rely on the federal authorities and had better make its own arrangements. Sherrill had done an archive search of the *New York Times* website that morning, reading up on the Intel Division and on Lake. Already it had up to a thousand officers at its disposal, a force within the forty-thousand-strong force of the NYPD itself. By comparison, the FBI, with just ten thousand agents to cover the entire United States, looked like minnows. The Feds resented them, of course; and the *Times* had reported a slew of complaints from civil liberties groups complaining that the Intel Division was not catching foreign terrorists but watching domestic political activists, bugging the phone calls and surveilling the homes of US citizens. It only added to the unfamiliar sensation now brewing inside Jay Sherrill, that he was badly out of his depth.

He knew how to interview cops, knew their foibles, their vanities, their sentimental weaknesses. But Lake had never been a cop. He was more like a politician, a veteran player of the Washington game. Why on earth had he taken this meeting? What message was he sending?

Sherrill had ten more minutes to wrestle with that question, sitting in the waiting area of the office of the man formally titled Deputy Commissioner for Intelligence. He knew this manoeuvre all too well: keep a man waiting, remind him who comes where in the hierarchy. Jay Sherrill's response in this situation – a refusal to flick through any of the papers or magazines on the table in the reception area in favour of simply staring straight ahead – sent a message of his own: 'You are wasting my time and I resent it.'

At last a grey-faced secretary gestured for Sherrill to come forward. He went through two successive doors, before being shown into an office which he instantly assessed as being slightly larger than the Commissioner's.

Lake was short by alpha male standards, five ten at most. His silver-grey hair was cut close and his eyes were chilly. He rose slightly out of his chair to acknowledge the detective's arrival, extended a hand, then began speaking even before Jay had sat down.

'So what is it we can help you with, Detective?'

'Well, sir, I really did not mean to trouble you with this. It's a matter way below—'

'What, my pay grade, Detective?' There was a mirthless smile. 'Why don't you let me be the judge of that? What are the questions you have for this department?'

'Sir, the UN security force opened fire on Gerald Merton at 8.51am yesterday. Two minutes earlier, the Watch Commander of that force had received a warning from his liaison within NYPD, offering a description of a terror suspect said to be about to enter the United Nations compound. It was on the basis of that description – for which Gerald Merton offered a complete match – that the UN officer opened fire.' He knew this account would have more punch if he added the words, 'thereby killing an innocent old man,' but he could not bring himself to do it. In spite of the indifference shown by the Commissioner, to Sherrill's mind the gun and fingerprints found in Merton's room remained the most compelling evidence in the case.

Lake rubbed his chin, apparently deep in thought. 'I see,' he said at last. 'And your question to me is what exactly?'

Sherrill could see that Lake was going to extend not the slightest help.

'I want to know how the NYPD was in a position to pass on what could only be live intelligence to the UNSF, sir.'

'*Live intelligence*? Are you sure you're not getting a little ahead of yourself here, Detective? Is intelligence an expertise of yours?'

Sherrill could feel a burning sensation in his cheeks; one he desperately hoped did not manifest itself. He tried to calm himself, to remember that this tactic of intimidation – the invocation of specialist knowledge – was just that, a tactic. 'I don't think it requires any great expertise, sir. Just as it would have required no great expertise to see that Gerald Merton was a man in his mid-seventies – hardly the profile for a terrorist.'

At that, Lake's eyes turned to steel. 'There are two answers to that, Mr Sherrill: the official one and the unofficial one. The official one is that this department never comments on operational matters, lest we compromise those working in the field to protect the great city of New York and, with it, the entire United States.'

'Of course, sir.' Sherrill wondered if he was about to make some headway. 'And what's the unofficial one?'

'We may have had our eye on the UN for a while, with evidence of a ticking time-bomb over there. Or we may not. But this was one hundred per cent a fuck-up by the Keystone Kops at UN Plaza. You try to roll the blame ball over to this department for that and you better make sure you're not in the path of travel. Because if you are, I will personally make sure that it crushes you into the ground so hard you'll think yourself lucky if you end up writing out parking tickets in Trenton, do I make myself clear, Detective?'

Sherrill swallowed hard. 'Doesn't this count as coercion of a law enforcement officer, sir?'

'Save it for the Kennedy School, Detective. The only words I have uttered to you in this meeting are as follows: that this department never comments on operational matters, lest we compromise those working in the field to protect the great city of New York and, with it, the entire United States. Any other words imagined by you will be denied by me. I will swear an affidavit to that effect and submit it to any court – along, of course, with a copy of your medical records showing your past history of mental illness.'

Jay Sherrill could feel the wind exiting his stomach as surely as if he had been punched. He barely managed to whisper the words, 'What are you talking about?'

Stephen Lake looked down at a single sheet of paper he now held between his thumb and forefinger. 'Seems, Mr Sherrill, that you once sought counselling for depression. Is that compatible with the role of a first grade detective in the New York Police Department? Hmm, I can't recall. Perhaps we should just check with the Chief of Detectives.' He reached for his telephone and began punching the keypad.

'No!'

'What is it, Detective?'

'It was years ago; I was a student! My brother had just died!'

'My condolences. I'm sure the human resources department of the NYPD would have been real sympathetic when you applied to be a fast track, high-flying, big swinging dick detective. Except, for some reason, you forgot to share that piece of information with them, didn't you? I've got your form right here in front of me.' He reached for another document. '"Have you ever sought professional help for a mental health problem, including but not confined to . . ." blah, blah, blah, oh there it is, "depression"? And here's the little check box you've marked with an X and guess which one it is. It couldn't be clearer. N-O spells no. That counts as a lie in my book. Might even count as perjury. Remind me to check that with a lawyer.' He threw the paper down onto the desk and fixed Jay Sherrill with a fierce stare. 'In case I haven't made myself clear, Detective, this is what I'm saying to you. You go take your blame ball and roll it onto someone else's yard – because this one's full of land mines and one of them will blow you right out of the sky. I guarantee it.'

# CHAPTER TWENTY-EIGHT

The instant the fire alarm sounded, the conversation halted. A secretary popped her head around the door to say that she was terribly sorry, but they had to evacuate the building immediately. Henry Goldman composed himself, packed his papers into a leather portfolio case and followed the secretary out.

Outside, there was a crush of employees, two or three of them donning fluorescent bibs, and a mood of nervous excitement. Tom and Rebecca walked the fifteen flights downstairs, neither daring to say much about what had just happened. One of the firewardens peered at their visitor labels and shepherded them to a different meeting point from the rest of the Roderick Jones staff. They stood there for twenty minutes in the early evening cold, Tom seizing the outdoor opportunity for a quick cigarette. He offered one to Rebecca, who pounced on it hungrily. Of course. Most of the doctors he knew were twenty-a-day types. Still she said nothing.

Then, with no announcement, no whistle or klaxon, merely directed by the herd instinct that grips every crowd, people began to drift back into the building. Apparently a false alarm.

They were soon back on the sixteenth floor and in the conference room. The secretary reappeared.

'Can I help?' she chirped, as if she had never seen them before.

'We were here before the alarm. Meeting Mr Goldman?' Rebecca offered a smile.

'Oh, but Mr Goldman's gone, I'm afraid.'

'Gone?'

She shrugged. 'I assumed you'd finished your meeting.'

At Tom's request, she called down to Security, who checked the executive garage: Mr Goldman's parking space was now empty. 'He wouldn't have done that in the old days, I can tell you,' she said, 'taking the chance to knock off early. Most partners never leave here before ten or eleven; the secretaries have to work in shifts! Mr Goldman was one of the worst. Before he retired, of course.'

Tom gave a full-wattage smile: charm mode. 'And that was a regular fire drill, was it?'

'Oh no. We only have those on Mondays. I thought maybe it was faulty wiring: that's what happened the last time. But I just spoke to Janice – she's one of our fire marshals – and she said someone broke through one of the "In case of emergency" things in the basement. Used one of the plastic hammers to break the glass and everything.'

'Gosh,' said Tom.

'You'd think there'd be a fine for that sort of thing,' the secretary added. 'Apparently Security have no idea who did it, but they're checking the CCTV already.'

'Perhaps it was a high-spirited prank,' Tom said, recalling the language the Dean had used back at Manchester when he and his mates had let off fire extinguishers. 'By one of the younger members of staff.'

The secretary looked appalled. 'But we don't have anyone like that here,' she said. And Tom believed it. That memory of his university days had incubated a new intuition and now it was nagging at him.

Rebecca was in no mood to prolong this chit-chat with Henry Goldman's assistant any longer than necessary. They excused themselves and headed out of the building. Letting Rebecca walk on ahead of him, Tom made a quick call to Jay Sherrill: he didn't like the guy, but he at least ought to look like he was co-operating. He wouldn't let on about Merton's Holocaust past: Henning had told him not to and that suited Tom fine. Sherrill might connect that with the gun and discover the DIN story for himself. Before Tom knew it, this whole business would be spinning out of his control. Managing the flow of information, that had been the secret of success in the UN: Henning Munchau had turned it into an art form.

'Hello, Detective Sherrill, it's Tom Byrne here in London.'

'Any leads on that weapon we found?'

'I do have something, as it happens, yes.'

'Go on,' said Sherrill.

'It's sketchy, nothing firm. It's possible that Merton may have had a past in some kind of armed group.'

'Jesus. What kind of armed group?'

'Like I said, it's sketchy at the moment. But I think he may have been one of a group of men acting as vigilantes. Taking the law into their own hands, punishing criminals.'

'When you say "punishing" do you mean—'

'Yes, Detective Sherrill. I do. But it was a long time ago and I'm not sure it sheds much light on the finding in the hotel room or the Russian—'

'No, but still. This is useful. What's the evidence?'

'Just a hint or two in some documents Merton left behind. Nothing explicit.'

'Anyone in this group ever get convicted?'

'Not one, as far as I know.'

'Are they still active?'

'That's the million-dollar question. I'll check in when I get more.'

He hung up and sprinted to join Rebecca, now unlocking the Saab. Once in the driving seat, she let out a gale of pent-up oxygen: 'Christ, that was frustrating! He's finally on the brink of telling us something we don't already know and you start *ranting.*'

'I did not rant. I was just making a point—'

'I don't want to talk about it.'

'—that sometimes justice—'

'I mean it,' she said, glaring. 'I *don't* want to talk about it.' And with that, she pulled out of the parking space and into traffic, the ferocity of her silence filling the car.

The arguments Tom wanted to make were running through his head, but they did not get very far. Rebecca was probably right; he had indeed scared Goldman off. He had made an elementary mistake, voicing his own views on a case when his own views were irrelevant. All that mattered was extracting information from a witness. He knew it was a mistake but that wasn't what unnerved him. It was why he had made it.

The daylight was fading now. Rebecca was gripping the steering wheel furiously, her gaze fixed on the road ahead. Tom stared into space. Neither of them paid attention to the wing mirror on Tom's side of the car: if they had, they might have seen the manoeuvre of the Mercedes three cars behind them – the move which confirmed it was following them.

# CHAPTER TWENTY-NINE

Now officially elderly, the boss could still outrun his staff. Given how little sleep he had had, he should have tired hours ago. It was always like this. While the men in their thirties and forties were already aching for a hot bath and a night's sleep, the boss was ready to crack open a bottle of the Scottish malt whisky he took with him everywhere, loosen his tie and begin some serious talk.

For the aide, it was a reminder of what everyone had said about his future employer when he took the job: that power was the purest form of adrenalin and this guy had it running, in neat form, through his veins. Forget adrenalin, he thought now; it was more like embalming fluid. Somehow, the decades this man had spent at the top of his nation's politics had halted the ageing process entirely; he looked the same as he had twenty-five years earlier. Even his shirts, the aide noticed, looking at his own rumpled effort, remained flat and unlined in the nineteenth hour of a twenty-hour day.

'So what do we have?' the boss began. His usual opening gambit.

'Well, our people in London managed to follow the subjects—'

'Subjects? Lets cut the bullshit intelligence language, shall we? You did about as much time in the army as I did.'

'They followed Rebecca Merton and Tom Byrne to a meeting at a law firm. Fortunately, it was in a tall, steel-and-glass building so, thanks to a highly directional shotgun microphone, we were able to carry out surveillance of the meeting.'

'I remember approving the budget for those devices. And?'

'The guy at the law firm spoke at length, detailing the background of the group—'

'DIN?'

'Yes, sir. But he did not in any way touch on, er, our aspect of the matter.' Then, delivered with a grimace: 'At least not in the portion of the conversation we monitored.'

'What the hell does that mean? You missed some of it?'

'The very beginning, sir. But everything that came afterwards suggests our aspect was not touched upon.'

'But you can't be sure.'

'The context makes that very clear, sir. And when there seemed to be a risk that it might stray into, you know, sensitive territory, we took action.'

'What kind of action?'

'We terminated the conversation.'

'How the hell did you do that?'

'We activated the fire alarm, sir.'

At that the boss gave his first smile. 'I'm glad machine politics still has some valuable lessons to teach. The fire alarm trick, eh? Always a winner five minutes before an awkward vote. We did that in the old days. Perhaps we should use it at the UN.'

The aide laughed loyally.

'And now?'

'It's under control, sir. Subjects are— sorry, the people involved are all under close watch. If the information we are concerned about is known at all, which I strongly doubt, then we will ensure it does not reach either Ms Merton or Mr Byrne. And if it does – we will make sure it goes no further.'

# CHAPTER THIRTY

The silence did not break, even as Rebecca parked the car, unlocked the front door and stormed up the stairs into her apartment. Only once she spoke did Tom understand that, in this respect if no other, Rebecca was like several women he had known: capable of bottling up her fury until she was home – here, in her kitchen – so that she would have the argument where she wanted to have it.

'Seriously, Tom, what the fuck was all that about?'

'All what?'

'Today, with Goldman.'

'I voiced an opinion, that's all. I—'

'No, you wrecked that meeting at the most crucial stage.' Her voice was firm and clear: she was Dr Merton, dressing down an anaesthetist who had administered an incorrect dose. 'You're meant to be helping me, remember? That was our deal. And there we were, listening to Goldman drone on, telling us what we already knew, and then, just as he's about to get to the—'

'You already knew all that?'

Her face formed into an expression Tom couldn't understand. 'No, of course I didn't. But we'd worked it out, hadn't we? From the box.'

'Sure, but we didn't know any of that detail. Or the context. Or the motivation. I thought you'd be fascinated to hear all that. To understand your father.'

'This is not therapy for me, OK? In case you hadn't noticed, someone trashed my place today. And we have no idea who they are or what they want. And no idea if they're going to come after me again.'

'I understand. This is very frightening-'

'You're damn right, it's frightening.' The volume was getting higher now. 'And then you start sounding off, defending vigilante murder, men going around killing people—'

'Well, can you blame them?'

'What?'

'Can you blame them? I mean it, Rebecca. Given everything that had happened to them. They were right: they weren't going to get justice any other way.'

'How can you say that? You're meant to be a lawyer, for God's sake.'

'That's exactly why I'm saying it!' He was shouting now. 'Oh, yes I used to believe all that crap about "the law" and "justice" and all the fine words. I was a true believer, Rebecca. I was just like your boy Julian.' He saw a look of scepticism cross Rebecca's face. 'I know that seems ridiculous now. But I wasn't always like this, you know.' He pulled at the cuffs of his Paul Smith suit. 'I used to believe that so long as you worked hard, gathered all the evidence, filed your briefs, then justice would be done. Why do you think I went to the UN? Because I was one of those saps who was going to change the world.'

He was startled to hear himself talk like this; he hadn't voiced these thoughts, even to himself, for so long. But he couldn't stop.

'I was right there, at the very top. The United bloody Nations. And then I was asked to lead for the UN on the Rwanda tribunal. It was a massive job: I was thrilled to get it. I'd be fighting the good fight.

'I began by reading the witness statements, page after page of them: they were just like your father's notebook. Stories that would make you weep. You know what happened there; everyone knows what happened. We knew it at the time. Minimum of eight hundred thousand people killed in the space of three months. Fastest genocide in human history, they reckon; even faster than the Nazis. And, as always, everyone, but everyone, is up to their necks in blood. It was neighbour killing neighbour, one end of a street rounding up the other and slitting their throats with machetes. Nuns stood by while children were herded into churches and torched alive. *Nuns,* for Christ's sake. And all the stuff that happens every time: teenage girls getting raped, boys having their balls sliced off, brothers forced to sodomize their sisters, men forced to kill their wives. Thousands of pages of it.

'On the evidence we had, at least a million people should have been in the dock. But guess how many Tutsis have been convicted.'

Rebecca looked down at the floor. 'I don't know.'

'Go on. Guess how many Tutsis have been convicted by the UN tribunal for the Rwandan genocide.'

'I don't know.'

'Just guess.'

'I don't *know*.'

'Just fucking GUESS, Rebecca!'

'Five thousand? A thousand? I don't know!'

'Twenty-six.'

She said nothing.

'Twenty-six. That's the grand total after a decade and a half of legal work by dozens of lawyers and God knows how many millions of dollars. Twenty-six people. It's bullshit, Rebecca. Bullshit. You know what they say about lies: the bigger the lie, the more people will believe it? It's the same with mass murder. If you kill ten people, you'll never get away with it. But kill a thousand and you'll never see inside a dock, let alone a prison cell. That's what I learned in Rwanda.' His voice was trembling.

'So what did you do?'

Tom steadied himself against the kitchen table. He wanted to sit down, but he knew it would look too much like defeat. 'The usual. Drinking, smoking, drugs – the things you do when you want to throw your life away.'

'You had a breakdown?'

'You could say that. In fact the UN personnel department *did* say that. *Byrne, Thomas – indefinite leave on health grounds*. I didn't believe in it any more, that was my illness. I couldn't do a day's work: I knew the whole thing was crap.'

'Did they fire you?'

'They would have. But Henning – my boss – he covered for me. Kept me on the payroll, looked out for me. I think he was worried that if they cut me loose, I might do something to myself.'

'And would you?'

'I thought about it.'

The silence hung in the air – until he broke it. 'And then I decided I wouldn't be a sap any more. I'd get wise, like everyone else. Law's a racket, so you might as well enjoy the benefits. Everyone else was doing it, so why not me?'

'What do you mean, it's a racket?'

'Put it this way, Rebecca. You wouldn't want to meet my latest clients on a dark night.' He tried to smile, but all that came was a wince. 'That's the difference between me and Julian, you see. He hasn't learned the lesson yet. But I have.'

'What's the lesson?'

'There's not going to be a brighter tomorrow, and no one cares what happened yesterday, so you might as well live for today.'

'No one cares what happened yesterday? You really believe that?'

'I do now. And it seems your father did too: he looked around the world and saw that no one gave a fuck what happened to the Jews. Not really. Not enough to bring the guilty to justice. So he and his friends did it themselves.'

'How *dare* you presume to know what my father felt about anything?'

'I'm just repeating what Henry—'

'You think I'm *proud* of what we found out today? You think it was OK to go around killing and killing and killing like that?'

'They were Nazis for Christ's sake!'

'What if they'd got it wrong, Tom? Eh? What if they'd accidentally killed the wrong man? You don't think that happened?' She took a step towards him so that they were standing and shouting at each other, just a few inches apart.

'I'm sure they were—'

'And who gave them the right to do it? Who set them up as judge and jury and executioner?'

'Oh, for God's sake. If they didn't have the right, who did? It's a bit much for us to sit here, judging the people who lived through all that. It was different for them, they—'

'Lived through it?' Her eyes were wild now. 'You don't think I've lived through it? Are you kidding? I lived through every *hour* of that war, over and over since the day I was born. Can you imagine growing up in a house that's dark even when the sun's shining? Can you imagine growing up knee-deep in blood, surrounded by all these ghosts? Where even the biggest drama in your life is *nothing* compared to this great big thing, this vast shadow that hangs over everything else?'

'I, I thought he hardly ever . . .' Tom stumbled. 'You told me your father didn't like to talk about it.'

'He didn't. But he didn't have to. It was in every room, without him saying a word. This *sorrow*. Do you know what one of the ghetto fighters once said? "If you could lick my heart, it would poison you." That's what my father was like. So don't tell me I didn't live through it, I lived through—'

And the sentence faltered, as she choked back tears. Without a conscious thought he closed the gap between them, placing his arms around her, trying to calm her with his embrace. But she would not be calmed, hammering instead at his chest, her fists two hard balls.

He could not help himself now. He lifted her chin and guided by an impulse he had held back too long, moved his lips to touch hers.

The kiss was urgent, hungry, powered by the desire that had thumped through him from the first instant he had laid eyes on her. At first she resisted, her hands clutching at his shirt, but it did not last. Her mouth was just as ravenous as his. The first touch of her tongue sent a current through him, a charge that made him harden in an instant. She could feel it as he pressed against her.

The smell of her was strong now. She pulled off his jacket and rapidly set to work on the buttons of his shirt, unpopping them one after another, then letting out a moan as she touched the warm skin of his chest. Tom placed a hand on her waist, feeling the naked flesh above her belt, when he heard it, a trilling sound that instantly sucked the oxygen from the room. Panting and breathless, she pulled away – and reached for the phone.

'Oh, hi, Julian.'

Of course, thought Tom, suddenly aware of the blood pulsing around his entire system. Young Julian's lovelorn antennae had probably been twitching the moment they had kissed. He watched Rebecca nod and 'uh-huh' her way through the conversation, eventually reaching for a pad to scribble down an address. As she leaned across for a pen, her trousers separated from her top, revealing a narrow sliver of her back and the barest glimpse of the top of her underwear. He wanted her with an intensity that frightened him.

She hung up. 'That was Julian, calling to ask how it went. He'd spoken to his father. Said he seemed "exercised" by our conversation.'

'Exercised? Is that good or bad?' It was a struggle to speak.

'Julian couldn't tell.'

'All right. Well, maybe we can go back and see him tomorrow.'

'Julian reckoned we should try to see him tonight.'

Those antennae were obviously well honed: even from a distance, Julian Goldman was conspiring to ensure Rebecca Merton and Tom Byrne did not get any closer.

She was biting her lip.

'What is it?'

'He said he got the distinct impression his father wanted to tell us something. Something important.'

## CHAPTER THIRTY-ONE

If nothing else, this trip was proving to be a first class tour of contemporary London. Rebecca had driven them back to Upper Street but instead of heading east into the grime of Essex Road en route to Hackney, she had headed up the Holloway Road and into the well-heeled charm of Highgate village.

Neither of them spoke, but the silence was different now. The tension between them had been building steadily, like a darkening sky on a close summer's day. Thanks to the stand-up row, and the kiss that followed it, the weather had broken. He sat alongside her, no longer fighting the urge to stare or, occasionally, touch her.

'Rebecca, we talked about the injury on your father's leg didn't we?'

'There was no injury; I told you. Why?'

'His body was found with a kind of metal shin-pad.'

'So you say.'

'Even though there was no injury.' He reached

around to the back seat. 'Can I get your father's notebook from your bag?'

She nodded, giving him another flash of the crooked smile whose power over him she surely understood. Tom thumbed through the handwritten pages. They looked like something altogether more valuable now, an authentic historical document of genuine significance. Gerald Merton had been one of the prime movers in a remarkable post-script to the Holocaust, a story that would shock anybody who had heard it. It would do to them what it had already done to Tom: force them to revise their view of an event about which they thought they already knew all there was to know.

When Goldman had used that phrase – sheep to the slaughter – Tom had felt a pang of shame. That was precisely the image he had long held of the Jewish victims of the Nazis, filing into the gas chambers without protest. He dimly recalled his history teacher at school using the phrase, and not unsympathetically. 'Pity those poor Jews, as defenceless as lambs sent to the abattoir'. That had been the teacher's meaning, Tom was sure of it. But today he had seen how insulting, how wounding that notion must have been to men like Gerald Merton.

There. He had found it: a passage describing young Gershon's involvement with the partisans, hiding in the forests. It was one of those Tom had had to skim read, but something had lodged. And here it was.

*For those months, I did not often serve as a fighter, at least not directly. As usual, my great value was my Aryan looks. So instead of simply firing a gun, I was involved in procuring guns. As I had sometimes done in the ghetto, I became a smuggler. I would run from our place in the woods to a meeting point, pick up a pistol or grenade or detonator, pay for it with whatever I had – sometimes cash, usually a watch or a ladies' necklace – and then creep back to camp. Often the supplier would believe he was arming a young blond volunteer for the Lithuanian resistance. He would not have sold weapons to a Jew so easily.*

*The trick with smuggling is to be prepared for getting caught. You need to let them find something on you. Once they have found it, they will usually congratulate themselves on having done a good job and let you go on your way. And only you will know that this 'something' was not the real thing at all. The real thing is hidden somewhere else and this you keep. So whenever I bought a gun, I would also make sure to pick up some cigarettes or perhaps some meat and these I would hide – but not so well. If somebody stopped me, they would find the cigarettes, maybe beat me a bit – but the gun strapped to my back by bandages, this they didn't find . . .*

Tom smiled to himself. So that explained the metal shin-pad. Gerald Merton was preparing himself for the metal detectors he knew would be at the entrance to the United Nations building. The alarm would go off and, with an apologetic shrug, the old man would reach down, roll up his left trouser leg and show the security staff the metal plate he had to wear for medical reasons. He would probably crack a joke – 'Airports are the worst' – and they would smile and nod him through. And no-one would think to check for the state-of-the-art weapon he had disassembled and bandaged to himself, with the steel inserts and ammunition stashed along his spine or in some other formation.

The gun hadn't been on him that day: it was still in the hotel bathroom. The Monday morning trip to the UN had surely been a reconnaissance mission, of the kind young Gershon had doubtless done down the backstreets of Buenos Aires or Bonn or Rome or San Sebastián or any of the other cities where he had conducted operations for DIN. He might even have acquired the reconnaissance habit along the crunching footpaths of the Lithuanian forests or in the fetid backstreets of the Viriampole district of Kaunas that became the Kovno ghetto.

It would have been a smart plan: if Merton had returned to the UN the next day, and the metal detectors had gone off again, chances are, one of the security staff would have recognized him: that nice old boy with the plate in his leg. More smiles and they'd have waved him through, no need to roll up his trousers a second time: 'You just have a nice day, sir.'

And then he'd have gone in and . . . what? If only he could speak to the shade of Gershon Matzkin, ask him who that gun was meant for. Tom had still not heard back from Henning with that list. Who might have been in the headquarters of the United Nations this week who would have warranted DIN's last, aged warrior to don his assassin's cloak one more time? Tom pushed back into his seat, wishing that those missing pages from the old man's notebook would somehow reappear. Had Gershon torn them out and destroyed them? Or had he hidden them somewhere? Is that what the thieves were after when they turned Rebecca's apartment upside down?

Now they were driving alongside Hampstead Heath, the vast green woodland and park on their left, houses of extraordinary opulence and size on their right. When Rebecca slowed down, Tom shook his head: 'Don't tell me he lives round here.'

Rebecca nodded.

'In one of these? No wonder young Julian's so screwed up.' Rebecca gave him a look of mock disapproval. To Tom's great pleasure, the expression seemed somehow complicit, as if the two of them were now together, with Julian on the outside.

'Here we go,' she said, signalling a right-turn into a steep, sloping driveway. The house was vast and absurdly palatial; Tom could see sixteen windows, half of them lit, before he lost count. Rebecca pulled the car up alongside a sleek Mercedes and turned off the engine. 'Remember, all charm this time.'

Rebecca pressed the doorbell. A traditional ding-dong chime sounded, unexpectedly suburban for a house so grand and Tom was reminded of the days when his mother had dragged him around the wealthier parts of Sheffield, carol-singing.

No answer.

'Try the knocker,' he said. 'Really hard. These houses are so big, they probably can't hear the doorbell.'

Rebecca reached for the brass knocker, fashioned as a bar of metal held between the jaws of a fierce lion. She pulled it back then banged it firmly down, twice.

The first knock gave nothing away, but the second rang oddly hollow and the door swung inward. It had not been locked at all.

Rebecca furrowed her brow at Tom, then stepped in. He followed her into a wide hallway, where their footsteps were muffled by a huge shimmering rug, an irregular checkerboard of different colours. Rebecca called out, 'Hello?' and walked further in, to a large reception area bordered on all sides by cream sofas, with two large, low coffee tables in the centre. The facing wall was covered with a vast picture that seemed part-photograph, part-painting. Recognizable were the faces of a forty-something Henry Goldman and, with buck teeth and curly hair, a teenage Julian.

Rebecca tried again: 'Mr Goldman?'

'Perhaps we should leave,' Tom suggested, glad of an excuse for an early exit – and perhaps a return to Rebecca's flat. 'We can call him tomorrow.'

'But Julian said he was definitely home.'

'Does he live alone?'

Distractedly, her head peering into the darkness of a corridor, Rebecca said, 'Yes. His wife died years ago.'

'Have you been here before?'

'Often when I was younger, but not recently. I'm just going to try the study and, if he's not there, we'll go.'

She stepped gingerly into the gloom, calling out 'Mr Goldman? Henry?' as she moved. She reached a door and as she opened it, the corridor was filled with light. Behind her by several paces, Tom felt vaguely disappointed: if the lights were on in the study, then the old boy was clearly home. He'd probably nodded off in his chair.

Rebecca's scream tore the air. She stood frozen in the doorway, then darted forward. Tom ran after her, only to find her hunched over a slumped body, her ear clamped to the chest of Henry Goldman, whose cold white face was staring upward. He looked aghast. Rebecca straddled his body and began pounding at his chest, bringing both hands, her fingers laced together, down in a series of massive thumps. Crouching at her side, Tom could hear her exertion as she sent all her strength plunging down in successive blows. But he could also hear a different sound, a kind of desperate whimpering issuing from her. Tears streaked down her cheeks like rain on a window pane.

Finally, she climbed off the unmoving body and let her head fall onto Tom's shoulder. 'He's dead,' she sobbed, the tears soaking into his shirt. 'He's dead. He's dead.' Her fingers were scratching at his side and his arms. 'He's dead, he's dead, he's dead.' Finally, she pulled back so that Tom could see her face. 'He's dead – and we killed him.'

## CHAPTER THIRTY-TWO

He wondered at first if it was some kind of joke. When he saw it, he had immediately looked around the rest of the office, to see who might be behind it, but there was no telltale sniggering. Besides, he was hardly ever in this office. He had no co-workers to speak of, still less work buddies. As a first grade detective, that's not how you operated. Out of the bag meant you were neither glued into a uniform, nor chained to a desk. Jay Sherrill worked as he imagined a top surgeon or lawyer might, running his own day, travelling around, with the cellphone and BlackBerry in place of an office.

Yet someone had put this here and they had done it in the last few minutes. When he had arrived an hour ago, seeking a quiet space to think through his next move after that none-too-subtle warning from Stephen Lake of the Intelligence Division, there had been no Post-It note stuck to his computer screen. He had gone to the vending machine for a cup of Styrofoam coffee, could only have been five minutes, and now there it was. The message was marked in block capitals: SUBWAY. ACROSS STREET. 4.15

He looked at his watch. It was 4.06pm. It could be a trap. He thought of some of the cases he had fought in the last two years, including one that touched on an outer ring of the mafia. Every cop in New York knew how those guys liked to exact their revenge. But his own role had been marginal; overwhelmingly, it had been an FBI operation. They surely wouldn't come after him. And in a crowded subway station, during the day?

He studied the note once again. It was cleverly worded. Someone passing by would have assumed it was not a message at all, but a reminder Sherrill might have jotted down to himself. The block capitals betrayed no clues. But how could someone have possibly got in here, one of the most heavily secured buildings in New York city, and got out again that quickly? He had no idea.

He also had no choice; he would have to go. You couldn't ignore a direct message like this; no cop would.

He walked out of the main entrance and was about to turn left for the subway station when he saw it, directly opposite him. Subway, the sandwich bar. He was almost relieved. It was the last place in the entire United States any mafioso would use for a hit: right opposite headquarters, it was an alternative police canteen, brimming with cops fuelling up on foot-long Philly cheese-steak heroes with extra everything. It was the kind of place a first grade detective like Sherrill always avoided, knowing the derision and resentment that would come his way from the old timers the instant he stepped inside.

He pushed the door open and scanned the room, hoping he wasn't making it too obvious. A line of customers, either cops or secretaries on lunch hour; a couple of middle-aged men on cellphones. None of them seemed to recognize him.

'Excuse me,' Sherrill said, still scoping the faces, as a blue-overalled cleaner shuffled into him, lethargically wielding a broom and a flip-open, extended dustpan. One of those ridiculous, preppie habits Sherrill couldn't shake: apologizing when someone bumped into him.

'No problem, Detective,' the cleaner murmured back.

Sherrill wheeled round to see the man, black, dreadlocked and with white headphones in his ears, raising his eyebrows in recognition: 'You wanna take a walk?'

Sherrill said nothing and watched, stunned, as the man propped his cleaning equipment by the front door and headed out. Once outside, the cleaner walked purposefully, not waiting for Sherrill to catch up. He remained a half-pace in front, looking ahead, so that he and the detective might just be two New Yorkers hurrying about their business, not communicating at all.

'Thanks for coming, Detective Sherrill. Sorry about,' he made a small movement with his hand, 'all this.'

'Who are you? How do you know my name?'

'We're co-workers. I'm an agent with the NYPD Intelligence Division. Undercover.' Still looking straight ahead, he smiled briefly. 'In case you hadn't noticed.'

'How did you—'

'Get into your office? That was easy. I've got an NYPD pass. Besides, cleaner's overalls? That's a regular invisibility cloak in this town. Fuck Hogwarts. Just gotta be a black man dressed as a cleaner: no one sees you then, trust me. Hey, Sherrill, pull out your cellphone.'

'My cellphone, why?'

'Just pretend you're talking into it. And don't keep looking at me.'

For the second time in six hours, Jay Sherrill was coming face to face with his own inexperience. He had never done undercover work. He realized now, he didn't know even the basics. He did as he was told and tried to fake a phone call.

'OK, what do you want?'

'I don't want anything. I'm risking my fucking job here—'

'I'm sorry, I didn't mean—'

'Want something? What is it with you people?'

'I'm really sorry. That was—'

'I have some information that might help you.'

The pitch of Sherrill's voice lifted. 'Information?'

'On the killing of Gerald Merton.'

'What kind of information?'

'The eye-witness kind.'

Sherrill couldn't help but shoot a glance at the man walking just ahead of him. Then, guiltily, he returned to the blank middle-distance stare adopted by all those talking on cellphones in the street.

'You were there?'

'I saw it all. From the beginning.'

## CHAPTER THIRTY-THREE

'First, I need you to calm down. We need to be really calm here.'

'We need to get away.'

'We can't do that. We need to stay and call the police.'

'I mean it!' Rebecca pulled away from Tom's embrace and glared at him. 'We need to get away. Far away. Somewhere where there are no people.'

'Come on, Rebecca.'

'Haven't you noticed?' Her voice was high, torn. 'Something very bad is happening here and it's following us. First my flat and now this.' She pointed at the corpse of Henry Goldman, stiff on the lushly carpeted floor of his study, his face still bearing an expression of open-eyed shock.

'I know, I understand,' Tom said, his mind jamming as one thought skidded and crashed into another. It was becoming impossible to deny: danger was stalking them. An image appeared before his eyes, punching him in the guts: he saw

Rebecca, brutally murdered. He pushed it away: the important thing was to stay focused. 'We can't go anywhere. We have to report this. Right away.' He was bracing himself for an argument, but they had no choice. Imagine how it would look if they didn't call the police. They had met Henry Goldman that afternoon, for a meeting that had ended inconclusively. Goldman had later called his son, sounding agitated; Julian would be sure to tell the police that. Tom cursed himself for losing his temper in the boardroom earlier: the secretary would confirm Julian's story, telling detectives about the raised voices she had heard. And Julian would then confirm that he had spoken to Rebecca this very evening, reminding her of his father's home address. 'You need to call the police right now.'

'Me?'

'It will sound better coming from you. You're a friend of the family. You have a reason to be here. And you're a woman.'

He picked up the cordless phone charging on Goldman's desk and instantly regretted it: fingerprints. Shit, Rebecca had left her prints everywhere, including all over Goldman's body. She had touched his wrist, his neck. He looked over at the corpse: she had ripped open his shirt, popping the buttons clean off. They would have to explain all this.

Too late to undo his mistake, he dialled 999 and passed the phone to Rebecca. 'Ask for the police.'

Still breathing fast, she spoke within a few seconds: 'I'm calling to report a murder.'

'No!' Tom shouted the word without making a sound, mouthing it with desperate urgency then shaking his head frantically. He stage-whispered: 'You're calling to report a dead body!'

She tried to correct herself but the damage was done. Tom imagined a recording of this call played to a jury in the future trial of Rebecca Merton and Tom Byrne for the murder of Henry Goldman. He knew how it would sound. He rubbed his temple.

Once the call was over, she looked at Tom. 'I'm sorry,' she said. 'I don't know—'

'You need to call Julian.' Any delay there would look even more suspicious. She took the phone and left the room, though he could still hear her speaking in the corridor. He was struck by how quickly she seemed to have steadied herself; he imagined this was her doctor's voice, used when telling families the worst.

Through the study windows he could now see the blue light of a police car and two uniformed men emerging. Local plods, Tom guessed; the first wave, sent to secure the scene. The big boys would come later, especially once they heard what had happened.

Tom went to the door, shut but unlocked, just as they had found it. He opened the door and gestured for the two men to come in.

They introduced themselves as constables, showed their ID and pulled out their notebooks.

They started with Tom, asking for his details, looking up when he gave an address in New York. Rebecca came in, the four of them standing together in the hall like hosts welcoming guests to a dinner party.

The older of the two men spoke. 'I would ask you to sit down, madam, but I'm reluctant to do that at this stage, in case you might alter anything that could be of importance.' As Tom had feared, they were treating this as a crime scene. 'So why don't you just tell me what happened?'

The policemen nodded as Rebecca explained that Henry Goldman was a friend of her late father's. To Tom's great relief, neither policeman seemed to recognize the name Gerald Merton, even though it had been across all that day's papers. They listened as she said that she had come here to carry on a conversation started earlier today. Then they both picked up their pens and scribbled furiously when she said that they had found the front door unlocked.

Of course, thought Tom. That was the crucial detail, the awkward fact that would turn this from the unfortunate discovery of a dead old man into a murder inquiry. He noticed the older officer firing regular glances his way, even when Rebecca was speaking. Wait, thought Tom, till you find out that I have known Rebecca Merton for less than twelve hours. Wait till you discover why I'm in London in the first place. He fought hard the urge to sink his head into his hands.

Soon a doctor arrived, to confirm that Henry Goldman was dead, followed by a second police car, this one containing a photographer, who immediately headed for the study, to capture images of Goldman's body in situ from every angle. Travelling with him was a plain clothes detective. Tom had now met two of these characters in the space of two days, a fact he kept to himself. This man was Asian, prompting Tom to think of Harold Allen, the one-time rising star of the NYPD who had become hobbled by a battle over police racism. That meeting with Sherrill and Allen seemed from a different age; New York felt far more than an ocean away.

The detective asked them all to step outside: he did not want any more footprints in the hallway than were there already. So they stood outdoors, in a huddle on the drive. Tom watched as the constables began cordoning off the entire perimeter with plastic tape.

This more senior man asked the same questions all over again, though now he loaded some with extra and, Tom felt, threatening emphasis.

'So you came here and let yourselves in, and you felt comfortable doing that because you had visited this house often as a child, am I right?'

'No, that's not—'

'And once you're in, you find the body. You find it in the study. Which means you had to go exploring, walking down the corridor and so on, to find it, am I right? And then you, Miss Merton, once you see it, you start trying to revive Mr Goldman. Kiss of life and so on, am I right?'

'CPR. Cardiopulmonary resuscitation.'

'All right. And this is because you suspect what?'

'I suspected major cardiac arrest. A heart attack.'

'And Mr Goldman was in what state when you made this effort?'

'He was dead.'

'I know that, Miss Merton, I know that.'

'Dr Merton,' Tom interjected. She placed a hand on his. *Don't.*

The detective now gave a hard look at Tom, as if eyeing a nasty stain on the carpet, before turning back to Rebecca. 'What I am driving at is that he obviously hadn't been dead for very long. Or you wouldn't have tried reviving him, am I right?'

'He was still warm, if that's what you mean.'

'That is exactly what I mean, *Dr* Merton. Exactly. Thank you. Now what about you, Mr Byrne? What were you doing all this time?'

'I watched Rebecca try to bring him round. I consoled her once we realized that it was too late. And then we phoned the police.'

'Yes, the phone call. I'm curious about that. The note I have says that the call that came at 9.55 this evening was to report a *murder*. Now what I don't—'

'Can I ask you a question, Detective?' Tom now drew up himself to his full height, more than a foot taller than the policeman. 'In what capacity are you interviewing us, exactly?'

Rebecca's eyes widened in warning: *Don't get hostile*.

'How do you mean, Mr Byrne?'

'I mean, are we witnesses or are we suspects?'

The detective suddenly allowed his expression to harden. 'That's exactly what I'm trying to work out.'

## CHAPTER THIRTY-FOUR

He wondered if he was about to get double-fucked. The punishment had become notorious inside the entire national bureaucracy. Civil servants in every department spoke about it: Defence, Education, you name it. That was the thing about the boss: he'd been around so long, he'd done every job. There was no one over twenty-five and under eighty with even the remotest connection to government who hadn't worked under him at least once. His dressings-down were legendary; there were schoolchildren in backwater towns who knew of them – though they surely did not speak of getting double-fucked.

No one knew when he had done it first, but there were multiple versions of the story. Some said the first victim was the luckless chump who had failed to square three crucial union bosses on the eve of a party election that the boss suddenly realized he was going to lose. 'What kind of fuck makes a mistake like that, you fuck?' he had asked at the meeting of his advisers that journalists later called a pre-mortem. Two fucks in one sentence: a double-fucking.

Now the aide who cursed his luck to be travelling with the boss during this crisis was ready to place a bet that he was in line for the same treatment. Never mind what the outside world saw – Mr Eloquent Orator and Man of Letters – he knew that his boss could be a crude and brutal bully. He hadn't stayed at the top for so long by being sweet.

Still, it was late afternoon and it had been a long day. And he was old. Maybe he wouldn't have the energy for such histrionics. The aide hoped.

He knocked on the door of the boss's suite and let himself in. Unsurprisingly, the old man was dressed in a suit and shirt without a crease between them, his face clean-shaven. He was sitting at a table set for afternoon tea – one of the boss's anglophile affectations – with a clear, picture window view of Manhattan easing its way towards dusk.

'Any news?' he said, before the aide had even crossed the room. No hello, no invitation to join him, not even a look round. These were not good signs.

'Some news, sir.' He cursed himself for not having rehearsed this moment; he should have sat down with a pen and paper and worked out precisely what he was going to say.

'Umm?'

'Good news and bad news, you might say.'

'What's the bad news?'

Damn.

'Well, it only really makes sense once you've heard the good news, sir,' the aide began, incredulous that he could have walked into so obvious a cul-de-sac. 'Which is, that Henry Goldman will be giving us no further trouble, sir. He did not manage to pass on the, er, critical information to the subj— sorry, the people we're following, sorry, I mean the people we're watching, that is to say, are interested in—'

'You're babbling. What's happened?'

'Goldman is dead, sir.'

'What? How?'

'Tonight. At his home, sir.'

The old man's face was reddening. 'Are we responsible?'

'Not in any way that could be proved, I don't think, sir.'

'You don't THINK?' The boss slammed his fist on the table, sending cutlery, plates and a milk jug leaping into the air. 'What do you mean, you don't *think*? What the fuck happened there?'

Here we go, the aide thought. It's coming.

'Was I not clear in my instructions?' Now the voice was low, calm – which only made it more terrifying. 'Was I in any way unclear? Or did I spell out, in words any moron could understand, that there were to be no casualties? We could persuade, even intimidate, but nothing more. Did I not make that CRYSTAL CLEAR?'

'Our men were following those orders, sir.'

'Don't be an idiot.'

'The trouble is, Goldman had a weak heart. The minute he saw them, there in his house, he started shouting, then clutching his chest. They didn't touch him. It just happened.'

'Did they try to save him?'

The aide hadn't even thought of that. 'I don't think so, sir.'

The boss was no longer shouting. 'I think in my day, men on such a mission would not just have left a man dying. They would have done something.'

'Yes, sir.'

The old man was slumped in his chair; he looked somehow smaller. 'Did they find anything?'

'Yes.' He was about to say that that was the good news, but thought better of it. 'As it happens, Goldman was going through some papers when our men arrived. They haven't had time to analyse them yet but they believe they relate to our issue.'

'What if there are other papers?'

'He was going through a box, sir. It seemed as if everything had been kept in one place. Probably hidden.'

'And those papers are safe now?'

'Perfectly.'

'Any mention of,' his voice trailed off, as if he were embarrassed, 'by name, I mean?'

'Don't yet know that, sir. There's some translation work to be done.'

'What about the girl and that man?'

'They discovered Goldman's body.'

'Are they in trouble?'

'Our information is that they've been taken away by police and arrested. They're in custody now.'

The old man rubbed his chin. Whether he was pleased or dismayed by this last item of news the aide could not tell. The boss was simply processing the information, calculating.

Finally, he threw down his napkin and pushed back his chair. Then, barely audibly, he muttered, speaking more to himself than to the official who was still standing by the table, like a waiter poised to clear away the plates. 'What have we started here?' he said. And with that, he waved the man away.

The aide receded from the room in soft steps, closing the door behind him almost noiselessly. No double-fucking then. The boss had been subdued rather than livid. And, in a curious way, that was altogether more frightening.

## CHAPTER THIRTY-FIVE

Tom could see the dilemma that must surely have formed in the detective's mind within a few minutes of getting here. Rebecca and Tom were clearly respectable folk, a doctor and a lawyer, and they had done the respectable thing, sounding the alarm immediately. In ordinary circumstances, the police would simply thank them for their act of public-spiritedness and send them on their way.

But there was the stubborn matter of that front door. People didn't just come home without closing their front door properly. Someone other than Henry Goldman must have come into that house, which suggested Goldman's death had not been entirely down to natural causes. And there was Rebecca Merton's phone call: why would she have said she was reporting a murder?

So the detective was faced with a quandary. He could work on the basis that a crime had been committed and treat Tom and Rebecca as useful witnesses. He would show great courtesy, of course, without ever losing sight of the possibility that these two might be the killers: iron law of any murder inquiry, don't rule anybody out.

But there was a risk to that approach. If he eventually charged them the information he had gleaned while treating them as mere witnesses would be compromised. Interviewing suspects was a wholly different business: they had to be formally cautioned and told their rights, with a solicitor present. So while the detective might very much like to have Tom Byrne and Rebecca Merton talk with their guard down, he couldn't get away with that indefinitely. This, Tom understood, was the policeman's dilemma.

A harsh beam of light swept across the driveway: it would be Julian. Without waiting for permission, Rebecca broke off and walked towards his car. Tom saw the look of apprehension on the detective's face: if he regarded Rebecca as a potential suspect, he wouldn't want her chatting with the son of the deceased, filling his head with her version of events.

'I'll tell you what I think we should do,' the detective said suddenly. 'Why don't we all go down to the station? We can have a chat, take a full witness statement from you both and then we can see how things look in the morning.'

'After the autopsy, you mean.'

'Yes. That should make things much clearer. Am I right, Mr Byrne?'

* * *

The police moved fast after that. Tom was sure it was because they wanted any time Rebecca had with Julian kept to a minimum.

'We have a car here. Why don't we take you down to the police station right away?' the detective said.

'We'll be fine. We've got our own car.'

'You've both undergone a traumatic experience tonight. Our guidelines on victim support say that often people who have experienced trauma are too shocked to drive. Even when they don't realize it.'

Tom acquiesced, though he could not abandon the suspicion that the detective's primary, if unauthorized, purpose was to give the Saab a quick once-over, before his not-at-all-suspects had a chance to clean it up.

They were taken to Kentish Town police station, a horrible, poky hole of a place, full of fluorescent-lit rooms and hard plastic chairs. They were interviewed separately, as Tom fully expected. And, no less predictably, the lead detective decided to interview Tom first. He soon realized Rebecca Merton's connection to events in the news. Tom explained that that was why they had been to see Goldman, because he was an old friend of her father's and, to Tom's great relief, the detective pressed the point no further. Doubtless, he was saving that line of inquiry for the day when Rebecca and Tom were upgraded to official suspects – rather than objects of mere, unofficial suspicion – and he could question them properly.

The prospect filled Tom with dread. As if this whole business was not complicated enough already. Where on earth would you start? With the gun in Gerald Merton's hotel room? With the notebook? With DIN? And how would Rebecca explain why she had not reported the burglary at her home?

Tom thought again of Jay Sherrill. He knew he ought to phone him, at least go through the motions of bringing him up to speed. But what the hell would he say? 'Oh hi, Jay. Look, funnily enough I'm helping some police with their inquiries here too. Isn't that a coincidence?' It would all sound too far-fetched, too wild. He had already thrown Sherrill the morsel about Merton as a former vigilante. The rest would have to come later. This was a puzzle, Tom was now convinced, that would only be solved by him and Rebecca – without any help or interference from a police department, whether in London or New York.

'Come this way, please.' A junior officer led them both to some electronic gizmo, like the one at American airports, where you press your finger on a glass and have your prints taken.

'Why do we have to do this?' Tom asked, earning a glare from Rebecca. 'Will these prints be entered on a database? How long will they be kept?'

The detective smiled. 'Once a civil liberties

lawyer, always a civil liberties lawyer, eh, Mr Byrne?' He told them they had nothing to worry about; this was only to exclude them from the inquiry, to enable the police to identify any prints they picked up from the scene. 'It's voluntary: you can say no if you want. But if you say yes, it will help.' The details would be destroyed and, no, they would not be added to the national database.

Tom was hardly reassured. He guessed that if someone had broken into Henry Goldman's home, the intruder would have taken the elementary precaution of wearing gloves. Which meant the only prints that would be on the door, the walls, the study desk and on Goldman himself would belong to him and Rebecca.

Finally, some three and a half hours after they had first driven past Hampstead Heath, the detective told them he would hope to have autopsy results in the morning: if Goldman had died from natural causes, no trace of any poison or narcotics in his bloodstream, then this would not be a murder inquiry at all. Tom and Rebecca would hear no more about it. And with that he sent them on their way.

They stepped outside into the chill air of a prematurely autumnal night and realized they had no means of transport. Tom was poised to go back inside the police station and ask for the number of a local mini-cab company when a taxi came by, its orange light glowing with the promise of refuge. They fell in and headed east.

His head was pounding. He had had only a few hours sleep since Sunday night, thanks to a combination of the Fantonis, Miranda and the flight from New York, and it was now officially Wednesday morning. And he wasn't thirty any more. But the exhaustion went deeper than mere lack of sleep. It was the fatigue that comes from long and sustained frustration, continued grappling with a problem that refuses to be solved.

Both he and Rebecca were too tired to talk. He looked out of the window. No matter how much had changed in London, it still seemed dead at night. Not in the bits they show the tourists, the West End or the theatre district, but in the London of Londoners, the places where people lived. That was still one of the obvious contrasts with New York: the absence of delis, coffee shops and bookstores that functioned late into the night.

A few hours ago Stoke Newington Church Street would doubtless have been humming, men in bicycle helmets emerging with a single bag of shopping from the organic supermarket, couples perusing the shelves of the Film Shop, 'specializing in world cinema'. Tom imagined the kind of people who lived here, the right-on lawyers and leftie NGO staffers. In another life, it could so easily have been him. But right now, there was nobody around. Just a couple of stragglers emptied out of the bars and a slow beast of a street-cleaning vehicle, flashing and beeping along the kerb.

He didn't want to be here, bouncing once more

up and down the speed-bumped, concussion-inducing streets of the London Borough of Hackney. He had wanted to go back to Rebecca's flat or, more ambitiously, his hotel, if only to get some rest, but she had rejected that idea instantly. In the police car, he had tried to touch her hand but she had brushed him away; not angrily exactly, but with a sort of suppressed irritation, as if now were not the time. He wondered if she had misunderstood him, if she thought he had been claiming an attachment that was not yet certain, rather than simply consoling her.

She had been terrified, that much was clear. He guessed that Rebecca Merton, hardened no doubt by a few years in A&E, had nevertheless not had much experience of either the police or the law. The very words – questioning, witness, crime scene – were enough to make most people lose their heads. Hence the error in the 999 call.

But Rebecca had already been in a fragile state when they pulled into Henry Goldman's oversized driveway. Tom was in danger of forgetting that not yet forty-eight hours had passed since her elderly father – her only family in the world, by the looks of things – had been shot dead thousands of miles away and in circumstances that remained baffling. Her home had been the target of a violent robbery, and now an old friend of the family lay dead – hours after revealing the secret life of a shadowy, lethal organization in which both their fathers had been players. He might try to reassure her that Henry Goldman's death was surely a coincidence, that he probably got out of his car with chest pains, lacked the strength to close his own front door properly and staggered into his study, clutching at his heart, before falling to the floor. Tom could argue that they certainly needed more information before they jumped to any other conclusion. But he had succumbed to the same nauseous fear as she had the minute he saw the corpse. The old lawyer had surely been murdered – and she could be next.

Someone out there was hunting for information about the life and curious career of Gerald Merton. They had upended Rebecca's apartment looking for it and, surely, they had come after Henry Goldman for the same reason. After all, wasn't that why he and Rebecca had travelled to Canary Wharf and then Hampstead, because Goldman was one of the very few men alive with detailed knowledge of DIN? The question that rattled around Tom's mind now was whether these pursuers knew of Goldman's knowledge independently – or whether they had simply trailed after Rebecca. He now thought it likely they had been followed as early as yesterday morning, that the thieves had been able to break into her flat because they had monitored her movements and knew she was out.

'I've worked one thing out,' he said finally, breaking the exhausted silence that had held since they had left the police station. 'The fire alarm.'

'What about it?'

'It wasn't a coincidence. The timing.'

'What do you mean?'

'It's an old tactic. The Trots did it all the time when I was a student. A meeting wasn't going their way, they'd just yank the fire alarm: meeting abandoned, live to fight another day.'

'You're saying Henry Goldman pulled the fire alarm because he didn't like what we were asking?' She was looking at him as if he were an especially slow child.

'Not him.'

'But no one else was in that meeting, Tom.'

'No one else was in the room, I grant you that. But that doesn't mean no one was listening.' He thought back to the notorious second resolution vote in the lead-up to the Iraq war, when the six waverers on the UN Security Council – the Swing Six, they were called – discovered they had all been bugged by the British and the Americans. 'I don't know how they did it, but they did it.'

'And who's they?'

'I wish I knew.'

Tom's phone rang. At this time of night, it could only be New York. He looked down at the display: Henning.

'Hi.'

'You don't sound pleased to hear from me.'

'Sorry. It's been a tough few hours.' Tom closed his eyes in dread at the mere thought of Munchau discovering what had just happened: a UN representative in the custody of the Metropolitan Police in connection with a suspected homicide. It wasn't enough that the UN had been involved in the death of one old Jewish man, they had to be tangled up with another. He wondered how long he would be able to keep it quiet.

'Well, maybe this will help. Your former colleagues here came up with a few names.'

'What?'

'You know, for your geriatric club? Seventy and over?'

'Oh, that. Right.' He had clean forgotten about it; that phone call to Henning, that hunch, felt like it happened years ago.

'Stay focused, Tom.'

'I'm sorry; with you now. What have you got?'

'Well, it's preliminary research, but they say they'd be surprised if anyone else turns up.'

'Go on.' Now that he'd been forced to click his mind back into gear, he was excited. This could be the breakthrough they needed: one elderly German, a plausible target for DIN's last mission, and they would have this whole business explained.

'Well, first, you won't be surprised to hear that there are none on the permanent UN staff. Retirement at age sixty, strictly enforced.'

'Sure.'

'But there are three visitors we've counted who are over seventy. All in town this week.'

Tom nodded, unseen; his pulse quickened.

'The Chinese have brought a veteran interpreter, Li Gang. Legend has it he did Mao and Nixon, though I don't believe it. I mean, they—'

'What about the other two?'

'Well, the President of the State of Israel is here. He's eighty-four.'

'And the other one?'

'Foreign minister of Ivory Coast. Seventy-two. Been in the job on and off since the seventies apparently.'

'Thanks, Henning.'

'No use?'

'It was only a hunch.'

Tom almost had to smile at the irony of it. He had noticed that before, how fate seemed to have a sense of humour. If you wanted to pick three people less likely to be Nazi war criminals you couldn't do much better than representatives of China, Ivory Coast and – just to put it beyond doubt – Israel. It was not just a dead-end. It was a dead-end sealed off with a bricked wall.

By now they had arrived at Kyverdale Road, home of the late Gerald Merton. Rebecca had insisted on it: if they couldn't find out whatever it was Goldman wanted to tell them from Goldman himself – and they couldn't – they would have to see if there was some clue, some hint, that her father had left behind.

As they pulled up and paid the fare, Tom wondered if this was the first time she had been back to her father's place since his death. He braced himself to see Rebecca hit by yet another emotional freight train: how much could one person endure?

He watched her produce a ring of keys, choose one and turn it in the lock. She did not linger in the hallway but strode up the thinly carpeted stairs. The smell was just as he expected: stale and musty. On the third floor, she made for the first door by the staircase. Tom noticed her hands trembling as she unlocked the door. As she switched on the main light, she gasped.

Tom peered past her. The place had been ransacked, worked over just as thoroughly as her own apartment. The cushions were slashed, the books strewn on the floor like casualties in a battlefield. Even the carpet had been rolled back to expose the dirty, dust-caked floorboards underneath. At least two now jutted out, as if they had been prised up, then banged roughly back into place. There were a couple of paintings on the walls, an abstract collage in the hallway and a sub-Chagall knock-off depicting what seemed to be a rabbinic violinist in the living room. Both were now badly askew.

Even with the light on, the place was cast in a stubborn gloom. Heavy brown curtains were drawn across the windows. Tom waded through the wreckage, trying to construct an image of how the place would have looked. The kitchen was small and off-white, the appliances museum pieces from the 1970s. There was a basic two-person table by the wall. Close by, also intact, was a catering pack of a dozen cartons of orange juice.

Next to it sat a similarly cellophane-wrapped bulk load of baked bean tins. Gershon Matzkin had clearly never forgotten the lesson of the Kovno ghetto: always keep food, just in case.

There was a radio and a vase and several framed photos, the glass broken on almost all of them. He peered closely at one holiday snap, showing a tanned man, his shirt off, with his right arm around a woman and his left around a young girl, all seated at a table in an outdoor cafe in bright sunshine. The girl was about twelve and gawky, all elbows and bony shoulders. But the crystal green eyes were clear even then. The woman was dark-haired, too, but her eyes were unlike her daughter's, warmer and darker.

Tom focused on Gershon. He looked at least ten years older than his wife, already bald, the prodigious crop of hair on his chest silver. But his body was in remarkable shape, the muscle firm and toned, the chest and stomach hard and flat. And his eyes were as luminous as his daughter's.

Tom went back out into the living room, examining the slashed remains of a single well-worn armchair by the window. Next to it stood a table bearing a telephone and a radio-cassette player, a hulking relic of the 1980s. All over the floor, emptied out from a large, glass-fronted cabinet, were candlesticks, assorted silver knick-knacks, a few books and many more family photos. One caught Tom's eye: Rebecca with a wide smile and a mortarboard, her whole life ahead of her.

He found her in the bedroom contemplating another depressing scene: clothes strewn across the carpet, cupboard doors flung wide open. Each sock drawer had been emptied; ties dangling like forlorn party decorations. Tom expected her to sink onto the bed and burst into tears, but instead she went back into the living room. A look of relief passed across her face. 'They're still here.'

She knelt down and began poring over the framed photographs dumped on the floor. Tom joined her, instinctively searching for any pictures from the 1940s, from the dawn of DIN. Perhaps they would find an image of the teenage Gershon Matzkin in the forests in his patched-together uniform, maybe with his lover and partner-in-grief, Rosa. But most of the snaps were of Gershon's post-war self, settled in Britain: the newly minted Gerald Merton.

Rebecca studied one of these images closely. It was in that peculiar shade of dull orange that seemed to veil all colour photographs from the 1970s and it showed five men beaming widely, four of them wearing large square glasses. Tom recognized Gerald, his wide sideburns flecked with grey. All five were in black tie, though they had their jackets off. The one on the far right was raising a glass.

'Joe Tannenbaum. He must have died soon after this picture was taken,' Rebecca murmured. 'And Geoffrey Besser, he died about ten years ago.' Her finger hovered over the last man in the shot, cheerfully drinking to the health of the photographer. 'I can't remember him though.'

'What is this picture?'

'These were my dad's best friends.'

Tom looked at her face, scanning it for a sign of nostalgia or reminiscence. But her brow was furrowed.

'I don't understand. What are you looking for?'

'Sorry. I should have said. This would have been my cousin's wedding in 1976. And this group here,' she angled the picture for him to look at it properly, 'this is the poker club.'

Tom took a step back, crunching a picture book of Jerusalem under foot as he did so. The photo showed five middle-aged men, their jowls thickening, their heads getting balder, probably laughing at a corny joke. They were five survivors of the inferno who had made new lives in London: Gerald Merton with his dry cleaning shop and Henry Goldman's father, wholesaler of ladies' outerwear. Looking at this photograph, no one would have guessed what these men had been capable of – the focused, unwavering campaign of targeted killings they had pursued across several continents. And no one would have known the hell they had endured to make them do it.

'There's Henry Goldman's father, just there,' she pointed, her voice still quiet. 'The only one I don't know about is this bloke here. Sid something, he was called.'

Tom looked hard at the man she indicated, the one with the raised glass. Now that he knew the story of this band of brothers, was he deluding himself or could he really see something else in these five faces? Gerald Merton had a wariness in his eyes discernible in every photograph Tom had seen. But there was something like it in gazes of the other men, too. A steel below the surface, despite the apparently avuncular smiles. And then Tom saw it.

'Is that what I think it is?' he asked, pointing at the blur of grey on the forearm of the Sid whose last name Rebecca could not remember. His sleeve was rolled up, his forehead twinkling with sweat, perhaps the aftermath of a strenuous dance. Tom had been to a Jewish wedding once, a friend from college. Those traditional dances were quite a workout.

'Yes, that's what you think it is. Sid was in Auschwitz.' And her finger hovered over the blurred image of a number, tattooed on the arm of a man, raising his glass at a wedding more than three decades earlier.

Tom couldn't help but stare into his eyes, barely visible behind the thick apparently tinted glasses. What horrors had they seen? Had the images lingered? Could Sid see them even then, on a night of dancing, sweaty dress shirts and toasts?

'Sid Steiner! That was his name. Sid Steiner.'

'Is he alive?'

'I have no idea. But I think we'd better find out.'

# CHAPTER THIRTY-SIX

The place was still not tidied up as they sat next to each other, in the dead of night, on the slashed remains of Gerald Merton's couch, both staring at the small, brightly lit device cradled between Tom's hands. It was his BlackBerry, though they were not using it for email. The machine also had an internet browser, even if it did move with painful sloth. They were trying to navigate their way around the online archive of *The Jewish Chronicle*, searching past editions of the paper's personal announcements. Tom was struggling to concentrate against the noise of the TV set. Turning it on had been his idea: if someone was eavesdropping on their conversations, as he was convinced they had at Goldman's Canary Wharf office, then at least they could make the eavesdroppers' job a little more difficult. It was a low-tech form of counter-surveillance but he couldn't think of anything better.

At Rebecca's suggestion, he had typed in the single word 'Steiner' and the website had come up with hundreds. They scrolled through looking for Sids and, to Rebecca's dismay, they had found a Sid Steiner easily, dated six years ago:

*STEINER. Sid. Passed away peacefully, aged 89, after much suffering. A much loved and special gentleman who will be sadly missed by wife Beryl, son David and daughter-in-law Gaby, grandchildren, Josh, Daniel, Richard, Simon and sister-in-law Helen. May he rest in peace.*

'OK, that's not him. Wife wasn't called Beryl.'

'You sure?'

'I'm sure. Hold on, here's another one.' This was more recent, just two years ago.

*STEINER. Sid. Our dear dad who is now at peace and reunited with his Ada. A strong, supportive and wonderful father who will remain in our hearts forever. May his soul rest in peace. Ruth and Jack.*

Tom looked at Rebecca, next to him on the couch, with an eyebrow raised. She shook her head. 'Kids didn't have those names.'

'How can you be sure? You didn't remember his last name a minute ago.'

'They had a son called Daniel. Dan. I remember because I had a crush on him.' Absurdly, Tom felt a stab of jealousy. Then, remembering their kiss just a few hours earlier, it turned into a pang of desire. He looked at her for a second or two longer, fighting the urge to touch her: he couldn't make a pass at her here, in the trashed apartment of her dead father, even if he desperately wanted to. He forced his gaze back to the machine: he could see no more Sid Steiners.

'OK, I think that's our lot,' he said.

'You haven't tried Social and Personal.'

'Those were the personal ads. That's what we've been looking through.'

'No, those were the classified personal ads. There's also Social and Personal; different column. Bigger type, different page. Costs more.'

'Two different classes of death announcement? You're kidding.'

'I'm not.'

'So death is not the great leveller after all.'

'Not in *The Jewish Chronicle*. There it is, Social and Personal. Enter Sid Steiner there.'

He did and three came back. Tributes to a 'Dear brother, now at peace and sadly missed' and 'thoughts with the family at this sad time', but none that struck Rebecca as the right Sid Steiner. Either the age or the family names were wrong.

Tom put the machine to one side and shifted position to face her. 'Is it possible he died quietly, without an announcement?'

'No. If you're as Jewish as Sid Steiner, you die in *The Jewish Chronicle*.'

'So where is he?'

'I don't know.'

'OK,' said Tom. 'We'll do this the old-fashioned way. We'll get some sleep and in the morning we'll start working the phones.

On an improvised bed of slashed cushions and a torn sofa, Tom tried to slip into sleep. Rebecca was next door, in her father's bedroom. He knew he was exhausted, that the days seemed to have merged into a single stretch of time without rest. And yet his mind was sprinting.

A succession of images was flipping through his head like the pages of a child's flick-book. He saw a boy in ghetto rags, then an old man shot on the steps of the UN, then a woman's body swinging from a rafter, then the smiling pathologist in New York, then Rebecca's crooked smile and then, without warning . . . Rebecca.

There she was, framed in the doorway, the bedroom light revealing her shape. She was wearing only a shirt.

Tom brought himself up so that he was resting on his elbows. He didn't say a word, and neither did she.

Their kisses were as hungry now as before – hungrier for having been thwarted. The touch of her skin, the scent of her, sent such a voltage through him he felt he might be burning. And there in the shadows, their sweat and their taste mingling, the moment he entered her was as if they had entered each other. The intensity of it, so great that it banished all awareness of their surroundings, frightened him.

Afterwards, the silence seemed to bind them together. Her head lay on his chest and it was the sensation of a tear falling onto his skin that made him speak.

'Rebecca?'

He could feel her trembling now, a quiet sob.

'Is this because . . . of here? Because of where we are?'

'No.'

'What is it?'

'I just wish this hadn't happened like this.'

He stroked her hair, certain that his first instinct had been right: it was madness for them to have made love here, in the home of her dead father.

She spoke again. 'With all this going on, I mean. I wish it could have happened another way. I'm so sorry.'

'I can handle it if you can.'

The silence returned, but this time Tom knew it was the prelude to another question.

'How come there's no Mrs Byrne?'

'Is it that obvious?'

'It is to me. Was there ever one?'

'No. I used to be married to the work. And then, after everything that happened, I sort of shut out the future, along with the past. Made my home in the present. I couldn't plan much beyond dinner reservations.'

'You're speaking in the past tense.'

'Maybe I've changed.'

'When?'

'In the last day or two.'

She got up, headed for the kitchen and returned with a glass of water. She drank from it, passed it to him, then lay back down, skin touching skin.

'How come there's no Mr Merton? Sorry, I mean—'

'It's OK. Well, there's the patients. They take a lot out of you.'

'But that's not the whole story.'

'No. The truth is, it was hard with my dad. I was his only child. And then, after Mum died, I was his only family. Marrying someone would have felt like I was—'

'—leaving him.'

'Maybe.'

'What would he have thought of me?'

'Well, you're not Jewish for a start.'

'So?'

'So, let's not get into it. That's a whole other psycho-drama you don't need to know about.'

'Rebecca—'

She turned swiftly to face him and placed a finger on his lips. 'Don't. Don't say anything.'

'Why not?'

'Because I'm trying to be like you. I grew up my whole life either drowning in the past or worrying about the future. I want to see if I can enjoy the present. Just for once.'

When he woke a little after eight Rebecca was no longer lying next to him. She was up and dressed, explaining that she had been too impatient to sleep. She wanted to start the search for Sid Steiner immediately.

She reached for the phone, tried directory

enquiries first, and in vain, then turned to the phone book. She circled one number and dialled it, only for the call to be fielded by an answering machine. The voice belonged to Sid Steiner – but it was an accountancy practice in Hendon, no connection.

'All right then,' said Tom, swallowing his pride. 'What about this Dan, then?'

'That was twenty-five years ago. I was about seven years old. I have no idea where he is now.' Tom was relieved: she hadn't said it was a childhood crush.

'You haven't stayed in touch at all? Do you know where he works?'

She shook her head. Then she brightened, instantly reaching over for Tom's BlackBerry. 'Can you get Facebook on this?'

Tom felt a sudden awareness of the age gap between them: he relied on old-fashioned, steam-powered email. Still, at least he knew what she was talking about. 'I'm sure I can. Why?'

'Because that'll be the easiest way to find Dan Steiner.'

Sure enough, once logged on, it took a matter of seconds in the search box to generate an image of a depressingly handsome man about Tom's age, with a full head of dark hair.

'I could just poke him,' Rebecca said. When she saw Tom's startled expression, she smiled. 'That's not what it sounds like. It's a Facebook thing.'

* * *

There was only one space left in the car park; the rest were taken up with three mini-buses which, Tom noticed, were equipped even on the outside with assorted ramps and handles for wheelchair access. The building itself was large, fashioned out of the grey concrete that seemed to have been the only material available to the architects working when Tom had come of age: Sheffield had been full of dull, faceless exteriors like this too. The housing benefit office, the local library, the council: in the 1970s all British buildings looked like this.

They walked up the ramp, pausing by the entrance for Tom to roll two quick cigarettes, both making rapid work of sucking them down to a tiny stub. Rebecca had only 'poked' Dan Steiner an hour ago. He had – entirely unsurprisingly in Tom's view – responded immediately, happily supplying Rebecca with a phone number. She had wanted to call him there and then but Tom had vetoed it: if they were being followed, if their meeting with Henry Goldman had somehow been bugged, then it made no sense to use the phone in her father's flat. If their pursuers had been in there to wreck the place, it wouldn't have cost them too much effort to put an ear on the phone line. They had driven instead to a phone box three streets away, bringing the admission from the thirty-one year old Rebecca Merton, child of the cellular generation, that she had never used one before. Once guided by Tom, glad for the excuse to be crammed in the booth with her, so close their faces almost touched, she placed the call. She accepted Dan's condolences, asked charmingly after his wife and children, then asked if she might make contact with Dan's elderly father. She screwed up her eyes with that last request, bracing herself for Dan breaking the news that his father had moved to Israel or Manchester or even that he had, despite *The Jewish Chronicle*, died recently – but instead he gave her the address of the old age home on Stamford Hill where his father now lived. It was a five-minute drive from her own father's place: the last two boys of the poker club had somehow stuck together.

They had not phoned ahead, but Dan had: the lady at reception said she was expecting two visitors for Sid. As it happened, they had picked a good time to come: there was bingo in the main hall and Sid would have come down from his room. They should just wait here and she'd find someone to lead the way.

Tom looked around, his eye settling on the glass display-case in the lobby. Inside were a couple of the eight-branched candelabra he recognized from New York: they were everywhere in Manhattan in the lead-up to Christmas, as Jews marked the festival of Chanukah. There were silver wine goblets in there too, engraved wth Hebrew lettering. Pride of place went to a commemorative shield, the kind that had so delighted young Tom Byrne when he and his mates had brought one back following the under-13 football championships for 'Sheffield and region'.

There were two trolleys laden with teacups, a few forlorn balloons and a noticeboard. He stepped forward to read it: 'Don't Forget: Chair-Based Exercise with Maureen at 3pm on Thursday'. Another promised 'Judith's Sing-Along'. Next was a condolence board, with a standard message and a blank space where the name of the latest resident to collide with mortality could be inserted.

'Hello!'

He turned to see a large woman in her mid-fifties, her chest a rock-solid shelf, striding towards them. From her ID tag Tom could see that her name was Brenda and that she was described as a 'facilitator'.

'We haven't seen you at the centre before, have we?' She sounded breathless. 'You're here to see Sid?'

The loss of the surname; the same thing had happened to Tom's father the minute he turned frail. Tom always used to correct them – nurses, doctors, all of them – referring to his own father as Mr Byrne, but they rarely got the hint. Mostly it would still be 'Ron's very good at his wees, aren't you, Ron?'

'We are,' said Rebecca, back in doctor mode. Her professional voice was deep, like a lake at night. 'We're not family. But he and my father were very close.'

'And has your husband met Sid before?'

'I'm not—'

'He's not—'

They shot each other a quick look.

'Well, I'm glad anyway. Visitors, he doesn't get so many.' The voice was part East London and part something else, something Tom couldn't place. It was musical, almost sing-song: a Jewish melody. 'The sons come every now and then, but you know how it is. Everyone's busy.'

She led them through double doors into a large hall, divided by what seemed to be a wooden garden trellis. Brenda pointed at it and said, 'This is our dining area. That side's meat, this side's milk,' as if that made matters clearer. Apparently to Rebecca it did.

On the milk side of the divide, there were perhaps fifteen old people seated at five or six round tables arranged in café formation. At the head of the room was a man at a table of his own, clutching a microphone and, with no expression in his voice, reading out a series of numbers. Occasionally, one of the old folks would scratch away at a card. Despite the absence of patter or laughter, Tom realized the man was a bingo-caller. The electronic sign on the table at his side, flashing each number as he called it, was for the benefit of those too deaf to hear.

'Ooh, I'm surprised,' said Brenda, laying a hand across her vast bust. 'I thought he'd be here. I hope he hasn't gone wandering. You know about Sid's condition? His son explained, yes?'

Rebecca flashed Tom a look of panic. 'No. No, he didn't. He said it might be difficult to talk to his father, but he—'

'Oh, I expect he didn't like to talk about it. But Sid's not the only one here, you know. Lots of them have it. I sometimes think it's a blessing. To protect them from remembering too much. Although the trouble is, they do remember—'

'Can we meet him, do you think?' Rebecca was getting impatient.

Brenda now led them out of the hall and down a small flight of stairs. 'This is the art room,' she announced, like a head teacher guiding prospective parents around a school. Tom saw a man with white stubble carefully add a stick to a model steam train made entirely of matchsticks. 'That's Melvyn,' Brenda announced. 'He used to be a watchmaker.'

Next, Brenda poked her head around the door of a room decked out as a hairdresser's salon, just like the one Tom's mother used to visit on alternate Fridays when he was a boy. It came complete with those sit-under, helmet-style hairdryers: Tom remembered manoeuvring himself as a five-year-old into one and pretending he was a cosmonaut.

'I didn't think he'd be here, but checking never hurt. It's mainly the ladies who come here. For a chat.' Tom saw a price list by the door: shampoo and set £5.

They ascended two flights of stairs. 'They do wander sometimes, I'm afraid,' Brenda said, catching her breath from the climb. 'When they're like that. Sometimes they leave the building altogether. And you know where we find them? Usually standing outside the house where they lived as a child.' A sad look changed the shape of Brenda's mouth. 'Although not in Sid's case of course.' Suddenly her face brightened. 'I think I can hear someone,' she sing-songed. She pushed open a pair of double doors and they walked into a large room whose floor was almost entirely covered in a mat the colour of a billiard table. At the far end was a solitary upright piano and, hunched over it, a man with white hair on both sides of a bald head, playing scales over and over.

'This is the room we use for mat bowls – oh, our gentlemen residents like that – and for line dancing,' Brenda said, not to be diverted from her tour. 'And there, at the piano, is Sid.' She smiled with satisfaction, as if vindicated that the system worked after all. 'Sid, visitors for you!'

The old man's gaze remaining fixed on his left hand as it moved up and down the keyboard.

'I say, Sid, these nice young people have come for a chat.' She turned to Rebecca and Tom, her back deliberately to Sid Steiner. 'Maybe now's not a good time. Could you come back tomorrow? Or at the weekend?'

'We'd love to, we really would.' The doctor voice again. 'But unfortunately I lost my own father this week and there's something urgent that has come up. I think Sid might be the only person who can help us.'

'I wish you long life, dear.' Brenda took Rebecca's hand. 'And you need to ask Sid something? You need to find out information?'

Rebecca nodded. Brenda's mouth formed itself into an expression suggesting scepticism verging on alarm. She looked at Sid, then back to Rebecca. 'Lets see what a cup of tea can do.'

At the mention of tea, Sid halted mid-scale. He lifted his arm up and placed it back on his lap. Gently, Brenda took hold of his shoulders and turned him towards Rebecca and Tom.

His face was liver-spotted and veined but he was still recognizable as the man who had toasted the poker club's collective good health thirty years earlier. His eyebrows had become overgrown, like an unkempt hedge, and his earlobes were long and furred. He was, Brenda had reminded them, eighty-nine years old. When DIN were in their first hunting season, Sid Steiner would have been in his twenties: fit, strong and fearless.

'Hello, Sid,' Rebecca said gently. She gestured towards a column of stacking chairs, and Tom pulled out two of them. Once she was at eye level with the old man, she spoke again. 'I'm Gerald Merton's daughter, Rebecca.'

'Who?'

'I'm Gerald Merton's daughter.'

'What do you say?'

'Gershon Matzkin.'

'Gershon Matzkin? You're Gershon's wife?'

'I'm his daughter.'

'Gershon's a good boy.'

Rebecca dipped her head and, as it hung there, low, Tom could see the sides of her eyes: they were wet. Was it despair at the pitiful state of Sid Steiner or the notion of her father as a boy that had done that? Tom didn't know, but he felt such a strong urge to touch her, to console her, that this time he didn't fight it. He squeezed her shoulder and, in thanks, she touched his hand briefly. Even now, even here, he could feel the crackle of electricity.

'Do you remember when you last saw him?'

'My mother won't like me talking to a girl like you, you know. She's warned me not to talk to girls like you. From across the river.'

Tom could feel Rebecca tensing. She reached out and placed a hand on Steiner's sleeve, a gesture which exposed how withered his arms had become. With a shudder, Tom thought of the skin that was concealed inside that too-large sleeve and, on it, the number etched in purple.

'Can you tell me anything Gershon said to you recently? Did he come and visit you here?'

'Now, did you get married in the end? Or wouldn't he have you?'

'Who?'

'What did you say?'

At that moment, Brenda pushed her way through the double doors, back first, holding a tray of tea. She must have caught Rebecca's expression, because she gave a small nod of recognition, as if to say: this is what I meant. Dementia.

'It's teatime, Sidney.'

'What time is it?'

'Teatime.'

'What's that?' He was pointing at the tray.

'That's a cup.'

'I know that's a cup. What's that?'

'Guess.'

The old man scrunched up his eyes, a child's caricature of concentration. Eventually, he opened them again and said three words which made Tom's eyes prick. 'I can't remember.'

'That's milk, Sidney. That's a jug of milk.'

Rebecca got to her feet and spoke quietly, almost inaudibly, to Brenda. 'I'm sorry to have taken your time, Mrs Jacobs. But I don't think this is going to work. We made a mistake, I'm sorry.'

'What is it you need him to remember?'

Rebecca looked over at Tom, with a question in her eyes: how much can we say?

'We need him to remember something from long ago,' said Tom, pulling an answer out of the air. 'Maybe fifty or sixty years ago.'

Brenda smiled. 'You should have said. Now come with me.'

They passed through a door set with patterned glass, the way front doors used to look. Next to it was a brass plate: *The Y Dove Reminiscence Room*.

The space had been divided into two areas. The first was wood-floored and done up like a hallway with a hat-stand and a sideboard cluttered with objects: a portable, wind-up gramophone; a Philips wireless; a Frister & Rossman sewing machine and a heavy, black mechanical cash register, the buttons marking amounts in shillings and old pence. Opposite was a small kitchen area, including a big square sink, a washboard and a stack of battered enamel saucepans.

Sitting on the counter was a biscuit tin decorated with the face of George VI, Queen Elizabeth and the two princesses, Elizabeth and Margaret. Above it, a shelf laden with products not seen for decades: Flor Brite Mop Furniture Polish, Lipton's No.1 Quality Tea and Victory Lozenges.

The main part of the room boasted a floral carpet the like of which Tom had not seen since childhood visits to his grandparents in Wakefield. There was a fireplace, its surround made up of beige ceramic tiles, and on a sidetable a heavy, black Bakelite telephone. On the wall was a framed poster showing a strapping woman striding across a meadow with a pitchfork in her hand: 'Come and help with the Victory Harvest'. A strapline at the foot of the poster read, 'You are needed in the fields'. Beneath it, Sid Steiner sat in a big armchair.

This was the place residents with dementia came for sessions aimed at giving their ravaged memories a workout. Because, while short-term memory was the first casualty, the experiences of long ago tended to be forgotten last, with recollections of childhood clinging on until the very end. People who could not find the word for 'cup' or 'jug', who could not recognize their own children, could come in here and, at last, remember.

Rebecca cleared her throat. 'So Sid, when did you come to this country?'

Brenda shook her head. 'Try to avoid factual questions, dates, that kind of thing,' she whispered. 'It can be stressful for them. Use the objects in the room, try to get him talking.'

Tom looked around and grabbed a packet of Park Drive cigarettes. He passed it to Rebecca who put it in Steiner's hands.

'Do you smoke, Sid?'

'We all do.'

'Do you like smoking?'

'It's warm.'

'Did you ever smoke these, Sid?'

He looked down, turned the packet over a couple of times, then shook his head. 'It's not easy to get cigarettes. Besides, when you get them, you don't smoke them. You use them. Don't you know that? Didn't they teach you anything in Warsaw?'

Rebecca leaned forward; it was the most coherent sentence they had yet heard from Sid Steiner. 'What do you buy with them?'

'Anything. To get in, to get out, to get past a guard. Cigarettes or jewels, it makes no difference.'

Neither Tom nor Rebecca knew where or when in his memory Sid had landed. Was it whichever ghetto he had been locked up in, or perhaps a camp; or was it the occupation zone of 1945, scene of DIN's first hunting season?

'What about this?' Hung up on a wall, among a display of documents and photographs, was the jacket from a British army uniform. Rebecca passed it to him.

'Not bad.' He assessed the three stripes on the upper arm. 'Sergeant. That could be useful. What we need are MPs. If you can get me one of those, we can use it.'

Tom squeezed Rebecca's wrist in excitement: MPs were military police. This fitted precisely with the testimony Henry Goldman had given them, that MPs uniforms were the ones DIN prized most.

'Use it for what, Sid?'

'I'm not going to tell you that. If you're meant to know, you know already. If you don't know then you're not meant to know.' Tom smiled: it was a smart answer.

'Did you work with Gershon in DIN?'

'You some kind of spy? I don't answer questions like that.'

'I'm with Gershon.'

'He's too young for a girl like you. He's only a boy.'

It must be 1945. Sid Steiner must have transported himself back to Allied-occupied Germany, probably the British zone. Maybe the uniform had done it. Tom looked around for another prop, something that might trigger a useful memory. In a glass case was a shoe-brush and, next to it, a Ministry of War Book of Air-Raid Precautions. That was no good; too British. He scanned the walls and shelves, desperate for anything that might light a spark.

Then Sid spoke unprompted. 'I know how to use that.' He was pointing at one of the display cabinets. Rebecca stood up, trying to follow the line of the old man's crooked finger.

'This?' She held up a tin of National Dried Milk issued by the Ministry of Food.

'No! Not that, that!' He aimed his finger leftward, until it rested on a rolling pin. Tom sighed: and just when we were getting somewhere.

Rebecca returned to her seat, her posture now deflated. They were heading back into la-la land.

'What did you use it for, Sid?' It was Brenda. She had pulled the rolling pin from its case and was handing it over.

'Well, I had to train as a baker, didn't I? If the plan was going to work.'

Rebecca leaned forward once more. 'What plan, Sid?'

'Ask Gershon, he'll tell you. He trained too. We both did. Kneading the dough, glazing the cakes. I was very good at doughnuts. Bread was hard, though.'

'And this was so that you could implement the plan?'

'Of course.'

'What's the name of the plan?'

'Plan B.'

'B for Bakery?'

'No. Wrong again.'

'Did Plan B work?'

'It made the papers you know. *New York* flipping *Times*. Nuremberg, April 1946. But we could have done more.'

'What was the plan?'

'Everyone needs bread, no?'

'You were making bread. Who for?'

'You may be pretty, but Gershon's picked himself a bit of a dunce if you don't mind my saying so. Who do you think it was for?'

# CHAPTER THIRTY-SEVEN

**Nuremberg, Spring 1946**

Our first task was to decide a target. This was not a decision for me; I was just a teenage boy. Others, the leaders, took those decisions. One of them was the man I had met in the cellar in the ghetto at Kovno, on that night of the candles. His name was Aron. The other two were dead by 1946, killed in the last Aktion which emptied the ghetto once and for all. I did not know that for sure, not then, but that was what I presumed. Unless you heard otherwise, unless you saw them or ran into them in the street or heard a rumour, it was best to assume this or that person were gone. In 1946 everyone was dead.

But a few leaders of the resistance had survived, emerging from the burnt-out ghettoes and the smoking ruins of the cities and they, along with a few from the camps, were the men who started DIN. I was still a teenager but I wanted them to think of me as a warrior, a man who had proved himself. Even though I was so young, they did indeed treat me like a man: anyone who had lived through what we had lived through was no longer a child, no matter how young you were. Your childhood was gone.

I was not the one who took decisions, but I had a good pair of ears and I listened. We were in a safe house in Munich and one night, as I was clearing away the dishes from our meal, I heard the commanders mention one place more than any other: Nuremberg.

They had heard that the Allies had set up a prison outside the city, to hold Nazis for 'questioning'. And not just any Nazis either, but the important ones. 'There are eight thousand SS in there,' Aron said. His eyes were dark and fierce, his hair thick and kinked: I never once saw him smile. 'No small fry,' he went on. 'They're being held for major war crimes. *Major* war crimes. They're all in there: senior staff at the camps, *Politischen Abteilungen*, Gestapo, Einsatzgruppen, everyone.'

It was obvious he was most excited by the men of the 'Political Departments', the *Politischen Abteilungen*. Among them would be some of the senior bureaucrats who had helped to organize the Final Solution. That was what the Nazis had called their killing. They did not call it mass murder, killing people by the hour, the way a factory makes products. No, they called it the Final Solution to the Jewish Problem.

But I wasn't thinking about these bureaucrats as I washed the plates, pretending not to listen. I was thinking about the Einsatzgruppen. The mobile killing teams who had gone from place to place murdering and murdering and murdering. These were the people who had killed my sisters at the Ninth Fort.

Aron had done some research, using a DIN volunteer who had ended up in Nuremberg. He had tracked down the source of all the camp's bread, a medium-sized bakery on the outskirts of town. The leaders talked some more, their voices becoming low and hushed. Then they fell completely silent. I was scrubbing the grease off a pan when I turned around to see that they were all looking at me, with that same look I had seen before, three years earlier, in the cellar in the ghetto.

They gave me a street address and told me which man to speak to at the bakery: the works supervisor. They had described him to me, short and barrel-chested with a face almost always flushed red. I was to clean myself up, find him and give him my story.

The description was good and I recognized him as soon as I walked in. 'My name is Tadeusz Radomski,' I began, 'and I need to learn how to become a baker.' I told him I was a Pole, with an uncle in Montreal who was himself a baker and was ready to give me a job. 'All I need is a visa, but for Canada it takes time. While I'm waiting, I want to learn. My uncle says I need experience—'

'I'm sorry,' the works supervisor said, wiping a flour-dusted hand on his apron. 'There are no jobs here.'

'I'm happy to work for free,' I said.

'No jobs.'

Then, as we had discussed back in the safe house, I continued: 'My uncle said I should show you this,' and I reached inside my canvas satchel. As soon as the man got a peek of what was inside, he gestured me to come into a back office. I had showed him a bottle of Scotch whisky and two bars of chocolate. Along with cigarettes, they were the currency of the occupation zone and he knew what they were worth. 'My uncle says you can have this now and there will be more for you when I have done a month's work.' I started that afternoon, with no pay.

And so I began as an apprentice baker, learning everything from kneading and rolling the dough to glazing and frosting cakes. I would volunteer for extra work, cleaning out the pans and scouring the ovens. If the manager needed a boy to run an errand, I would do that too. I said little and worked hard. I wanted there to be no complaints against me and for the manager to trust me completely, so that he would let me work anywhere in the bakery. My job was to find out exactly how the system worked, to understand every aspect of it: when the allocation of flour was received from the Americans, where it was stored, which shift came on when, when they came off and how the place was guarded. Above all I needed to discover how the thousands of loaves for Stalag 13, the holding centre for Nazi prisoners, were baked and when and how they were transported.

I did as much as I could, never asking a single direct question. I just watched and listened. I didn't chat to anyone – as far as I was concerned every worker in that place was a Jew-killer – but I wanted them to think the only reason for my silence was that I was a lonely orphan boy working hard for a new life abroad. The strange thing I realize only now, as I set down these words, is that I was not really acting at all: a lonely orphan boy was exactly what I was.

Then one day, the American army trucks arrived at usual, just before dawn, to pick up the bread. I had been doing the night shift – I had volunteered for it – and I was there, on the outside loading platform, when I heard one of the American drivers complain that his usual partner was off sick: he needed someone to help unload at the other end. The manager took one look at me and with an index finger guided me towards the truck. 'He'll go.'

And so I rode up front in the cab, next to the American, trying not to stare at his uniform, refusing his offer of chewing gum but accepting a cigarette, even though I did not smoke, because

I did not want to look like a kid who did not smoke. I held it between my lips, sucking every now and then, looking out of the window and saying nothing, passing the bomb site that was Nuremberg. My memory now is of a landscape that looked like the surface of the moon. So much rubble, long stretches of it on either side of the road, interrupted by the odd building that had escaped the bombing, looming over the rest like an adult in a kindergarten.

When we got to Stalag 13, waved through by the American guard on the gate, I felt prickles on the back of my neck. This site, I knew, used to be a concentration camp. It was surrounded by barbed wire and filled with row after row of wooden huts: barracks that once housed Jews, worked like slaves and taken to their deaths, and now filled with the men who had tortured and killed them. I had to clench both my fists to get a grip on myself and stop myself shivering.

'OK, here we go,' the driver said in English, parking up and jumping down from the cab. He told me, in gestures and signs, to start unloading the wheeled trolleys, each stacked with a dozen racks, each rack containing two dozen loaves. We were parked outside the camp kitchens and I was unloading for a long time: I estimated that, along with the other trucks, we delivered around nine thousand loaves of bread. All black bread.

'What about the white bread?' I asked in German.

The driver shook his head, his brow furrowed. He did not understand. Somehow, through a combination of hand signals and pidgin German and English, I got the question out. Eventually he nodded and pointed into the distance, at a single truck unloading at the other end of the camp. So that was how it was done: nine thousand loaves of black bread for the Nazi prisoners taken in several trucks to the prisoners' kitchen, including the one I had just unloaded. And then a separate truck carrying one thousand loaves of white bread, delivered to a different kitchen for the American guards. The driver pointed at the black loaves and made a retching expression. Then he gestured in the distance, at the white loaves, and patted his stomach. He was telling me that the Americans couldn't stand the coarse, thick black bread and needed white, like they had at home.

I worked hard to hide my smile as we drove back to the bakery and, after that, as I walked home. Only once in the apartment we had rented in Nuremberg, a new hideout, could I let out a scream of delight. 'This will be easy,' I said. 'This will be easy.'

I briefed the commanders that night, proud of the discovery I had made. We had only to direct our attention to the black loaves; anything we did to them would never affect the Americans. It would be DIN's simplest, but greatest, operation.

But then Rosa brought bad news. All of us had had to get jobs. My friend Sid Steiner – his first name then was Solomon – had also trained as a baker in Munich, because we hoped we would be able to repeat the Nuremberg operation there, perhaps even on the same night. Rosa's job was no less important. She had been told to find a boyfriend. Not any boyfriend, but an American. Plenty of women in occupied Germany were doing the same thing. Some were Germans, but some were Poles or Czechs or Hungarians, women who had washed up and landed in Berlin or Nuremberg like so much driftwood on the shore. They made themselves friendly with any man in an American uniform, a man who could provide attention, as well as coffee, cigarettes and corned beef in a tin. These women were desperate and would not hold back their affection. Rosa's task was to pretend to be one of them. What nationality she would adopt, I had no idea. But she did not look so Jewish – except for the deadness in her eyes, dead from all that she had seen, which would have been obvious to anyone who had looked. Luckily, these men were not looking so closely.

No one ever asked whether she minded being used in this way; it was simply her duty. The order was given and, as a fighter and partisan and now a soldier for DIN, she would obey. No one asked me either, even though, by that time, Rosa and I were together. Perhaps no one knew; perhaps people would have assumed I was too young for such things.

So Rosa set about throwing herself at the GI Joe responsible for the guards' canteen at Stalag 13. Did she sleep with him? At the time I told myself that she did not, but now I see something else: I imagine him on top of her, pounding away at her flesh, not noticing the eyes, still and glassy, in her face.

Anyway, this sergeant was joking about some of his officers, health-conscious types from Boston or New England. 'You'll never believe this,' he said, 'but they refuse to eat American white bread. They want the brown stuff the Krauts eat!' So each morning he has to arrange for one hundred loaves of Nazi bread to be separated from the rest and delivered to the American kitchen. 'Crazy, they are.'

I received this news as you would word of a disaster. If we tampered with the black bread we would hit some Americans and they would not let such an attack go unpunished. They would hunt us down.

There were more complications. In what I imagined was an idle moment of pillow-talk, Rosa's boyfriend explained that he'd had a rough day. Not only had he had to keep his own mess running, but he'd had to do a spot-check on the prisoners' kitchen. They were meant to do it once a week or so: checking equipment, making sure no knives had been stolen and, more important, ensuring that the food supplies were not being used as cover for any smuggling. It had been known for prisoners to hide weapons, even cyanide tablets, inside a loaf of bread or a bag of sugar. Everything that went into that kitchen had to be checked, not every day, but often. What a drag it was; it added hours to his day. Rosa probably stroked the sergeant's brow in sympathy, quietly noting what she would tell the DIN leaders back at the flat: that they would have no guarantee that any tainted bread would not be probed, examined and, quite possibly, discovered.

Both Rosa and I did as we were told, uncovering every detail of the process and then relaying it to our commanders. I was asked to come up with a thorough blueprint of the bakery, including all measurements, as comprehensive as any architect's drawing. And of course I had to bring back several loaves of bread, black and white, so that they could be studied.

After two months of this, we were summoned for another meeting. This time, though, a man I had not met before was there. I remember him as an elegant, older character come to us from Paris – but that may be just how he looked to me, a fifteen-year-old boy who knew everything of the world and also nothing. This man was never introduced by name, but he was treated by the commanders as an expert. They showed him respect. It turned out that he was an experienced player of the black market – and that he had made contact with a chemist.

Aron asked this man to tell us what he knew.

'Comrades,' he began, in an accent that seemed only half-French. 'The decisive question is how we introduce the poison to the bread.'

Poison. It was the first time the word had been uttered. We preferred a codeword: *medicine*. 'If we're to treat the disease,' Aron would say, 'we need medicine.' We avoided saying 'poison' out loud. Why? Because we feared it would betray our secret? That it might jinx our mission, that it would somehow bring bad luck? That we did not quite want to admit, even to ourselves, what we were about to do? All of the above.

But now he had said it, it gave us a strange confidence. This man, this adult, would make this crazy dream of ours come true.

'Now,' he continued, 'the obvious method would be to make the poison an ingredient stirred into the mixture for the black bread from the very beginning. This would be simple. Sadly, it is *impossible*. We now know that one hundred loaves of this bread go, in fact, to the Americans. If these Americans die, it would be a disaster! So we need another method, yes?'

Aron began shuffling in his seat.

The Frenchman reached into his bag, an oversized doctor's case of battered brown leather, and with a great flourish produced a huge, thick paintbrush.

'You have seen it used by the house decorator, yes?' He was smiling.

'What's the idea?' asked Aron, his patience dwindling.

'To *paint* the poison onto each loaf.'

'Paint? With those?'

'The young man knows all about it, I am sure.' He nodded in my direction. 'The pastry chefs call it glazing, I think.'

He picked up from the table a loaf of black bread I had put there earlier for exactly this purpose. 'First, you dip the brush into the liquid – for now we use only vinegar, of course – you paint one stroke up, one stroke down and there: *Voilá!*'

There was silence as the semi-Frenchman sat down, his demonstration completed. Our leader was frowning. None of us wanted to speak before he did. He picked up the bread, examined it, then placed it back on the table.

'And that's enough?'

'It is.'

'You're sure the poison will have no taste?'

'No taste.'

'No colour?'

'No colour. It's an arsenic mixture, odourless and colourless. I have seen it myself.'

I was nervous about speaking, but as the only baker in the room I felt I had some authority. 'Won't the crust on the top be moist?'

The man from Paris widened his eyes into a smile

and pointed at me. 'Our young friend has asked a good question! This, for me, is our biggest problem.'

Aron was alarmed. 'You mean he's right? The bread will be wet?'

'For a while. But not for long. After an hour or so we think it is dried out.'

'You think?'

'If there is some dampness it would be so slight, no one would think anything of it. Remember, this is not the Ritz Hotel. What are the Nazis going to do, ask their waiter to take it back?'

Aron ignored the joke and turned to Rosa. 'What time do they start eating breakfast?'

'At 6.15 a.m.'

Now to me. 'And the loaves are picked up at five?'

'Yes. But most are baked by three.'

Aron turned to the not-quite-Frenchman. 'And this method works?'

'There is a dead cat in Paris who says it works very well.'

We waited as Aron picked up the bread once more, then placed it back down on the table. He rubbed his chin. Finally he gave his verdict, looking at each of us, his gaze steady. 'The first night with a full moon, we do it.'

As it happens we did not choose the very first moonlit night. We waited for a Saturday. That was because of the way we had chosen to stage the operation.

It was the Frenchman's idea. I call him that because I never found out his name. Rosa said he was a Communist, or at least had been, and that he had been part of the resistance in Krakow. He had found his way to Paris, a place where it was possible to get hold of anything: cars, forged papers, douche syringes, poison. Why he was in DIN, what bitterness he stored inside, I did not know. But he covered it well, with his semi-French accent and his performance. Not many men in DIN smiled as often as he did.

Once Aron had said the operation could go ahead a new discussion began: how? When the commanders first hatched the plan, they assumed it would be a simple business: I would smuggle some poison into the bakery and, when no one was looking, would tip it into the vat of flour, stir and that would be that. But painting poison onto nine thousand individual loaves was a mammoth task even if it were done by several people working at once.

For the hundredth time I was called on to explain the process.

'As soon as the bread comes out of the ovens, it's placed on a series of trolleys here.' I was standing over the table, pointing at my own drawing of the bakery. 'They're then wheeled, into the drying room – here. There's a door out onto the loading area here. Just before five a.m., the trolleys are wheeled outside for the Americans to pick up.'

Aron now questioned me the way he had questioned the Frenchman. 'Once the bread is in the drying room, is the room empty?'

'Not for long. People come in and out constantly.'

'Even at four in the morning?'

'Even then.'

He nodded. 'And there's no way anyone could be discreet, working with that thing.' He pointed at the housepainter's brush, still on the table. 'You would have to be there, undisturbed, for hours. Damn!' He slammed his fist down on the table.

Then the Frenchman spoke to me. 'How many workers are there at that time of night?'

'Normally it's about ten.'

'Normally? And what is not normally?'

'On Saturday night, once the work is almost finished, before three a.m., about half the workers go off. To drink.'

'Leaving how many people in the bakery? Five, maybe, including you?'

I nodded.

'In which case I think I have a plan.'

The preparations took weeks. After our meeting in the apartment, the Frenchman returned to Paris to meet with the chemist: between them they had calculated the amount of arsenic mixture we would need for nine thousand loaves. It took some time to prepare. Once it was done, the Frenchman despatched a courier, another DIN volunteer, to carry the liquid personally from Paris to Nuremberg. 'There is no other way,' he said.

When the courier appeared at our apartment, he was wearing an American uniform under a heavy overcoat. Rosa answered the door, but I remember wondering how such a man who had survived what we had all survived, a soldier of DIN, could be so fat. He was not just tall, he was enormous. But once the door was closed, I understood. He ripped off the coat and his jacket to reveal at least a dozen hot water bottles, all made of sweating rubber, strapped to his body. Before he had a chance to say a word, he took one look around and collapsed onto the floor: he could carry that huge weight no longer.

That night Rosa and I transferred the mixture into smaller bottles. We used whatever we could find: medicine bottles were the best, so long as they could fit inside my satchel. Each day I would take one or two into the bakery and, when I was alone in the drying room, I would stash them under the floorboards. In my head I kept a mental map of that room, memorizing each board, so that I would know exactly which boards to lift in the few minutes we would have to prepare the mixture.

When Saturday April 13 1946 came, I was more nervous than I had ever been before. Don't ask me why. Perhaps it was because, in the past, I had pretended to be this or that person for just a few minutes, long enough to get past a guard or onto a train. But I had been Tadeusz, the Polish baker boy, for several months now. I was part of the team at the bakery. You can't work alongside people every day, week in, week out, and remain a complete stranger. Sometimes one of the women, in hairnet and gloves, would tousle my hair, as if I were a playmate for one of her sons. The first time it happened, I had to run outside. I was gasping, as if I had been strangled. (Later I said I had had a coughing fit). Now that I am older I understand what I did not understand then. Maybe I had to be a father to understand what that fifteen-year-old boy felt that day, a boy who had not felt the loving touch of a mother for so long that even a hint of it was enough to turn him upside down. I read once of a prisoner who had been in jail so long that, when he was released, he was allergic to fresh air. Perhaps I was that way with a mother's love.

Tonight they were about to discover the truth of me and I think that was what made me scared. I had to force myself to remember what this operation was really about, to remember the men inside Stalag 13, to think of the Einsatzgruppen. When I did that, I could make my heart turn to flint.

I checked my watch. I had been on shift since five o'clock that afternoon and the hours had dragged. I was desperate for three o'clock to come. I did my work but I could not be distracted. I kept asking myself, will we have enough of the mixture, will we have enough time, will this crazy scheme work? I even began to wonder about the

Frenchman. What did we really know about him? Could this all be some elaborate trap?

At seven minutes to three I heard the words I had been waiting for, spoken by the manager himself. 'Come on, the beer is calling!' He and seven others took off their overalls, hung them up and headed, as usual, for the tavern down the street. They said goodbye to me and the other 'saps' who had to stay behind.

I checked my watch again. Precisely six minutes from now and I would do what we had planned. For now, I had to stay put.

I knew what was happening outside. Once she had got the signal – they've gone! – from Manik, serving as lookout across the street, Rosa would have appeared from the opposite direction, wearing a short dress, in black and red; God only knows where she had picked it up. She had been given money to buy bright lipstick, too. Her instructions had been to look appealing and available – for the right price.

I can picture her strolling up to the gate in high heels, waiting for the night-watchman to emerge, as I had told her he would. She would have had just a few moments to make her impression. She was not the blonde these Germans liked, but she was beautiful and her body, at least, was young. I can see him unlocking the gate, then stepping forward to give Rosa a proper looking-over. She would have probably let him grope a bit, just to close the deal, and as he touched and squeezed, she would have moved nearer, more intimate until he was so close she would only have had to push the blade a few inches forward to find his heart.

Then Manik would have run from his hiding place across the street, his shoes soft-soled and quiet, to help Rosa drag the dead body out of the way. Then they would have given the signal to the truck over the road. The vehicle was from the British Army transport pool, signed out by a friendly member of the Jewish Brigade, using forged papers. With its lights switched off, it drove through, Manik closing the gate after it.

That was when I headed for the drying room and, from there, to the outside loading area. By the time I was there, keeping the door open, they were all out of the truck, five of them, their faces blacked up with boot polish. With Manik and Rosa, it made seven. All were armed.

I guided them through the drying room until they were huddled around the far door that led into the bakery proper. Silently, Aron counted the group off then one, two, three – they burst through, shouting '*Achtung!*' and training their guns on the half dozen bakers, my fellow workers, they found within.

I did not go inside, but watched through the glass window in the door. The bakers offered no resistance. They had been sitting around, either playing cards or finishing up for the night: they were in no position to fight against a gang of armed men. All of them raised their arms in the air, a group of Germans surrendering to a gang of Jews. It should have been a sweet moment but it had come at least three years too late.

Three of the group began to bind and gag the bakers, tying their ankles and wrists and finally tethering each of them to a pillar or table leg.

I saw our leader swivel around, looking for me. He needed me to show him where the supplies – the sugar, yeast and flour – were kept. I emerged, ready to point at the storeroom. I tried hard to avoid meeting the eye of the men tied up all around me, but I could not do it. I looked into each pair of eyes, most of them aghast with surprise, some ablaze with hatred. So, the little Polish boy betrayed us. They could say nothing, but they did not need to.

Aron and one other set about emptying the storeroom, taking turns to go back and forth between there and the loading area, filling up the truck that was waiting outside. They took their time, making sure this activity lasted as long as necessary.

I was back in the drying room. Once the bakers had all been restrained, I set about prising open each memorized floorboard, bringing out the concealed bottles of poison. Earlier I had brought in a set of metal mixing bowls, the biggest I could find. Rosa and I began filling them as fast as we could. The Frenchman had been right: the fluid was clear and smelled of nothing.

The other four in our group opened up their

bags and pulled out the paintbrushes. The first dipped the bristles in one of the full metal bowls, letting them absorb the liquid. He looked at me, waiting for guidance. I showed him to the wheeled rack, gesturing at the top row and, methodically, he started painting on the poison, loaf by loaf.

Soon we had a rhythm, a veritable production line as Rosa and I ensured at least five bowls were full of poison at any one time, shuttling again and again to various hiding places under the floor for fresh supplies.

Every ten minutes or so, Aron passed through the drying room but he could not stop for long: he had to maintain the charade of loading up the truck with sacks of sugar and flour. He could not let the bakers, gagged and bound inside, know that anything was going on inside the drying room. For that reason, we worked in silence and only occasional whispers.

The day itself had dragged but these two hours – less, of course, by the time we actually started – flew by. We were sweating through it, each of us possessed by the same fierce desire: to poison as many of those loaves as we could in the time. I counted the racks we had done and I estimated we had painted arsenic onto about three thousand.

Then Aron joined us, gesturing at his watch. It was quarter to five; the American trucks would arrive in fifteen minutes. He urged us to pack up. I began putting the unused bottles of poison back in their hiding places under the floorboards. Of course they would be found eventually, but by then, with luck, it would be too late to matter.

I hid the last bottle and caught my hand on a spike sticking out of the floorboard I had been trying to replace. My hand began to bleed. I was pressing the board in, harder and harder, but it would not stick. And now a pool of blood was spreading.

'Come on!' Aron said in a loud whisper, glaring at me. It was three minutes to five. The trucks would be here any second. Yet I couldn't leave, not while blood and an uneven floorboard were calling out to be noticed, advertising the poison hidden below. If I at least removed the bottle, then, even if they looked, the Americans would find nothing. They would assume this was just damage caused by the intruders as they went about their business.

I looked around. Everyone else had gone, Rosa and the rest of the poison team were all outside, in the truck by the loading platform waiting to go. Only Aron remained, now looming over me. I was on my knees, trying to retrieve the hidden bottle. He looked as if he was about to knee me in the face, to knock me out and drag me into the truck.

But when he saw the blood and the stubborn floorboard he understood. He shoved me out of the way and, in a single jump, he let his entire weight land on the uneven plank of wood. Still, it would not settle. We now had less than two minutes.

He stepped out of the way and gestured for me to remove the poison. Once I had, he wheeled over one of the racks and placed it over the board and the bloodstain. There was nothing else we could do.

He then marched out, heading for the truck. I was behind him and was already outside, in the loading area, when I saw it – lying on one of the steel counters, too close to the loaves not to be suspicious. An oversized paintbrush, too large and crude to be used for glazing pastries. In all the haste to rinse out and hide the mixing bowls, clearing them of arsenic, as well as filling our bags with the empty bottles that had once contained poison, someone had forgotten the biggest and most obvious piece of equipment. I rushed back and grabbed it and when I turned around I saw our leader, now crouching with the others in the back of the truck, aiming his pistol at me.

I realized then that if I had taken even a second longer he would have shot me in the back. Any further delay caused by me would have been simply too costly: better to kill me and leave me on site. It would not even have looked suspicious. The apprentice boy killed in the course of an armed robbery on a bakery. That, after all, was our cover story.

The Americans would untie the workers and draw the obvious conclusion. Armed thieves had come to steal the sacks of flour and sugar and huge quantities of yeast they knew were held within, filling their truck with the hoard and making off just before the Americans arrived at dawn. It would be no great surprise. Foodstuffs and raw materials fetched a good price on the German black market of 1946. The workers, gasping for breath and nursing the welts on their wrists, would tell them all about it. 'It was an inside job,' the manager would say. 'That little Polish bastard let them in.'

The others would explain how the robbers had taken their time, stripping the place of everything that had value. The Americans would offer consolation, shake their heads at the loss of such costly resources and, perhaps, call for a military policeman to come and investigate. But they would not be diverted from the task of the morning. They had thousands of men to feed in Stalag 13 and – yes, look over here – as luck would have it, the intruders came in after baking time. The loaves are all here, stacked and ready for loading: the bread, at least, they did not steal. Well, our sympathies, gentlemen, but we need to be on our way.

That, anyway, was the plan, dreamed up by the Frenchman and pushed and pulled, kneaded and twisted, over weeks and weeks more thoroughly than any loaf I ever made in that bakery. Aron attacked the plan from every angle, each day thinking of new objections. But once he had thought of answers for everything – Rosa for the night-watchman, Manik for his corpse – he had decided that it was the only way. We would commit one commonplace crime – common at least in the chaos that was Germany after the war – in order to commit a much greater, more noble crime. One that was not, of course, a crime at all.

The truck travelled south, where Manik found a deserted spot to hide it. We would be fine so long as no one found the truck, or connected it with the robbery in Nuremberg, until it was too late. It would be a mystery why black market thieves had simply abandoned such precious booty, but that was a mystery we could live with. Besides, that little puzzle would be a perfect decoy, a false trail that would delay anybody coming after us.

The rest of us got out a few miles from the bakery and simply waited by the roadside: the city was already waking up by then, men making their way to the morning shift and, before long, a couple of taxis came by. We got in and Aron handed the driver a wad of notes and told him to take us to the Czechoslovak border.

Only Rosa stayed behind, to do one last job. Once more she had to act, but this time she would not play a slut or a whore. Instead she simply had to wander among the quiet, residential streets that surrounded Stalag 13, homes rented by the wives of the Nazis waiting to stand trial. She would pretend to be just such a wife as she stopped to ask women whether the rumours were true, that many of the prisoners had suddenly been taken ill. Some of these loyal maidens of the Reich stood sobbing with her, as they told her she was right: the hospital was full of their brave men. The doctors couldn't cope, more men were admitted than they could treat, all of them suddenly struck down by the same terrible plague. 'What is it?' Rosa would ask. A complete mystery. Food poisoning, the Americans said, but who knew whether to believe them. But it was serious. 'I don't want to worry you, dear, but some of the men seem close to death.'

Rosa reported all this back to us, together with whatever scraps of information she could pick up. She had broken off with the mess sergeant a few weeks earlier. I liked to think that was because she had extracted all the information we needed and she ran from him as soon as she could. But I think Aron had told her to do it: if they were still together, he might become suspicious.

And, eventually, there were official accounts, in the newspapers and so on. We didn't believe every word: we knew they were censored and suspected the Americans would want to cover up what had happened. If they had not managed to protect the men they were holding, it did not look so good.

But the reports, including Rosa's, left no doubt. The poisoned loaves had got through and the Nazis, in their thousands, had eaten them. How many had died? We never knew for sure. It might have been three hundred or seven hundred. It might have been a thousand or even several thousand. Aron said the exact number did not matter. What was important was that the Nazis held in Nuremberg would have understood and, eventually, the world would have understood, too, that the Jews had not accepted their fate, but had come back to claim their revenge. That the story of Stalag 13 would live on and that no one could say again that we had been sheep to the slaughter.

I tried to accept what Aron said but I cannot lie. I wanted to know, and I never stopped wanting to know, even years and years later, exactly how many Nazis had tasted that bread I had helped bake, that bread I had helped poison, how many had tasted it and died from it. I wanted to know if their death was painful. Above all, I wanted to know that among the thousands or hundreds or even dozens dead, was the man who killed my Hannah, my Leah and my Rivvy, my sisters.

# CHAPTER THIRTY-EIGHT

Jay Sherrill wanted nothing more than to sit down. The information from Agent Marcus Mack of the New York Police Department Intelligence Division was coming too fast to take in, at least too fast to take in like this, walking on a busy Manhattan street in late afternoon, jostled by shoppers and commuters and street vendors, pretending to talk into a cellphone, unable even to look his source in the eye. This was not how Detective Sherrill liked doing business.

'So when you say, from the beginning, you mean from the beginning.'

'Uh-huh. Reckon I was the first agent put on it. In the morning, anyway. Obviously surveillance had been monitoring him since the previous night.'

'When he met the Russian?'

'Right.'

'And they put that together with his location—'

'Near the UN.'

'—and on that basis he became a suspect. A terror suspect.'

'Which is why I was following him.'

'And you say there was another man, another agent?'

'At least one.'

'What do you mean, "at least"?'

'Well, I know for certain there was one other guy, because I saw him when we got to UN Plaza. We saw each other; we both had the same reaction.'

'But?'

'But my handler said, when I asked whether there was back-up, "There's a team". Now, he coulda been shitting me, they're not above that, these guys.' For a fleeting second, Mack eyed Sherrill, at his left, then looked forward again as he kept walking. 'You know what I mean, Detective? Saying "there's a team" when really they mean, there's you and me – we're the team. So it may have just been me and this other guy, the one I saw when I got there.'

'Did you speak to him, this other agent?'

'Yes and no.'

'What does that mean? Oh, excuse me, sorry.' A woman carrying a cappuccino-to-go, and also talking into a cellphone, had banged into him and, naturally, he had been the one to apologize.

'It means we didn't exactly have a conversation, but we spoke.'

'To each other? To someone else? Who?'

'No, we said something at the same time. That's

when I realized. Look: back up a second. Remember, I told you that when I got to the Plaza, I could no longer tail the guy, because he had entered another jurisdiction? He was on UN turf so I just had to hang back?'

Sherrill nodded.

'OK. So I watched what happened. I saw the suspect walk into the centre of the Plaza, kinda looking around and then I see the UN guard reach for his weapon. And exactly at that moment, the suspect turns around and faces my direction. And that's when I see it. What I hadn't been able to see the entire time I was tailing the guy.'

'You saw his face.'

'Exactly. I saw his face. And I realized it instantly, the mistake we had made. I mean this guy was old, really old. There was no way he was a terrorist. He was a senior. And I know what's happening here. The guard's had the warning, the description, and this old man fits it perfectly. Black hat, black coat. He fits it. And he's just got our warning, my warning, that the suspect is about to enter UN territory and so he's reaching for his weapon. He's thinking to himself, I got Muhammad Atta here, I gotta blow him away.'

'So you try to stop him?'

'I try and stop him from shooting. I wanna shout, "You got the wrong guy!" Now that I've seen his face, I know he's the wrong guy. But there's no time. The only word that comes out is "No!"'

'And at the same time, another man does the exact same thing.'

'Right. The same word at the same moment. And that's how I know that that guy, maybe five yards from me down the street, is also a cop, an intel agent. Because he's realized what's going on, same way I have.'

Jay clenched his teeth. He was remembering Felipe Tavares's testimony two days ago. Why had he started shooting? 'Because of the faces of those men I saw. The way they looked so shocked, and the black man screaming "No!" like he was desperate.'

'The black man he saw, that was you,' Sherrill murmured.

'What's that?'

'Nothing.' Sherrill was turning it over: Tavares had worked it out afterwards, when it was too late, after the bullet was already plunged deep inside Gerald Merton's chest. Only then had he understood that the black man, and the white man near him, had been trying to stop not a bomber but him, Felipe Tavares, from shooting an innocent man.

'Did you talk to the other agent?'

'No. We kinda looked at each other, as if we both understood. Then we did what the rules say you do in that situation.'

'Which is?'

'You scoot. Opposite directions. You never want to make contact, not if you're both undercover. Could blow it for both of you.'

Sherrill remembered his last exchange with Tavares, how the security guard had said that both men had vanished. 'OK,' he said, unsure where to move next. 'And you've been thinking about this ever since?'

'You could say that. Look, it was me who called in that the "suspect" had moved into UN Plaza. And it was me who freaked out the UN guy by shouting "No". It was those two things that made him think he was dealing with a suicide bomber.'

'So you feel guilty.'

'The word I would use is *responsible*. That's what I am, responsible. And it's not just me. That's what you gotta understand. I was only on this guy's tail because we had intel on him connecting him with the Russian and all that bullshit. So it ain't just me who's responsible here, you know what I'm saying?'

'Who else?'

'Who do you think? I'm talking about the New York Police Department Intelligence Division, that's who. I can see what's going on here. I've noticed how Intel have suddenly gone very quiet. They're not saying a word, nah-uh. Letting a few fucking Belgians over at the UN take the rap. Well, that, my friend, ain't right. And I don't intend to let them get away with it.'

## CHAPTER THIRTY-NINE

Tom was staring. Not, for once, at Rebecca, but at a man sitting two seats away from her.

There was no reason to gawp. He was just a guy tapping away at a computer screen. But something about him had stopped Tom short. He seemed out of place here; too well dressed, not poor enough . . .

They were in an internet café on Kingsland High Street, just a few hundred yards from Julian Goldman's shabby legal aid practice and only a ten minute walk from the Brenner Centre, home of the near-senile Sid Steiner.

It had been Tom's idea to come here. They could hardly go back to Rebecca's flat, he had said: whoever was pursuing them could be there, waiting. It was a risk even to use his computer there: their stalkers would doubtless be able to hack into it and see whatever they were seeing.

So he had suggested coming to this place. 'Internet café' was not quite an accurate description. Coffee was available from a sorry-looking vending machine in one corner, a mess of sachets, crusted sugar and discarded stirrers. But otherwise it looked no different from any other shabby shop, the display window entirely covered in stickers promoting discounted rates for calls to Nigeria, Sierra Leone and Addis Ababa. One wall was divided up into telephone booths, each partitioned off by the flimsiest, palest, plastic imitation of wood. They were all full, the soundproofing so basic that the babble of conversation, in a dozen different languages, was loud and constant. Inside were young men, none older than thirty-five, Tom reckoned. He could imagine the longing expressed in these phone-calls to wives, mothers and children back home, people whose livelihoods depended on cash remittances sent from London and whose hope depended on these phone calls. The sound of it was unmistakable. It was the sound of desperation.

The terminals were all in use too, with pretty much the same clientele. Tom's years at the UN meant he could make a pretty good guess at the range of nationalities gathered in the room: Kenyan, Somali, Sudanese would have been his initial estimate. Their presence here said something depressing about their presence in London: that they had not come anywhere close to settling in, that everything they cared about was elsewhere. They were like landless people, just passing through, and this place, this internet café, was a way station.

All except for the one white man, two seats away from them.

Rebecca began with a cursory check of her email, Tom watching over her shoulder, trying to sniff out any sign of a boyfriend. It was a deluge of condolence messages, mainly from acquaintances as far as he could tell. She clicked her way through them, then called up NYTimes.com, finding the page which promised to open up the archive of *The New York Times*.

'All right,' Rebecca said, her fingers hovering over the keyboard.

'Now remember,' Tom whispered, conscious of the man close by. 'He told us the date. April 13th 1946. So let's start with that.'

'It wants keywords.'

'Try "Nuremberg, poison".'

She typed the words in slowly, with two fingers.

*Your search for Nuremberg, poison in all fields returned 0 results.*

Tom bit his lip. 'Try Nuremberg, SS, deaths.'

*Your search for Nuremberg, SS, deaths in all fields returned 0 results.*

They tried Stalag 13, bakery, loaves. Still nothing.

'Look,' Rebecca said at last. 'Steiner's memory is shot. What are the chances he'd remember an exact date?' She keyed in a new entry in the date field, suggesting not a single day, but a range of a week: April 12th to April 19th.

Nothing.

Tom fell back into his hard plastic chair. Maybe they'd got excited over no more than a daydream spun by an old man who no longer knew the word for a jug.

Rebecca's face suggested she had arrived at the same state of resignation: a lead had become a dead end. She reached around her chair to collect her coat.

Tom's eye scrolled down the screen, looking at the other stories on the page, none of them even close to what they were looking for. He clicked on one at random, marvelling as the screen filled up with words written from the heart of occupied Europe more than six decades ago. He was about to click on the red circle that would close down the browser altogether: he had decided he would leave no details on screen, where they could be glimpsed. He shot another look at the man he'd noticed when they first walked in: if he was watching them, he was doing a good job of concealing it.

Just as Tom's cursor hovered over the red circle, a phrase leapt out at him: 'This report filed by arrangement with the military censor.'

Of course. News from occupied Europe did not come out instantly. This was not the age of cable TV, satellite feeds and the internet. News crawled out back then, delayed by technology and military authorities who filtered out anything they didn't like.

Now he sat in Rebecca's chair, still warm from her. He repeated the keywords – Nuremberg, poison – but this time keyed in a three-month range for the dates, March to May. Five items filled the screen, each headline fascinating. There was a story datelined Munich from April 24th – *Nazis in Bavaria Regaining Position; Hitler Youth Aide in Key Job* – and another from Frankfurt: *Haushofer, Hitler's 'Geopolitician', Commits Suicide With His Wife*. But it was the first and second items that drew in Tom almost instantly. He clicked on the first.

> **Poison Bread Fells 1,900 German Captives in US Army Prison Camp Near Nuremberg**
> April 20th 1946, Saturday
> Page 6, 351 words
> FRANKFORT ON THE MAIN, Germany, April 19 (AP) – Nineteen hundred German prisoners of war were poisoned by arsenic in their bread early this week in a United States camp and all are 'seriously ill', United States headquarters announced tonight.

Tom turned to Rebecca whose eyes were growing wider with each sentence she read. And now he clicked on the second item, filed three days later:

> **Poison Plot Toll of Nazis at Stalag 13: 2,283**
> Arsenic Bottles Found by US Agents in Nuremberg Bakery that Served Prison Camp
> April 23rd 1946, Tuesday
> Page 9, 347 words

NUREMBERG, Germany, April 22 (AP) – United States Army authorities said tonight that additional German prisoners of war have been stricken with arsenic poisoning, bringing to 2,283 the number taken ill in a mysterious plot against 15,000 former Nazi elite guardsmen confined in a camp near Nuremberg.

# CHAPTER FORTY

He hesitated before suggesting a return to her father's flat. Hard enough to be among the worldly remains of a dead parent: harder still to be in a place that had been trashed, a subliminal reminder that her father had not been allowed to die an old man's death, but had been murdered.

Besides, it was making things easy for their pursuers, returning to a place they had already targeted. And yet he knew there was a flaw in that logic. For if they had intended to kill them, why had they not simply come out and done it? It couldn't be moral scruple: the corpse of Henry Goldman was testament to that. Nor could it be lack of guile: whoever was after them was patently efficient enough to have followed their movements over the last twenty-four hours, to have bugged their meeting with Goldman so precisely that they had managed to terminate it at the crucial moment and, for all he knew, to be aware of everything they had discovered since.

He and Rebecca Merton were clearly enemies of somebody, but those people had not shown themselves or made any demand. Tom's best guess was that he and Gershon Matzkin's daughter had become like the Russian arms-dealer in Brighton Beach. Their job was to play it out, to do whatever they were doing so that those watching could watch. Were they meant to lead them somewhere? Were they meant to find out something these men didn't already know? Could that explain the envelope that had mysteriously arrived at Rebecca's apartment yesterday? Was that the gesture of an enemy or a friend?

As they left the internet café, hopping on the 76 bus, Rebecca took the decision out of his hands. 'The answer is somewhere in his flat, I'm sure of it.'

'They've turned it upside down. Don't you think that if there was something there, they'd have found it?'

'No. That's why it was so trashed. Because they hadn't found it. If they had, they wouldn't have needed to start slashing cushions.'

Tom was about to say that made no sense, when Rebecca's phone rang. He sat up. She looked at the display and shook her head: not connected with this.

'Nick, hi. No problem, I can talk.' She nodded. 'OK, that sounds good. Let's hope her luck's beginning to change. Check to make sure she's still in remission, change out her lines, and let the transplant team know she's a go. We can tee up her brother's harvest for next week. Speak soon.'

Tom was only half listening. He was concentrating instead on a man in his twenties who had just boarded the bus, wearing iPod headphones. Tom was trying to see if they were plugged into a music player or something else.

Rebecca put aside her phone and resumed her argument with Tom precisely where she had left off. 'Anyway, there's nothing else we can do. We don't have a Plan B.' Even then, despite everything, that 'we' warmed him.

And so they made their return visit to Kyverdale Road, to see if there was something that, no matter how improbably, had been overlooked by the burglars. The pair of them tiptoed around the place, picking up every remaining photograph, peering inside every ornament, including the broken ones. Rebecca stayed in the bedroom, working through her father's jackets, probing into each pocket. Tom went, methodically, through the old man's books, shaking each one by the spine just in case some long-forgotten note from 1946 would tumble out.

All the while he was thinking of what had happened in that room just a few hours earlier. Not just the sex, but the way she had finally dropped her guard in the minutes afterwards. She had felt guilty about it all, to be sure, but if he could choose to be anywhere in the world, Tom decided, he would choose to be inside that moment once more, the two of them together and naked, telling the truth.

He was flicking through the pages of an *Antiques Roadshow Compendium* for 1981 when he came across something: yellowing, handwritten and impossible to understand. Tom could make out no more than a few of the letters. All he could tell for certain was that these were not regular English words. Perhaps they were names, German names.

'Rebecca! Come here!'

She ran from the bedroom and was by his side in seconds. She took the paper from him, bringing it closer to her eyes for deciphering. Tom was breathing faster.

Finally, she turned towards him with a smile. 'These are names all right. May even be German. Trouble is, these are the names of dry-cleaning fluids. This is one of my dad's old shopping lists.'

Tom scrunched it up and fell into a chair with his eyes closed. When he opened them Rebecca was staring at him coldly.

'Not that one.'

'What?'

'Don't sit there.'

'Why not?'

'That's Dad's chair.'

Tom immediately leapt up, and tried to pretend the moment hadn't happened. 'So what do we know?'

'We know that my father, Sid Steiner, Goldman and the others from DIN went round killing Nazis.

They did it in two phases, straight after the war in occupied Germany and then again in the fifties and sixties all over the world, Europe, South America, everywhere. And now we know that their biggest operation was at the Nuremberg bakery, where they may have killed thousands of Nazis.'

'OK.'

'What we need to work out is why any of that would matter now. Even if DIN was out to kill one last Nazi – which is obviously what you suspect my father was doing in New York – that's over now. My father was . . . stopped.' She paused. 'And he was the last one. He was always the youngest. There's no one after him. Goldman wasn't going to do anything. So why kill him? Why do all this?' She was gesturing at the scene of destruction in the flat.

'To stop the name getting out,' Tom said. 'Maybe it's a Nazi everyone's forgotten. Or he's got a false name. Or your father knew his address. If I was a Nazi and I knew Gerald Merton had been coming to get me, I'd also want to make sure he hadn't left any clues behind.'

'No, that can't be it,' Rebecca said, biting her lower lip. 'Goldman had something else to tell us, remember.'

'Might have been the name.'

'What, and this geriatric Nazi has been spying on us, breaking into my house, tearing up—'

'You can get people to do these things.' Tom sat up. 'What's that?'

'Oh.' Rebecca turned to face the picture in the hallway. Barely lit in the windowless space, and obscured by the coat-rack, was an abstract painting, a formless collection of greys and blacks at least three feet wide and two feet tall, the paint piled on thick. Tom had not paid attention to it before. Nor, it seemed, had the intruders: it didn't appear to have been touched.

'Rosa did that. I think it was the only thing my father had left of hers. I hated it as a child, so dark and depressing. My mother hated it too. She'd only let him have it in the basement.'

'But when he had his own place, he hung it on the wall. That's interesting, isn't it?'

'Maybe he felt he owed her something, I don't know.' Rebecca moved closer to the painting. 'As a child I always resented the idea of Rosa: you know, "the woman who came before mummy" and all that. But you look at this and realize what an awful life she had. When she died, she was younger than I am now.'

'What's it called? The painting.'

'It's called Aleph. See the grey lines, they just about make the shape of an Aleph. The first letter of the Hebrew alphabet.'

'Right.'

The two of them stood there, gazing at it, the shape of the letter now obvious. Tom was trying to imagine the world these two young-old people, a boy and a girl, inhabited those sixty years ago. A world of massacres and constant death and cruelty which, they believed, could only be redeemed by more death. He imagined Gershon in the bakery, doubtless praying that the tainted bread would touch the lips of the man who had murdered his beloved sisters.

And then it struck him, an idea thudding into his brain with such force he could barely grasp it.

He turned to Rebecca, grabbing her arm. 'What was it you said before, when we were arguing about coming here? On the bus.'

'I said that we had to come, we might have overlooked something—'

'Not that, something else, keep going.'

'I said, we didn't have any other option—'

'That's it!'

'—we had no plan B.'

'Exactly! That's it: Plan B. What happened at the bakery wasn't the main operation after all. It was Plan B. That's what Sid called it.'

'I thought B was for bakery.'

'So did I. *Brot,* German for bread; or *Bäckerei* for bakery. Remember, that's what I said to Sid. "B for bakery". And he said "No. Wrong again". I thought that was the dementia, but when he was talking about the bakery operation he was perfectly lucid. He even remembered the exact date! Don't you see, he was telling the truth. Of course he was. Think about it, why would all these Jews from Poland and Lithuania use German for an operation's codename? They wouldn't. They would use Hebrew, just like they did with the name of their organization. Goldman told us, DIN was Hebrew for judgment. What's the Hebrew for bread?'

'*Lechem.*'

'Right. No "b" there. And what's the second letter of the Hebrew alphabet?'

'*Bet.*'

'You see! Plan Bet. Plan B. And it was called Plan B because it was plan b. It was the fallback plan.'

'So what was the main plan?'

Tom smiled. 'Plan A.'

'Oh, well done, Sherlock.'

'Or rather, as I think DIN might have called it, Plan Aleph.'

Slowly, they both turned to contemplate Rosa's assemblage of baleful blacks and night-time greys.

## CHAPTER FORTY-ONE

They took the painting down as carefully as their impatience would allow. One holding each end, they carried it into the centre of the room, where they leaned it in a forty-five degree angle against a chair.

They had already examined the picture microscopically, looking at it from an inch away, studying the thick accretions of oil paint, searching for clues – but they had found nothing.

Rebecca had returned from the kitchen with a steak knife and set about scraping the paint away from random sections of the canvas. Tom tried to divine whether the fierce energy she brought to the task was the urgent desire to see what the picture might conceal – or simply a long-repressed fury at the painting and indeed the artist who had created it. For all her efforts, they had found nothing, just the smudged blankness of the canvas underneath.

Now they were looking at the back. It had been expensively framed, with a thick wooden border, the canvas secured at the rear by copious amounts of binding tape. Tom took the knife from Rebecca and slowly sliced around the edge. He half-expected the picture to pop out, but it had been in too long for that. He began removing the tape, layers of it, soon realizing that the back was not the back of the canvas after all, merely a mounting that bulged out by a good quarter of an inch. He would have to remove this too.

He fought the urge simply to slice through the layers of cardboard backing, operating more gingerly instead. Eventually the surrounding tape was gone and he could see the edge of the card. Slowly, he lifted it off.

The second he had, they could both see his work had not been in vain. Stuck to the back of the painting, not glued but pressed there by time, was a set of papers. His hands trembling, Tom reached in and peeled them loose.

There were five sheets inside, all roughly the same size, about A3. When Tom turned the first one over, he almost pulled back in surprise. It was not what he was expecting – a photograph or a list of names that would at last unlock this mystery – but a drawing, something between a map and an architect's blueprint. The next was not identical but similar and so was the next and the next.

'What the hell are these?' he said, but Rebecca was too stunned to answer. Of all the revelations about her father, this one seemed to have blindsided her most.

Tom stared hard at the first drawing. He wondered

if it was an old-fashioned electrical diagram, a sketch for a circuit board perhaps. Then he wondered if it was, perhaps, a map of an underground railway; it certainly seemed to depict pathways and routes.

He looked more closely, his eye now just a matter of inches from the paper, close enough to smell the must. In a tiny hand, he could see numbers written at various intervals. They were, he decided, measurements.

And then Rebecca spoke. 'Of course,' she said quietly.

'What is it?' Tom said, his voice rising. 'What?'

'Do you remember from the notebook, how Rosa and the others escaped? From the ghetto?'

Tom shook his head. That would have been in the section he had skimmed, the pages dealing with the final stages of the war, the flight into the forests awaiting the arrival of the Red Army. The first mention of Rosa Tom could remember was when she and Gershon became lovers, which would have been long after she had broken free of the ghetto.

'Sewers. Rosa and the others, the leaders of the resistance – they all got out on the last day of the liquidation of the ghetto. The Jews were being rounded up and sent to the camps. But the resistance always had a plan for the last day, when there could be no more fighting back.

'So Rosa and the rest, they went down into the ground. Not my father. He was already on the road by then, spreading the word. But later Rosa told him what had happened. And he told me.

'The stench down there was just terrible. It had been raining that day and apparently that made it worse. And the pipes were so narrow, not much wider than their bodies, that they had to crawl through all that shit and piss on their hands and knees. And then, in some places, the pipes got even smaller, so they had to slither along on their stomachs – tilting their heads back just to gasp at the few inches of air. The liquid was giving off all kinds of gas; people were fainting. Not Rosa, though. She just pressed on. That's what she said anyway.

'They did that for nearly two miles, until they got to an opening outside the ghetto walls where two fighters from the Communist underground were waiting to pull them out.'

'And so—'

'It took a lot of work. There was one senior member of the resistance who had been working on it for months, mapping every inch, every tunnel, every manhole cover. The sewers weren't just an escape route; the resistance used them for smuggling too, bringing in weapons. Plenty of people died down there: some were overwhelmed by the stench; others simply got lost.'

The words were just flowing out of her now, as if on a tape recorded long ago, waiting to be played back. For a moment, Tom could see Rebecca as a child, listening intently in the darkness to bedtime tales of resistance, heroism and war. She seemed to have memorized every word.

'So these—'

'These must be the maps of the sewers.'

Tom looked hard at the maps which, he now realized, were indeed hand-drawn. He ran his fingertips across the paper. What an extraordinary document this was. Not just a precisely rendered map but a testament to an almost superhuman resourcefulness. And to think that, according to the late Henry Goldman at least, even the most senior of these people, these warriors, had not been a day over twenty-five years old.

But now, as he squinted at every inch of the paper, he examined more closely what had seemed to be a pattern, a printed stamp, in the bottom right-hand corner. Now he could see that it was not a printed badge at all but a block made up of words, written in a tiny, fine-point script. He could decipher none of them, except for one in block capitals: NURNBERG. He looked in the same place on the next map. München. The next three were Weimar, Hamburg and Wannsee, a suburb of Berlin.

He gestured for Rebecca to take a look and her brow instantly furrowed. 'I don't understand.'

'Your father was never in those places, was he?' Tom hesitated. 'I mean, there were no ghettoes in Germany itself, were there? The Nazis kicked the Jews out and set up the camps and the ghettoes in Eastern Europe, right?'

'Yes.'

They both stared at the diagrams trying to decipher their meaning. Tom regrouped and spoke again. 'But we do know that they were there after the war. We know that he was in Nuremberg.' He pointed at the Nuremberg drawing. 'And we know that this, all of this, somehow relates to Plan A. That's why it was hidden in the painting.'

But Rebecca was no longer listening. Something in the pile of discarded binding and paper had caught her eye. It was stuck so flat as to be barely visible, but taped to the backing board was a square of card whose edges had turned almost yellow. With great care she pulled at one corner, feeling the tug of adhesive as it came away. She moved slowly, as if she knew that to move too rapidly was to risk losing whatever buried message from the past was contained here.

She turned it over and Tom found himself staring at a line of random squiggles, half-squares and incomplete hieroglyphs which looked like no language he had ever seen.

'What is it?'

Rebecca was gazing at it intently. 'It's either one or the other.'

'I don't understand.'

'The characters I recognize,' she said. 'I'm just not sure of the language.'

The noise of the TV was even more distracting now, but it was his own fault. He had turned up the volume as soon as Rebecca had realized the postcard carried a message: if someone was listening, now was the time to stop them. But the background chatter of a daytime soap made concentration all but impossible.

Tom prided himself on his facility for languages. Even those he couldn't speak, he could at least recognize – he knew his Korean from his Thai – and he would have liked to think he could have identified a sentence of Hebrew when it was set down in front of him. But Rebecca had had to explain that the printed alphabet was not the same as the script used in everyday handwriting: the shape of each character was vaguely related, but not identical. Even to someone who would recognize a bible printed in Hebrew, a sentence of Hebrew handwriting could look like a string of corrupted computer icons.

Although Rebecca could make out each character, she wasn't sure she could do much more. 'I can just about read Hebrew,' she said, adding that she had endured basic Hebrew classes as a child. 'Kind of like Jewish Sunday school.'

'So what's the problem?'

'The problem is, this might not be Hebrew. It could be Yiddish.'

'I thought Yiddish was like German.'

'It is, mostly. But it's written in Hebrew characters.'

Tom had to smile at that. Yiddish was surely tailor-made for undercover communication. A German might understand it if he heard it, but he would not be able to make head or tail of the written version. How many non-Jews knew the Hebrew alphabet at all, let alone in this hand-written form? Almost none. It meant DIN would have had no need of cryptography: their own language, written down, was sufficient.

'OK,' Rebecca said finally. 'This much I've worked out. It says, *Fargess nicht*!'

'OK, said Tom. 'That's simple enough. That means "Don't forget".'

She read on. '*Yir-mee-ya . . .Yirmiyahu*! It's a name: Yirmiyahu, like Jeremiah.'

'Keep going.'

'*Yirmiyahu vet zine* – and now there's the number twenty-three – then there's the word *dem* and then another number, fifteen. And then it finishes with another exclamation: *Lomir zich freien!*'

'*Lomir zich freien*. It's some kind of exhortation, like "Come let's party, come celebrate". Read the whole thing again.'

'*Fargess nicht! Yirmiyahu vet zine* twenty-three *dem* fifteen. *Lomir zich frein*.'

'Don't forget, Jeremiah turns twenty-three on the fifteenth. Let's celebrate!'

Rebecca shook her head. 'Don't tell me all we've got is a party invitation.'

Tom got up to pace, but it was no good. Finally he marched over to the TV set and stabbed at the off button. In the quiet, perhaps twenty seconds later, it came to him. 'Oh, that's very neat. Very neat indeed.'

'What's neat?'

'Do you remember, in your dad's notebook, the message they gave him to take to the other ghettoes?' Just as Rebecca was about to answer, Tom placed a finger over his lips – and turned the TV back on.

'"Aunt Esther has returned and is at Megilla Street 7, apartment 4".' She paused. 'Oh, I see.'

'We need a Bible.'

It took them a while, wading through the rubble of books and junk heaped on the floor, but eventually they found one, a volume much larger than the Bibles Tom was used to. Not that he was an expert: his militantly atheist father had always refused to have 'that sodding book' in the house, since it had only brought 'misery to millions'. This was perhaps twice the size of a hotel-room Bible, as large as a volume of an encyclopedia.

Rebecca turned the pages hesitantly, eventually turning back two pages, then forward one, like someone narrowing down to a single reference in a dictionary. 'Here we go. The Book of Jeremiah, Chapter 23, Verse 15.'

'Read it.'

Tracing each word with her finger, she read aloud: '"Therefore, this is what the Lord Almighty says concerning the prophets: 'I will make them eat bitter food and drink poisoned water, because from the prophets of Jerusalem ungodliness has spread throughout the land'".'

# CHAPTER FORTY-TWO

**Nuremberg, 1945**

Aron never wanted me to be part of it: he did not believe I had enough hate inside me.

In the autumn of 1945 he told me that DIN was over, that from now on, justice would be up to the courts and the lawyers. We were to put down our guns and grenades and head off to the next front in the war for Jewish survival: Palestine. The British masters of the country were keeping a tight lid on Jewish immigration so entry would not be easy, but an underground network would smuggle us in. Another war was coming: the new Jewish homeland would not come without a struggle – against the British, against the Arabs – and the Jews would need all the soldiers they could get. I was barely fifteen but I counted as a veteran.

I was ready to leave when Aron called me in to see him. He asked me, for the first time, about my family and how they had been killed. I told him how my father had been burned to death in his own barn by a mob. How my mother had hanged herself the day the Nazis arrived in Lithuania. Finally I told him about my sisters, shot into the pits at the Ninth Fort.

I did not cry as I told my story and he nodded, saying nothing. When I finished, he stared at me for many minutes, occasionally rubbing his chin. Eventually, in a quiet voice, he told me I should stay in Europe, that DIN had one last mission for me. I must have persuaded him that I had enough hate to be trusted.

There was never any briefing. To keep the plan secret, Aron told each of us only what we needed to know. It took me some time to put the pieces together so that I could see the entire picture.

It began with the Frenchman, then idling in post-liberation Paris. He ran into a former resistance fighter, a scientist, who told him the greatest threat in the second half of the twentieth century would not be the mighty atomic bomb but something much smaller, a weapon that could be carried in a briefcase. It would not be deployed on the traditional battlefield, but on the morning commuter train or in a theatre or in a soft drinks factory. Poison, that was the weapon of the future.

The Frenchman's curiosity was piqued. Discreetly, he began his own inquiries, speaking to chemists who told him of toxins that retained their potency even when mixed with great volumes of water. It was in those conversations that Tochnit Aleph, Plan A, was born.

The day after Aron had told me that I should stay in Europe he sent me for what he called 'training', with a man I had not met before, a Jew from Palestine. He came from Germany but had left in the middle of the nineteen thirties. The moment I knew this about him, I hated him. What did he know of DIN and of vengeance, this man who had saved his own skin and got out early? I felt superior towards him and jealous of him, all at the same time.

But I had to keep silent and be his pupil. He introduced himself only as 'the Engineer' and it turned out that he was a real engineer, an expert in construction and so on.

Within one minute of meeting me, he threatened to walk out. 'It's absurd to teach you these things, you are a child!' But Aron's orders were final and so he taught me.

He spread out a number of complex blueprints on the table. They seemed to show pathways or underground tunnels. He explained that this was the water system for the city of Nuremberg. And that I was to seek employment with the Department of Filtration.

'But I don't—'

'I know. You know nothing. That's what I'm here to teach you.'

And so this engineer taught me to speak of regularized pressures, saline clearance and filtration residues. At night, one of the DIN commanders drilled me in German, ironing out weaknesses in my vocabulary and accent. In these night classes, we devised yet another cover story – that my late father was Polish and that we had lived some time in the east – to explain any lapses.

I was handed a set of forged papers, including documents showing sterling service in the Hitler Youth and then the Wehrmacht. We worked out the youngest age that would be compatible with this life story and decided that I was eighteen. Luckily, I was not just blond, blue-eyed and uncircumcised, but also tall for my age.

On all this I was tested and tested again. 'Where were you born?'

'Leipzig, sir!'

'What was your mother's maiden name?'

'Fischer, sir!'

'What was the name of your troop in the Hitler Jugend?'

After six weeks of this, Aron arrived one night at midnight. He examined my papers, walked around me, inspecting the suit I would wear for the job interview, and finally said, 'Apply for the job tomorrow.'

My palms were sweating as I sat in the waiting room. Even though I had done it so often, I never got used to lying. I was summoned by a young secretary who, I noticed, swayed her hips more than was necessary as she walked in front of me, then gave me a smile over her shoulder. If only she knew, I thought, that I am only fifteen years old. If only she knew that I would not hesitate to strangle her brother, her father or even her if I had even the slightest reason to do it.

The interview was mainly about my war service. The boss was in his early fifties and had missed the draft himself: he was envious of me, blessed with a chance to serve the Fatherland. I nodded but did not smile. I let him think I was a hardened soldier, too tough to chit-chat. As with most weak men, that only made him talk more. And at the end of it, he said how much he had enjoyed our conversation, even though I had said next to nothing. He told me to start at the beginning of the following week.

I still did not know what I was supposed to do. The commanders had told me nothing. Dressed in the overalls of a lab technician, I checked pressure gauges, lowered dipsticks and entered figures onto a form attached to a clipboard – and wondered what it was all for. You may ask whether, when I did understand, I ever questioned it. But the thing no one can appreciate, not unless you saw what we saw, is how deep our hatred had become. It was larger than any of us; we could swim in it and sink into it and we knew it would endure long after we had gone.

Who did we hate? We hated the people who could pick up a screaming baby by his ankles and smash his infant skull against a brick wall. We hated the people who could herd human beings into fetid, medieval streets and starve them to death so that their corpses would be chewed by stray dogs. We hated the people who told us we were to be resettled in the east, tricking us into train trucks that were built for cattle, then separating us – to the left and to the right – making themselves angels of death, deciding by the ramp of a just-arrived train still exhaling steam, who should live and who should die. We hated the people who beat us and whipped us and pushed us, our children and our elderly, into concrete shower-rooms, saying they were 'delousing' us because we were infected like so many flea-bitten animals – still lying even at the very end – and watching us as we waited for the cleansing water that never came, watching through a spy hole as the gas generated by a canister of Zyklon B gas hissed into the room, the men and women and the young inside climbing over each other to get to what they thought, in their desperation, might be an opening in the ceiling or high up in the wall, a source of unpoisoned, breathable air. We hated the people who would pull the rings from our fingers and the gold from our teeth, who would melt them down for the money they could make. We hated the people who would tear the clothes off the backs of our dead, sending them home to be worn by their own wives, sons and daughters. We hated the people who, once they had mined the wealth from our very flesh, shovelled us into incinerators, choking from the ash that could rise up and descend like snowfall for miles around. We hated them for their plan to remove us from the face of the earth, to smash our gravestones and to rip out the wombs of our women so that today's generation would be the last. We hated them for their insatiable hatred of us.

When a man burns with a rage as white-hot as this rage, made hotter still by the knowledge that the rest of the world is ready to shrug its shoulders and move on – he is prepared to do almost anything. If it will sate this fury, he is ready to do it. As I was ready to do it.

This is what Aron must have seen in me. He must have seen that mine were the eyes of a man who had seen his own blood spilled too often. Because he trusted that when I discovered the truth of Tochnit Aleph I would not hesitate.

And he was right. When I finally understood that DIN's plan was to poison the water supply not only from the plant where I worked in Nuremberg but in four other German cities – Munich, Hamburg, Weimar and the Wannsee suburb of Berlin – I did not baulk. I understood that we were going to kill at the turn of a tap, making no distinction between active Nazi and ordinary German citizen, no distinction between direct war criminal and silent bystander, no distinction between adult male and young child, no distinction between the guilty and the innocent. We were, in other words, to do to them what they had done to us – killing them not one by one, but without discrimination and as systematically as we could. And even then our slaughter would only be a sixth of theirs.

For this was Plan A. It aimed to kill, in a single stroke, no less than one million Germans. And I did not question it for a moment.

# CHAPTER FORTY-THREE

He marvelled at his boss's ability to do this. He was on – what was it? – his fourth meeting of the morning, listening, nodding sagely, offering rounded little aphorisms for each occasion, leaving each person he met convinced that the great statesman had focused on his or her problem at the exclusion of all else. No one would have had a clue that the great man was, in fact, distracted beyond measure, that he was thinking throughout of a topic a world away from the one under discussion. His face could continue making all the right expressions, his mouth forming the right words, entirely on automatic. Meanwhile, like a computer programme running behind the screen, his brain was processing a different issue entirely. Compartmentalization, the business magazines called it, the psychological state required for high-powered, CEO multi-tasking. But that was far too mechanical a description for the magic this man was able to pull off. This was not compartmentalization. This was sorcery.

In the intervals between meetings – the 'bilaterals' that always took place in the margins of any international pow-wow, with UN General Assembly week no exception – the boss would turn to his aide, letting his rictus smile disappear and pick up the conversation they had been forced to abandon some twenty or forty minutes earlier. Always, the aide noticed, at the exact same point, as if there had been no interruption.

'There's no point waiting for definitive proof,' he said, pushing back to the junior official the exact phrase he had used before the half-hour discussion with the President of the World Health Organization.

'Why not, sir?'

'Because if you're able to get definitive proof it usually means you've left it too late. An example: if you're worried I'm going to kill you, then a bullet in your chest is definitive proof.' He smiled a laughless smile. 'But you wouldn't want to wait that long, would you?'

'No, sir.'

'No. So we don't wait. If we even suspect—'

Instinct made him stop even before he could have heard the light knock on the door of the suite. It opened a crack to reveal the pretty assistant who was handling logistics. 'The Italian foreign minister is here, sir,' she said.

He showed her the hand gesture, peculiar to his country, that indicated she would have to wait a moment. She closed the door, taking care to pull it to quietly.

'If we even suspect they are getting close, then we will have to act. No point waiting.'

'Act?'

The boss inspected his counsellor, his eyes scoping upward, starting with the younger man's shoes. His manner was less regimental colonel reviewing the troops than high school girl checking out a rival. His mouth curled in derision. Could now be the moment, the aide wondered. Would the double-fucking strike, apparently unprovoked and when it was least expected?

'Try not to make your squeamishness quite so obvious. A man of your age should not reveal his fear quite so easily.'

'It was just that I didn't—'

'When I say act, I don't mean anything rash. Nothing hasty. I mean only that we should,' he paused, the ostentatious searching for the right word that was part of his standard performance. 'We should open up a dialogue. How's that?'

The aide knew better than to ask how he was meant to do such a thing. Perhaps the phrase was simply a euphemism deployed by the old guard to cover up heaven knows what ghastly practice from the early days. Interpreting it literally was bound to be a schoolboy error, for which he would receive another scalding reprimand. But he could not think about that now. He would get through the next meeting and find a way to ask after that was over, some form of words that would not expose his own uncertainty, one that would not reveal what he felt most intensely in the company of his boss: his sheer lack of worldliness.

So he got up, opened the door and gestured at the neatly moustached man waiting, with leather portfolio case on his lap and comely interpreter at his side, to come forward. He gestured him into the room where the boss, the elder statesman, was already standing, his arms outstretched in readiness for a politician's hug:

*'Signor Ministro degli Esteri!'*

# CHAPTER FORTY-FOUR

**Nuremberg, Winter 1946**

My job in the filtration plant should have been boring, but it never was: I had to concentrate too hard for that. I had to make sure my German did not let me down. I had to avoid letting slip a remark that would contradict my false life story. And, most of all, I had to watch my face, to be sure I did not betray what I truly felt about the German murderers who surrounded me.

I kept turning up each day, doing my shift, eating my sandwiches, listening to the jokes in the canteen – including the ones about the kikes and the yids. People imagine that everything changed the day Hitler shot himself in the bunker, the day Berlin fell, but it was not like that. They were still the same people, it was still the same Germany.

Each day I would return to the safe house and wait for my orders. But in the end it was other news that came.

First, a message arrived that the plan had changed. The DIN man in Berlin had failed to get inside the water plant there: he had gone for an interview but he hadn't got the job. No one knew why; he had as much training as I had. But that was that. We were down to four cities.

Three weeks later, more bad news, this time from Weimar. Our man there had got inside the plant but he had been shifted to a desk job that allowed no access to the filtration areas. To get near them would run a high risk of getting caught. The commanders discussed it and decided his exposure would jeopardize the entire mission. He was ordered to stand down.

Not long after came word from Hamburg. Our most qualified man, an engineer in his own right who had required only minimal training, had been sacked. The managers of the pumping station had checked his documents. Apparently, they discovered a discrepancy which convinced them the papers were forged – which they were. Luckily, they assumed he was a common criminal seeking to hide his past. They did not guess he was a Jew.

The plan of five cities was down to just two: Nuremberg and Munich. The commanders did their sums and calculated that a total of one million three hundred and eighty thousand people drank the water supplied by the plants in those two cities. The target of reaching – poisoning – one million Germans could still be achieved.

But when I was established in my post in

Nuremberg, and Manik was installed in the water plant in Munich, the commanders hesitated. As they stood on the brink of a decision that they knew would reverberate around the world and change the history of nations, a decision for the ages, they paused. I look back on it now and realize what I could never see then: that they were only young men.

They decided they could not make such a fateful decision themselves. They needed to act on some higher authority. A similar conundrum had pressed in on them when they had first formed an armed resistance to the Nazi invaders: 'By what right do you act in our name?' Back then they had waved the question away with a simple answer: 'If not us, who?' No one else was fighting back; it was their duty to take up arms and save Jewish lives. But this was different. Tochnit Aleph would not save any Jewish lives, at least not directly. Perhaps it might generations from now, by warning that Jews could not be slaughtered with impunity. No: Tochnit Aleph's purpose was to take German lives, the innocent with the guilty. One million of them.

The commanders were not religious men; they would take orders from no rabbi. The higher authority they had in mind was the sovereign Jewish people: the men and women who were fighting for Jewish independence in Palestine. They were three years away from statehood then, but the apparatus of Jewish sovereignty was already in place.

DIN would seek the guidance of the elders of the Jewish nation before they acted in that nation's name. In their quest for a blessing, Palestine would be their destination.

The British rulers of that land had closed the gates to the Jews in 1939 – even in their darkest hour – and the limit on Jewish immigration remained. The only way in was via the secret and illegal network that criss-crossed Europe: a system that relied on backwoods paths through forests, then midnight rendezvous at tiny fishing ports, followed by the chartering – in cash – of trawlers for long, perilous voyages dodging storms, sickness and British gunboats, hoping, eventually, to reach the shores of Palestine.

That was Aron's journey to the promised land. I picture him, finally jumping off an old rust-bucket of a vessel into the cool Mediterranean, wading, along with perhaps two hundred other ragged refugees from old Europe, onto a beach in the dead of night – these new, secret migrants then smuggled out to the network of kibbutzim and farming villages of northern Palestine, the place the Bible speaks of as Galilee.

I can see our leader on that first night, hiding, like an item of illicit cargo, in the back of a lorry as it drove away from the shore. I imagine him, his eyes burning up the darkness, trying to see what he could in the gloom, trying to catch a glimpse, however fleeting, of the land of Israel. For he had reached the place he believed would, at long last, serve as the haven for a people who had just faced extinction.

He did not make his move straightaway. His reputation, as a leader of the Jewish underground in Nazi-occupied Europe, preceded him and there were many in Palestine who wanted to meet him. They honoured him as a hero, the epitome of the new Jew they wanted to create in Palestine: a Jew who fought back, who refused to go to his death like a lamb to the slaughter. He told none of them that the work of resistance had become the work of vengeance. They believed that his fight against the Nazis was in the past. They knew nothing of DIN.

He would reveal that to only one man and, after two weeks of moving in the circles of those set one day to govern the new Jewish state, he came face to face with him. He was seventy, a founder of the movement for a Jewish homeland, regarded first as its chief emissary and now, in old age, as its figurehead. No man carried greater moral authority. In an earlier age in the land of Israel, thousands of years earlier, he would have been revered as the Hebrews' chief elder.

The younger man sat with him in the private study of his home and told him what, until then, this elder had only read about in reports and cables. He told him the story of the whirlwind that had engulfed the Jews of Europe. How the Germans had set out to remove the Jews from the face of the earth, pushing them into the death factories of Auschwitz and Treblinka as if they were products on a factory assembly line. He told him of the torture, the 'experiments' conducted without anaesthetic on screaming women and terrified children in the name of science. He told them of the world of death he had inhabited for nearly five years – and how the men who had created it had emerged unpunished.

And then he told him of Tochnit Aleph.

Now there was a reason why DIN's leader had chosen this man in particular. It was not just his seniority, the power his blessing would carry. It was also because this man, this leader, had earned distinction in an earlier life as a great scholar, specifically in the field of chemistry. Indeed, he had now retired from frontline politics and diplomacy and returned to his laboratory.

The elder listened throughout, his eyes darkening with each new tale of catastrophe. His head seemed to bow lower. Aron considered stopping or at least slowing the flow: give the old man a break, don't force it on him at once. He considered that and then suppressed the urge. It needs to be told, he said to himself. He needs to hear it.

So he carried on, sparing no detail, even as he saw the aged leader wince as if the grief of it was his own. By the time Aron spoke of Tochnit Aleph, the elder did not recoil or tell him to gather his things and get out. He simply nodded. And then he spoke.

'If I had travelled the road you have travelled, if I had seen what you have seen, then I would do the same.'

Aron dipped his head, as if in grateful acknowledgement. But he was uncertain. The elder's statement had been ambiguous: it was quite possible to empathize with a man whose wife, say, had been murdered, swearing that you too would want to strangle her killer if you were in his shoes, and nevertheless believe that it was not the right thing to do. Was the elder simply expressing understanding for DIN's state of rage? Or was he doing what Aron needed him to do, namely offering moral approval for the plan to extinguish a million German lives?

An ambiguous answer was not sufficient, but Aron would not push the old man. He would tell the others that the plan was off. If the blessing did not come easily, then it was not a real blessing.

By the time Aron was standing, he could see that the elder had removed a fountain pen from his breast pocket and was writing a note. It took him a long two or three minutes to finish it, the scratch of nib against paper a loud accompaniment to the ticking clock in this room thick with books and wooden furniture – a corner of Europe in the sweat and heat of the Levant.

'Here,' the old man said eventually. 'This is the name of the finest bacteriologist in Palestine. He is a student of mine, at the Institute in Rehovot. He is young but very brilliant. I have written him a message, telling him what you need. And I have told him it his duty to give it to you.'

'Thank you,' Aron said.

Then the elder, still sitting, clasped Aron's hand, like a grandfather on his deathbed, desperate for the touch of those who would live on. His eyes closed and he began to incant what Aron thought was a prayer. He said, '*Dam Israel Nokeam.*' The blood of Israel will take vengeance.

# CHAPTER FORTY-FIVE

Tom looked up at Rebecca and saw that the far-away distraction of a few moments ago had vanished. He followed her gaze to the blueprints, depicting in precise detail the layout of the water supply of five German cities, and then back to him.

'Tell me the quote again.'

Tom reached for the piece of paper he had scribbled on. '"I will make them eat bitter food and drink poisoned water".'

She nodded, still staring at the diagrams of the waterworks.

'It can only mean one thing, Rebecca.'

'I know.'

'It would have been so many people.'

'I know.' She turned away from the drawings, preferring to stare at the floor.

Tom got up from the slashed remnant of a chair he had been sitting on and moved across to her. When he placed his hands on her shoulders, she leaned into him, welcoming his touch.

'Look, we know it didn't happen. Everyone would know about it if it had. We know that Plan B happened because Plan A failed. The key question is, why did it fail? What happened?'

# CHAPTER FORTY-SIX

Aron went to meet this young scientist, Eliezer was his name, who took the note as if he were a pharmacist handling a prescription. He read it quickly, glanced up at Aron, then looked back at the note and read it again, and again. At last he said, 'This will take some time. You will hear from me when it's ready.'

I don't know what Aron did in the days of waiting. I like to imagine that he wandered around the country that was then taking shape. I like to picture him on the beach in Tel Aviv, holding an ice-cream cone. Or buying a falafel from one of the corner kiosks in Jaffa. Or running his hand along the pale-gold stones of ancient Jerusalem. But such things would have been a distraction from the work in hand. He would not have been able to allow himself joy and delight while others had suffered such pain, at least not until that pain had been avenged. Above all, I suspect he would have been frightened: frightened that if he let in even an hour of comfort, a few minutes of happiness, then his resolve would weaken. His will would soften and he would be unable to go ahead with the mass slaughter of Tochnit Aleph.

So I assume he spent his time in further meetings with the leaders of the Jewish state-in-waiting, still wearing the dark suit and white shirt of Europe. It's not just the character of the man that leads me to this assumption. It's also my knowledge of what happened next.

Perhaps a fortnight passed and Aron met again with Eliezer. The young chemist handed him the canisters filled with toxin, steel flasks cased in a protective netting. They could pass for camping equipment: Aron would be able to take them back to Europe in his rucksack.

He had arranged his passage with the men of the Jewish underground. He needed their help because he had entered Palestine illegally: he had none of the requisite papers to get past the British guards at the ports and board a ship. The underground told him of the British transport ships that sailed from Haifa. He could be smuggled onto one of those, with forged papers suggesting he was one of the Free Polish soldiers who were knocking around Palestine at the time.

I can see Aron on his voyage, alone with his notebook, planning and scribbling while the other men drank or sang. I picture him drafting his place in Jewish mythology: he would be the slayer of the Germans, the avenger of the Jews. He now had the deathly potion in his bag. I was in Nuremberg, ready to pour the lethal liquid into the water supply for that city. Manik would do the same in Munich. Tochnit Aleph would soon transform itself from a plan into one of the landmark events in history.

The journey was nearly over, the ship about to dock in Toulon, France, when Aron heard the noise from above, the footsteps and the barked inquiries as British MPs, military policemen, boarded the ship. Did he have the instinct in the pit of his stomach that told him what they were there for? Did he know, as they rattled down the stairs to the lower decks, that they were after him? I bet he did. Did he reach for the rucksack? What did he do with the canisters?

They dragged him off the ship without explanation and later sent him back to Egypt, to a cell in Alexandria. Eventually they transferred him to jails in Palestine, including Jerusalem. Aron – our leader who had ducked and bobbed for five long years, escaping the clutches of the Nazis, who had dashed down ghetto side streets and hidden himself in hollowed-out tree stumps in the forests, who had never been caught by anyone – was now a prisoner.

The British interviewed him but their questions were vague, unfocussed. He came to the conclusion that they knew little about him or about Tochnit Aleph, that they had not picked him up on their own evidence but on a tip-off, suggesting that Aron posed some kind of security threat. But who was the source?

I know the question gnawed away at him through those endless days and nights he spent alone, whether in a dank British prison cell in Jerusalem or held, like a captive knight, in an old Crusader fort in Acre. He would have assumed that he had been betrayed, that the informant was someone he had once trusted. He would have drawn up lists in his head of all those who knew of Tochnit Aleph – the elder who had given his blessing; the young chemist; the most senior underground leaders he had met in those last weeks. What might they have revealed? Had they blabbed to the British inadvertently or had it been deliberate? If on purpose, why? Why would any Jewish patriot have sabotaged this audacious attempt at justice?

Or had the British received their information from somewhere else entirely? Tochnit Aleph was, after all, a plan to kill a million Germans. It was Germany that stood to benefit most directly from Aron's arrest. Was it even possible that the British would collude with the enemy . . .? No. Surely, it was unimaginable.

We – Rosa, Manik and me, even the DIN commanders – knew nothing of this, of course. We were simply waiting for Aron to return to Europe with the poison. Finally, a messenger arrived with a note that Aron had somehow smuggled out. It said simply, 'Arrested. Proceed with Plan B.'

# CHAPTER FORTY-SEVEN

'But if it didn't happen, what's the connection with everything that's been going on? Why would they be killing Henry Goldman or smashing up my flat? It doesn't make any sense.'

Tom wished he had an answer for her, but she was right. Each time they approached what promised to be a solution, the whole conundrum only seemed to get more complicated. It was clear their pursuers were after something and this – the secret Plan A – surely had to be it. In a way, they had been proved right: the evidence, probably the only remaining evidence in the world, had been hidden here, bound and taped inside the painting. There couldn't be anything else, some other secret concealed in this flat: every inch of the place had been probed and examined, if not by the thugs themselves then by Tom and Rebecca. Plan A was surely it. This must be the secret their enemy was striving so hard to suppress. Why else had they killed Goldman, if not to prevent him revealing it?

And yet, it lacked all logic. Plan A had not happened. There had been no mass poisoning of Germany's major cities. It was a pipe-dream from sixty years ago. How could it possibly matter now?

Unless they had been looking in the wrong place. Unless he, Tom, had been making everything too complicated. 'Lets go back to basics,' he said, pacing. 'Your father was obviously after someone in New York. Whoever that person is reckons your father had evidence against him. That maybe your father had a list of names – like that list that came to your flat, except up to date, consisting solely of Nazis who are still alive. Maybe the person in New York knows he's on this current list. He needs to have that document. And that's why he was so frightened of Goldman talking. Because this person, this old Nazi, suspects Goldman had the list too.'

They had reversed positions, Rebecca now perching against the ex-sofa. 'So this won't stop until we find that list.'

'If there is such a list. There might not be. Let's face it, Rebecca. If we haven't found it yet, where's it going to be? It probably doesn't exist.'

'Not any more.'

'What's that?'

'Not any more. Years ago, you could draw up lists of ex-Nazis who were still alive. You could fill a phone book with them. But there are hardly any left now. Everyone's too bloody old.'

'Exactly. Which means whoever your father

was after was just one person, one name he had kept in his head. I think the only way we're ever going to settle this is by finding out that name.'

'How the hell are we going to do that?'

Tom was all but forming his reply, that he had no idea, when it struck him. Of course: what an elementary mistake. *Too bloody old.*

Tom quickly folded the blueprints and postcards back inside the picture frame – reckoning that since they had escaped detection there so far, there was probably no safer hiding place – and crudely taped the thing back together. 'We're going.'

'Where? I don't understand.'

'Neither do I. Not yet. But I think we're about to.'

## CHAPTER FORTY-EIGHT

He would have preferred to have gone somewhere else, somewhere with more people, but without the car they couldn't be choosy. So they would take their chances and simply make the ten-minute journey back to the internet café on Kingsland High Street. The second Tom walked out of the front door, he scanned the street. He saw two woman pushing buggies, one on a mobile phone. It could be an ingenious cover – or nothing at all. He looked in the other direction. A postman – or was that a disguise for a lookout? Thudding over the speed bumps was a white van with two young men inside. Had it been parked until Tom emerged? Did it contain not plungers and pumps, as promised by the 'DrainClearers' sign painted on the side, but state-of-the-art surveillance equipment? Tom shook his head, aware that all he could do was keep looking over his shoulder, cross the road at the first sight of anyone suspicious and stick to busy streets.

It made him feel grateful that Gerald Merton had stayed in Hackney, even to the end. Well-to-do areas were almost always deserted, especially at this time of day. Kids ferried to and from school in the sealed capsule of a four-by-four; fathers returning from work in a sleek, insulated BMW; any chat with neighbours done indoors and by telephone or, for all he knew these days, computer. But in a poorer part of town, a place like Hackney, life was lived on the street. There were always people around, waiting for a bus or picking up a bottle of milk and a packet of fags from the shop. In the residential areas kids still played football in the middle of the road. They weren't told by their mothers to stay indoors, for fear of what other, rougher lads might do to them. They were the kids other kids were frightened of.

Tom appreciated it all, as they made the three or four turns towards the high street en route to the grandly titled Newington International Call Centre.

'I've been thinking,' Rebecca said, looking left and right as they crossed Cazenove Road. 'Shouldn't we have heard from the police by now? About the autopsy.'

'No news is good news. If they'd found anything, we'd know about it. If there were drugs or poison in Goldman's bloodstream, you, Dr Merton, would definitely know about it.'

'So the police will say he died of natural causes?'

'And therefore it's not a murder inquiry.'

'But it should be.'

Tom thought about repeating his earlier reassurances – that Goldman's death might have been no more than a coincidence – but he couldn't do it.

They'd reached the internet café where he was gratified to see the same melancholy clientele gathered for the afternoon shift. The fake-wood phone booths were again filled to capacity; most of the computer terminals were in use. As Tom handed over a couple of pound coins, reserving the machine at the end of the row, an older, bearded man, in traditional ultra-orthodox Jewish garb, got up from the next seat along. Now there were two spaces, one for each of them.

He went straight to Google and typed in the two words which had struck him with such force in Gershon's flat. It had been such a basic error of logic he was almost embarrassed by it. What had been his request to New York? To come up with a list of everyone over seventy who was present for the week-long General Assembly. He had drawn a blank, presented with a roll-call that included a Chinese interpreter and an Israeli head of state, among others. The opposite of a list of Nazi war criminals.

But when Rebecca had complained that 'Everyone's too bloody old,' he had instantly seen it. Just as she had been raised in the shadow of the events of the Nazi era, so had many others of her generation. And not all of them were children of the victims. Some were the children of the perpetrators. They too might have been drawn into this strange, left-over riddle, still unfinished after all these years. They might have been enlisted into this posthumous battle just as Rebecca had been, fighting the wars of their fathers. Except these men, the ones Tom was imagining, would be fighting on the other side.

Which is why Tom so badly wanted his hunch to be wrong as he typed into the Google search field the two words that made his heart heavy.

*Henning Munchau.*

## CHAPTER FORTY-NINE

Most of the pieces that appeared were in German, starting with a news story from the *Frankfurter Allgemeine Zeitung* when Munchau's appointment at the UN was announced and several others from the specialist legal press. In English there was an interview with *New World*, the magazine of the United Nations Association in Britain, and a diary item from the *New York Observer*, noting Munchau's legal summons to the Manhattan magistrate for failure to pay a parking fine. Not what Tom was looking for.

He put his head in his hands. He knew there was something else he wasn't remembering. Think. *Think.*

Tom closed his eyes trying to visualize the office of the legal counsel, plush with an outer area containing two secretaries and a window view over the East River. There was a sign on Henning's door. He had gone past it a thousand times without ever looking at it properly. Slowly it formed, in his mind's eye, the lettering taking shape. There it was: *W. Henning Munchau.*

*W.*

Now it came back to him, both of them in the queue to leave Dili, East Timor waiting for their papers to be checked and approved. They had swapped documents, so that Henning could examine Tom's passport photo and mock him on his visible decline.

'Once so handsome. What went wrong, eh, Tommy?'

Tom had seen nothing that provided counter-ammunition in Munchau's photograph: the man had barely seemed to age. But he had seen his colleague's full name for the first time.

'Ah, we have a Kaiser in our midst, no less. Pray silence, Mein Herren, for Kaiser Wilhelm Henning Munchau.'

Henning had shut him up. Tom hadn't questioned that at the time. He was getting lary, there were people around. But now, replaying that memory in his head, Tom wondered if Henning had suddenly lost his smile for a different reason.

He retyped the name into the computer.

Once again, the first two entries were in German. They seemed to be from formal legal gazettes with Henning's name in among a long list of others: probably the announcement of various awards and promotions.

Tom decided to narrow it down. Not allowing himself to stop, lest he change his mind, he reentered the name into the search field – *Wilhelm Henning Munchau* – this time adding one more word: *Nazi.*

It took the machine less than a second to scour the world and find the sentence Tom had dreaded. But there it was, the first few words of an entry intelligible even in the opening list of results. It came from a website attached to the Department of History at the University of Maryland.

*Captain Wilhelm Henning Munchau, 1898-1975; served in the SS's Totenkopfverbände or Death's Head units; received suspended sentence from West German court in 1966 for service at Theriesenstadt (Terezin).*

Tom followed the link on the word 'Totenkopfverbände'. It took him to the website of something called the Museum of Tolerance. There was a definition: *SS Units who guarded concentration camps. On the right collar of their uniform they wore the death's head symbol, from which they took their name. They became an elite unit within the elite SS.*

Tom scanned to the end of the entry.

*. . . they were put in charge of killing Jews and partisans.*

Now he pushed back his chair and reached, instinctively, for the pouch of tobacco in his inside pocket. If there was anywhere left in London you could get away with smoking, surely it was in a hole like this. With one hand, his eye still on the screen, he rolled himself a cigarette and put it between his lips. Even this sensation, before he had lit a match, felt like a hit of soothing nicotine.

Jesus Christ. What part of his brain had not thought of this earlier? Had he suppressed the very thought of it? It had been under his nose. The minute he had opened Gershon Matzkin's journal, he should have at least considered it. Everyone else would have. He'd been despatched to shut down the case of an aged Nazi-hunter by – guess who – a German! You didn't have to be filled with prejudice to see the connection, just common sense. Why had he been so stupid? He had allowed his personal affection for Henning to cloud his judgment. It had obscured the most obvious line of enquiry. His friendship had barred his synapses from even twitching at the possible interest a German diplomat might have in suppressing the Nazi past. Or perhaps it was that Tom no longer even saw Henning as German, but rather as some internationalized quasi-Australian.

His mind sprinted ahead, trying to keep up with the implications. Surely it meant that Henning had tricked him by sending him on this mission. He had claimed to know nothing of Gerald Merton but he had known everything that mattered, starting with the old man's motive.

But that was the least of it. The chief legal counsel of the UN had somehow masterminded an intelligence operation in a foreign capital, able to track down – and trash – the homes of both Gerald Merton and his daughter, to say nothing of eavesdropping on, then murdering, Henry Goldman. How would Munchau possibly have such power? Unless he was part of something much bigger.

At first Tom had felt a slight sense of disappointment. Specifically, disappointment in Gershon Matzkin. He had expected more of him. It seemed beneath him to have travelled to New York simply to track down the son or, more likely, grandson of a Nazi war criminal. Tom had, despite himself, sympathized with DIN's determination to hunt down the guilty men, but this – visiting the sins of the fathers on their children and grandchildren – was impossible to defend. The only way it could make sense was if this was not simply about Henning Munchau and his Nazi grandfather, but something in which the UN lawyer – Tom's old boss and great friend – was just a minor player.

He turned to Rebecca, expecting her to be looking over his shoulder, reading the potted history of Munchau Snr that still glowed on the screen. But Rebecca wasn't looking at his terminal. She was looking at her own. And her face was white.

'What is it?'

She simply pointed at the display, open to her Facebook page. She indicated the Friends column down the left hand side.

'I don't understand,' Tom said, once again aware not only that Rebecca was ten years younger than him but that the latest wave of the internet revolution had mostly passed him by. Everyone else might have been forming social networks but these days his own personal community consisted of the models he dated, the Mafia men he worked for and the British-born tailor he had discovered on Spring Street: and none of those relationships happened online.

Rebecca made a few key strokes, going back several pages. Tom was distracted: he had spotted a new customer.

'See this guy here?' She was pointing at a square filled not with a photograph but with a question mark. 'He asked to friend me earlier.'

'To *friend* you?'

'It's a Facebook thing. Anyway, I said yes.' She saw Tom's look of disbelief. 'Lots of people were getting in touch, mainly to send condolences about Dad. It just seemed easier to say yes to everyone.'

Tom was looking again at the new arrival. Something about him was familiar.

'Look at these status updates.'

Tom looked down at the list. *Jay . . . is dining in York – again. Zoe . . . can't wait till she gets off work so she can have a stiff drink.* His eye went off the screen and back to the man, now sitting at the end of the row. White, iPod headphones nestled by his collar.

Rebecca's finger took Tom back to the list of status lines on the Facebook page, directing him to one five lines down. 'That's him.'

*Richard needs to meet Rebecca urgently – so he can explain everything that's going on.*

# CHAPTER FIFTY

Tom had barely read the words when Rebecca began typing furiously: *Who are you? How do you know what's going on?*

Tom rubbed his chin, 'I wonder if you should say—'

'Too late,' Rebecca said, coming down hard on the return key. 'I've already sent it.'

'For God's sake, we needed—' He stopped himself: he couldn't afford to pick a fight now, not with what he was about to tell her. He glanced over to the man with the white headphones: he had his head down and was banging away at the keyboard, apparently oblivious to them and everyone else. 'Rebecca, there's something you need to look at.' He turned his screen towards her, so that she could see his discovery for herself. 'Remember my old boss, Henning Munchau? Legal Counsel to the Secretary-General of the United Nations and all that? OK. Take a look at this.'

He watched as Rebecca's face lit up in the blue

glow of the computer screen, her eyes skipping across the few lines of biography on Wilhelm Henning Munchau he had just called up. She didn't look surprised, Tom decided; she just seemed to be concentrating very hard.

'You think this could be what this is all about?'

'I don't know. It seems crazy. OK, Henning plays hardball, no doubt about it. But underneath the cynical exterior, he's on the side of the angels. Serious humanitarian. If you'd seen him in East Timor, when the rebels were getting pounded, he—'

'But it would explain a lot. His father's a Nazi—'

'Probably grandfather.'

'—and he doesn't want it to get out. Maybe he knows my father knew about his family and he's determined to prevent us discovering it. It would explain a lot.'

'I know. But I can't believe he would go to those lengths: sending men over here to wreck your father's home, your home, to bug our meetings—'

'To kill Goldman.'

'Even if he wanted to do that, he wouldn't have the capacity to do it. People always imagine the United Nations is some global power. But it's got nothing. If it wants ink for the photocopier it has to go begging.'

'Have you got a better explanation?'

Tom rubbed his eyes until they emitted an

audible squeak. He had no good answer. After all, what did they know? That there had been a plan to poison the water supply of post-war Germany that had clearly been abortive. That, instead, DIN had killed hundreds, perhaps thousands, of former SS officers while they awaited trial for war crimes. But how this related to now, to the present day, he could not say. Despite everything they had learned, he and Rebecca could not even state for certain what Gerald Merton had been doing in New York two days ago.

'No. I can't think of—'

'A-ha. Here we go. He's replied.'

*I'm a friend and I really want to help.*

Instantly, Rebecca hammered out a reply: *Of my father's?*

It took perhaps thirty seconds but then Facebook announced a new message had landed. She clicked it open. *I never had the privilege of knowing your father. But I knew his work.*

She turned to Tom. 'What the hell does that mean, his "work"? My father was a dry cleaner.' She pounded the keyboard. *What 'work' do you have in mind?*

The reply came back in a matter of seconds. *I am an admirer of DIN.* Rebecca looked back at Tom, hesitating. 'What do you think we should do, Tom?'

Again, that 'we' sent a thrill through him. He wanted to hold her, to stroke her, to spend hour after hour meeting the gaze that seemed to see him so clearly. It required a great effort to bring himself back. 'I think we should meet him,' he said. 'Somewhere public, somewhere safe.' Tom glanced over at the man at the end of the row, squinting to make out what was on his screen: he appeared to be immersed in some kind of gothic video game.

Rebecca was typing again, breaking off for a moment to check her watch. *I'll be in Starbucks, Portland Place at 6pm.*

'Say you'll be with me. As protection.'

*We'll be in Starbucks, Portland Place at 6pm.*

'Here.' Tom leaned over and started pressing the keys himself. Rebecca did not pull back. Tom had the sense she was breathing in the smell of him. 'Best not be subtle.'

*I'll be with a friend: he's helping me.*

Then, as an afterthought, Rebecca typed five more words: *How will I recognize you?*

The reply took only a few seconds to come back.

*Don't worry about that: I'll recognize you.*

# CHAPTER FIFTY-ONE

It was Tom's idea to be early. You always had an advantage in any negotiation if you owned the room: that's why, back at the UN, there was such an elaborate protocol over where colleagues would meet, even for the most mundane exchange. Standard practice was for the official on the lower grade to travel, as if in supplication, to his superior. If you were in the latter position you got to rock back on your own swivel chair, to fiddle with your own pencils and rubber bands and act like the wolf in his lair. Meanwhile the other guy had to operate from a stiff-backed chair, ideally one that had been chosen precisely because it was lower than yours.

This was neutral territory, a café in the middle of a busy street. But by being here ten minutes early, Rebecca and he could simulate the office politics of UN Plaza, if only a little bit. Tom scanned the place looking for the cosy armchairs that had originally made Starbucks' name, back in those distant days of the early 1990s when the handwritten blackboard signage and pierced noses of the baristas deluded people into thinking the cafés were vaguely alternative, even grungy – what with the Seattle connection and all – rather than a corporate chain bent on global domination. The Tom of the last couple of years would doubtless admire the capitalist ingenuity of it all. But today he couldn't help but lament the sardine economics that provided only a couple of soft chairs, using the rest of the floor space to cram in ever more punters.

'There,' he said pointing at a round wooden table which could just about accommodate three people. It would be awkwardly intimate, even claustrophobic, but it did have the advantage of ensuring that they could talk with this 'Richard' quietly. If they were being followed, any eavesdropper would struggle to hear the conversation. That the place was so full had its advantages.

Now that the territory was marked as theirs – jackets hooked over backs of chairs, Rebecca's bag firmly planted on the table – Tom dug into his pockets for some change. 'So what will it be, mademoiselle?'

Rebecca managed a taut smile. She clearly dreaded what they were about to hear. Speculation was one thing. But to hear finally and irrevocably the nature of the quagmire they had waded into, to hear spelled out exactly what her father had done – as 'Richard' had promised they would – well, that that was much more frightening. It suggested finality.

Tom went over to the counter to order a cappuccino and a latte, hesitating when asked whether he wanted *venti* or *grande*. He handed over the money to the button-nosed, blue-eyed blonde: Polish or Lithuanian or Slovenian, he couldn't tell; maybe even Latvian.

While he waited for them to pour, scoop, froth and steam the concoctions, he looked over at Rebecca, now gazing into middle distance. If he had found these last few days inflicting a fatigue he had not experienced outside a war zone, how much more exhausted must she have been. She had lost her father, in every sense. Each day, each hour, she had had to assimilate some new, more astonishing aspect of his story. The latest addition had been her own father's readiness to commit mass murder, to take the lives of God knows how many hundreds of thousands of Germans without discrimination, at random. And yet, as he gazed at Rebecca now – on the phone, no doubt checking in once again with the hospital – he had to marvel at her resilience, marching forward as if there was no time to rest, as if she would bind her wounds only later when the battle was over. He realized that he felt for her a sentiment that, painful to admit, he had rarely felt for a woman. Not just desire or affection or even love, but deep admiration.

Maybe she sensed his eyes on her. She came over to the counter, even though she didn't need to, and he was about to open his arms to her, or smile, when the girl announced that his drinks were ready, gesturing him towards the elliptical side table where they placed the coffees once brewed. He picked up the two oversized mugs and had turned back to Rebecca when he saw a man standing directly in front of her, his eyes wide in greeting.

'Rebecca Merton?' He stuck out a hand. 'It's Richard.'

He was, Tom would have guessed, a couple of years older than her and several years younger than him. His brown hair was longish, almost tousled, even though he was wearing a suit. He looked healthy, as if he worked out.

He turned to Tom. 'Where are you sitting?'

Tom paused, uncertain what tone to adopt. Eventually, and with his hands full with coffee, he used his head to indicate, twisting a look over his right shoulder and saying 'Just there.'

'Great. I'll just get a drink and join you.'

They took their seats, Tom furrowing his forehead into a question for Rebecca. She shrugged, as if to say, 'I don't know. Not what I expected.' They sipped their coffee and waited, the hot liquid that slid down Tom's throat a comfort.

'Thanks for meeting me here,' the man said once he had come back with a mug of his own, tucking his chair tight under the table to ensure no one had to shout to be heard. 'And at such short notice.'

Rebecca said nothing. She brought the mug up to her lips and drank her coffee. Tom could see it was a stalling tactic: force this man to talk.

'And I'm sorry about the whole Facebook thing.

I just couldn't see any other way to get in touch with you.'

'That's OK.' She smiled. Tom was surprised by that; it seemed oddly eager to please. *Don't reward him too early: he hasn't given us anything yet.*

Tom extended a hand. 'Tom Byrne.' He shot a look over at Rebecca, checking that she was not about to take a lead. She seemed happy for him to do it. Hadn't this, after all, been their deal, that he would navigate through what was, for her, the alien territory of negotiations and information trading?

'So you say you know what's going on with all this mess?' He had vowed not to sound aggressive and he was pleased with the result: the question had come out casual rather than rude.

'Yes, and we will talk about that. About that and everything else. We really will. I have to say Rebecca, you do look very tired. Do you feel tired?'

'As a matter of fact, Richard, I'm really exhausted.' She smiled again, showing even more of her teeth. Tom was amazed by this sudden show of friendliness. 'Does it show?'

'I'm afraid it does, Rebecca. And what about you, Tom? Are you feeling tired?'

Tom wanted to tell him to mind his own business and to get on with telling them what they needed to know. But that urge gave way to another feeling. Maybe it was the warmth of the room or the restorative power of a hot drink or just the sight of Rebecca at last relaxed. Whatever the source, now didn't seem the moment for a fight.

This man was being friendly and mellow. Tom felt he should be friendly and mellow too.

'You know what? I am really tired. Isn't that funny?' And Tom gave a smile that turned into a small chuckle.

'Do you want to get some fresh air perhaps? Would you like some fresh air, Rebecca?'

'Yes, Richard I would.'

'And you, Tom? How about you? Would you like some fresh air?'

'I think I would, Richard. Thank you.'

'OK. Well, why don't you drink up and we'll get some fresh air. That's it, finish off those coffees and we'll take a walk.'

Both Tom and Rebecca did as they told, taking a sip, then keeping the mug close by their lips to down some more. They did that more or less in silence, until there was no coffee left.

'All righty then,' Richard said, so that now all three of them were smiling. 'About that walk.'

They got to their feet, Tom giving Rebecca a quizzical look that was nevertheless pleasant: this is odd, isn't it? She gave a semi-shrug back to him that said, *Let's just go with the flow*.

'Pick up your handbag, Rebecca.' It was Richard, his wording – direct, as if he were giving an order – surprising Tom. But Rebecca, who had been such hard work with him, didn't object to being bossed about by this strange man, this 'Richard'. Tom wanted to criticize or complain or at least make a sarcastic remark, but he didn't have the energy.

They were outside now, stepping into an immediate and fast-moving stream of pedestrians, rushing in such haste, barking into their phones so loudly, Tom felt his head spin. Some were carrying umbrellas which meant, Tom realized after a delay, that it was raining.

'Tell you what,' said Richard, his voice still calm and smooth. 'Maybe this isn't quite the right atmosphere. Since we all want fresh air, maybe we need to drive somewhere.'

'Drive?' Rebecca said.

'Yes, drive. And guess what, here's my car.'

Tom had noticed it already, a split second earlier: a silver Mercedes saloon, hugging the kerb. It was not quite a limousine; more like a very upmarket hire car, the kind his high-paying clients – including those whose tax returns claimed they were in the New Jersey construction industry – would occasionally send to collect him. He noticed the windows were blacked out.

At that very moment, just as Richard stopped speaking, Tom felt a firm and sudden push to his lower back, a robust nudge, the kind busybodies used to administer on the Tube to ensure the passengers moved into the carriage. It obviously worked because, without quite knowing how it had happened, it was no longer raining. He was in the dry. A second or two later, he found himself on the back seat of the Mercedes. Rebecca was on the other side and Richard was in between them.

He wasn't sure if it was real, or just his woozy imagination, but the car seemed to be gliding forward. There was no outside noise at all. Tom could see nothing more than the ear of the driver and that seemed to be filled by some kind of device. It was flickering with a blue light.

'Rebecca, would you just roll up your sleeve for me.'

Tom watched, though he seemed to be looking through a gauze. Was it especially dark in this car? Tom tried rubbing his eyes. No, it made no difference. His vision still seemed soft, as if someone had rubbed Vaseline on the lens.

'There we go,' Richard was saying, as Rebecca obliged, offering him the flat surface on the underside of her right elbow. She didn't even flinch when Richard produced a syringe, pushing a small squirt of fluid from its needle as a test. 'You'll feel a small jab and that will be that.'

Tom watched all this as if it were being played back to him on videotape. He tried to tell himself that it was happening right now, that it was strange and probably not a good idea, but somehow he couldn't get the words out. It wasn't just speaking that was the problem. His thoughts themselves seemed to have slowed down, as if they had to travel through a thick, viscous treacle of lethargy. No matter what he was seeing happen in front of him, he couldn't rouse himself to feel that strongly about it. He had a vague sense that he should, but mainly he just wanted to relax.

He heard a distant voice say, 'I'm just going with the flow.'

'That's really good that you're going with the flow, Tom,' Richard said. 'Really good.' He produced another syringe and nodded in the direction of Tom's right sleeve. Automatically, Tom unrolled it and presented the patch of exposed skin, offering this man he had met perhaps ten minutes earlier his vein.

'By the way, Tom, I'm sorry I had to drug your coffee.'

Tom felt the tiniest prick and watched as the needle tucked under his skin, the vein now protruding.

'Not nice to have tainted two perfectly good cappuccinos like that. Or was one a latte? Anyway, sorry about that.'

The man's voice was getting more remote, as if he were speaking on a cellphone and had just gone into a tunnel. As a matter of fact, that was just how Tom felt. He imagined himself on a first class train, stretching his legs forward and pushing his seat back, ready for a really good sleep. And all around, the light was falling away, replaced by darkness. A tunnel of darkness, enveloping him, covering him. What harm would it do to surrender and allow himself some rest? He would tell this man, this Richard, that that was what he was going to do, that he was going to sleep. If only he could find the energy to open his eyes, then he would tell him. He would tell him . . .

# CHAPTER FIFTY-TWO

The journey west took more than two hours, with the crawl out of London accounting for most of that time. Once they were on the M3, the traffic moved along pretty briskly and Richard could relax.

Richard. It wasn't a bad name; he'd had worse. And it had done the trick, hadn't it? Rebecca Merton had not challenged him to say more; he hadn't given her the chance. He'd been more worried about this UN lawyer she was with. But neither of them had noticed the spray of GBL – gamma-butyrolactone, the industrial solvent which had found a niche as the date-rape drug of choice in the seedier corners of the London club scene – which he had administered before they'd barely exchanged a word. It had not been difficult: one quick spray and job done.

He had been given only the barest instructions and certainly no clue as to the purpose of the mission. That was standard practice but this job was anything but standard. He was used to taking out men rather than women or couples; and they tended not to be middle class professionals but intense, bearded young men who'd spent too long watching beheadings on the al-Qaeda version of YouTube. So this had been an extra challenge. And the level of resources was unusual, too: he'd been told he could spend whatever he liked, just so long as he got the subjects out. No one had said anything explicit, but the way his controller had spoken suggested this was a job authorized from the top. Or close to it.

The driver's satnav announced they were less than a mile away. Soon they'd be arriving at the rendezvous point. He checked over his shoulder at the two sleeping beauties in the back. They were out cold.

The satnav spoke, a woman's voice, oddly soothing: *You have arrived at your destination*.

They were at the Invincible Road industrial estate, just outside Farnborough in Hampshire – a bleak place of tarmac and corrugated steel. He read the signs, counting off the unit numbers.

'There. Seven A.'

The gates opened as they approached. It meant their contact was here, watching them on CCTV. The driver let the Merc purr towards the steel-shuttered garage door. It too opened electronically and he inched the car inside. As the shutters came back down, overhead fluorescent lighting flickered on. In the adjacent bay was an ambulance, its rear doors open. All was going to plan.

'Welcome,' said a voice. And welcome indeed it was. They had worked on several previous jobs together and had come to like each other. Neither knew the other's name.

'You've got the clothes?'

'Yes. All the stuff's inside.'

Between them, with help from the driver, they withdrew two stretchers from the ambulance, then placed them on two wheeled gurneys. Then they pulled Rebecca Merton and Tom Byrne from the car and laid them on the stretchers, face up, arms at their sides.

'You two do him, I'll do her,' Richard said.

'Surprise, surprise. Keeping the best job for yourself.'

Richard started with the woman's boots, easing them off from the heel. Her feet were small, their shape clear in the thin socks she wore. He moved around so that he could get to the top of her jeans. He undid the first button easily, noting the taut flatness of her stomach. As he undid the next and the next, he fought the arousal that was stirring inside him. Even asleep like this, inert on the stretcher, she was a very attractive woman.

With the fly undone, he grabbed the denim at the hips and began to tug. It required some strength, and at one point he had to slide his hand under her bottom, to give himself the elevation necessary for the jeans to slide down her legs, but eventually they were off.

Now she lay before him, naked from the waist down save for a pair of black briefs. He tried to keep his eye from the small triangle of material that covered her most private part, but it was a losing battle. He could see the contours of her through the material; found himself breathing heavily.

Next, he turned to her top half: a V-neck sweater over a white shirt. He had to lift each arm, dead with unconsciousness, and pull it through a sleeve, then lift the sweater over her head, cradling her skull from the back, his hand caught up in her thick, dark hair.

Finally, the shirt, a vintage style, slight thing with delicate buttons. He worked up from the bottom but as he got to her chest, his fingers began to tremble. Drugged like this, she was breathing slowly, her chest rising and falling. As he fumbled with the last button, by her neck, he had a clear view of her breasts. In a black bra that matched her underwear, they were full and, even in this position, firm. His hand hovered a few inches from them. The prospect of a touch was enticing.

'Here are the scrubs.' It was his contact, throwing him a cellophane-wrapped packet of hospital clothes. He stepped back, taking in a full view of the sleeping woman. If only he was alone . . . He tore off the cellophane and pulled out the green cotton trousers. He scrunched them and hooked them over Rebecca Merton's feet, then tugged them up the length of her legs. He tied the drawstring into a bow just below her navel. He was almost glad he could no longer see anywhere below: he needed to collect himself.

Next he propped her up, using the palm of his hand in the small of her back to keep her sitting upright. He pushed her arms through the smock, tying the two strings at the back before lowering her flat once more. The final touch was to gather her hair, then scrape it back into a tight cap. There, it was done.

He looked over at the stretcher alongside his one. His colleagues had worked faster than he had. That was not so surprising. True, their subject was heavier but he had offered fewer . . . distractions. Lying there, oblivious, the anaesthetic holding strong, the two subjects looked ready for the operating theatre.

'OK, let's get them in.'

The contact lowered the ambulance's electronic ramp, manoeuvred the gurneys inside and locked them into position.

'Now, us,' he said. He retrieved two garment bags from the vehicle, unzipping the first to reveal a green paramedic's uniform, equipped with assorted pieces of kit: visible was a whistle and walkie-talkie, and even a metal badge with what appeared to be a royal crest. Underneath was a name: 'Executive Medical Assistance Inc.' He had another, apparently identical, which he passed to the driver.

'And this is yours.' The contact handed Richard a hard plastic photo-pass attached to a metal chain.

Richard looked at the picture of himself, one in which he was wearing a white coat and was identified as Dr Rick Brookes, Specialist, EMA. It was amazing what Photoshop could do.

'You got their passports?'

The contact held up two, both in the maroon leather of Her Britannic Majesty. 'Hers was in the apartment, no problem. We went to his hotel two hours ago. He hadn't even checked in, so we knew he had it with him. In his jacket pocket.' He smiled, gesturing at the pile of clothes he had just removed from Tom Byrne's unconscious body.

The driver then scooped those up, along with Rebecca's, and stashed them in a kit bag which he shoved into the ambulance. The three of them did a quick check to make sure nothing had been left behind. Richard and his contact took their seats by the patients inside the vehicle and the driver turned the ignition on. A press of a button on a remote control unit and the steel shutters came back up, closing after them. Richard checked his watch. They were on time.

The drive to Farnborough took no more than quarter of an hour. They followed the instructions they had been given, sweeping past the well-appointed business terminal, reserved exclusively for private jet users, and drove direct onto the tarmac. The Bombardier Challenger 604 was waiting for them, the jet engines looking massive on the plane's short, torpedo body. The retractable seven-step staircase was already down, suggesting the work of internal transformation had already been done. The usual configuration, favoured by CEOs and pampered rock stars, of half a dozen plump leather armchairs and tables, would have been stripped out and replaced by flatbed mattresses and a bank of flickering, beeping medical equipment: ECG monitors, pulse oximeter and, of course, a defibrillator. There would be IV stands carrying sacks of saline solution, intubation equipment, suction devices. Everything, indeed, that you'd expect from a mobile Intensive Care Unit.

Only now, in the dark, did Richard spot the two staff, one uniformed, at the foot of the staircase. They reminded him of those people you saw on the news, politicians nervously waiting for the arrival of a visiting head of state. Richard got out of the car, ID around his neck like a pendant, and strode confidently towards them.

The civilian, a woman, stretched her hand out. 'Welcome to Farnborough, Dr Brookes. I'm Barbara Clark, head of corporate liaison.'

'Thank you.'

'I appreciate the hurry you're in, doctor. We're going to make this as quick as possible. I'll do the security checks myself. Now I take it, you packed these bags yourself?'

She proceeded with the usual set of questions – 'No one could have given you anything?' – and then cursorily waved a wand over him and his colleagues. There was a beep for a cellphone and some keys and nothing else. In Richard's bag, she saw only syringes and various vials, which was no more than she expected.

She checked the holdall by hand and assured him that ground staff had already thoroughly examined the aircraft using sniffer dogs.

'I need to have a quick look at the patients, I'm afraid. But I'll keep it very quick.'

Richard turned back to the ambulance and gave a nod. The two 'paramedics' wheeled the gurneys to the foot of the plane, both holding saline drips aloft in their right hands.

Clark looked down at the sleeping patients and slowly moved her wand over each one. There was a loud beep when she came half way down the man's body. Richard shot a look at his contact. Was there something they had forgotten? Had some telltale object been dropped there?

'Would you mind?' Clark said, pulling the sheet back. Richard held his breath.

'Of course.' It was the buckle of the belt, strapping Byrne into place. The sound was repeated when she checked the woman.

'Well, all seems to be in order, Dr Brookes. I just need to ask you a little about their condition. Is there any more you can tell me about this trip beyond—' she glanced down at some paperwork, '—"medical need"?'

'I'm afraid, I really can't, Ms Clark. Doctor-patient confidentiality and all that.' He smiled apologetically, but in such a way that conveyed there was no room for negotiation.

'Of course. A quick word with my colleague here from immigration and you'll be free to fly.'

Richard presented the passport of Dr Rick Brookes. He then showed the ones belonging to Byrne and Merton. The official checked the photos against the people lying, like resting saints, in front of him and then gave a nod. Richard gestured to his colleagues, who released the stretchers from their chassis and carried them, the man first, up the narrow staircase and into the aeroplane.

'Strange isn't it,' Clark said, as she watched the paramedics come back for the second patient. 'They look almost peaceful. Is it terribly serious, then, doctor?'

'Well, it's not great, put it that way. But they're in good hands now, have no fear.'

'Nothing our own NHS could do, then?'

'Well, you know how the very wealthy are, Ms Clark. They want the most personal treatment. Personal – and discreet.'

The woman blushed a little, Richard thought, though it was hard to see in the evening gloom.

A light drizzle was falling, picked out by the yellow glow of the terminal building.

'Of course.' She paused. 'Sorry.'

Richard could see the contact talking with the pilot, who tucked a clipboard under his arm, suggesting any final checks had been made. 'My thanks again, Ms Clark, to you and your team here. We'll be on our way.'

Richard nodded farewell to his driver, who headed back to the ambulance. He then climbed inside the plane, followed by his contact. They watched as the staircase retracted in a stately, electronic movement.

He strapped himself in, giving a last check of his two unconscious charges. Clark was right: they did look peaceful. They might need a top-up during the flight, but they were out.

He settled back into his chair, the leather soft and easy against his flesh. His colleague was already flicking the pages of *Forbes* magazine, doubtless left on board by the last high-paying customer to have chartered this jet. He deserved to relax, Richard thought; he had done a good job. They both had.

As they took off, angling into the sky, the engines screaming, he looked down at the ground below. Somehow the flying experience was always more intense on one of these small planes. The necklace of lights down below, the villages and roads of Hampshire, somehow felt within reach, even as they soared away from them.

A voice crackled onto the PA system. 'Good evening, gentlemen, this is your captain speaking.' The voice seemed amused by the absurdity of the situation. 'Welcome aboard this Challenger 604. Flying conditions are smooth tonight. We should be at our destination in approximately seven hours.'

# CHAPTER FIFTY-THREE

Jay Sherrill placed a protective hand on the laptop, covering up the Apple symbol; he knew what the NYPD numb-skulls would make of that. It would be one more confirmation that he was a college boy, a white-wine sipping Volvo driver – some homo who should have been a graphic designer rather than a cop.

Though there were some fellow Volvo types around here. This was the Commissioner's office, after all. Bound to be some policy advisers and media specialists in the operation. They wouldn't all be hard-boiled gumshoe cops moulded in the 1950s.

He wanted to open up the machine again, just to be sure the item was still there. What if there wasn't enough power? What if the programme crashed?

'The Commissioner will see you now.'

He gathered up his things and went straight through, aware that his shirt was creased and that there was a small stain on the right leg of his chinos. He had known that when he put the trousers on this morning. But he had no choice. They were the only semi-clean clothes in the entire apartment. The truth was, he had barely slept or eaten or washed since this whole nightmare of a case had landed in his lap on Monday morning. He was ragged.

'Good to see you, Mr Sherrill.'

'My pleasure, sir.' My pleasure? 'I mean, thank—'

'Relax, Mr Sherrill, take a seat. My office said you needed to see me urgently. That sounds like good news.'

'I hope so, sir.' *Calm. Breathe.*

'Why'd you bring that thing in here? You got something to show me?'

'Yes, I have.' He flipped open the lid of his computer, clicked open the iMovie programme and selected the most recent project. Only then did he get up and move round to Riley's side of the desk. 'May I, sir?'

'What's this gonna be, *Debbie Does Dallas*?'

'Not quite, sir, no. But still pretty interesting.'

A window opened up, a small video screen. Sherrill, hovering at the Commissioner's side, leaned down to expand it. And then he pressed play.

Instantly an image appeared of a silhouetted man. He was seated against a window. The visual grammar was obvious: it was the style of an undercover interview designed to preserve the subject's anonymity. There was a voice on the film, though it was off-mike. It was Sherrill's own.

*Please identify yourself.*

Then a reply: *I am an agent of the New York Police Department, Intelligence Division.*

That was enough to have Chuck Riley spin round in his chair and look up at the man over his shoulder. The excitement visible in his expression was what Sherrill had been hoping for. Now, at long last, he began to relax. He heard his own voice on the computer again.

*Can you verify that, without revealing your name?*

*Yes. I can reveal operational details that would only be known to an officer in Intel. I will do that to the Commissioner or any investigating authority.*

*I appreciate that, but perhaps you could say something now, that might establish your credentials?*

The silhouetted figure paused, moving slightly in his chair. The change in profile revealed an unexpected hair style: long, Riley thought, like a woman's.

*I could tell you about our operation during the Republican convention when it was in the city, monitoring protesters.*

*That would be excellent.*

The voice proceeded to give details of how he and his fellow agents had travelled beyond New York, to New Mexico and Illinois, to Montreal and even to Europe, snooping on political activists who were planning on demonstrating outside the convention. He spoke about how he had worked undercover, going to left-wing and anti-war meetings, making friends, eventually getting himself on electronic mailing lists – all the while filing reports back to headquarters.

*The thing is, everyone thinks we were just watching foreign terrorists. But I gotta tell ya: we were spying on people who had no intention of doing violence to anybody. I even infiltrated some street theatre company, for Christ's sake. Church groups too. And here's the thing: these people were US citizens.*

The Commissioner was listening closely, turning his face from the screen so that his ear could be nearer to the computer's speaker. Occasionally, he closed his eyes, as if he wanted to avoid all distraction. He then signalled for Sherrill to stop the machine. 'You sure he couldn't have got all that from the papers? From the internet or somewhere?'

Sherrill smiled and released the play key.

*We all had different code names. My one was Tenzing. Another was called Simpson. And there was Hillary. All famous climbers, apparently. They say the boss is some mountain freak.*

At this, Riley sat back and exhaled. That much was true: Stephen Lake was a fanatic, challenging himself by climbing ever more improbable peaks. But Lake was hardly known outside the CIA or, more recently, the Intelligence Division of the NYPD. His penchant for mountains was certainly not public knowledge. The silhouette couldn't have just picked that up. Besides, the Commissioner knew at least one of those codenames was accurate. When *The New York Times* had started digging into the Republican convention story, he had made some inquiries of his own. He had heard about the unit called Hillary. He'd never have made the link to mountains though; he'd just thought the units had girl's names. Like hurricanes.

'OK,' he said finally. 'I believe him.'

'I'm glad, sir. Because I think what this man goes on to say explains how Gerald Merton came to be shot dead on the steps of the UN.'

'And—'

'And, more importantly, sir, who was responsible for that happening.'

'That's very good, Sherrill. That's very good indeed.'

# CHAPTER FIFTY-FOUR

He was dreaming of Rebecca. She was scraping something from a wall, it could have been paper or paint, it was hard to tell. But the more she scraped, the more the wall began to crumble. Whole hunks of plaster were coming off, crashing onto the floor. But still she carried on, apparently oblivious to the rubble piling up around her and the dust powdering her face. She occasionally looked over her shoulder, so that he could see her. She didn't seem angry so much as determined. Finally, the wall gave way, a huge oval opening up like a mouth. Somehow the ceiling stayed in place, but Tom could see through the hole and so could Rebecca. They both could see it, the light bouncing off the ripple of solid black and deep red. There, on the other side, was a grotesquely oversized swastika.

His eyes snapped open, his breathing hard. He squinted, trying to focus on the wall ahead. It seemed to be plain white. There was no window, just a cross-hatched square in the door on the left.

He swivelled his head around to the table at his side. A small wooden cabinet, with a plastic jug of water. Above it, fastened to the wall, was a sign warning of the correct evacuation procedure in the event of a fire. Where the hell was he?

He tried to get out of bed, but his legs were thick and leaden. He pulled away the tight, starched sheets covering him and saw he was wearing green surgical scrubs. *My God.*

His mind raced. Had he had some terrible traffic accident? Is that what this was, the intensive care unit of a hospital? What had happened? And then, halting this torrent of thoughts with a thud: *Rebecca.*

He had to think back. What was the last thing he could remember? He could picture her: jeans, boots, a white buttoned shirt. He felt a sensation that was wholly unfamiliar: the anticipation of great sadness, a kind of pre-grief. He was imagining the pain he would feel if he could not see her again.

They had been in Starbucks. He had been buying the drinks, he had turned to her. There was a man there, the man they had arranged to meet . . .

Tom tried again to get out of bed. This time he picked up his legs with his hands, grabbing his own thighs as if they were someone else's, but once his feet were on the ground, he buckled and had to grab the bed to stay upright. He steadied himself. Now, his jaw clenched in determination, he headed for the wall and shuffled his way along it to the door. Stretching up, he got a view through the rectangle of glass of an empty corridor and, opposite, what he guessed was a nurses' station. It all seemed too uncluttered, too neat and hi-tech to be an NHS hospital. Was this some private clinic?

He would step outside and find a nurse or a doctor to explain everything. And maybe he would see Rebecca. Perhaps she would be sitting there, flicking through a magazine, waiting for him. Unless . . .

He reached for the door handle. The metal was so cold in his hand, it made him shiver. But it would not turn. Perhaps whatever accident he had suffered, or treatment he had endured, had weakened him. He tried again and came up against the hard metal stop of a lock. He was locked in.

He stayed there, leaning against the door, too exhausted to risk the trek back to the bed. He was panting. He needed to think.

Starbucks, Rebecca and him at the counter. He could see the woman who had taken their drinks order, the tiredness in her face, the streaks in her otherwise blonde hair. The man who had greeted Rebecca. So the meeting had happened as planned. But then what?

A remembered emotion bubbled upward, arriving somewhere in his chest: jealousy. Instantly, he could picture Rebecca's smiling face, warm and friendly towards the newcomer. Richard.

And now Tom could see the three of them, stepping outside the café. There was a car, a silver car . . . he could see no more.

Tom rubbed his temples. It was like trying to dredge up a dream, a fragment would appear, only to slip through his fingers, sand from the bottom of the sea. He could not remember. Weary of supporting himself upright, he slid to the floor.

He had not noticed the small camera in the far corner of the room, nor the other one diagonally opposite. Nor did he know about the motion sensors placed under the mattress of the bed, which sounded an alarm as soon as the normal ups and downs of breathing ceased for more than thirty seconds – and which were, of course, triggered when the patient left the bed entirely. So he wasn't to know that he had set off an alarm at the nurses' station. He couldn't hear it because his room was thoroughly soundproofed – chiefly to ensure that no sound ever got out, but which, naturally, also ensured no external sound ever got in. Such were the demands necessitated by this ward's usual patients.

Tom reached up for the doorhandle, using it to haul himself up. He winced as he tugged at it, the memory of early mornings on the monkey bars at the overpriced gym on Lafayette and Bond returning to him. That seemed like a different age. In truth, it seemed like a different person. Finally he was standing, his back resting in the corner where the two walls met. Now, with one last push, he heaved himself around so his eyes were level with the window-hole in the door. It was filled entirely with a face.

Tom rocked back with shock. The face had been just an inch or two away from his, separated only by glass. And now he could hear the sound of the door unlocking, an electronic release.

Two men walked in, accompanied by a nurse putting away a swipe card. 'Thank you,' said the less bulky of the two men. 'We can take it from here.' He waited for the nurse to close the door behind her before he spoke again. 'I hope you slept well. In fact, I know you slept well because I've been watching you.'

Now that he heard his voice, Tom remembered him. It was Richard, the man they had met in the café.

'What happened? Where am I?'

'It's a long story, Tom. Put it this way. We were in London, we needed you to take a little trip. And so we took it.'

The smugness of this man, his smooth, chatty manner and his studiedly relaxed hair, sent the rage thudding through Tom's arterial network; the veins on his neck began to throb. Without planning it, and despite the sluggishness of his limbs, he brought back his right arm and curled his fingers into a fist.

He got within six inches of Richard's face but no closer. The bodyguard, or whoever the other man was, simply lifted up a hand and caught Tom's arm as if it were a stray twig. He didn't merely block the punch, but pushed Tom's arm back, twisting it in its socket. Tom let out a yelp of pain.

'No need for any of that, Tom. Now as it happens, we—'

'What have you done with Rebecca? Where's Rebecca?'

'Let me finish.' The bodyguard was still holding onto Tom's arm, keeping it in a half-nelson behind his back. 'As it happens, I was going to come and wake you anyway.'

'Where's REBECCA?'

'She's here. In this same city.'

Tom gasped his relief. Then: 'What city? Where am I?'

'Don't you know? I'd have thought you'd have worked it out. You've been fast asleep in the city that never sleeps.' He paused. 'No? You're in New York, Tom.'

*New York?* It made no sense. How could he have been in Starbucks in the West End and now be in New York? He didn't remember flying anywhere.

'Who are you?'

Richard ignored the question. 'I'm sorry we had to do it this way, Tom. But the boss will explain everything soon enough. And look.' He lifted the travel bag he had been holding at his side and placed it on the bed. 'I even have your clothes.'

A few minutes later, Tom was in a wheelchair, watching as nurses and orderlies busied past him.

Any risk of him crying out was tempered by the presence at the wheelchair's handlebars of the bodyguard: Tom did not doubt that, were he to cry out, he would soon be silenced, by a fist if not by some stray item of medical equipment.

Richard hadn't been lying. All the voices and accents he heard confirmed this was, indeed, the United States.

He was wheeled into an elevator. Richard pressed the button for the basement. It took them to a service area, the plush carpets and furnishings now replaced by steel doors and grey concrete. He wondered, for the first time, if they were planning to do away with him here, to crush his body in some industrial waste machine.

In silence they wheeled him out through a pair of double doors; he felt a change of temperature. He was in a car park.

They went into a side bay, one marked by a disabled badge. There was the electronic squawk of car doors opened by remote control.

The meathead pushing the chair now tucked his hands into Tom's armpits and lifted him. In a single movement that was more efficient than brutal, Tom was loaded onto the back seat of an empty car. Richard stepped into the passenger seat, the bodyguard took the wheel and fired up the ignition, letting the engine idle. Richard turned around and with a smile that renewed in Tom the urge to punch his lights out, he said, 'We're just waiting for one more and we'll be on our way.'

How had he let himself get into this position? Somehow he had been so careless, so lacking in basic vigilance that he had allowed himself to become a helpless prisoner in the hands of . . . whoever the fuck these people were. That was the worst of it: he had no idea who was holding him or why. All those years detailing the human rights abuses of this regime or that tinpot dictator, compiling reports on 'the disappeared' of Latin America or Africa and look at him: he had learned nothing. He had made himself a victim.

Now there was a clunk and the opening of the passenger door opposite. He looked up and felt his heart squeeze.

## CHAPTER FIFTY-FIVE

He studied her face closely. In the dull twilight of a locked car in an underground car park, it was almost impossible to discern anything but an outline. To make sure she was really there he touched her, running his fingers gently over her skin, her cheekbones, her chin.

'Are you, OK? Did they hurt you?'

'I'm fine,' Rebecca said. 'Woozy, bit nauseous, exhausted. Like being a junior doctor really.' She smiled weakly, sending a stab of pain through him that felt very close to love.

Now the car took off, emerging up an exit ramp and into the daylight. Their captors had not been lying. They were in New York. It took him a while to realize it, but Tom was back on the very street he had driven down hours before he had left for London. There was the Bellevue Medical Center and there, still open for business, was the Office of the Chief Medical Examiner, where – how long ago? – he had gazed upon the staring, blue-eyed corpse of Gershon Matzkin.

They were driving in the opposite direction from his last journey, heading north up First Avenue. A sensation that was part bafflement, part dread began to rise inside him. They were travelling towards the United Nations.

A picture of Henning Munchau floated into Tom's head. Could this really be his handiwork? What terrible secret could he, or those he served, harbour that he would do this – and to one of his oldest friends? It seemed so idiotic. Didn't Henning realize that he would simply have had to say the word – ordering rather than suggesting Tom's return – and Tom would have jumped on a plane back to New York? Instead he had gone to these extreme lengths. Tom looked over at Rebecca, absorbing the sight of her in profile, a corkscrew curl of hair tucked behind one ear. *Unless, it was not Tom that Henning had needed to get to New York . . .*

They were descending again, down another slope into an underground car park. Damn. He hadn't been paying attention at the crucial moment: he didn't know precisely where they were.

Once more they parked up by an elevator shaft. This time there were no wheelchairs. Richard and the bodyguard simply guided Tom and Rebecca into the lift, flanking them to prevent escape. Saying nothing, Richard pressed the button. The top floor, Tom noticed.

The lift doors opened and now he understood: they were in a hotel, on what, he guessed, was the penthouse level. They walked down a corridor until they reached a door where two young men in dark blue suits, curled wires in their ears, stood as sentries on either side. Richard gave each of them a nod and the door was opened.

Inside was the sitting room of a suite, clearly one of the best in the building. Tom had seen hotel rooms like this only a couple of times, travelling with the UN high command. In his memory, they were always strewn with piles of paper, the odd, hastily installed fax machine and several uncleared trays of room service food. These quarters, he noted, had much less clutter.

He and Rebecca were invited to sit down and they did so in silence. Rebellion was wholly pointless, he reasoned: they would soon meet the 'boss' Richard had mentioned.

Finally, another young man entered the room, darting only a quick glance in their direction: Tom guessed he saw something in his expression, a reluctance, perhaps even an embarrassment. Richard and this man exchanged a few words. Tom strained to hear what they were saying, even to hear what language they were speaking. He couldn't make it out; he wasn't sure he recognized it at all.

The minutes went past, Rebecca occasionally turning out her palms as if to say 'What the hell is going on?' All he could do was shrug.

And then there was the sound of shuffling on the other side of the dark wood door. Someone had arrived. The flurry of activity, the pulse of adrenalin passing through the room, told Tom it was someone important. The boss.

More delay and then Richard spoke. 'I can show you in now.'

The two got up and followed him through the connecting door, into a larger sitting area. This room was spotless. They could see the figure of a suited man, his back to them, standing at the large picture window, apparently taking in the view of Manhattan and the East River in the morning light.

At last he turned around. 'Welcome to the Presidential Suite,' he said.

Tom took in that voice, and the face he instantly recognized, and felt his veins turn to ice.

# CHAPTER FIFTY-SIX

He knew the smart thing to do. That much his Harvard education had given him: he was at least sharp enough to know the precise course of action he needed to follow if he was to please the Commissioner and advance his own career.

Better still, it was remarkably, enticingly simple. All he had to do was do nothing and say no more. He simply needed to end his presentation, close the lid of his laptop and shake his superior's hand and be on his way. Any one of his colleagues would consider that a very good morning's work – and take the rest of the day off.

But something nagged at Jay Sherrill. It would have been pompous to call it a pang of conscience. And wrong too. It wasn't his conscience that was speaking so much as an irritating personality trait: this anal desire of his for neatness and completeness. He simply knew that it would niggle him all day and for the rest of the week if he didn't give Commissioner Riley the full story. Of course it made no political sense; the boss had already told him as directly as he could that he did not want to know anything more. He had a narrative in mind and he did not want it disrupted by inconvenient facts.

Still, though, Sherrill did not want to take that decision alone. He wanted to let Riley decide. *Tell him everything, then, if he chooses not to use the information, the responsibility will be his. I will have done my duty.* Sherrill knew that was playing it by the book, but he couldn't see any other way. He had been raised on the book.

'There are a couple more elements to the story, Commissioner.'

'Always are, Detective. Lots of chaff in any investigation. Our job's to put aside the chaff so all we got left is wheat.'

'I know that, sir. But I thought you ought to know—'

'Sure. Maybe you can speak to Donna outside and arrange another appoint—'

'This won't take long, sir. It's simply that identifying the dead man, Gerald Merton, as a terrorist may not wholly have been a mistake.'

'Well, that's a mighty interestin' theory. I'm sure. Now if you just—'

'It's not only a theory, sir. There's the weapon – the hitman's friend, you called it – hidden in Merton's hotel room. He had been consorting with a known arms dealer. The UN's man, who's been in London, says there may be a history of vigilante killings.'

The Commissioner's expression changed instantly. Gone was any trace of avuncular warmth. 'What UN man?'

'Tom Byrne. He's the lawyer the UN put on the case.'

'Yes – to *oversee* your investigation. What's he doing investigating?'

'He's not. Not officially of course. But the UN sent him to London to mend fences with the family. To head off any compensation—'

'Never mind that. You say he's uncovered what?'

'He's given me very few details. But he believes the weapon in the hotel room might be explained by—'

'*He* knows about the gun?'

'Yes, sir.'

Riley now sat upright and began to straighten the papers on his desk. 'I see,' he said, in a voice now drained of all southern bonhomie. Sherrill instantly understood what it meant: the Commissioner had concluded that his little game – blaming the Intelligence Division for the death of an innocent old man – was now over. If it had just been Sherrill, it wouldn't have been too tricky to find a carpet under which they could have swept any awkward facts. But now the circle of knowledge had unexpectedly widened. His scheme couldn't work.

'Detective, a thought has just struck me; 'pologize for not thinking of it earlier.'

'Yes, sir?' Sherrill could feel his throat turn arid.

'This killing took place inside the environs of the United Nations, correct?'

'Yes, sir.'

'Is that inside the jurisdiction of the United States of America?'

'I'm sorry, sir, I don't—'

'Is it on American *soil,* Detective?'

'I suppose, technically speaking, it doesn't count as—'

'Nothin' technical about it. It's not. And I know what the District Attorney of this city, or a US attorney for that matter, would say about that. He would say that no crime has been committed here.'

'Excuse me?'

'No crime has been committed. There is no offence he or any prosecuting authority could pursue. Yes, a shooting has taken place. But it did not happen on US soil. Which means there is no crime under US law and nothing here to trouble any US law enforcement agency – such as the New York Police Department.'

'But you said this was a high priority case, you said I should report directly to you.'

The Commissioner adopted a faux official voice. 'In the post 9/11 environment, I didn't want to take any chances. In case this might have had implications for the rest of the city.' Then he leaned forward, fixing Sherrill with a stare. 'But the basic point still stands, as a quick call to the DA's office or any one of our legal advisers here would instantly confirm. No crime here, Detective. You're off the case – because there is no case. This meetin' is over.'

# CHAPTER FIFTY-SEVEN

Tom looked over at Rebecca. She was as shell-shocked as he was.

'I'm sorry about the way this meeting has been arranged. Not my usual style. Not my usual style at all.'

Tom was too stunned to speak. To see this man, in this context, talking like this – it was dizzying.

'I never actually met your father, Rebecca. Though our paths crossed. I wonder if he knew that. I'm not sure.'

The accent was even stronger than Tom remembered it. Did he usually soften it? Why was he allowing its cadences of Eastern Europe to be heard now? Was he making some point? *Remember who I am.*

'We're getting ahead of ourselves. We need to set some ground rules. We need to talk about the terms of this meeting.'

Again, Tom felt the ire boil inside him. First this man was talking about how things had been 'arranged' and now this – as if Rebecca and Tom were taking part in a routine New York business appointment, the slot in the diary mutually agreed.

Tom wanted to scream about abduction, about involuntary sedation, about the thousand violations of basic human rights law and international standards that this 'meeting' represented. He wanted to be the angry lawyer he had once been, warning his antagonist of the depth of the shit he had waded into. But he couldn't bring himself to say any of it to this man simply because of who he was. All he could manage was to squeeze out the words: 'This will destroy you.'

And at that the man gave a slight nod, the same rueful, thoughtful gesture Tom had seen him give on TV interviews going back – what? – forty years. Anyone who watched Newsnight or Nightline or who had ever opened a serious newspaper would have recognised it. It was the expression of the man who had, at different times, served as education minister, foreign minister and even prime minister of his country. And even though he was well past eighty years old, the career of this veteran politician – one of the best-known statesmen in the world – was not over.

Now Tom was facing him across this room, just a few yards apart. He was staring at the President of the State of Israel.

# CHAPTER FIFTY-EIGHT

'I admit, I am taking an enormous risk here. Some think I'm being reckless.' He gestured in the vague direction of the door, which Tom took to indicate the clutch of young aides milling about in the other room. 'People say that I have been cautious throughout my career. "Cautious" is the kind word. One of my biographers preferred "cowardly". "The boldness of his rhetoric has always been in inverse proportion to the courage of his actions. In a nation of warriors, his great misfortune was to have been born a coward." That's the full quote.'

Tom looked over at Rebecca, hoping that she might be able to make sense of this bizarre scene. But she was simply staring intently at the President, as if waiting for him to explain himself.

And then he remembered it, Munchau's list, the list Tom had asked him to compile of all visitors to this week's UN General Assembly over the age of seventy. Tom had waved aside the mention of the Chinese interpreter and the foreign minister of the Ivory Coast. And he had not given it a second thought when Henning had said, 'Well, the President of the State of Israel is here. He's eighty-four.'

Henning. Tom brought his hand to his head, a flush of shame passing through him. He had succumbed to the crudest of stereotypes, blaming his old friend – the man who had given Tom second, third and fourth chances when he had cracked up and when the rest of his colleagues had written him off – and he had been just as crudely wrong. Henning was German so Tom had decided he must be doing the work of the Nazis, even if that meant sending thugs to bug and burgle their way across London. He would never be able to look Henning Munchau in the eye again.

The President had come forward now, away from the picture window. He stepped past the couch and pulled over a plain, straight-backed wooden chair, its cushion covered in chintzy red and white stripes. Once he was seated, Tom drew breath: it was an image familiar from a hundred photographs on the foreign news pages. All that was missing was a matching chair directly opposite, seating an American secretary of state or pro-Western Arab leader. Tom was all but waiting for the old man to reach across and perform a sustained handshake for the cameras.

'But people misjudge me. I was always cautious in that I always made a *calculation*. Before every move I ever made. Sometimes the calculation called for boldness or bravery. Even recklessness. This meeting comes into that category.'

'You keep calling this a meeting.' It was, to Tom's delight and relief, his own voice. The fury that had been coursing through his bloodstream had, with no decision on his part, finally burst out. He was glad of it. 'But you abducted us to bring us here. You drugged us and restrained us with force. This is not a *meeting*. This is a crime.'

'As I said, Mr Byrne. It is high risk. But I hope you'll soon see why I had to take it. Like a lot of actions taken by my country, and misunderstood by the rest of the world, this is a case where we have performed one regrettable deed in order to avoid having to do much worse.'

'Regrettable? *Regrettable?* What you've done—'

'Mr Byrne,' the President said, deploying a single index finger pointed upward. Somehow, Tom could not have explained why, it worked; it silenced him, the way a politician's raised palm can silence a hostile interviewer. 'Please let me explain. There is something I need to know. To be more precise, there's something I need to know if you know. The simplest method – and there are people who would have done this without hesitation – would have been to send in men who could have asked you in a fashion designed to make you tell them. Do I make myself clear?' He did not wait for an answer. '"Coercive interrogation" the Americans call it. I've no idea what term of art our intelligence use these days. I've been away from such things, from the front line so to speak, for too long. This is a ceremonial post I have now. Lighting the Chanukah candles, handing out prizes, funerals of world leaders younger than I am.' That wistful look again. 'I had to call in a favour just to get this operation done. They did it for old times' sake.

'Anyway, the point is there were shortcuts that could have been taken to find out what you know. We could have asked directly and not in a nice way. But I wouldn't do that. Not to a daughter of the Shoah.' And for the first time he looked properly at Rebecca.

Tom could see that she was meeting his gaze and holding it. Was it possible that she knew what the old man was talking about?

She spoke. 'You did this to be kind? Is that what you're saying?'

'I apologize, Dr Merton. To you especially. Of course I don't expect you to see what I have done as a kindness. Just as no one credits Israel with gentleness when our soldiers go into some vipers' nest looking for terrorists on foot, searching house to house, opening one booby-trapped door after another and losing dozens of our boys in the process – when the Americans, or the Brits for that matter, Mr Byrne, prefer to drop bombs from fifteen thousand feet. That's how it's done in Iraq or Afghanistan, isn't it? So much cleaner than our way.

'So, no, Dr Merton. I don't expect thanks. But

I want you to know that the distress you've experienced these last few days was because I refused even to consider the alternative. I chose the lesser of two evils.'

'You *killed* a man. You killed one of my father's friends. Henry Goldman is dead because of you.'

The President dipped his head. 'I have to apologize to you again. This was never meant to happen. It was a terrible accident. You're a doctor. I hear you came across the body. I hope you examined it. I hope you saw that Henry Goldman died of natural causes. From heart failure.'

'Caused by you!'

'He had a weak heart and he suffered a great fright. But he was not meant to die. He too, remember, was a son of the Shoah. I never meant him to come to harm.'

Tom wondered if this was just politician's theatrics. If it was, it was very good. But he had seen his fair share of diplomatic and high-level bullshit and this seemed different. In the President's eyes he believed he saw something different: an old man's sadness.

'I don't know how I can make amends for this tragedy. But I want to. And it was after his death that I decided enough was enough. It was time for me to be candid. No more games. We would have to meet face to face.'

Tom's blood began to bubble once more. 'So you thought you'd drug us—'

The President raised his voice. 'What else was I meant to do? There was no way to make contact without exposing myself. No other way of ensuring we met face to face. And this is how it had to be done. You'll soon see. You'll understand the calculation I made.'

'But we'll go straight out of this room and tell any reporter who'll listen what you've done. You'll be finished.'

'Of course I weighed up that risk. I concluded that it was not as great as you suggest. You see, what evidence would you have?'

Tom hesitated, his mind scrolling back through the events of the last – he didn't even know how many hours. He thought back to Starbucks, the meeting with Richard. Any witnesses would only have seen Rebecca and him leave voluntarily, still standing. The drug Richard had slipped into their drinks had made them pliable and obedient. There had been no scene: they had got into his car of their own free will.

And then what? Tom had nothing to show for the events that followed. Not the surgical scrubs, not so much as a tag from the hospital. How would he prove he had been there?

Which is when it struck him. With excitement, his voice rising, he all but exclaimed it. 'But we're in New York! And there'll be no record of how we got here! How will you explain that? No boarding pass, no stamp on our passports?' He was aware of speaking too loudly.

'I'm afraid that has all been taken care of. When you leave here, your passports will be returned to you, stamped in all the right places. Check your bank statement when you get back home, Dr Merton. You'll see that you withdrew the right amount of cash to pay for two tickets to New York. There are two boarding pass stubs as well. My young associate tells me you'll even qualify for frequent flier miles.' He offered only the smallest smile. 'The technology makes so much more possible these days. In your father's time, for him and his comrades, it was only what they could forge with ink and paper. And still they did remarkable things.'

Tom got to his feet and took a step forward. He was now just a few feet away from the President. He towered over him, yet the old man – whose biographer had branded him a coward – did not look in the least bit scared.

'I won't insult you, Mr Byrne, by reminding you of the risks of physically assaulting a head of state. Especially an eighty-four-year-old one. Even a very good lawyer like you could not talk your way out of that.'

Tom stepped back, though he remained standing. 'None of what you're saying matters. You've admitted to us that you ordered our abduction, that you burgled Rebecca's home and the home of her father, that you were involved in the death of Henry Goldman. We just have to tell the world what you've already confessed!'

'And who would believe you?' The emphasis was on the last word. Tom was startled.

'What the hell do you mean?'

'I mean, who would believe a Mafia hack like you? The paid servant of organized crime, the hired help of the Fantoni family of Newark, New Jersey. Who, in case you've forgotten, have been charged with racketeering, money laundering, drug-trafficking, of course, prostitution – need I go on?'

Tom swallowed, hard and visibly. He could feel Rebecca's eyes on him. He could not bear to see her; his face was hot.

'Oh, I'm sorry. Perhaps this is something you've not yet shared with Dr Merton. I gave more detail than was strictly necessary. I apologize. The point is, no one will believe a word you say. A lawyer who freaked out then sold his soul to Don Corleone.'

Rebecca spoke, her voice low but wavering with anger. 'Your thugs obviously injected us with something. There'll be traces of it in our blood-stream. There'll be puncture marks on our skin.'

'Are you sure this is a point you want to make, Dr Merton?'

Tom turned around to see Rebecca whiten. 'What are you talking about?'

'I mean that your skin has probably quite a few marks on it.'

She shook her head in disbelief. 'That was ten years ago. How could you possibly—'

'You can find out anything about anyone, if you really want to. That's all intelligence work really amounts to. You once had an intravenous drugs habit which means—'

'I didn't have a habit! I injected drugs but I was never an addict.'

'Is that a clinical definition?'

'It was a mistake, I was at a very low—'

'Doesn't matter to me. I'm a liberal on these issues. But it could make your position – as a doctor, I mean – *complicated*. Let's put it no more strongly than that.'

Tom fell back into his chair. Rebecca, of all people. He would never have guessed. He contemplated the unhappiness that would have driven her to it; he remembered what she had said about growing up in a house of permanent darkness. Still standing, he stretched a hand across the space between them and found hers, the first time they had touched since they had come into this room.

He could see the old man had them cornered. Neither could say a word to anyone about anything. If they did, they would sound delusional: no saner than the people who send emails to the national press, insisting they have been abducted by aliens or are the personal victims of the royal family. They had been comprehensively outmanoeuvred. Tom sunk in his chair and waited for the next blow.

It was Rebecca who spoke, softer than before. 'I don't understand. You used to be the leader of

Israel. We learned about you in school. Why would you be my father's enemy?'

The old man sighed and took slowly to his feet. It was the first time he had showed his age. He walked in deliberate steps over to the window. The city seemed to glitter in the morning sunlight.

Without turning around he spoke quietly. 'You're right to want to move beyond these preliminaries. We've set the ground rules. It's time to get to the heart of the matter. We need to speak about DIN.'

# CHAPTER FIFTY-NINE

'This is the second mistake my aides would warn me about.' He paused to turn around and face them. 'I say "would" because, of course, they know nothing of this. Not the real reason. I have kept it from them, the way I have kept it from everyone. My family, my friends. My country. My aides – the team out there – think only what I have told them: that you hold information that compromises the security of our country.

'The problem is, I don't know if that's true or not.' He cocked his head to one side, a gesture designed to show he was about to correct himself. 'Of course, I know that you know nothing that directly threatens Israeli security. But I don't know if you know something else. Something that threatens me. And therefore threatens my country.'

Tom felt a wave of exhaustion coming over him. 'What are you talking about?'

'I knew Gershon Matzkin was still alive. I'd

always known it. I'd been keeping an eye on him: I had people who could do that for me. And I waited. I waited for the day I'd hear he had been hospitalized, or had fallen ill. But the day never came. I thought about it more often than I like to admit. I'm not proud of this. Maybe a few days would go by when I didn't think about it. But never as much as a week. Especially in the last few years, when he was the last one left.

'Aron, the leader, he died long ago. Such a strong man, such a hero. He didn't even reach seventy. What's his name – Steiner – he lost his mind years ago. I knew he couldn't hurt me. But Gershon was still fit. He still had everything up here.' He tapped the side of his head. 'I hope I don't offend you, Dr Merton, if I tell you that I was, in a way, waiting for your father to die. Not out of cruelty, please don't misunderstand me. Out of worry. Out of an old man's anxiety. I needed *relief,* you see. I needed to know that I had outlived him. I have spent all these years needing to live in a world where no one knew our secret but me. Because then it wouldn't be a secret any more, would it? The memory would have gone. I would be free.

'But not while Gershon was alive. Not while he carried our story in his head. And then Monday happened. I was here, in New York, for the General Assembly. And I hear that name, on the local cable news. "A British man has been killed on the steps of the UN. He has been identified as Gerald

Merton." Can you imagine what was going through my mind? My hands were trembling.' He held up his right hand, giving it an exaggerated wobble. 'I wondered who would want Gershon dead. They were saying it was an accident, but I didn't believe it. Gershon always took care of himself. All those killings – I'm sorry, those executions – and never once did he let anyone get near him. Others from DIN were not so skilful, but Gershon was different. It's not an accident that he lived the longest. He was the best.

'But then I began to get queasy. Why was he in New York? Could he have started,' he paused, unsure what word to use, 'work again? Who could he possibly be after? He must have known I would be here. Was it me he wanted to see? And then my hands trembled some more. Had Gershon come to New York to kill me?'

Tom wanted to interrupt, to ask what motive Gershon Matzkin would possibly have had to murder the President of the State of Israel, a fellow Jew, a comrade, it seemed, from the secret crusade that was DIN. But he bit his lip: this torrent of words from the old man would eventually explain everything. He just had to let it gush out.

'You see—' He was about to speak but stopped himself, giving a smile that was as brief as a wince. 'But this is to take the greatest risk of all. This is often how it is in politics. The only way of preventing a revelation is to make the revelation yourself. But maybe this is crazy.'

'What's crazy?' It was Tom, his voice no longer confrontational. The same voice he had used when counselling very senior members of the UN bureaucracy, including the Secretary-General. Outsiders had no idea of the extent to which aides to the highest ranking politicians served as counsellors, surrogate spouses, paid best friends.

'What I'm about to do. Having worked so hard to ensure you don't have a certain item of information, I'm about to give it to you. But I can see no other way.'

'No other way of doing what?' Tom felt as if he was hitting his stride now.

'Of being sure there's no other evidence. If it's just you, your word based on what you hear from me now, today, then it's nothing. I will deny it and the press will learn that you are simply not credible witnesses – for reasons I don't think we need to repeat. But I need to know if there's something else. This is what I have always needed to know. Every day any member of DIN was alive, I needed to know it. Now that Gershon is gone, I want this thing to be over. I want to sleep for more than three hours at night.'

'So you need to ask us what we know.'

The old man nodded.

'OK,' Rebecca said. 'Ask.'

The President examined his fingernails which, Tom couldn't help but notice, were in perfect condition. And it wasn't just his nails. His suit hanged impeccably; the shirt was pressed exactly.

How this elegant statesman, welcomed into every chancellery in Europe, must have hated the notion of a stain, hovering somewhere in the great 'out there', waiting to spill all over his reputation.

At last he spoke, the reluctance making the slightest downward twist to his lips. 'What do you know about Tochnit Aleph?'

# CHAPTER SIXTY

Tom tried to make a calculation, to work through his options, but he kept colliding with a wall of fog. His brain felt soupy, still thick from sleep and sedative. It was easier when he simply had to listen to and prompt the President, but this was different. Now he needed to think fast, for his sake and, more important, for Rebecca's.

The word *Tochnit* had thrown him, but *Aleph* was now familiar enough for him to work it out. He had guessed there would be a Hebrew expression for Plan A and this had to be it. So this was the aspect of DIN's work that had given this man sixty years of sleepless nights.

If they said nothing, who knew what extra punishment he could inflict on them? He had already shown what he was prepared to do. To defy him could spell calamity; he would surely find a way to make them speak.

And yet, to say what they knew was to give away whatever leverage they currently held. At this moment, the President needed something from them: once he had it, what other protection would they have? He had already confessed his yearning to be the only man in the world with this secret knowledge: once he was sure of that, he would rest easy. If Tom and Rebecca told him what they knew, he would have every incentive to ensure they went the way of Gershon Matzkin and Aron, DIN's leader, or at least the way of Sid Steiner, their memories obliterated. How would the President achieve that? Tom had no idea. But that he would be prepared to do whatever it took, he had no doubt.

His heart was beginning to thump. He needed to think of another way. He somehow had to make the old man believe Tom and Rebecca were speaking the truth, that they were saying all they knew, and yet supply him with an incentive for keeping both of them alive.

'We've seen the papers,' Tom said.

'What papers?'

'The blueprints. The blueprints of the city water-works. Of Munich, Weimar, Hamburg, Nuremberg and Wannsee.'

'So you know.'

'We know.'

'And you know about me?'

Tom stared hard. He didn't want to go for an outright bluff: no one would be better at sniffing out bullshit than a veteran politician; bullshit was their most traded commodity. But Tom wanted at least to keep the old man guessing.

'Do the papers point to me in any way?'

'I think that if someone knew what they were looking for, they could work it out.' He had crossed the border into the danger zone, the land of the lie.

'That's what I supposed. And where are these papers now?'

'I think you can understand why we'd be reluctant to tell you that.'

The President assessed the faces of the two people before him. He lingered over Rebecca and then directed his next sentence to her. 'I think you need to hear what happened. Then perhaps you'll see this differently.'

Tom exhaled silently. This is what he had wanted: for the President to start spilling.

'I was not a member of DIN. I was not even in Europe during . . . during those times. I left Russia in 1936. I got out in time. I came to Palestine: to be a pioneer. Our aim was to create the *Ivri,* the Hebrew. A wholly new Jew. Strong, a worker, a soldier: no more cowering, no more passivity in the face of our enemies. We used to say that all that awaited the Jews of Europe was death.' He dipped his head. 'We had no idea how right we were.

'So I arrived in Palestine as a teenager. I went to university there: I studied chemistry. And of course, I joined the youth movements and before I knew it, I was elected to this and then that. I was a politician even then. But I learned from the best. People don't realize this about me. They call me arrogant, but they don't understand. I was always a student of great men. I showed them only humility and respect. Which is why they trusted me. Including him.'

Tom raised a quizzical eyebrow, a gesture he immediately regretted. He should have pretended to know.

But the President had passed the point of no return; he was not about to stop the flow now. 'The professor at Rehovot: the man who had brought us to the Promised Land. Imagine it, the Moses who had led the Jewish movement for a homeland. He had returned to his laboratory and I was one of his students. So what do you think I said when he asked me to make up this mixture? What would you have said? Would you have denied him? I was a child, in my early twenties. Of course I said yes.'

The fog was beginning to clear. Tom could see Rebecca was sitting stiff and upright. 'So you made up the poison.'

'What can I say? That I was only obeying orders? As you know, that line of defence is rather discredited.'

The air in the room was heavy; Tom could feel it pressing down on him. He spoke: 'Did you know what it was for?'

The President gave him a smile. 'It would be nice to say I didn't. But it would be nonsense. What else could such a request be for? The note from the professor was clear. "Give this man a toxin that has no colour and no smell, and yet will not lose its power in water." What else could it be? And the volume! Only an idiot would not have realized that this was designed for a mass water supply. And it was Aron who bore the note. Even if you had never heard of DIN, everyone knew about him. He was the hero of the Jewish resistance, one of the few who had emerged from the fire. You only had to look at that cadaver of a face to know what business he had with me and my poisons.'

'But you did it.'

'I did it.'

'And this is your great secret.'

The old man took a sip from the glass of water that sat on the table between them, until now untouched. 'Not just my secret. Think of the State of Israel. There are many in the world who hate my country, who believe its very existence is a crime. Imagine what they would do with this information: that the founders of the state – including the man who is today the country's president – were ready to cause so much death. Would we ever recover?

'But I do not deny there are personal considerations here. I don't know how much you know of my career, Mr Byrne. I am the advocate of peace and reconciliation. I am the man who has preached putting war and violence behind us. I have been garlanded in every capital, in Bonn and

Berlin especially. I am the holder of the *Großes Bundesverdienstkreuz*, the first non-German ever to be awarded that title. My honorary rank is Kommandeur. Try to imagine what happens to that reputation if now, more than sixty years later, the world finds out that I was an accomplice to an attempt at mass murder. You've seen those blueprints, both of you. You know what Tochnit Aleph would have meant. Death at the turn of a tap. To a million people. Not just Nazis, but children and women, too. Random, senseless killing.'

Rebecca leaned forward: 'Why didn't it happen?'

'For the reason I've just said. In the end, cooler heads prevailed. The leadership in Palestine realized that Tochnit Aleph would be a disaster for the Jewish people: we would no longer be the victims of the greatest crime in human history. We would be guilty of mass murder. Tochnit Aleph would have destroyed our moral advantage. And, remember, this was 1945: the moral high ground was the only ground we had.'

Rebecca spoke again: 'Did the leadership order DIN to call off the operation?'

The old man stretched, his first sign of fatigue. 'It wasn't quite as simple as that. DIN was a movement that had the highest righteousness on its side: it spoke for the six million. What were a few politicians in Tel Aviv next to that?'

'So how did they stop it?'

'Aron was on a boat leaving Palestine, on his

way back to Europe with three canisters of my poison in his bag. British military police boarded the ship and arrested him. Threw him into solitary confinement.'

'Somebody had tipped off the British authorities?'

'That's right.'

'Do you know who that was?'

'Of course I know.' He paused and took another sip of water. Then he looked back at Tom and Rebecca with an expression of mock puzzlement. 'It was me.'

## CHAPTER SIXTY-ONE

Rebecca was ashen. 'Why? Why on earth would you have done that?'

Tom could see strain on Rebecca's face, draining it of colour. She was visibly struggling to make sense of what they were hearing. Each revelation had shaken up the kaleidoscope and then, just as it was resettling into a new picture she could understand, it was thrown into chaos all over again.

'I've asked myself that same question. Many times.' The President fixed Rebecca with a steady gaze. Tom noticed his eyes were reddening around the edges. 'I knew the leaders were desperate to stop Aron. But they didn't know where he was or how to get to him. No one did. Then he contacted me, at the last minute. He was in a hurry: he had a question about storage of the poison. Was he meant to keep it cold, in the dark? We met and he let slip that he was leaving the next day. We knew he was going by

British transport ship. So the British had to watch the port only for that single day. It was easy.'

'I still don't understand why.'

The old man let out a deep sigh. 'My disease. I suppose that's the answer. My disease.'

'What disease?' Rebecca's doctor voice.

'The same disease I've always had.' He paused, as if they were expected to know the answer. After a few moments of silence, he filled the space. '*Ambition.* I knew that the very highest echelons were determined to stop Aron and they couldn't do it. And then, thanks to me, they could. Within a few weeks, I was out of that laboratory, appointed as a personal adviser to the old man. The man who became my country's first leader. Funny, we all called him the old man. But I am now much older than he was. Anyway, I've been at the top ever since.'

Tom was struck by the man's honesty. Self-criticism was not usually politicians' strength and this went much further.

'All right,' Tom said, aware he was interrupting a conversation between the two of them. 'Why don't you just tell the world what you've told us? You're the man who stopped Tochnit Aleph. That should win you a few more prizes.'

'Oh, the world would be delighted, I agree. I could be a hero. Except the world is not Israel, Mr Byrne. In Israel, Aron of the Ghetto is a hero. And not some passing idol either. I mean a *gever*, a hero on a Biblical scale. He is the man who defended the Jews against their greatest enemy. He will be remembered in thousands of years, like Judah Maccabee or the boy David who slew Goliath. His name is already a legend in my country. Jews around the world read his poetry. Against him, I am an ant. A politician, cutting deals. And that's before they know what I know. And what you now know. That I betrayed him. The great Aron of the Ghetto. And to the British! The hated imperial masters, who shut the gates of Palestine in our hour of mortal peril!'

'So what are you going to do?'

'I think the question is, what are *we* going to do? We all need an exit strategy.'

'What the hell is that supposed to mean?' It was Rebecca.

'It means, my dear, that we need a way out. You need to leave here safely, with a guarantee that you will not be troubled by any of this again.' He let the words hang in the air a while, so that Tom and Rebecca could weigh them. They sounded emollient and reasonable, until you stepped back – and realized they were a threat.

He went on. 'And I need a guarantee that what you know, what we have discussed here, will never be made public. That you will take this secret to your grave.'

At last, thought Tom: a negotiation. Some lawyers did nothing else. Tom had not been one of them, not when he started. But at the UN there had always been a bit of bargaining involved in the job, even if it was a departmental tussle within the UN. He had once had to resolve a dispute over a Pacific island – in truth a glorified rock, smaller than the average New Yorker's bathroom – claimed by two rival, and slightly larger, islands. It was an arcane and hair-splitting dispute but it had ended in a negotiation. Besides, his work over the last few months, including for the Fantoni family, had been nothing but deals.

Tom sat up stiffly, an attempt to establish some authority in the room. His mind was revving. He had planned for this moment, but only over the last few minutes. He would have to improvise. 'OK. We each know what we want and what we have. You will give Rebecca safe passage back to London. Once there, she'll arrange to give you the papers that you want. They will be originals. Once you have them, you will know that there is no more hard evidence of what happened. No evidence of your role.'

'Except what's in your heads.'

'Yes. But how likely are we to use that? Why, realistically, would we want to cause trouble? Now that we know what you can do to us.' This was the first move.

The President rubbed his chin, then began a slight rocking motion, forwards and backwards, like a family patriarch on the porch, taking his time. Tom decided to press the point, see if he could close the deal.

'If you can inject us with anaesthetic just off

bloody Regent Street, then you can inject us with something worse.' He watched the old man. 'We have no interest in causing you embarrassment.'

'And in return?'

'You let us have our lives back. You call off your thugs and give back our passports and wallets.'

'And you will give me back those papers.'

'They will be yours. And so long as nothing happens to us, no one will ever see them.'

This was the second move, the one Tom hoped would be decisive.

'What does that mean?'

'It means that I have already made an electronic copy of those papers and scanned them into a website. A dormant website, programmed to stay dormant so long as I log in, with my password, every seven days. If for some reason I don't log in – say, I've been incapacitated in some way – then the site goes live. And sends an email alert to a few chosen addresses. Editor@NewYorkTimes.com would be one. Editor@JerusalemPost might be another. Oh, and we wouldn't want to leave out the BBC or CNN.' Tom looked over at Rebecca. Her eyes were wide; she looked startled.

The President spoke again, his pitch now rising. 'You've done this?'

Tom nodded, a bead of sweat forming on his upper lip. 'We spent a lot of time at that internet cafe, as I'm sure your friends have told you.'

'How dare you?' The old man examined both

faces then, with effort, hauled himself upright. 'What if something goes wrong with this website, what if it accidentally—'

'No need for you to worry about that. It's secure. Just so long as nothing happens to us.'

The President was pale, unsure what to say. Rebecca leaned forward, as if keen to exploit this moment of weakness. 'I have one more condition.'

Tom swivelled round and glared at her: *Don't ruin this.*

She ignored him. 'In return for keeping what you have told us safe and secret, in return for keeping that website dormant, I want you to use your influence to get me a meeting. With the Secretary-General of the United Nations.'

'Oh, for God's sake, Rebecca—' Tom couldn't help himself. What the hell was she playing at, risking the wrath of a man who had already proved he would stop at nothing to get his own way, and for what?

With a half-smile, which Tom interpreted as sheer disbelief at the cheek of the woman, the President held up a hand to silence him. 'Tell me again. What is it you want?'

'What Rebecca is trying to—'

'I asked the lady myself, Mr Byrne.' She had gone too far, Tom was certain of it. Any moment now the President would summon the heavies to come in and close this problem down once and for all.

Rebecca spoke again. 'What I want is for you to get me a meeting with the Secretary-General. I want him to look me in the eye and admit what the UN did to my father. Then this nightmare can be over. My father did not survive all that he survived to be treated like this, as if he were nothing.' Her voice was cracking. 'Dirt on someone's shoe.'

'I understand,' the President said quietly. 'Dr Merton, I truly understand.'

Suddenly, as if snapping himself out of a trance, he turned to Tom and shook his hand, giving him no chance to refuse the gesture. 'I am prepared to accept these terms. I will contact the Secretary-General's office right away. And so long as you come to no harm, this internet site of yours will remain locked. Yes?'

'Yes.'

'And it stays locked and hidden even after my death: my future reputation matters to me just as much, you know. I can make arrangements that will hold after I'm gone. If that information is ever released, our agreement will be void. There will be people ready to act on that fact.'

'I understand.'

'Good. And now I would like to have a private word of remembrance with Dr Merton.'

He headed for the doorway: Tom wondered if he was about to usher Rebecca into the outer suite. Was he going to ask her to pray with him? But he gestured for her to stay behind, leaving

Tom and Rebecca alone. Neither dared speak, fearing the old man would come back at any moment. He was gone for no more than twenty seconds, no doubt preparing his aides for the departure of his two 'guests'.

When the President came back, he immediately placed an arm over Rebecca's shoulder, guiding her towards the window. Tom could only see their backs but he could hear the old man muttering something in a language he guessed was Hebrew: judging by Rebecca's low nod of response, it was probably a word of condolence for her father, perhaps even a memorial prayer. The President then removed his arm so that he could face Rebecca directly, clasping her hands in a double-handshake, the kind of showy gesture politicians saved for the special occasion. Tom was sure he had seen this very man do just that at the signing of a peace treaty a couple of decades earlier. There were more inaudible words of farewell, then the door opened and Tom and Rebecca were shown out – leaving the eighty-four-year-old President of the State of Israel gazing out of the window, quite alone.

# CHAPTER SIXTY-TWO

They were in his old office. It had been Henning's idea: the new occupant was away, in Slovenia on some EU-related business, and the room was empty.

When it had been his, Tom had found it cramped and dull. The shelves were cast in grey metal, as was the desk. It had the utilitarian appearance of a foreman's cabin watching over the factory floor.

But now he wasn't looking at the furniture. Nor was he focusing on the fact that there were only two window panels for this cubicle, unlike the three to be found in the more senior offices at each end of this corridor. Now he was gazing outward, enjoying the generous and direct view of the Chrysler Building, easily his favourite New York landmark. Perhaps it was the simple relief that this strange ordeal was at last over; that he no longer had to look over his shoulder, no longer had to fear which flat was about to be ransacked, which old man was about to wind up dead. But he could not take his eyes off the view. To him, it shimmered.

Rebecca was behind the desk, sitting in a graphite chair far grander than the creaking, fake leather contraption he remembered.

'All that time,' he said at last. 'We were looking in the wrong place.'

She gave the smallest frown, two lines in the space above the bridge of her nose.

'I was thinking Nazis. That's all I could think. Once I read your father's journal, I was certain that the only people who would be doing this – smashing up the house, stalking us around London – would be some bunch of old war criminals. I never once thought of . . . his own side.'

'Why would you have thought of it?' She gave him a smile, one that warmed even this metallic room. 'Anyway, even if you're not much of a detective, you're a helluva negotiator. That was quite a move you made.'

'He gave us time to think. All that talking; it wasn't difficult to come up with something. We just had to give him a reason not to get rid of us once he got the papers.'

'Oh, yes. The papers.' She was still smiling. 'What exactly are these mystery papers?'

Tom looked back at the window. 'You know your trouble, Rebecca Merton? Too little faith.' He turned back, so that he could face her. 'We can choose. It could be the blueprints of the waterworks—'

'But those have no link to him.'

'Not now, they don't. But it wouldn't be difficult for you to add a few words to that postcard, now would it? Some clever little play on a Biblical verse that happens to name our old friend. There must be plenty of characters in the Bible with the same name as him.

'I'm not convinced. What's the other option?'

'Your father's notebook. You could fake his writing, add a section about Plan A, explaining how the now-famous Mr X brewed up the potion. We hand over that page and the blueprints. Enough stuff to make him realize we weren't bluffing.'

'Except we were—'

'Ssshh.' Tom placed a single finger across his lips. 'All that matters is that getting rid of us is now less attractive than it was. Or getting rid of me. He wouldn't lay a glove on you: you're a "daughter of the Shoah".'

Rebecca sat back in the chair. They had gone to the Nations' Café first, straight after they had been escorted out of the presidential suite at the UN Millennium Plaza hotel, from where Tom immediately phoned Henning. He wanted to break it gently, but it just splurged out: he and Rebecca had come on a hastily arranged trip to New York because the resourceful Dr Merton had made an end-run around the UN bureaucracy, deploying her own contacts to get her precious meeting with the Secretary-General.

'I know,' Henning had said. 'I just got a call from the SG's political office.' He was furious. 'I'd won the battle on this, Tom. The SG had some ludicrous idea about meeting your Dr Merton and I got it blocked. And now I'm undermined by an intervention from the bloody Israelis. You've made me look a prick.'

'She's made you look a prick, Henning.'

'Thanks a lot, that makes a big difference.'

Tom tried to placate his old friend. At least this way, there would be no publicity. He put his hand over the receiver and checked that Rebecca was happy for there to be no photographers. She nodded immediately, looking terrified at the very prospect of facing the media. 'She agrees. We'll have no one there, no press, no advisers. Let's keep it simple, Henning – and leak-proof. By the time the media know about this meeting, it'll be over.'

Munchau told Tom the only reason he wasn't resisting this insane idea more strenuously was that he had been notified the previous day that the NYPD were dropping their inquiry into the Merton killing altogether. 'Since it falls outside their jurisdiction, the DA says no prosecutable crime was committed.'

'So the coast is clear?'

'I suppose so. But I still want her to sign a comprehensive end-of-claim agreement. Can't have her throwing a meeting with the SG back in our face in some future civil action, claiming it as admission of liability. And a gag agreement, promising no publicity, no interviews, nothing.'

'I'll draft something right away,' Tom said, confirmed in his view that Henning was one of the best men the UN had, protective of the institution and its reputation even when the boss was cavalier. Tom felt a sting of guilt at how quickly he had doubted him.

'I'm impressed,' Rebecca was saying, swivelling her chair and alternating her gaze from the Chrysler building back to Tom. 'You got it all worked out.'

'Not quite everything.'

'No?'

'There's one thing I've never understood. Barely had a minute to think about it in London. But I still don't understand it.'

'Don't understand what?'

'The envelope that arrived at your flat. The list of names. I don't get who would have done it. It can't be the Israelis, or whoever was working for the Pres—'

There was a knock on the door. Henning.

Rebecca leapt up from the chair, re-adopted the expression of grieving daughter, and extended her hand.

Tom did the introductions and Henning got straight to the point, too professional to show that his teeth were gritted. 'Dr Merton, the Secretary General is so appreciative of the gesture you've made in coming here that he has asked if he can see you right away, in accordance with the conditions I have discussed with Mr Byrne.' He looked towards Tom, who nodded. 'He has cleared his next two appointments.' He raised his hand in a beckoning gesture.

'Hold on,' Rebecca said. She took a deep breath, then exhaled. 'Can we just take a minute?'

'Of course.' Henning shot another look over at Tom. *She's not going to start crying, is she?*

Rebecca collected herself. 'Mr Munchau, I'm not used to this sort of thing. Meetings with world leaders.'

Tom looked at the floor.

'From what I hear, you're pretty well-connected. Quite something to have the president of the state of Israel in your corner.'

'Still, I think I might find it intimidating to walk into the Secretary-General's office, with him sitting behind some giant desk. Do you know what I mean?'

'I think so.'

'Is it possible that we meet somewhere, I don't know, less *grand*? Somewhere a bit quieter?'

'Of course, Dr Merton.' Henning's diplomatic veneer was back in place. 'I can think of a place that will be ideal, wholly suitable for an encounter of this gravity.'

'I really appreciate it.'

She stood up and visibly girded herself, like a candidate about to give a speech. Tom stepped forward, ready to follow her out. But Rebecca raised a single palm to block his path.

'Tom, you've helped me so much. But I think I need to do this on my own.'

Tom nodded and retreated. Henning gave him a brief smile, then ushered Rebecca out. 'Don't worry, I'll bring her back,' he mouthed with the tiniest gleam in his eye.

Tom watched them go, giving Rebecca an unseen nod of encouragement, then looked back around the office, trying to remember what it had been like when it was his. There had been even less decoration then than now. He had not stuck up any photographs or garlanded the shelves with bandanas picked up on visits to some exotic, 'developing' hell-holes, in the style favoured by colleagues down the corridor.

A leaden memory surfaced, like a hunk of rusting metal on the end of a fishing line. It was in this room that he used to do it. It was here that he would read the testimonies, one after another, detailing the most horrendous war crimes. Sure, the language was different each time. The place-names changed. But the story was always the same: the most blood-curdling human cruelty.

At first, he always reacted the same way: revulsion, anger, a terrible, weighty sadness. But after Rwanda, he could feel no longer. After all, those emotions had been roused to full alert when he served on the Rwanda tribunal and what good had it done? How many killers had they actually prosecuted and convicted? Twenty-six.

After that, he stopped reading the accounts. He would skip over the human testimony and just get to the bottom line figure. That's what he had done with the Darfur paperwork that had come into this office. He had trained his eye to skip over the eye-witness stuff, the individual case-studies, and just find the hard number at the bottom of the page. Why read it? He knew what savagery human beings were capable of. And, much worse, he knew that there was nothing that anyone – not even the sainted bloody United Nations – could do about it.

Tom needed to get on with drafting the agreement for Rebecca and Henning to sign. He sat at the desk and switched on the computer. It asked for a name and password: his old one didn't work. He smiled and remembered the 'system administrator' code Henning had taught him when they had once had to hack into the machine of a colleague who had gone on vacation without first sending them a draft text he had been working on. He tapped in the password – *UThant*, the name of a past Secretary-General – and so, thanks to the sentimentality of the United Nations IT department, he was in.

He opened up a Word document and had tapped out a first sentence when he hesitated. Another lesson from Henning: for anything truly confidential, don't use the internal UN system. Anyone could access anything. If Munchau's chief objective was the avoidance of publicity, it made no sense to risk a leak. He would draft a text by hand.

He reached into his inside pocket, but there was no pen. Perhaps it had been taken during his unconscious flight. Or left behind at the hospital.

There were no loose pens on the desk and the drawers were locked. He saw Rebecca's bag: she had left it behind on a chair, along with her coat.

Guiltily, he walked around to get it. He never liked so much as peering inside a woman's handbag: it felt too much like going through his mother's purse. He opened it quickly, saw a fountain pen and grabbed it. There was some paper in the laserprinter: he took a couple of sheets and prepared to write.

*Agreement between* he scratched without leaving a mark. He gave it a shake but still no ink would flow. He unscrewed the barrel and saw the explanation: there was no ink cartridge.

Perhaps it had become detached and fallen back into the barrel. Tom held it up to the light and saw that there was indeed something inside – but he knew instantly it was no cartridge.

At first he wondered if it was some kind of cigarette, perhaps even drugs. From what he'd heard in the presidential suite, it would be no surprise. Tom tapped the pen barrel on the surface of the desk and it popped out. Not a cigarette, but a neatly rolled sheet – perhaps two sheets – of paper.

It took Tom no more than a second to understand what he was looking at. As he rolled them flat, the size of the pages, the faint lines, were instantly familiar. And the handwriting was unmistakable.

Tom scanned the words.

*I received the list of names and worked my way through them methodically. I could not get to them all at once. Some of these men lived very far away; they had hidden themselves well. Each mission required papers, a fresh passport, money and a cover story. In San Sebastián, Spain, I pretended to be a tourist. I followed Joschka Dorfman, a senior SS officer at Treblinka, for days before I had a chance to 'meet' him away from his wife. She came back from a shopping trip and found that he had not taken an afternoon nap as he had promised. Instead he was hanging from the ceiling of their hotel room . . .*

Tom's head began to pound. So these were the missing pages torn from Gershon Matzkin's notebook. They had not been missing at all. Rebecca had had them all the time. She had known all along the truth of her father's life. She had known about DIN.

Of course she had. What had Julian Goldman said when Rebecca had introduced them? *'You have never seen a father and a daughter who were closer. Even when it was just the two of them, they were a family. A two-person family.'* They were a pair, the Mertons; they worked together. But Tom had been so blinded by sympathy, by warmth towards her, by his desire for her, that he had not seen the obvious. Whatever it was Gerald Merton had been up to, Rebecca Merton had been his confidante and accomplice.

But she had also sat there in Henry Goldman's office, stunned by the story the lawyer had revealed as much as Tom had. Hadn't she? A memory, brief and fleeting, came to him. He had wondered about it at the time, but the moment had passed. It was when they had argued, back in her flat, straight after the Goldman meeting. She complained that the old lawyer had been droning on, 'telling us what we already knew'. *What we already knew.*

Had the whole thing been a charade, one long act? She must have decided it from the very start, tearing the key pages from her father's notebook long before Tom had shoved it in his bag. She had probably done it the instant she heard her father had died.

But he had discovered the truth anyway, he had learned about DIN and their work of vengeance, seeing the evidence for himself, stashed away in the box at Julian Goldman's office. They had gone straight there after the envelope arrived.

*Of course.* No wonder he had never been able to work out who had sent over that faded, crumbling list of names. It was the piece of the puzzle that could never fit. The person who had sent that letter – delivering it by hand, in an envelope that was not stamped – had surely been none other than Rebecca Merton herself.

He pictured her, sealing the envelope, then presenting it as if it had come from out of the blue. How clever she had been, standing out of sight, alternately hiding or disclosing the crucial clues that would unlock the mystery of her father. She clearly had wanted to put Tom on the path towards DIN – without ever revealing how much she knew.

But why? Why lead them both on such a pointless charade, pretending not to know what she knew perfectly well?

He thought back to the meeting with Sid Steiner, the almost absurd lengths they had gone to, first to find him and then to dredge up his memories. Rebecca had seemed no less baffled than Tom had been, desperate to know what Sid knew. She had been the same during the last visit to her father's flat, the secret papers hidden in the Aleph painting apparently as much of a revelation to her as they had been to him. Could all of that have been a sham? Or was this more complicated than that: had Rebecca known part of the strange, murderous life-story of Gershon Matzkin – but not all of it?

Tom rubbed his eyes, forcing himself to concentrate. He looked back at the hand-written pages in front of him. Sure enough, at least on the basis of this skim-read, Gershon seemed to be recounting only his work as an unofficial executioner of individuals – hunting down specific, named men who had once, just a few years earlier, been part of the Nazi killing machine. There was no reference to the bakery at Nuremberg and none to the water plot. Tom looked hard for the name of the man whom they had met just a few hours earlier, the Israeli president. What if Rebecca had, after all, harboured the crucial evidence Tom had promised when bargaining for their safety, evidence whose existence he had conjured from nowhere for the sake of a bluff? What if such evidence existed right here, rolled up in the barrel of her own fountain pen? But there was no sign of the Israeli's name. The man who was now the president of Israel, along with Plan A and Plan B, was unmentioned in the journal of Gershon Matzkin.

The ink on the last sheet was thicker and fresher and the handwriting spidered across the page. It was obvious that these lines had been added long after the rest of the journal had been completed. Gershon now wrote in the unsteady hand of an old man.

*DIN's work finished many, many years ago. For nearly forty years, none of us has taken on any more of this duty. We tried to remove Mengele, but as you know, we failed. We came close, but not close enough.*

*Rebecca, I promised myself – for your sake and for the sake of our family – that I would stop. And I kept my promise to you. For all these years, I have only been a normal, loving father to you. I have certainly tried.*

*But a long time ago, I made another promise, a promise to a young woman just as full of life and of beauty as you are today. I never thought I would have the chance to honour my word to her. I thought it was too late.*

*Now I have the chance and I cannot let it pass. This is why I am going to New York. If you want to understand, you must do as I say – and remember Kadish.*

# CHAPTER SIXTY-THREE

A new wave of electricity flooded into Tom's brain; he felt as if his neural circuits were about to crash. He tried to process this latest surge of information. It meant that Rebecca had known not only that her father had been an assassin for DIN, but that this had been his purpose in New York. The meeting with the Russian, the gun secreted away in the bathroom at the Tudor Hotel: they were indeed all they had seemed. Gerald Merton, seventy-six-year-old Gerald Merton, had come to New York to kill. And his daughter, who had carried this information stashed in her fountain pen, had known that all along. Her number had been on his phone: he might even have been updating her on his progress. No wonder she had not wanted to call the police after the break-in; no wonder she had barely mentioned pressing a full legal case for compensation against the United Nations. She didn't want anyone probing too deeply into a story she knew only too well.

Now Tom was convinced: Rebecca Merton knew whom her father had come here to kill. But who was it?

Could it have been the Israeli president? Had the aged politician, whose antennae had doubtless become finely tuned after so long, intuited Gershon's intentions correctly? Maybe this was the 'chance' Gerald thought he had to seize, the visit of the President to New York.

But it made no sense. The Israeli had been visible and in public life for years and years. And Gershon Matzkin was a first-class hitman: if he had wanted to get his revenge for the betrayal of Aron, he would have had countless chances – plenty of them easier than targeting a head of state in the security-saturated environment of the United Nations.

Besides, this passage in the notebook did not, surely, relate to Aron. It spoke instead of a promise to 'another young woman'. Was it Rosa, his benighted first love and early comrade in DIN? But there was no specific connection between her and the Israeli that had to be avenged, at least none that the old politician had hinted at. And he hadn't seemed to hold anything back.

Tom looked down at the torn page which, anxious to become a scroll once more, had recurled on the table. He laid it flat and read it, lingering on the last sentence.

*If you want to understand, you must do as I say – and remember Kadish.*

Tom now saw that there was another word, written in brackets and in pencil so that Tom had missed it the first time. It seemed to be a time reference of some kind: *(March)*. Perhaps that was when Gershon had made the note, a few months back.

Tom looked again at the final, inked phrase, realizing that he had seen it before. It had been on a note pinned to Rebecca's noticeboard at home, written in her father's hand. It referred to the Jewish memorial prayer for the dead, she had said. He remembered now how the poignancy of it had struck him, as if the newly dead Gershon Matzkin was pleading from the grave to be remembered. Rebecca's explanation had been less dramatic: it was simply a request by her father to say prayers for her late mother.

But the tone here was more urgent. It suggested that this 'Kadish' would somehow explain Gershon's mission to New York: *If you want to understand, you must do as I say.*

Tom looked back through the two pages. The writing was so small it was hard to read fast. He went back to the account of the Dorfman killing in San Sebastián, deciphering the script as it told of leaving the Nazi hanging in his hotel room, walking past Dorfman's wife as she came into the lobby, knowing what she was about to find. The writing became crabbier but, squinting, Tom could make it out.

*After the Dorfman job I went to the seashore, picked*

*up a single stone and said Kaddish for all the Jews of Treblinka. It was the first time I had said Kaddish since I had been a child in Kovno, where I learned to say Kaddish for my father. I had not forgotten the prayer.*

So that confirmed it: Kaddish was precisely what Rebecca had said it was, a memorial prayer. Tom fell back into his chair, closed his eyes and grabbed his head. What on earth had Gershon meant: *If you want to understand, you must do as I say – and remember Kadish.*

And then it struck him, a creeping realization that made his skin tingle. He tried to calm himself. It was probably nothing, just a simple mistake. After all, the post-script had been written only recently. Gershon was in his late seventies; it might be an error of old age.

But the difference was clear. When referring to the prayer, Gershon had used two ds: *Kaddish*. But here in this final message, there was just one: *Kadish*. And that, Tom was sure of it, had been the spelling in the note on the pinboard. *Kadish*.

Slowly, his hands trembling, he turned back to the computer keyboard. He opened an internet browser, dragged the cursor over to the search window and typed in those six letters. Instantly Google made the same assumption he had.

*Did you mean: Kaddish?*

He said yes and saw entries for the 'Jewish Mourner's Prayer' and the like. Then he went back to the single 'd' spelling: Kadish.

The list of entries seemed barren: a professor

of electro-chemistry in Indiana, a bass guitar teacher in Texas, a federal government official in Washington. He had expected something with an instant and clear connection to Gershon Matzkin and to DIN.

Aware of the clumsy crudity of it, he went back to the search window and wrote: Kadish Holocaust. If this narrowing down did not work, he would go back to his earlier hunch – that Gerald Merton had simply had a senior moment and spelled the word wrong. He hit return and as the screen filled he felt the flow of his blood quicken.

All of these entries seemed relevant. An artist called Reuben Kadish, who had done Holocaust-related work: perhaps Gershon had one of his paintings, perhaps he had hidden some papers there, just as he had in the backing of the Aleph canvas. There were a couple more references to the artist's work, including an exhibition and an archive.

But what Tom read below those entries, halfway down the screen, made him shiver.

> *George Kadish – Wikipedia, the free encyclopedia*
>
> *George* **Kadish** *was a Lithuanian Jewish photographer who documented life in the Kovno ghetto during the Holocaust, the period of the Nazi German genocide . . .*

He read it twice to be sure that, in his fevered state, he had not imagined it. But the crucial five words were still there. They had not disappeared in some hallucinatory vapour: *life in the Kovno ghetto*.

Tom began to click frantically, hopping from one website to another, learning that Kadish had kept a home-made camera under his coat, secretly photographing his fellow Jewish inmates of the ghetto. Now the screen was filling up with photographs Kadish had taken. Two boys, toddlers, no more than three years old, sitting on a threadbare cushion in front of a filthy, cracked wall, their faces as dirty as those of young children anywhere. Except sewn to these two boys' clothes, covering their hearts, were oversized yellow stars.

The pictures kept coming. A young couple, looking like they might be engaged – except they too were wearing the yellow star. Jews pushing wagons in the snow, their possessions loaded up in bundles, all of them yellow starred as well. The caption: *Moving into the Kovno Ghetto. Credit: George Kadish, photographer.* Tom remembered Gershon's bracketed, pencilled addition: *(March)*. He looked for dates: perhaps the key photograph would be labelled March 1942. But most were undated.

Now Tom was in a section of a website on Kovno titled plainly: Ninth Fort. There was a Kadish photo of Jews gathering in a square, a 'final muster', the caption explained, before they were taken to the Fort. Another showed a clump of men and women, their rags almost indistinguishable, one person from another, in the muddy black and white of the photograph. It said these were Jews inside the Ninth Fort 'after their arrival there and prior to their execution'.

Tom was clicking in a fever, as if he knew what he was looking for even though he did not. He knew only this: that whatever he was meant to find, it would not be in the faces of the victims. Gershon Matzkin had come to New York to do one last killing. His target would not have been one of those engulfed by the fire, but one of those who had set it aflame.

Next Tom came across a photograph of Kadish himself, grim-faced, determined, in a peaked cap – the kind that radical chic students had worn in Manchester when Tom was a student – holding a simple camera, about to bring it to his eye. Tom wanted to stare at this man, this bringer of eye-witness testimony from the past to the present, but there was no time.

He clicked again and again until one image stopped him. The caption labelled it as 'The March: Lithuanian militia members leading Jews to their death at the Ninth Fort'.

Tom's pulse was galloping. There was no date on this photograph either. But this one had a title: *The March*. Surely this was the picture Gershon had had in mind, the one that he was urging his daughter to remember. It showed the Jews marching in a ragged column, identifiable as Jews only from their tatty clothes and baleful expressions. At the head and at the sides of this human herd, wearing black jackets, were the Lithuanian militiamen. There was no mistaking them because they were carrying sticks and wearing armbands, marked with some kind of insignia. It was hard to make out the exact pattern, but it was surely a nationalist symbol. Most were smiling.

Tom's eye was drawn to the left of the picture. There were two men there, one taller than the other, the first beaming with what seemed to be pride. He was watching the man next to him, who, on closer inspection, was no more than a boy, perhaps his son – a tall, rangy teenager. This younger man was brandishing a truncheon. It was raised into the air, held at the same height as his ear. His front foot was forward, in the manner of a cricketer about to play a shot. Except his target was no ball, even if this was some kind of sport. For the teenager was about to beat one of the Jews marching towards his death. He was about to bring his truncheon down onto the Jew's head where, if the shutter had waited just a second longer, it would, no doubt, have caught the smashing of a skull.

There was a strange delay in how Tom absorbed what he was seeing. His brain seemed to know what it was about to take in even before his eye had glimpsed it. When Tom's gaze, at last, moved away from the truncheon and towards the young assailant's face, it was as if it was merely to confirm what some sixth sense of Tom's already understood. There was no mistaking it. The features were sharp, unambiguous. It did not matter how many years had passed, this was the same face. It was the same person.

Tom felt a shudder ripple through him. He kept staring at the picture, as if hoping that somehow the very act of his observation would change what he had seen. But it did not change. He was gazing at the boy who had become the man, even if the two appeared to be from two different historical eras, ancient and modern. They were two different species and yet, there could be no doubt, they were the same person.

And then he remembered: *Rebecca*.

# CHAPTER SIXTY-FOUR

Tom hurtled out of the office, heading first for the lifts then, thinking better of it, shouldering his way into the fire escape: taking the stairs reduced the risk of a collision with someone he knew.

He ran down the stairs as fast as he could, clutching the banister so that he could vault the final three or even four steps, leaping into the air and pounding onto successive landings. He emerged from the fire escape on the third floor, disappearing as invisibly as he could into the throng. He couldn't afford to run; too noticeable. Instead he walked at his briskest pace, past the gifts of Maoist kitsch from the People's Republic, past the glass case displaying a traditional Thai logboat. He took the stairs to the second floor, ignoring the memorial exhibit of molten bottles and charred coins salvaged from Hiroshima. One more flight down and he was, at last, by the ceiling-high stained-glass Chagall window with its pale moons, eerie blues and desperate mothers clinging to their swaddled babies. The Peace Window, they called it, even though it had always struck Tom as reeking of the sadness of war.

He stopped, breathing heavily. There were no tourists milling around; he was alone. Only a hunch had brought him here. Rebecca had asked Henning if the meeting could be somewhere quiet, somewhere that was not 'grand'. If he knew Henning, and he did, the German would have brought her to this place.

They called it the meditation chapel. It was a plain dark room. There were no religious symbols, no holy texts, no books or artworks at all. It was meant to be 'multi-faith', even if that meant it was essentially an empty space. There were benches to sit on but they were rarely used. Tom had come here once or twice, including late at night after a particularly terrible session in his office, wading through eye-witness testimonies. But most UN staff could work in the place for twenty years and not even know it was there.

Not Henning though. He had been one of those adamant that the entrance to the area should become a memorial for those who had fallen serving the UN. There was a plaque for Count Bernadotte, the diplomat assassinated in Jerusalem, as well as the torn flag of the United Nations mission, bombed in Baghdad in 2003. To Henning at least, the meditation chapel meant something. Besides, he probably calculated that this location would give the UN some precious moral high ground for its meeting with Rebecca.

Tom tried to steady himself. He didn't know what he was going to find. He wanted to think, to work out what he would say or do, but there was no time. He walked through the partitioned walls – there was no door – and he knew he had been right.

They were both there, Rebecca and him. No one else, just as Henning had promised. No aides, no advisers – precisely as Tom had requested. Him and her alone, facing each other.

The change in the light meant they both turned around as Tom walked forward. Tom could see that Rebecca was aghast – with surprise, with confusion, he couldn't tell – but his gaze did not linger. It was not her he wanted to examine.

Instead he peered hard at the features of the man. Tom had never worked with him; his appointment had come long after Tom had fled for the corporate hills. But his face had become familiar in the last few weeks, at least to those who followed the politics of this place. It had been in the papers, on TV. The high forehead, the combed back, silver-grey hair, the wide mouth and firm, sharp nose. He was tall, too, elegant in a dark, tailored suit and perfectly knotted tie.

But it was not the similarity of the real man to the TV likeness that Tom was trying to make out. Rather he was comparing the face before him with the image he had seen just five minutes earlier on the computer screen. Was there room for doubt? Even in this gloom, Tom was sure there was not. He would have been ready to swear under oath that the man he was looking at and the teenage Fascist thug of Kovno's Ninth Fort were one and the same man. He knew that the eager participant in the massacre of the Jews of that town, a minor but murderous accomplice in the greatest crime of the twentieth century, was standing before him as the Secretary-General of the United Nations.

# CHAPTER SIXTY-FIVE

'Tom, get away. This has nothing to do with you.' Rebecca's tone was different, harder than he had ever heard before. And yet there was something else in the voice too. Not just anger, but anxiety. The muscles around her mouth seemed to be trembling.

'Rebecca, just talk to me. What are you doing?'

'I mean it, Tom.' She was restraining herself, striving hard not to shout. 'Just turn around and go away.'

Tom looked over at Paavo Viren, who stood frozen in his suit. For the first time, Tom could see that his face, usually a model of statesman-like composure, was drawn, ashen.

'Rebecca, I've seen the photographs. *Remember Kadish.*'

'So you know?'

Only then did he realize, in a fleeting moment of self-awareness, that he had assumed she did not know. He had *wanted* her not to know. He had told himself that, despite the pages stashed in the fountain pen, she had never fully understood her father's message, that she had not looked at the photographs of George Kadish. He had, Tom understood now, clung to the belief that Rebecca had demanded to see the Secretary-General for the sole purpose of hearing an official apology for the mistaken killing of her father. Now he could see the truth. He nodded to Rebecca. 'Yes, I know.'

'I'm sorry, Tom. I'm really sorry.'

'Why are you apolog—' And then he stopped himself. 'Oh I see. Now I see very well, Rebecca.'

'It's not like that, Tom.'

'Is that what this whole thing was about? Is that what I was to you: a ticket into this place?'

'Don't, Tom.'

His brain seemed to overflow with a whole new set of understandings, arriving in waves, one after another. She had wanted to be rid of him at first, but then suddenly she had softened, pleading with him for his help. He had thought that was simply because she was frightened by the break-in. Now he realized she had seen his potential: with Tom at her side, she had a chance of penetrating the heart of the United Nations, reaching the Secretary-General himself – with the chance to complete her father's unfinished business.

He remembered their kiss: it had come once he told her that he not only understood what her father and DIN had done, but that he agreed with it. *Given everything that had happened to them, they were right: they weren't going to get justice any other way.* Perhaps that was the moment she let down her guard, seeing Tom as a kindred spirit, a comrade in the struggle for vengeance. Or maybe it was more calculating than that. Maybe she had concluded that to rely absolutely on Tom to get her inside UN Plaza, she would first have to cloud his judgement . . .

When had her deception begun? Was it the moment he confronted her with evidence of Gerald Merton's meeting with the Russian and the discovery of an assassin's weapon? That was when she had thrust the notebook in his hand, telling him to read it in full. At the time, he'd assumed that had been aimed at making Tom and the UN back off from accusing Merton of being a hitman. But she had torn out the crucial pages: she was playing a game even then.

And the robbery? That was surely when she understood that this went way beyond her and her father and that she would need some serious help. Who better than a man who knew only those parts of the story she chose to reveal to him – a man backed by the heft of the UN and with the ability to bring her face to face with her ultimate target?

'How many others know about this wild story of yours?' Paavo Viren stepped back and raised himself to his full height, trying to take command of the room. His accent was somewhere between Scandinavian and international diplomat, that peculiar brand of English as global *lingua franca*, all traces of geography flattened out.

'I've not told anybody,' Rebecca said. 'Tom worked it out for himself. Like I said, this is between you and me.' And she turned to glare at Tom, her eyes imploring him to back off.

Viren spoke again. 'Since Mr Byrne is here, perhaps you can explain to him what it is exactly that you want. Because I am still unclear.'

Rebecca leaned closer towards him. 'I want you to tell me the truth. That's all you have to do. After all these years, it's too late for anything else. But the victims deserve that. They deserve at least that.'

'You want me to start confessing to you, in this chapel?' He gave a snort of mockery. 'Are you some kind of priest?'

'I've told you, we have the evidence. There is a photograph of you, herding Jews to their deaths in the Ninth Fort. No one noticed it before because no one knew your face, at least no one who cared. But now people care very much.'

'I know this photograph.' He paused then let his mouth widen into a joyless smile. 'That surprises you, yes? Of course, I have seen it. Perhaps there is a vague resemblance, but nothing more than that. The idea that this would count as evidence is laughable. You're too young to remember the Demanjuk trial, Ms Merton. But perhaps you, Mr Byrne, remember it?'

Viren turned to Tom. It was a familiar

manoeuvre, the attempt to co-opt the minor opponent, in order to isolate the major one. He wanted Tom to side with him against Rebecca.

'I remember it.'

'They called him Ivan the Terrible. Some car worker in Ohio.' He pronounced the name as if it were an exotic, fairytale place, separating each syllable: O-hi-O. 'All because of a photograph of him as a young man. Even the court in Israel could not convict him. A case of mistaken identity, that was the final judgement. And the Demanjuk photograph was of an adult. This picture you have is of a boy, a teenage boy. People's looks change so much between this age and adulthood. You don't have "evidence". You have a baseless accusation.'

'So why don't you walk out?' It was Tom, standing in the shadows.

'What?'

'If this is all baseless nonsense, why are you still here? You've been talking to Rebecca Merton for—' Tom made a show of checking his watch, 'quite a while. If this was all slanderous rubbish, you'd have walked out by now. You'd have summoned your aides. Henning Munchau would be here, drafting a writ of slander. You'd have called Security. But I'm looking around and I don't see anybody here. Now why would that be?'

Viren lifted his chin, as if making a more thorough assessment of Tom Byrne. 'I'm trying to be humane to Ms Merton. She's clearly a lady in some dist—'

'Really? Or is it because you don't want anybody else, not even a security guard, to hear what she has to say?'

The SG began to pace, half-turning his back on Rebecca. The movement made her flinch. For the first time, Tom wondered whether the man was armed in some way – an absurd thought, he realized, as soon as he had formulated it. Even so, Rebecca had been brave confronting him alone like this. He was not young, that was true, but he was not frail; he could have overwhelmed her, he could have—

'Do you know how old I am?'

The question hung in the air. The longer it lingered, the more it made Tom feel unsteady. The physical resemblance in the photograph had been so striking, he had not even considered basic matters like age and chronology. Now, though, his memory spooled back to the way he had come across the picture: the discovery of the name 'Kadish', the search in the photographer's online archive for an image that might connect to Gershon's story, then finding one that seemed to make sense of everything, right down to the word 'March' in the caption. A snapshot that showed at last why Gerald Merton had embarked on a final mission to New York, to the steps of the United Nations headquarters.

But perhaps Tom had made an elementary error: perhaps he had seen what he had wanted to see. Police officers did it all the time, following a pattern of apparent evidence to a conclusion that fitted their first assumptions. It was a universal, human failing; we are suggestible creatures. How else did optical illusions work, except by relying on the eye's habit of seeing what it expected rather than what was actually there?

Rebecca broke the silence. 'Your official biography says you're sixty-eight.'

'Good, Ms Merton. You have done your homework. My biography says I am sixty-eight because I am sixty-eight. And how's your mental arithmetic? Because mine is quite good and it says that I was five years old when the war ended. Five! We can agree that the man in your photograph was more than five years old, yes?' The smile again, this time with more enthusiasm.

'You lied about your age.'

'What, for all these years? Do I look seventy-eight to you?'

Rebecca shot back. 'My father didn't look his age either. He was fit and strong. He could have passed for sixty-eight too.'

Tom could feel his knees weakening. What if Rebecca was wrong? What if Gershon Matzkin had got it wrong? There had been no DIN organization any more, just an elderly, lonely Gerald Merton at home, probably scouring the internet, struck by the physical similarity of a newly public figure to a hated face in an ancient photograph. They were making a terrible mistake.

But Rebecca had not budged. Instead she was standing even closer to Viren, examining him as if he were one of her patients.

'Oh, there's no hiding that, though, is there, Mr Secretary-General? That line around the ear always gives it away. You've had some work done here, I can tell.'

'So what? A little cosmetic surgery is nothing to be ashamed of in this day and age. Just ask the prime minister of Italy. Human vanity is no crime, Dr Merton.' Then, as if he could sense Tom wavering: 'Besides, and this you must know already, I am not Lithuanian. I am Finnish, for heaven's sake. I served as the foreign minister of that country. I am the wrong age and the wrong nationality – which means you have the wrong man.'

Tom looked down at his feet. He would need all his lawyerly skills to resolve this situation. He would have to offer an apology, explaining that both he and Rebecca Merton had been under extreme stress, and that they withdrew their accusation, undertaking never to repeat it. None of this would be put in writing, lest such a document itself, even in refuting the charge, be taken as grounds for suspicion. And Dr Merton would waive any claims for compensation for the death of her father. Tom would sketch out the broad terms to the SG now, then work out the detail with Henning later.

He stepped towards Rebecca, aiming to place a gentle hand on her arm and guide her out of the chapel. He hoped she would not make a scene. But the instant he moved, she wheeled around and gave him a look that froze him.

'Don't disappoint me, Tom.'

'What do you mean?'

'Don't think so little of me. Or my father.'

'I don't under—'

'Do you really think he would have come here, ready the way he was ready, if he wasn't certain? Dead certain, that this man is exactly who he thought he was? Do you think I would be here now if *I* wasn't certain?'

'But it's just one photograph.'

'Oh no, Tom. There are many more photographs of this man. He was one of the stars of the ghetto, weren't you, Mr Secretary-General?'

Tom looked at the SG – who had the same pitying expression fixed on his face – then back at Rebecca. 'There are more photos?'

'Yes, there are more. They weren't all taken by Kadish either. Lots were taken by the Nazis themselves. Half a dozen at least, some quite formal, some casual, the boys joshing around. Like a team photo. And young Paavo Viren, or whatever his name was then, always in the middle: the team mascot.'

'But he's just sixty-eight.'

'He lied about his age. Plenty of the young ones did. They got new papers, adding ten years to their date of birth. Once they were in their late twenties, it all sounded plausible enough. It was easy.

Remember, they had a whole lot of people to help them.'

'He's from Finland.'

'He *went* to Finland, Tom. Not the same thing. Some went to Canada, some to Ohio,' she glanced back at the SG, 'some even went to Germany, for Christ's sake. They started over: new lives, new names. Finland was a good choice: hardly any Jews there, and certainly no survivors of Kovno. No one who would remember.'

Tom looked at her, imagining how she appeared in Viren's eyes: a crazed, deluded young woman. 'Where is all this evidence, Rebecca?' Tom hated how his voice sounded, sceptical, prosecutorial – as if he were doing the SG's work for him.

'It was all there, in London, in a file. But it was taken. One of the first things they took.'

'From your father's flat or from yours?'

Her delay in answering suggested she understood the significance of the question. 'From mine.'

'So you've known this all along.'

'My father told me what he was doing before he went to New York.'

Tom nodded, a gesture that was not meant to convey acceptance so much as a pause, a time-out in which he could digest what she was telling him. 'And what else did you know, Rebecca?'

'I knew about DIN. But not the rest, I swear. The break-in made no sense to me. The bakery, Tochnit Aleph – I never knew anything about that. You have to believe me.'

'It makes no sense, Rebecca. Why would your father tell you about DIN and keep the rest secret?'

'I've tried to work that out, Tom, really I have. All I can think of is that my father was ashamed. Plan A was *random*. It was indiscriminate. The DIN I knew of only went after the guilty. But if I knew about Plan B I'd find out about Plan A. And if I knew that, then I think my father believed I'd stop loving him.'

Viren cleared his throat, as if he were politely requesting his moment at the podium. 'You say this so-called "evidence" has vanished? It has been stolen?'

Rebecca did not answer. Tom said nothing.

'So we are back where we started, correct? Back with a wild claim?'

Tom was struck again by the simple fact that Viren was still here. Rebecca did not have him at gunpoint; she had no physical leverage over him at all. Yet here he still was. Why?

Rebecca now walked back a couple of paces, coming closer to Tom. Once there, she faced the SG and raised her voice a notch. 'I'll leave you alone. I'll drop these claims. I'll never make them again.'

'Dr Merton, I'm glad to hear—'

'On one condition.'

'What? What condition?'

'That you let me examine your left arm.'

The features of Viren's face remade themselves, from initial confusion to horrified indignation. He looked aghast. 'How dare you suggest such a thing. Do you have any idea who you are addressing? I am the elected representative of the entire world community!'

But still he didn't leave. What was he frightened of? Did he fear that if he stormed out, Rebecca would rush into the lobby of the UN and start shouting that the SG was a Nazi war criminal? She would be bundled out by Security and that would be the end of it. Why did he care what she said?

Was he waiting for something that would change her mind? And then a new thought struck. The SG was waiting for *him*, for Tom. If he, her escort on this trip to New York, agreed that Rebecca was just a traumatized, grieving daughter, then her claims would be discarded. But if he, a former senior lawyer at the UN, lent her any credence then the charges would gain at least some currency. And mud like this needed to be hurled only once to stick. Tom wondered if the new Secretary General was one of the few people in this building who did not know Tom Byrne's history: otherwise, he surely would have known what the Israeli president had known – that any claim Tom Byrne made about anything could be dismissed with a wave of the hand. *Mafia hack.*

Now Tom understood. He had been forced into the role of referee; the SG wanted Tom to agree with him that Rebecca Merton was a maniac. Only then would he risk stepping back into the outside world, letting this woman rant and rave with her accusations.

'I think you should let her see your arm,' Tom said softly. 'Then this thing can be over.' And he stepped forward and took hold of Viren's left wrist. The Secretary-General desperately tried to remove his arm from Tom's grasp. But he did not shout or scream.

'OK, Rebecca,' Tom said, suddenly aware that he was assaulting an innocent, eminent old man – an old man with a shocking degree of strength. 'Take a look at his arm.'

She stepped closer, her own nervousness clear. She couldn't look Viren in the eye, focusing instead on his wrist. Slowly, with great care, she pushed up the sleeve of his jacket, then began to unbutton the cuff of his shirt. She was cautious, like someone handling a suspicious package.

'What are you looking for?' Tom said, the words squeezed out between short breaths as he struggled to keep the older man restrained.

'I'm looking for a scar,' Rebecca said, her voice low and steady, a doctor in surgery. And then she looked up, so that she might fix the writhing Viren in her gaze. 'I'm looking for the scar my father's sister left on the arm of a young man who raped her, a young man who terrorized the children of the Kovno ghetto – a young man they called the Wolf.'

# CHAPTER SIXTY-SIX

Tom wasn't sure he felt Paavo Viren's muscles go rigid at the mention of that word. It could have been another trick of the mind, Tom imagining what was not there. But now Rebecca had the old man's sleeve rolled up to his elbow and she was staring hard.

*Wolf.* It had taken Tom a beat, no more, to remember that name. It had been one of the most chilling details in the Kovno journal of Gershon Matzkin. Indeed, it had been one of the few occasions when the Nazi enemy had a face.

As Tom felt the strain in his arms from keeping Viren immobilized, he tried to see again those handwritten lines. The Wolf had not been German; Gershon had been describing the son of one of the Lithuanian guards in the ghetto. The Jewish inmates had feared him especially – or perhaps that was, as Rebecca had suggested just now, merely the memory of those who had been children at the time. It was easy to see why the young would fear him so intensely, a killer and tormentor with the face of a boy.

When Tom had sat in the cafe around the corner from Rebecca's flat, reading the faded pages of Merton's journal, he had tried to picture the cruelty of this Wolf, the smiling, teenage sadist who had asked for the pleasure of punishing Gershon's sister, Hannah, for the crime of smuggling a crust of bread. He had stripped off the clothes of a girl his own age, beaten her with a truncheon, then forced himself inside her. *Hannah was wounded. Not just her face, which was no longer hers. But her soul.*

So this was why Gershon had broken his own rule, ending his retirement from the work of DIN. The Wolf was a special case, a personal score to settle. What had the torn pages, concealed in Rebecca's pen, said? *A long time ago, I made another promise, a promise to a young woman just as full of life and of beauty as you are today. I never thought I would have the chance to honour my word to her. I thought it was too late.*

No more than a boy, Gershon must have promised his older sister that he would avenge her, that he would, one day, make the Wolf pay for what he had done. Somehow he had kept alive the memory of that single act of brutality, even amidst all the killing and carnage he was to witness in the weeks and months and years that followed. He had seen such horrors, yet this one act had burned inside him.

Rebecca was peering intensely at Viren's forearm. Tom was trying to work out the expression on her face. Finally she spoke, uttering words that seemed to suck the air out of the room.

'There is no scar.'

# CHAPTER SIXTY-SEVEN

He tried to remember what this feeling was like and the comparison, when it came to him, was a surprise. But the combination of anxiety and anticipated relief – the sense that while he was about to endure something painful and risky, things would be better afterwards – was indeed similar. Jay Sherrill felt now just as he had when he first stepped into the office of the therapist who had counselled him after the death of his brother. Now, as then, he had concluded that the very act of taking action had to be better than enduring another anguished, unending night.

It was good that he had had so little time to prepare. He had contacted Henning Munchau late last night, asking to see him urgently. He didn't like going over Tom Byrne's head, but he had little choice: he hadn't been able to get hold of Byrne since yesterday lunchtime.

Munchau had seemed reluctant to take his call. Maybe he didn't like to undermine Byrne: more likely, he wanted arm's length deniability on the whole Gerald Merton business. Doubtless that was why he had contracted out the case to a lawyer who had left the UN more than a year ago. 'I'll see what I can do,' was the most Munchau had promised. Besides, he had no reason to bother with Sherrill: by now he would have had word from the DA's office that there were to be no charges in the Merton case. No crime had been committed; the UN was off the hook.

And then a call from Munchau twenty minutes ago, saying that a window in his schedule had suddenly opened up. If Jay could be in UN Plaza in the next fifteen minutes, they could have coffee in the delegates' lounge.

'Sorry to spring that on you like that,' the German said, in an accent Sherrill struggled to place. Was it European or Australian?

'Not at all. Just glad you could make the time.'

'Unusual situation. Secretary General just asked me to clear an hour of his schedule, which suddenly gave me an hour I didn't have.'

'Right.'

'He's meeting Rebecca Merton, as it happens. One on one.'

'She's in New York?'

'Didn't Byrne tell you? They flew in together.'

'So he's alive then.'

Munchau arched an eyebrow.

'It's just I've had no word from him for twenty-four hours. Despite multiple messages.'

'That's Tom for you. So: what can I do for you?'

'This conversation is strictly confidential, yes?'

'If you want it to be.'

'Well, my career – which is probably over – might depend on it.'

'What's on your mind, Detective?'

'Two days ago I had a meeting with the head of the NYPD Intelligence Division.'

'With Stephen Lake?'

'Yes.'

'I'm listening.'

'He said something I barely noticed at the time, but which I can't quite figure out.'

'What was it?'

'It could have been a simple slip of the tongue . . .'

'Detective?'

'He said,' Sherrill read from his notebook, '"We may have had our eye on the UN for a while, with evidence of a ticking time-bomb over there".'

'He said that?'

'"Or we may not."'

'Are you saying that the intel division knew there was a terror threat to the UN and didn't pass it on?'

'No, sir, I'm not. That's what I thought it meant too. But listen to the exact wording. Lake didn't say a "a ticking time-bomb *on its way* to the UN" or "a bomb *aimed* at the UN". He said "a bomb *over there*".'

'As if it were already here.'

'Exactly.'

Henning looked around, watching delegates chat and smoke. 'But NYPD wouldn't sit by and let this place be blown up. It would be their fuck-up, apart from anything else.'

'I agree, Dr Munchau. Which is why I think he didn't mean it literally. He was using the phrase metaphorically.'

'So intel knows something about this place that counts as a time-bomb.'

'Something that could destroy the UN, yes, sir. That's what I suspect.'

The look of recognition and then alarm that spread across Henning Munchau's face meant that when he silently got to his feet, Jay Sherrill knew he had no option but to follow.

## CHAPTER SIXTY-EIGHT

'What do you mean there's no scar?' Tom instinctively loosened his grip.

Now Viren spoke. 'Good. I'm glad this farce is over. I should, of course, report you—'

Rebecca cut him off. 'Or rather there is not the obvious scar.'

The Secretary-General tried to shake himself free. 'What the hell are you talking about?'

'You see,' Rebecca said, pointing at the pale skin of his forearm, 'there is no line there. But, unluckily for you, plastic surgery was not able to do then what it can do now.'

'You're talking nonsense.'

'Back then, when they did skin grafts like this one, to cover up a scar, they couldn't help but leave a mark around the edges, where the new skin was placed. It's like the outline of a patch sewn on a suit. See it? Right here.' She was being unnervingly calm.

'So what if I did have a skin graft? It was for a burn I had twenty years ago.'

'Was it?'

'Yes. It was an, an, an accident. At home. With a stove.'

'Well, that's very odd. Because, in fact, the marks you have on your skin in this area are clear signs of stretching. And the only way you could have got those is if you had a skin graft when you were young, when your skin was still growing. And you weren't growing twenty years ago, Mr Viren, were you?'

At that, Viren shook Tom off, so that he was now inches away from Rebecca. He raised his hand, high so that it was level with his ear, and it was about to come down on Rebecca when Tom grabbed him around the middle, a crude wrestling move that left the older man's fist flailing in the air.

And then Viren let out a shriek.

Tom's view was obscured at first by the body of the man he was restraining, but now he could see the source of his alarm. Rebecca had produced from somewhere, a sleeve or a pocket, a hypodermic syringe. She was now raising it into the air, at eye-level, so that she could test it against the light.

Tom gasped. 'Rebecca, what the hell are you doing?'

She ignored him, addressing only the Secretary-General. 'Your great misfortune is that I'm a doctor. I know about scar tissue and skin grafts

– and I also know about poisons. This one, for example, is odourless, clear and instantly effective. I don't know how painful it is but, given its source, I'm an optimist. Which means I hope it's very painful.'

'Rebecca, where did you get that?'

'Let's say it was a gift from someone we just met. A former comrade in DIN.'

In an instant, Tom pictured the lingering farewell he had witnessed between Rebecca and the Israeli president: how he had muttered to her in Hebrew, how he had held her hands in a double-grip, one that could easily have concealed the handover of, say, a needle and a measure of deadly fluid. *Now I would like to have a private word of remembrance with Dr Merton, in honour of her father.*

If Gerald Merton had been able to work out the truth of Paavo Viren's past, it would not have eluded Israeli intelligence. Once the President was reassured Merton had not been after him, and once he had heard Rebecca request her face-to-face meeting with the Secretary-General, it would have confirmed it: Viren had been DIN's last target. And what better way to assuage his guilt over Aron than to give DIN what it needed from him once again – a vial of deadly poison? Even if Rebecca had been caught, the President would have known that this young woman – a daughter of the Shoah and a daughter of the Avengers – would not have betrayed him. She would have been bound by the code of DIN.

Viren was making a half-hearted effort at writhing out of Tom's grip. But his eyes were only on Rebecca. 'There must be a way we can resolve this. If you insist, we could have an independent review, to examine the claims you've—'

'Oh no, I'm far too unreasonable for that. You see, your second great misfortune is that you picked the wrong people to murder and maim. You raped and nearly killed my aunt, Hannah Matzkin, who, thanks to you, I never met.' She squeezed the syringe, holding it still as it squirted a brief jet of fluid. 'And you took part, an eager part from what I hear, in the massacres at the Ninth Fort. I wonder if you remember any of the thousands of people you and your friends shot into those pits. My aunts were three of them.'

Tom was frozen, still holding the old man but doing so now out of sheer paralysis. He was watching Rebecca as if he were viewing events at a distance, played back on a video monitor. Perhaps it was the near-darkness of this room. More likely it was the shock of everything that had happened, everything he had heard, over the last few minutes. He seemed to be on some kind of delay, each new item of information taking a few seconds to register. Now though he realized that he had been co-opted into what was about to become an act of homicide – without even having a moment to consider it. He was restraining Paavo Viren, holding him down so that Rebecca could inject him with poison.

Yet he had not wanted to let Viren go. He wasn't sure about Rebecca's analysis of the scar tissue on his arm. But the old man's reaction had settled it. His tone had changed. He had stopped protesting his innocence and begun pleading for a deal. When innocent people were faced with punishment for a crime they did not commit, they did not start plea-bargaining: they insisted all the more loudly that they were innocent. It took time, often a long stretch of it, to grind down people's essential belief in fairness; only then were they ready to negotiate a compromise penalty for something they had not done.

Viren had required no such time. He had been ready to deal within a few seconds. Tom was an experienced enough lawyer to know that that – along with his failure to walk out as soon as Rebecca started making her charges, his unexplained decision to stay and listen – was not the action of an innocent man.

Tom was still holding Viren in place, frozen, as Rebecca carried on speaking.

'You killed the wrong people, Mr Viren. You killed the family of Gershon Matzkin and he was not the kind of Jew you bargained for. He was one of the Jews who refused to die. He was one of the Jews who were determined that their blood be avenged. He was part of DIN, the movement whose Hebrew name means judgment. But it also stands for three words. *Dam Israel Nokeam.* "The blood of Israel will take vengeance".' She was speaking faster now, the urgency in her voice accelerating. She held the syringe vertically between her index and middle finger, as if it were a cocked weapon. 'He was an avenger, Mr Viren – and I am his daughter.'

With that, Rebecca leaned forward and placed the tip of the needle on Viren's neck, expertly finding the jugular vein.

The certainty of that action, the finality of it, seemed to snap Tom out of his state of disconnection. Rebecca intuited immediately what he was about to do.

'If you make any sudden movements now, Tom, the needle will go in. Really, even a slight jerk and Viren will be dead.'

Tom could see that she was right. His job now was to hold the SG stock-still – for his own sake.

Viren managed to squeeze out a few words. 'What do you want from me? If you want to kill me, just kill me. Get it over with.'

'Oh, but that wasn't your way of doing things, was it, Mr Viren? From what I understand, you and the men from the Lithuanian militia enjoyed the whole performance. Get the Jews to come to the collection point, packing all their bags as if they were off on a journey. Then a long wait. Then a long truck ride. Then another long wait. Then a march to the pits. Then watching the women undress, lining them up by pits you'd made the Jews dig for themselves. And then only a single bullet, so that – what, one in ten, one in five? – did not even die straightaway, but had to choke to death, buried alive under a pile of corpses. So don't start bleating about "getting it over with". If this is trying your patience, Mr Viren then I don't apologize.'

Tom was wincing, watching Rebecca standing so close to the SG, her finger capping the plunger of the syringe as if it were a detonator.

'My father would have done the job much faster, that's true. The way he'd worked it out, getting you on your own meant there would be no time to speak to you: he'd have had to kill you in a split-second. But that was not the normal DIN way.'

'Rebecca, listen to me. You can't do this.'

'Shut up, Tom.'

'I mean it. This is not right. Not like this.'

She didn't take her eyes off Viren. 'For DIN it was very important that the target know the identity of his executioners, to know that the Jews had sought justice. But I want something more. I want an admission. I want you to tell me the truth.'

Viren began to stammer. He could surely see that this woman would not be swayed by a confession into an offer of clemency; she had already made clear that she was going to kill him. Tom suspected that her father would have been more skilful, tricking his victims into believing they had an incentive to talk.

'Listen to me, Rebecca. This can't work. You'll be caught. Even if people sympathize with you, you'll spend years in jail. Is that what your father would have wanted, to see his beloved daughter behind bars?'

'I could get away.'

'Come off it, Rebecca. Henning knows you're here. He'll be here soon. If he finds the Secretary-General dead, you'll be blamed.'

'We'll say he had a heart attack.'

'There'll be a needle mark. Bruises on his arms where I've held him. Please, Rebecca. Think what your father would say, the idea that the Nazis would destroy the life of another woman in the Matzkin family.'

Rebecca's eyes were on fire, two braziers of flame in the murk of this room. 'How dare you talk to me about what my father would have wanted.'

Tom's arms were tiring from keeping his captive dead still. 'Your father never got caught, Rebecca. None of them ever did. I bet that was important to them: that a Jew would not suffer again because of the Nazis, not even for one more day.'

'I need to hear him say it, Tom.' She was staring at him, hard. 'There needs to be a reckoning.'

'I understand.' His voice softened. 'But this is not the way.'

'But I heard you in Goldman's office. Saying that DIN was right, that the law had always failed the victims. "The bigger the crime, the worse it is,” that’s what you said. I remember it because I agreed with you. “There is no law,” you said, “just politics”. Remember?’

Tom found it unbalancing, to be reminded of his own words like this. It was true, he had said those things, angered by Goldman’s pettifogging, pedantic deference to the law when he, Tom, had seen the law’s failure again and again, in Rwanda and East Timor and God knows where else.

Yet at this moment, an elderly man in his grip, holding him still while a needle at his neck threatened his life, Tom could not stand by what he had said. The prospect of killing a man like this repelled him. Theory was one thing; the actual physical deed was quite another. This was not justice. It was everything the law was meant to stop: the descent into barbarism.

‘Rebecca. It can’t be like this. DIN killed people because there was no other way. But you have evidence. You can take this to a court. There could be a trial.’

She made a snort, her head tilting back in mockery. Tom waited for Viren himself to say something, to agree that, yes, he would submit himself to a trial. His silence suggested he was as smart a politician as his reputation promised: he understood that if he endorsed any strategy of Tom’s it would be the kiss of death. Rebecca would reject it.

‘You think they would ever put this man on trial?’ she said. ‘They would come up with the same bullshit they always come up with. "He's too old. The evidence is cold. The witnesses are dead. The statute of limitations has passed. It didn't take place on our soil." I've heard every argument in the book.

'Even so, Rebecca, the alternative is to sink to their level. You won't be killing them; you'll be turning into them. Remember, Plan A? It didn't happen. In the end, the Jews couldn't do it.' He sighed. 'The law is all we've got, Rebecca. It's not perfect. Christ, I know that better than anyone. But it's all we've got.'

'I need to end this.' She was trembling now, her whole body shaking. 'I've lived with this my whole life, Tom. Can you imagine that, knowing your own life is trivial compared to everything that happened? Can you imagine that? Of course you can't. No one can.'

In a brief change in the light, Tom could see there were tears slipping slowly down her cheeks. He wanted desperately to touch her.

'Your life is not trivial. It matters.'

She said nothing.

'Your life mattered to your father, Rebecca. He named you after his mother for a reason.' He swallowed. 'I think you were meant to be her second chance.'

She reeled back, her clenched hand finally coming away from Viren's neck. The old man now seized his opportunity, using all his strength to shake Tom off. As Tom fell backwards, he stumbled, hitting his head on the edge of one of the benches. He was stunned.

In that same instant, Viren lunged at Rebecca. He reached for her wrist, pulling it upward. She was still clasping the syringe, now terrified that the old man was about to turn the needle back on her. She let out a scream as he tugged at her arm.

The light in the room suddenly changed. Two men had come into the doorway, casting new shadows. Viren looked up to see Henning Munchau staring at him, his face aghast. The Secretary-General seemed frozen.

That moment of delay, of paralysis, was all Tom needed. He hauled himself up and surged forward, crashing into the space between Viren and Rebecca, pushing the pair apart. Rebecca staggered backwards, at last out of the old man's reach. But the needle was no longer in her hand.

Tom turned, only to find Viren coming at him, his eyes wild, clutching the syringe and aiming it directly at Tom's heart. Tom reached for Viren's wrist, but the old man had remarkable strength. Even in Tom's grip, he was pressing forward, the tip of the needle getting closer and closer until it was no more than an inch from Tom's chest.

With an almighty surge, Tom shoved Paavo Viren's wrist backward – listening to the roar of horror as the Secretary-General of the United Nations realized he had plunged the needle deep into the jugular vein of his own neck.

# EPILOGUE

**One year later**

'And how many displaced people are we talking about?'

'Maybe a million.'

'Mainly in Chad, or elsewhere?'

'Chad mostly.'

'Conditions in the camps?'

'They are very overcrowded. Shortages of food. Disease. The biggest problem is panic. Everyone is terrified.'

'And what are the aid agencies saying?'

'They have their own problems. Some say they cannot do anything for the victims, when they have the security of their own staff to worry about. The Janjaweed target them, too, you know. Deliberately. And it's working: many of the NGOs have withdrawn.'

Tom pushed back into his chair, chewing at the top of his pen. His concentration was total. But once this meeting was over, he would allow himself the same thought that kept occurring these days: it was good to be back, absorbed once more in the work he was born to do.

'I need to look at all the documents you have, all the paperwork. So that we can assemble a cast-iron case. First we need to establish the general circumstances, so that we can paint a picture of the overall humanitarian situation, just the kind of details we've been discussing now. Then we move onto the specifics of each individual. OK?'

It was the fifth Darfur-related meeting Tom had had in the last month. He wondered how long these problems had festered before reaching his desk. He held up his hand, in a request for patience, and turned in the direction of his assistant.

'Lequasia!'

During the silence that followed, Tom turned to his client and raised his eyebrows – a gesture that conveyed long-suffering patience. He tried again, this time raising his voice. 'Lequasia!'

At last she appeared, emerging from the back corridor where Tom had added a decent coffee maker to the battered old kettle that used to sit there. In the light, he counted at least four strands of radically different colours in her hair, some plaited, some straight. Or were they simply hair extensions, purchased in that black women's salon just off the Holloway Road?

'Lequasia, thanks for gracing us with your presence. I hope we're not keeping you from some urgent appointment with your stylist. Let me introduce you to Ismael Yahya Abdullah.'

She reached over to shake Ismael's hand, her false nails digging into his palms.

Tom went on: 'He's here on behalf of himself and five other people seeking asylum in this country from Darfur. He's studying at UCL. Since he's been here the longest, and has the best English, he's going to be the point of contact for the whole group. Could you give him six copies of the basic asylum form please?'

Tom said goodbye, leaving Lequasia and Ismael in the waiting area. He turned back to his computer – there was an email to Henning he wanted to finish – when he heard the door open. In truth, he sensed it more than he heard it. First, the chill draught from the street, then the unmistakable shuffling sound that could only mean one thing.

'Hello, Lionel.'

'Hello, Mr Byrne.'

'Julian's actually in court today, but he'll back soon.'

'Julian's in court? Why, what did he do?'

'He didn't do anything. He's a lawyer. He's acting for somebody.'

'They going to send him to jail?'

'They might.'

'Julian's going to jail? Oh—' and he began to sob.

'No, Lionel. Not Julian. *Julian's* not going to jail. His *client* might be going. If the court finds him guilty.'

'He's not guilty.'

'Well, he might— No, no, you're right. He's not guilty.' Tom shook his head. Not for the first time in the last few months, he was filled with admiration for his partner in the Kingsland Law Centre. Julian Goldman had endured conversations like this with Lionel and the rest every working day for the last seven or eight years.

'Do you fancy a cup of tea, Lionel?'

'That would be nice, Mr Byrne.'

'It's Tom.'

'That's a nice name, Mr Byrne.'

Tom was grateful for the chance to retreat to the back corridor and what was laughingly referred to as the 'kitchen'. No wonder Lequasia was to be found here so often: it was the only hiding place.

As he waited for the kettle to boil he smiled at the absurdity of it. There had been a documentary about Orson Welles on TV the night before: it showed the onetime cinema wunderkind grinning as he confessed that he had started at the top – and worked his way down.

It hadn't been quite like that for Tom. But little more than two years ago he had been one of the top international lawyers in the world, in the inner circle of the Legal Counsel of the United Nations. And now he was here, in a Hackney legal aid practice where the carpet came in thin squares and the client base consisted of the dispossessed and the unhinged, 'the migrated and the medicated' as Julian put it. He was earning around a fifth of his previous UN salary, if that wasn't too generous an estimate – and a much, much smaller fraction of what the Fantonis had been ready to pay him for just a few weeks' work.

When he first met Goldman Jr, Tom had assumed he was a naive young man who would soon learn the ways of the world. But it had been Julian who had taught Tom a lesson: that even if Justice with a capital J was elusive, you could still remedy a thousand little injustices every day – one asylum applicant, or one plastic-bag carrying mutterer, at a time.

It felt much longer than a year; so much had happened. These days Tom struggled even to remember those few, crazed hours in New York. Sometimes he wondered if he had imagined it; his memory of the scene in the meditation chapel particularly so murky. His recollection tended to begin with the immediate aftermath.

Rebecca had not been wrong: the poison had been instantly effective. By the time Henning Munchau and Jay Sherrill were at the Secretary-General's side, he was dead: Tom had killed him before their very eyes.

Tom had had to adopt an almost unnatural calm to explain what had happened. Luckily, there was no time for deception: he had to tell it straight – and he did.

Henning proved himself all over again that day, not only as a good friend but as a first-class lawyer. He methodically ingested all that Tom was telling him, visibly organizing the information he was hearing, even its wildest elements, without losing his steady focus. He summoned two United Nations security officers into the chapel and told them to clear the lobby. The pretext was easy: another security alert. They removed Viren's body – and Henning began to draft a statement.

As Legal Counsel, he insisted there would be no cover-up. The deputy secretary general held a press conference, announcing that Paavo Viren had been killed by former UN lawyer Tom Byrne, the latter acting entirely in self-defence. Viren had lashed out violently at Byrne and his female companion after they had confronted him with evidence of a grave secret, one that an internal UN investigation had now confirmed. Legal Counsel Dr Henning Munchau and NYPD Detective Jay Sherrill had witnessed the killing.

The New York police held Tom and Rebecca for a day, before releasing them under caution. Tom testified that even though the syringe and poison was Rebecca's, she had not intended to kill Viren; she had merely been threatening him, in a bid to elicit the truth. The District Attorney rapidly concluded there was little mileage in prosecuting the daughter of a Holocaust survivor for the death of a man who, posthumously and overnight, and thanks to archive photographs reproduced on newspaper front pages, on the internet and screened endlessly on twenty-four-hour TV news, had become the number one hate figure in New York and around the world. Besides, the DA added for the second time in a week, since the killing had taken place on UN soil, no crime had been committed under either New York or US law.

In Finland, there was a call for a national day of atonement, so great was their shame in having allowed a war criminal to have sullied their collective good name. In Lithuania, a few thousand ultra-nationalists marched in Vilnius with banners displaying Viren's face, including – incredibly, as far as Tom was concerned – pictures of him as a young man, posing in his black blazer in Kovno. It turned out that Rebecca had been right on this too. There were lots of photographs of the Wolf and they had not been difficult to find.

In Israel, there was a brief flurry of controversy when it emerged that the country's aged president had used his influence to broker the fateful meeting between Rebecca Merton and the Secretary-General. The President said he had simply responded to a request for help from the daughter of a brave survivor of the Holocaust. He was as shocked by the turn of events as everyone else. Truly shocked.

A few weeks later Tom saw an article in *Time* magazine alleging that not everyone had been so surprised by the Viren revelations.

*Sources in the Intelligence Division of the New York Police Department claim division chief Stephen Lake had picked up chatter about 'gaps' in the UN boss's resume. Lake had reportedly kept these leads to himself, in a bid to have future leverage over the UN supremo. 'If you can blackmail the Secretary-General of the United Nations, that's some pretty serious power,' one NYPD Intel insider told TIME, speaking on condition of anonymity. Lake's own position is now said to be hanging by a thread, with NYPD Commissioner Chuck Riley 'livid' that elements within his own force did not share such sensitive information with the international community prior to Viren's appointment.*

Tom only half-followed these developments. Once the police had granted their release, he accepted Henning's offer of a hot shower and a bed for the night: Rebecca in the spare room, him on the couch. He had assumed he would fall into a deep, exhausted sleep. But it had not come. Instead his mind had raced.

He had imagined the Israeli president nodding with satisfaction as he watched the TV news in his Manhattan hotel room. In a single day the old man had had both iron confirmation that Gershon Matzkin had not, after all, come to New York to confront him over his betrayal of DIN – and a chance, at long last, to expiate the guilt he had carried for more than six decades. A chance he had seized with both hands.

Accordingly, Tom detected more than a hint of embarrassment in 'Richard', the man who had drugged and dragged them to New York, when they met up with him a week later, as arranged. He had barely been able to make eye contact as he relieved Tom and Rebecca of the papers they had prepared for him, including an extra postcard which featured a cryptic sentence, pencilled in Yiddish. If the president studied it, deciphering the faded markings, he would find the Biblical verse that alluded to his own name. That should be enough, they reasoned, to persuade the aged politician that what could damage him was now in his own hands.

Tom felt a vibration in his pocket. It took a second or two to snap out of his reverie and realize it was his phone. He looked at the display and then looked at it again, just to be sure: Rebecca.

She had only been back in London for a month, after spending most of the last year travelling. She had needed to clear her head, she said. She had been all around Europe and Latin America with a brief stint in South Africa. For a while, Tom had wondered if she was retracing her father's footsteps, a morbid revisiting of his travels as an assassin. But Rebecca insisted it was nothing of the sort: she had been volunteering as a doctor in most of those places. By way of proof, she told him she had gone nowhere near San Sebastián.

'Tom? It's me.'

He didn't know how to reply. Her voice alone could still send a charge through him, but now it made him feel wary rather than excited. There was still so much they hadn't said.

Without waiting for him, she spoke. 'I've just had some sad news. Do you remember Sid Steiner? The man in the old age home?'

'Of course.'

'He died last night. In his sleep.'

'Oh, I'm sorry to hear that.' He remembered the old boy, playing the piano, his hands fluttering along the keyboard as if he were a teenager.

'He was the last one, Tom.' He could hear her voice wavering. 'There are none left now.'

'I know.'

'There's something I need to discuss with you.' She paused, girding herself. 'I want to do what my father did, to continue what he started.'

Tom felt his chest seize up. What was she saying? 'Look, Rebecca. I'm sorry Sid's gone. But DIN has to end sometime. It's not up to you to carry—'

'No, I don't mean that. DIN is over, Tom. I don't expect you to forgive me for how it ended, but I need you to know that it has. And to know that I will never lie to you again.'

'I want to believe that, Rebecca.'

The silence held between them. Eventually she spoke again. 'This is something different I need to do, for Sid's sake. Something my father always did when this happened. I've never done it before. I'm not even sure I know how. But I'd like you to be with me. At my side. Because you're the only one who knows everything that happened.'

'What is it you need to do?'

'I want to remember them, Tom. Sid, my father, Hannah, Rivvy, Leah, all of them. I want to remember them. I want to say Kaddish.'

# AUTHOR'S NOTE

*The Final Reckoning* is a novel – but the story at its heart is true. A group of Holocaust survivors did, in fact, seek revenge for the Nazi slaughter of the Jews in the months and years that followed the Second World War, and they did so along the lines described in this book. They were known in Hebrew as the *Nokmim*, the Avengers, and they consisted of a hardcore of around fifty men and women, most of them former resistance fighters from the ghettoes. Others name the group after its motto – *Dam Israel Nokeam* – which translates as 'The blood of Israel will take vengeance' and which abbreviates as DIN.

Their story was first told in English in a truly remarkable book, *Forged in Fury*, written by the former BBC correspondent in Jerusalem, Michael Elkins. Published in 1971, when many of those involved were still alive, it provides perhaps the fullest account of DIN's post-war activities. More detail has come in subsequent years in memoirs from those involved, including *From the Wings* by Joseph Harmatz, and in Rich Cohen's excellent account, *The Avengers*. An interview with Harmatz published in the *Observer* on March 15 1998 also sheds much useful light.

These sources differ on many of the details but all make clear that there was indeed both a Plan A, a scheme to introduce toxins into the German water supply, and a Plan B, aimed at poisoning former SS officers via a Nuremberg bakery. There is some debate about the number of Nazis killed in the latter operation, but Harmatz – who was directly involved – and others leave no doubt that it happened. *The New York Times* articles from April 1946 detailing the consequences of that effort, articles which Tom and Rebecca read in the internet café, are not made up: they appear in this book exactly as they were published. They can be retrieved from *The New York Times* database.

The record also shows that the Avengers' leader, Abba Kovner, travelled to Palestine – as Aron does in this book – seeking the moral authority of those poised to lead the Israeli state-in-waiting. Kovner met Chaim Weizmann, not only the former leader of world Zionism and soon-to-be first president of the state of Israel, but also a renowned chemist. According to Cohen, Weizmann listened to Kovner before declaring, 'If I were you, having lived as you have lived, I would do what you will do' – much as 'the elder' in this novel gives his blessing to Aron. Indeed, Weizmann put Kovner in touch with a young chemist to supply the poison. In Cohen's book, Weizmann knows only of Plan B rather than the much deadlier Plan A; but Elkins implies that the old man was aware of, and backed, the more lethal scheme.

Aron's fate in this novel reflects the fate of the real-life Abba Kovner, who did board a British ship bound for Europe carrying canisters of poison only to be arrested by British military police late in the voyage, forcing him to abort Plan A. Historians of the episode debate who precisely might have betrayed him, but they are convinced – as Kovner himself was – that it was a fellow Jew and Zionist. The individual who gives up Aron in this novel is wholly fictitious. Indeed, I should stress that my imagined President of the state of Israel is not to be confused with the current occupant of that ceremonial office – even though they are both men in their eighties.

Gershon Matzkin is also my own creation, but he is rooted in reality. He is an amalgam of several figures, including Lebke 'Arye' Distel – the blond, blue-eyed Avenger who, according to Harmatz and Cohen, applied the poison to the loaves destined for Stalag 13 – and also the man Elkins calls Ben-Issachar Feld (most likely a pseudonym to protect his identity), whom he later dubs 'Benno the Messenger'. As a young boy, Feld was charged with spreading word of the Nazi plan to exterminate the Jews. The coded sentence Matzkin carries

– 'Aunt Esther has returned and is at Megilla Street 7, apartment 4' – was, according to Elkins, the same cryptic line delivered by Feld.

The description of the Kovno ghetto, and the circumstances leading to its creation, as well as the mass killings at the Ninth Fort, are also entirely grounded in documented fact. The pogrom of June 1941 is detailed in many sources, including *The Vanished World of Lithuanian Jews* by Alvydas Nitzentaitis, Stefan Schreiner, Darius Staliunas and Donskis Leonidas. For the account of the 'Great Action' of October 28 1941, I was guided especially by *Surviving the Holocaust: The Kovno Ghetto Diary* by Avraham Tory, as well as from eye-witness testimony collated at the HolocaustResearchProject.org website. The image of the pit that seemed to breathe for three days comes from the Rev Patrick Desbois, quoted in 'A Priest Methodically Reveals Ukrainian Jews' Fate', published in *The New York Times*, October 6 2007. George Kadish, the photographer whose work helps Tom finally unravel this story's mystery, is no invention either: all but the last of the Kadish pictures Tom sees can be viewed online.

The fading DIN list of targeted individuals, apparently hand-delivered to Rebecca's flat, features here just as it appears in *Forged in Fury*, with the addition of two fictional names: Joschka Dorfman and Fritz Kramer. The statistics presented by Henry Goldman, detailing the huge numbers of Nazis who escaped justice, are drawn from the work of Raul Hilberg; the table of figures appears as a footnote in David Cohen's essay 'Transition Justice in Divided Germany after 1945', published in *Retribution and Reparation in the Transition to Democracy,* edited by Jon Elster. Inevitably, given the intense secrecy under which DIN operated, it is close to impossible to verify whom exactly the Avengers managed to kill. Some of the names Elkins cited in 1971 would not survive historical scrutiny now. But it is hard to dispute that Nazis across the world were hunted down and killed in their homes, on the streets and in the dead of night – by a group of men and women determined to show the world that Jewish blood could not be spilled cheaply.

## ACKNOWLEDGEMENTS

As the preceding note stressed, I am especially indebted to those who have already, in non-fiction, charted the extraordinary events that stand at the core of this novel. Besides works by Joseph Harmatz and Rich Cohen, I want to emphasize the gratitude I feel towards the late Michael Elkins for bringing the DIN story to light. His book, *Forged in Fury*, had an enormous impact on me when I first read it two decades ago and it retains its power today.

A long list of others gave personal help in bringing this project to fruition. Ian Williams, Marc Quarterman, Andrew Gilmour and Sam Daws were all extremely generous with their insiders' knowledge of the United Nations, while Philippe Sands QC lent invaluable advice on international law. Dr Nick Haining shared his copious medical expertise, while Raymond Shaw let me benefit from his serious brainpower on the criminal law. Jim Dwyer of The New York Times gave me more time than I had any right to ask and deserves his reputation as the leading police reporter in America. Steve Coombes gave excellent tips on the tough business of surveillance and security, while David Learmount of Flight International opened a window on the shadowy world of private aviation. I'm grateful too to Lester Harris and his team at the Brenner Centre; once again to the indefatigable Anna Tzelniker for her mastery of Yiddish; to Eric Silver and Ruth Tzur for sharing their memories of Michael Elkins; and to Cordelia Borchardt, Jon Henley, Vic Keegan, Seumas Milne and Jay Rayner, for letting me raid their deep knowledge bank.

Special thanks go, once more, to Jonathan Cummings for his energetic ability to research even the most elusive fact. Jane Johnson, along with Sarah Hodgson and Fiona McIntosh at Harper Collins, brings sheer professionalism, skill and wisdom to everything she does. It was a conversation with my agent Jonny Geller that first inspired this book and I still marvel at his loyalty, insight and unerring faith in me.

Finally, I must thank my beloved wife Sarah and my two young sons, Jacob and Sam, whose patience has been stretched during the gestation of this book. If this book dwells on a dark past, I know that with them I am building a bright future.

# The Righteous Men

## Sam Bourne

**Someone is killing good people ... why?**

A series of murders as far apart as the backstreets of New York, the crowded slums of India and the pristine beaches of Cape Town can't be connected. Can they?

Rookie *New York Times* reporter Will Monroe thinks not – until his beautiful wife Beth is kidnapped. The men holding her seem ready to kill without hesitation.

Desperate, Will follows a sinister trail that leads to a mysterious cult, fanatical followers of one of the world's oldest religions – right on his own doorstep. Now he must unravel ancient prophecies and riddles buried deep in the Bible to find a secret worth killing for, a secret on which the fate of humanity may depend. But with more victims dying every hour and each clue wrapped in layers of code, time is running out ...

'Compulsive reading ... successfully blends ancient teachings with the highly charged ways of the 21st century ... bears all the hallmarks of a blockbuster' *Daily Express*

'More readable than *The Da Vinci Code* – the sense of menace is darker and the characters more believable' *Esquire*

# The Last Testament

## Sam Bourne

**A missing clay tablet..a dead assassin..buried secrets in the land of Christ..will these trigger the war to end all wars?**

April 2003: as the Baghdad Museum of Antiquities is looted, a teenage Iraqi boy finds an ancient clay tablet in a long-forgotten vault. He takes it and runs off into the night …

Several years later, at a peace rally in Jerusalem, the Israeli prime minister is about to sign a historic deal with the Palestinians. A man approaches from the crowd and seems to reach for a gun – bodyguards shoot him dead. But in his hand was a note, one he wanted to hand to the prime minister.

The shooting sparks a series of tit-for-tat killings which could derail the peace accord. Washington sends for trouble-shooter and peace negotiator Maggie Costello, after she thought she had quit the job for good. She follows a trail that takes her from Jewish settlements on the West Bank to Palestinian refugee camps, where she discovers the latest deaths are not random but have a distinct pattern. All the dead men are archaeologists and historians – those who know the buried secrets of the ancient past.

Menaced by fanatics and violent extremists on all sides, Costello is soon plunged into high-stakes international politics, the worldwide underground trade in stolen antiquities and a last, unsolved riddle of the Bible.